NEXT OF KIN

BOOKS BY OLIVER LANGE

Defiance—An American Novel (formerly titled *Vandenberg*)
Incident at La Junta
Red Snow
Next of Kin

NEXT OF KIN

Oliver Lange

SEAVIEW BOOKS

NEW YORK

Library of Congress Cataloging in Publication Data

Lange, Oliver.
    Next of kin.

    I. Title.
PZ4.L2764Ne 1980   [PS3562.A485]   813′.5′4   79-66080
ISBN 0-87223-560-2

For Nancy, with love

NEXT
OF KIN

ONE

The pickup, carrying a homemade camper knocked together out of painted plywood and sheet metal, moved down Interstate 40 at a steady fifty-five. Past Old Dad Mountains and the Devil's Playground, headed toward Ludlow.

Outside, it was over a hundred degrees. Inside the cab, even with the windows rolled down and the vents popped, it felt hotter. Heat mirages distorted the desert flatlands, and far ahead the straight ribbon of the highway shimmered and seemed to melt into quicksilver.

The driver was a tall, thin man named Jesse Slade. He was seventy-two. In his time he had been known for his meanness and hard-nosed ways. Now he was just old and decrepit. Like a lot of elderly types who live solo, he had the habit of talking aloud to himself. The conversation wasn't inspiring, but it helped pass the time: "Needles to Barstow, plumb in the middle of July! Whatever gov'ment asshole got the notion to use up taxpayers' dollars pavin' this stretch of hell-hole oughtta been stood up against a wall and shot. The Mojave Desert. Christ! Why any human being with a lick of sense'd want to live in this goddamn state is a mystery."

Another side of his mind spoke. "Needles! Need*less* is more like it. Ninety-nine degrees at six A.M. this morning. Shit!"

He glanced at the instrument panel and noted angrily that the temperature gauge was almost kissing the red warning line. "Wished I'd brought along a couple of chickens to put under the hood. 'Long about now, they'd be barbecued."

AT BARSTOW, WHERE the Interstate cuts south for the long uphill climb that eventually drops down to San Bernardino, he pulled off and parked at a roadside restaurant. Walked through swinging glass doors, into air-conditioned comfort.

The place was crowded with summer tourists. It was noisy and busy. There were plenty of kids. The adults were dressed for hot-weather travel, mostly in the junk clothing of the American road traveler: Bermuda shorts, emblazoned T-shirts, sandals, sneakers.

Jesse Slade made his way among the tables, toward the counter. One kid, wearing a Mouseketeer hat with black cardboard ears, looked up and poked at his mother's arm. "A cowboy. Hey, is he a real cowboy?"

The mother, a pretty young woman wearing sunglasses with rhinestone-ornamented frames, glanced up from her hamburger and shake. Saw an emaciated old man, dressed in tight, faded jeans, a frayed denim work jacket that was bleached almost white, pointed high-heeled boots, and a big gray Stetson. His face was narrow and fleshless and burned brown, and his mouth was set in an angry line. He carried a Rand McNally road atlas in one hand and a small paper sack in the other. The mother watched as Slade took a seat at the counter. She said, "How do I know if he's a cowboy? Maybe he is. You going to eat those fries or just fool with them?"

At the counter, Slade inspected a glossy fold-out menu. He took his time about it, donning reading spectacles, and moving a forefinger slowly across the meals that were described. A passing waitress left him a glass of water, which he drank. Presently another waitress stopped, pad and pencil in hand. She said, "Morning. What'll it be?"

Slade said, "Coffee." He removed his eyeglasses.

"Just coffee?"

"That's right, miss."

"Breakfast Special's still on," the waitress said.

"I can read."

"Just coffee, then?"

"At these prices, coffee'll do fine," Slade said.

When the coffee came, he tasted it, then put his glasses back on and spread the road atlas open, checking his route into Los Angeles. Still looking at the map, he opened the paper sack and took out a baloney sandwich on rye, and began eating. About halfway through the sandwich he glanced up. The waitress who had brought his coffee was standing on the other side of the counter, watching him. She said, "Sir, we have a rule."

"You do."

"Yes."

"What rule?"

"Patrons aren't allowed to bring food in."

Slade took another bite of his sandwich. "At the prices you charge, I'm surprised more folks don't try it. Hell, girl, three dollars for a couple of eggs an' a little ol' sliver of bacon. Back home, eggs is sixty-five cents a dozen. Why, you people in here got a license to steal."

"I just work here, sir."

"Well, I'm sorry for that."

The waitress left, and Slade continued eating his sandwich. Over at the cashier's desk she conferred with the hostess. "I told him," she said, "but he acted kind of nasty."

The hostess looked at Slade. Finally she shrugged and said, "Probably a road bum. Leave him alone."

Slade finished the sandwich and slowly drank his coffee. He took a red foil package of Prince Albert from a pocket and rolled a cigarette, crimped the ends, then smoothed the thin cylinder with an oddly graceful—almost elegant—gesture and placed it in a corner of his mouth. He lit it, and puffed leisurely. The kid with the Mouseketeer hat sidled up to him. "Hey, mister. You a for-real cowboy? You carry a gun?"

"I ain't a cowboy," Slade said sourly, glancing down at the boy. "Not anymore, leastways."

"Can you ride a horse? You got a horse outside?"

"Nope."

"Why ain't you got a horse?"

"Whyn't you git lost?"

The kid said, "You look real old. How old are you?"

"Old enough to hate kids," Slade said, putting his glasses in a shirt pocket and closing the atlas. He got up. " 'Specially smart-assed little brats like you."

The boy thought this over, frowning. Then he gazed up at Slade and smiled. "Hey, mister, can I tell you something? Come here . . . bend down. Listen."

Slade paused by his counter stool, then leaned over as the boy stretched on tiptoe, one hand cupped to his mouth, and whispered, "Go fuck yourself, you freaky old bastard!" He jumped back quickly, ready to run.

Slade considered this, then stood erect. He and the boy regarded each other. Slade said, "Son, you keep on that way, you'll probably end up President. Maybe even Secretary of State."

He made his way toward the cashier's desk to pay for his coffee. He paused momentarily at the table where the boy's mother sat. She looked up and smiled. "I hope Freddy wasn't bothering you."

Slade said, "Missus, first thing I'd do if'n I was stuck with a kid like that, I'd kick his no-good rotten ass plumb into the middle of next week." With that, he walked on.

ON I-10, BETWEEN San Berdoo and Pomona, still miles out of Los Angeles, Slade got into trouble in traffic. It seemed that all the vehicles on the highway were huge rigs, hauling meat and produce and building materials, and they were moving fast.

His hands, clutching the pickup's steering wheel, were sweaty. By this he judged he was nervous. Slade was not a man to sweat much. It was as if his skin had been too dried out and tanned by the sun and the years to have any moisture left in it.

Nor were his reflexes that good. The closer he got to Los Angeles, the spookier he felt. Watching the tractor-trailer rigs roar past on his left, he said, "Sweet Jesus, Mary, and Joseph, ain't any of these idiots heard about the speed limit? Seventy-five, eighty. Mebbe more! They must be in a hurry or something."

He had a bad habit when driving, a tendency to ride with his left wheels on the median line dividing the inner and outer lanes. He got away with this until a four-ton stake-bed sped past in the inside lane, its air horn blasting a warning, seeming only inches away as it thundered by. Slade spun the steering wheel to the right, went too far, then swung left, overcompensating, and careened in a wild skid, ending up on the dirt shoulder of the highway. The pickup wasn't hurt, but he was frightened. His hands were trembling.

Behind the pickup, a California Highway Patrol car pulled onto the shoulder and stopped. A CHPer got out. He walked up to where Slade was sitting in the cab and said, "You all right?"

"Course I'm all right," Slade snapped. " 'All right'! You blind? Whyn't you go chase that wild man who just steamrollered me off the road? Ask him if *he's* all right."

"May I see your license?"

"What for?"

"Let's see your license, please."

"You think I ain't got one?"

"Sir, I'll have to see your license," the officer insisted.

Slade sighed and shook his head exasperatedly, and reached for his wallet.

The officer said, "I've been following you for the past couple of miles. Don't you know it's an offense to straddle the median?"

"What median?"

"The white line dividing the lanes," the CHPer explained. "That's one offense. I could cite you for another. Failure to exercise due caution."

"How about those goddamn lowlife truckers who've been runnin' me off the road?" Slade said furiously. "Go cite them! Quit quotin' law at me. 'Due caution'!"

"Mister, you were giving them a worse time than they were giving you."

"Oh, shit!"

"It's also an offense to use abusive language to an officer of the law," the CHPer said, frowning.

"Goddamn it, son, I wasn't sayin' it to you," Slade argued. "I was just sort'a sayin' shit in general."

After glancing at Slade's license, the officer took out his ticket book. "Sir, your license expired three months ago. I'm going to have to write you up."

"It did?" Slade thought this over. He got less cranky. "Well, you know how things are. Man my age is liable to forget."

"May I see the pickup's registration?" Slade produced it. Unfortunately, this had expired too. The officer said, "You New Mexico people sure forget things, don't you?"

"I had the Chinese virus back then," Slade explained. "Laid up flat on my back for nearly a month. Thought I was goin' to die. Ran a temperature of a hundred-and-three."

"Old-timer, I wish I could just give you a warning," the officer said, "but so far I've got you on not observing a median, lack of caution, no license, no registration, and maybe a couple of other things. I could take you in, you know. How long have you been driving?"

"Since way the hell before freeways was invented, that's how long," Slade said. His crankiness returned. "And that means since before you climbed into your first pair of diapers."

"What're you doing here, all the way from New Mexico? All by yourself."

"What d'you mean, 'all by myself'?" Slade snapped. "Do I look like I need a nursemaid or something? It's a free country, ain't it? I happen to be here on business."

"What business?"

"Official business," Slade replied. "Hell, boy, you think I'd come fartin' around way out here just for the pleasure of it, where you California maniacs drive like you was all in some kind'a demolition derby? Shoot! I may be old, but it don't follow that I'm stupid on top of it."

"What kind of business?" the officer insisted.

"I got to git a kid."

"You what?"

"I said I got to git this kid," Slade said again. Finally, still looking furious, he reached into the glove compartment and took out an envelope. "For an officer of the law, you're real snoopy, ain't you? Here, see for yourself."

The letterhead bore the imprint:

**GREATER LOS ANGELES
DEPARTMENT OF HUMAN SERVICES
CHILD WELFARE DIVISION
BURBANK OFFICE**

The text of the letter said that a juvenile, Clement L. Slade, sixteen, was being detained in the Burbank Juvenile Detention

Home, on charges of car theft and breaking and entering. It said too that young Clement, with one parent dead and the whereabouts of the other unknown, had not responded to various foster-home situations, and had in fact exhibited behavior of a severe antisocial nature. The last paragraph asked for assistance in locating any of Clement's relatives who might be able to provide a home environment for the boy.

It was a routine tracer. Signed by a Miss Marsha Macguire, Supervisor, District Five, Field Office.

The CHPer said, "This boy related to you?"

"Grandson."

"Looks like he's had himself a few problems."

Slade's expression grew stonier. He did not reply, as if by silence he was indicating that family matters were private.

"The date's over a month old," the CHPer noted.

"I ain't easy to track down," Slade said evasively.

"You and your family going to take him over?"

"I'm alone," Slade said. "Widower. Over twenty years now. Listen, you goin' to stand around here all day, gassin' away at me? I got to git movin'. You goin' to write me a ticket, boy, git on with it."

"Don't call me boy."

"Well, what else are you?"

"I'm an officer of the law."

"Well, sonny, law officer or not, git the hell on with your business."

The CHPer was angry, but he tried to keep a professional attitude. He said, "All right. If you're going to Los Angeles, though, you better sharpen up your driving skills."

"Nothing wrong with my drivin' skills."

"You planning on staying in L.A.?"

"Not five seconds longer'n I have to."

"I see. Going to take this juvenile back to New Mexico?"

"That's the general idea," Slade said. "Just as fast as this old heap will move."

"Well, I wish you luck, mister," the officer said. "I'll still have to write you up, though."

Slade gave him a hard look. "You California cops got Christian charity just oozin' out'a your pores, ain't you?"

The officer let this go by. Went about writing his citations. Then he said, "Where're the boy's parents? Or the one that's still alive?"

"It's a long story," Slade said sourly. "I wouldn't want'a keep you from your appointed task."

The CHPer gave the old man an irritable look, as if he was ready to hand Slade a dressing down. Then gave up on it. He explained that the fines could be paid by mail, that California had a reciprocal law with other states to prosecute non-resident offenders, and then added, "What I'd do, if I were you, Mr. Slade, I'd get back to New Mexico as fast as I could. I'd go straight to my department of motor vehicles and get my license renewed. I'd get a current registration. And I wouldn't cross the Arizona-California border again until my papers were in order."

"I'll do just that," Slade said.

"Sign these, please, where I've marked X's."

Slade signed the citations.

"And I'd be real careful about these highways."

"I surely will," Slade said. "I'll do all those little chores the minute I git back home. Well, son, you been fair enough. I got to say that much. I was dead-sure in the wrong. You was just doin' your job. Right is right. Yessir. And I'll surely stay off that medium line."

He accepted the tickets and smiled at the CHPer. Almost friendly. Drove off. Five miles down the highway he took the citations the officer had written, crumpled them into wads, and tossed them out the window as the pickup passed a sign warning that a hundred-dollar fine would be imposed on litterers.

MARSHA MACGUIRE WAS a trim, marvelously pretty woman in her middle thirties. She looked somewhat nonplussed now as she listened to Jesse Slade. Jesse sat in a chair on the other side of her desk.

They were in her office, and he was into one of his tirades: "Listen, don't git the notion I want'a be saddled with this lousy kid! Probably one of them dyed-in-the-wool perpetual delinquents. No sir! I don't care much for kids. Never have. Only good kid is a dead kid, them's my feelin's. This boy's got a relation, my niece, by my late sister Helen, she died in 'fifty-four. She's someplace over in Germany with her big-shot Air Force husband and family. He's a colonel. They'll be coming back to the States pretty soon. So, it's just a kind of temporary arrangement with me, as they say. I already wrote her. She'll take the boy. I don't have enough time left in my life to go foolin' around with some troublemaker. I don't mind doing what's right, but I ain't no professional do-gooder. You might as well git that straight, girl. How'd you ever get a line on me anyway? You're supposed to be in welfare work. Detective work's more like it. FBI could make real use of a girl like you."

"Among Clem's father's effects there was a notify-next-of-kin card," Miss Macguire said. "It was routine." She paused, and then spoke, choosing her words carefully. "What you should know, Mr. Slade, is that Clem—your grandson—is not exactly a run-of-the-mill child. Actually, of course, none of the children we work with could be considered routine. They're all special."

"So was Adolf Hitler," Slade remarked. He began rolling a cigarette and lounged back in the chair, the gray Stetson propped on one crossed leg. "I once had a three-legged dog. He was special. Name was Clyde. What was special about him, he used to bite left-handed people. Smartest damned dog you ever saw! Could smell a left-handed person a country mile off. Well, this Clyde, he finally bit me. I'm right-handed, you see. Bit the livin' hell out'a me, for no reason at all!"

"What happened?" Miss Macguire asked.

"That evening I called him from the back door of the kitchen," Jesse said. "He came smoochin' up, all friendly and wagging his tail. I had this soup bone held out in my right hand, so's he could see I was okay and wasn't holdin' no grudge against him. He come up and took it, and I shot him right between the eyes with the forty-four I had in my left hand. He never knew what hit him. His tail was still wagging when he went down. I guess he was right about not trustin' left-handed folks."

Miss Macguire stared at the old man, half convinced that it was just a story. Yet another part of her wasn't so sure. She got back to business. "And you say you never had any contact at all from Clem's mother?"

"Not a word. She was bad news," Slade said. "All I ever heard about that woman from my son, one time when he was passin' through, was that she took off when the kid was about a year old." He lit his cigarette. "My son wasn't a talkative kind of man, see? Oh, he'd talk about himself all the time, but it was all brag. He told me I was a grandpa, but not much about her. I got the im-

pression she was one of these low-trash bar floozies. If you git my
meaning. Like mebbe he married her 'cause she got one in the oven,
and he didn't know what else to do. You know how such things go.
Five minutes' fun, twenty years' regret. That's life, these days. I
never exactly had the feelin' that she'd be a candidate for Mother
of the Year."

Miss Macguire was going through a dossier spread open on her
desk. "Your late son paid into Social Security. That'll be a help.
Do you know if he had any life insurance, real estate, or other
equity?"

"Well, miss, if you're out to cross the *t*'s and dot the *i*'s, I suppose
you'd have to say he didn't amount to much either," Slade said.
"I'm not a person to talk about what goes on inside a family. But
I guess you got to ask questions. When you git right down to it, my
boy never lifted a finger or sent five dollars to help me or his mother,
when she was alive. He lived for today, and let tomorrow take care
of itself. He never made anything of himself. Worked as a long-haul
trucker—that is, when he was sober enough to see out the windshield. He was a mite quick with his fists, and he had a thirst to go
with the temper, if you follow me. Wore sideburns and long hair.
Cowboy boots. Hell, he couldn't have ever stayed on a horse that
didn't have a steerin' wheel. You probably got it all down there
in those papers. I do know he did time at Soledad, eighteen months,
for something or other. Claimed it was somebody else's fault."

"When was the last time you saw your grandson?" she asked.

"Me? Why, lady, I ain't never seen him," Slade said. "He's been
out here in California all this time. His daddy never brought him
home."

The social worker considered this. Lit a cigarette, too. Looked
across the desk at the old man. "You've never seen him?"

"Never laid eyes on him."

"Snapshot? Surely."

"No, ma'am. We never went in much for that kind'a stuff."

"Mr. Slade, we have something of a problem here," Miss Macguire said. "For you to have come all the way from New Mexico
. . . to suddenly just appear like this. Everything could have been
worked out via regular correspondence. I suppose what I'm trying
to say is that a relative, asking to assume custody, frequently needs
counseling as much as the child in question."

"What else'd you expect me to do?" Slade demanded. "I don't see any problem. I'm the kid's grandpa. Doesn't mean I *want* him. But I suppose I'll have to take him. Ain't nothin' else to do, is there? That's why I come. Kin is kin." He considered this. "I don't take him, what're you goin' to do? Leave him sit in that jail? You got my identification. You got to have the kid's birth certificates and all that garbage in your folder. Probably you got his daddy's death certificate, too. You folks kind'a go in heavy for paperwork, I understand. Got to make sure everything's on the up and up, right?"

"Yes, but—"

"You think I'd drive near to a thousand miles to git some rotten kid that wasn't blood kin?" Slade said angrily. "No one'd do that, less'n he had to."

"I'm not arguing that," the social worker said.

"Well, then, what the hell problem is there?"

"Oh . . . it's difficult to explain," she said. "What do you think your grandson is like, Mr. Slade? I mean, in your mind?"

"Jesus H. Christ, what difference does it make?" Slade snapped. "Some noisy, snot-nosed kid. Trouble on the hoof. If his luck is against him, he may have his daddy's features. What're you drivin' at?"

Miss Macguire stared at him. She said, "Clement is almost seventeen. He's quite tall for his age." She glanced at the dossier. "Almost six feet four."

"You're kidding! Six four? Something that size is too big to keep in the house."

"Weight, one ninety."

"Must be from his momma's side. I'm tall. But six four. That's real tall!"

"Here. You might like to see for yourself." She handed him a form to which was stapled a passport-sized photograph.

Jesse Slade took out his glasses. Put them on. Glanced at the photograph. He looked again. Then he held it out at arm's length, as if to see better. He frowned. Shook his head, and stared up at the ceiling. Said slowly, "Well! Goddamn my ass!"

Miss Macguire said, "I beg your pardon?"

"That miserable, two-faced, double-dealing son of a bitch of a son. It's a travesty, that's what it is! A sure-enough travesty on life, that's what he went and did."

"What do you mean?"

"He never once bothered to tell me what he was up to, that's what! That sneaky, mealymouthed bastard!"

"I don't understand."

"Miss Macguire, cut it out! Don't come on all sweetness an' juicy-Lucy with me," Slade said. He held up the sheet of paper. "You know what I'm talkin' about. This here goddamn kid's a nigger!"

"Mulatto."

"Mulatto, my ass." He stared at the photograph, with an expression close to amazement, confoundment. "Hell! Looks as black as the ace of spades to me!"

IT TOOK A while for her to get him calmed down. Or as calm as could be expected. She watched him and listened.

"I surely didn't expect this, I can tell you that!" Jesse exclaimed. He went into a sullen reverie. "I should'a knowed! Never a word, no letter, all these years. Last time he stopped by, that would have been 'seventy-one or, no, mebbe it was 'seventy-two. It was in the autumn. I was gittin' ready to take in my corn. He was comin' out'a Oklahoma City, with a brand-new truck his company had sent him up there to buy. Comes walkin' into the house, with those sideburns and boots, smokin' a big cigar, easy as pie. 'Just wanted to look in and see if the old place was still standin',' he said to me. I told him, 'What'd you expect this one-whistle dump to turn into, something like Chicago mebbe?' I asked him how his life was going. 'I'm a success, Poppa,' he told me. I knew right off he was lying through his teeth. 'Trucker is the only free man left in this country,' he said. 'I got to be free and on my own.'"

Jesse paused, staring again at the photograph attached to the form. The boy in the picture was handsome, with a light-brown complexion, a broad, friendly mouth, and eyes that stared right into the camera. "Listen, miss, you sure there ain't some kind'a mistake here?"

"The documentation is adequate," Miss Macguire said. "Far more than we have on some of our other children. The papers you brought indicate that Clement Senior was your son. Since we have no way of tracing the maternal side, that seems to make you next of kin."

Jesse frowned. "Couldn't there have been some kind'a mistake? Hospital records git all mixed up. Why, babies can be switched, by accident."

"Nonsense. For years newborns have gotten a handprint and a footprint, minutes after delivery. I'm satisfied that a blood relationship exists between the two of you. My question, though, is, 'What now?' "

Jesse looked at her suspiciously. "Meaning what?"

"Meaning do you want the boy?" Miss Macguire said. "Because I am not about to release him to any relative who isn't prepared to care for him."

Slade thought about this. He rolled another cigarette. Finally he said, "I got to hand it to you. Always liked a woman who could spit out what was on her mind without goin' all around the barn. Well, now that you ask . . . no, I don't. What in hell am I goin' to do with a colored kid back home, taggin' around after me? Why, an ordinary normal kid would be bad enough. But this! I just don't know."

"I see," she said.

Jesse said complainingly, "I mean, y'know, I live in a real small town, way up in the mountains. A kid like this would be out of place. You see my predicament?"

"I can see that it would be difficult for you. And for Clem, too. You said that this niece of yours, who's stationed with her husband in Europe, has agreed to take Clem when they return to this country?"

"Well, kind of." Then he said, "I mean, I ain't heard back from her yet."

"When will they return?"

"Less'n a year. That was what she wrote on her Christmas card, anyway. She's one of those types who're always sending cards. She goes to the toilet, everybody gits a card. Usually one of those Kodacolor snaps with her and her big-shot husband and her stinkin' kids, wavin' and grinnin' at the camera, y'know, like they're goddamn glad they're *there* and you're *here*. Some people! They got kids comin' out'a the woodwork, and still, they're smilin' and wavin' all the time. Livin', breathin' proof that Christian decency pays off." He thought about this. "I don't know. When I first got your letter, I figured I could mebbe handle this boy till they got back. Just temporary, y'know. But this situation's different. You see my point?"

"I do."

"Hell, I ain't young no more," Jesse complained. "I'll be seventy-three next April. What am I goin' to do with a half-breed kid like this? I got a sneaky hunch he'd be a real can of worms to handle."

"That's true, I'm afraid," Miss Macguire said. "We've had Clem in three foster-home situations in the past four years. He's had some serious problems."

"Oh, with him bein' an intermix and all, I can see that," Jesse said.

She glanced at him. "The interracial aspect doesn't amount to that much out here. It may, where you live. California has a little of everything."

"It sure does. Drugs, hippies, livin' in sin, and crime, from what I hear."

"The worst problem, really, is that he's never had any kind of family, especially when he was small. The father apparently unloaded him on friends or casual acquaintances for most of the first six or seven years. We don't have the entire story. But apparently Clem has built up an inventory of feelings about being rejected and unwanted. Unloved."

"That's understandable. Who'd want something like that around?" Jesse said. He frowned again, moved restlessly in the chair, and then fidgeted with the brim of the Stetson. "An' now you're sayin' I'm doin' the same thing."

"I'm not saying anything, Mr. Slade. You seem to be the one who's expressing doubts. All I'm interested in is what's best for Clem."

"What'll happen to him?"

"You mean, if you don't take him?"

"Yes."

"He'll stay at the D-Home. He's been there quite a while already. Eventually, he'll appear in juvenile court."

"And then what? Reformatory?"

"Perhaps not. If we can find another foster-home arrangement, well . . . that's something we can at least hope for. You have to understand, Clem isn't exactly what most prospective foster parents have in mind when they come to us. People have an image of cute, cuddly youngsters. Clem, I understand, is into karate. And a few other things as well. With his emotional makeup, he's quite capable of exhibiting aggressiveness toward a father figure. Or authority. Or school. He knows the street scene. 'Street people' . . . that's an expression we have. He's a pretty tough kid. He knows an awful lot for someone his age."

"What's this here D-Home like, that you got him in?"

"Well, the windows have bars and the cells are locked," Miss Macguire said. "It's a maximum-security facility, Mr. Slade. It's not especially pleasant."

"Sounds like the ol' *calabozo* to me."

"*Calabozo*? Oh . . . jail. Yes, you could say that," she agreed.

"Reckon you got some really hard cases in there, eh?"

"Oh, yes."

"So," Jesse mused. "I guess this kid'll just have to sweat out his time. In a sense, it could be said he's gittin' what he deserves. I mean, you don't buckle down and shape up, well, you got to take the consequences. Probably some folks would say it served him right."

"Probably some would," she agreed.

"Probably he'll go from bad to worse. Prison. Down the drain. One of them lifelong criminals, like you see on television."

"If I agreed with that, there'd be no need for my profession. All we'd need is bigger prisons. Lots of them."

"But can you see my predicament?"

"I certainly can."

Jesse shook his head, and set his mouth in a grim line. Looked as dangerous as an old turkey buzzard. Finally he snapped, "Goddamn it all to hell and back! If there is one thing I hate like poison, it's bein' whipsawed."

"I don't understand."

"You heard me, girl. Whipsawed! Plain and simple," Jesse cried. "If I take this goddamn kid, there's no tellin' what kind'a ruckus he'll stir up back home. People'd talk. Hellfire, back there you can't scratch your ass at the south end of town without folks at the north end knowin' what hand you're usin'. I've lived in Brazos for goin' on fifty years. Ranched there when I was younger. Ol' Jesse Slade. Bringin' home a wood's-colt nigger. 'Bad blood, comin' back home,' that's what they'd say. Not that that bothers me. The hell with 'em. People back there don't like me much, and I don't like 'em neither. Kind'a mutual, you might say. Still I got to live there. I ain't got many years left. I'd like to spend them peacefully. I got a few friends. Not many. Man doesn't need many friends. Man collects too many friends, he's liable to find out he don't need no enemies. Now, on the other hand, if I leave this kid here, assumin', that is, he's a relation, like you claim, legal an' all . . . well, miss, I don't like that much. No, I'd have to say I don't like that at all."

"We'd do our best for him."

"Oh, surely," Jesse said, looking sourer. "And how you fixin' to do that? By keepin' him locked up? My own grandkid?"

Miss Macguire looked across the desk at the old man. Then she said regretfully, "Well, Mr. Slade, over the long mile that might be best, for all concerned. For the boy—and for yourself, too."

Jesse glared at her. "If that's true, then how come I don't feel right in my mind about it? Answer me that! How come I feel whipsawed? Trouble with being whipsawed is that no matter which way a man turns, he loses. There ain't no justice and there ain't no winnin' with that kind'a deal. I leave that kid here, I ain't goin' to feel right with myself, that's for goddamn sure. I couldn't look any of my friends in the face."

"They wouldn't have to know, would they?" she said. "Unless you told them, before you left home."

"You think I'm some kind of ravin' lunatic?" Jesse said. "I keep my business to myself. Nossir! Far as anybody is concerned, I could say I come out here for a little vacation, mebbe to Disneyland or something. There'd be no problem at all."

"Well, then? Maybe that's the best course of action."

"Girl, you miss my point. You're smart, and you're educated, but you miss my point entirely."

"What's that?"

"*I'd* know, damn it," Jesse said simply. "This boy wouldn't even have to know I'd come out here. But I'd know! I wouldn't care for that one bit. Leavin' my own flesh and blood in a fix. It ain't right."

"Mr. Slade, why don't I step outside and have a coffee and let you sit here and think it over," Miss Macguire said. "Take your time."

"No need to," Jesse said mournfully. "I could sit here thinkin' until cows laid eggs, and it would still come down to the same thing. Whipsawed. If he had some uncle or auntie here in California, why, I'd be outta here in a flash. But that don't happen to be the case."

"So?"

"What papers you want me to sign? How soon can you git him over here? Is this detention home far? Should I just go pick him up?"

"There are forms," she said. "Lots of them. The Home is nearby. However, I'd rather you waited here."

"Do I have some kind'a tab to settle up with you people for food and shelter?" Jesse asked. "I got about a hundred and forty bucks travelin' money on me, but that's all. If the bill comes to more than that, you'll have to take an IOU."

"The state takes care of everything, Mr. Slade," she said. "I'll also be arranging with New Mexico's social services for them to pick up the case at their end."

"No need to trouble yourself. I ain't much for havin' the gov'ment stick its fat nose into my affairs."

"I'm afraid it's obligatory. We can't just close the case without a final disposition. Clement has Social Security benefits, from his father's employment. The application is pending. It'll take time. We can advance you money for his immediate expenses."

"Don't bother. I ain't lookin' for no handout. Just git him over here, pronto."

Miss Macguire looked at him. Then she said, "You're sure, Mr. Slade?"

"Trot the bastard out."

THE BOY'S CELL was eight by five. Lidless bowl in a corner. Roll of paper. Cot, neatly made. On it, magazines—mostly beaver pictorials. Grilled window, letting in hazy, soft, Los Angeles light. Opposite, a steel door, with a hinged pass-through window. Outside, a faint hum of traffic, far off, on busy Burbank Boulevard. The boy rarely came out of the cell except for trips to the cafeteria, interviews with the psychiatric worker, and workout time in the "golden fields," which was what the inmates called the exercise yard. The whole compound was walled in with chain link, twelve feet high, topped with barbed wire.

The boy didn't look as good as he had in the photograph Jesse Slade had seen. He had a black eye. One cheek was puffed.

The steel door opened. A man in a short-sleeved shirt—a tall, rangy black—stepped in. "Clem?"

"Yeah."

"Come on."

"You got something on your mind?"

"You're going out."

"How come?"

"Relation, over at the main office, wants to pick you up."

"Ain't got no relations."

"You do now."

"Tell whoever it is to fuck off."

"Hey, baby."

"That goes for you too, Ralph."

"What's all this here fuck-talk?"

"Just what I said. Just what it means. I been fucked. More'n I can remember." He grinned at the counselor. " 'Cept here. Staff time here. Get the staff, straight between the ol' cheeks."

"That how you got the mouse?"

"Maybe."

"They try to gang you?"

"Wasn't nothing. Different strokes for different folks. Take a shower, it pays to look in all directions. That's all."

"Three kids was in the infirmary this morning."

"Well, you know how it goes, Ralph. I just don't like somebody thinking they can lean on me. I don't put up with that."

"From the looks of them, you were doing most of the leaning."

"Just takin' care of my own business. I mean, like, if I grooved on all that Browning Queen shit, it'd be no hassle. I got no kind of respect for that."

"I guess they dig that now."

"You said it, I didn't," the boy agreed. "Just 'cause I'm here, it don't follow that I'm trash. You look at these dudes, Ralphie. All they doin' all day long is tattooing themselves with a needle and a ballpoint. Printing all kinds of raunchy sayings on themselves. Walking signboards. You don't see me marking up my skin, do you? Ain't a mark on my skin anywhere! It's clean. I got respect for my body."

"Move your gorgeous ass," the counselor said. "You want to wash your face?"

"No need."

"Come on, then."

"You mean, I got to?"

" 'Fraid so."

"I like it here."

"We like you too. You're just like family by now."

The boy ran his fingers through a bushy Afro. "What relation?"

"How would I know?"

"That's shit, Ralph. I ain't got no people. It's in my records. That's a proven fact."

"Clem, quit screwing around. Let's go."

"Deputy out there?"

"Two of them."

"Cuffs?"

"No."

"How come? They don't think I'm dangerous, or something?"

"I asked 'em not to. Told 'em you'd mellowed out in here."

"Good. I don't like cuffs."

"Stay cool, Dillinger."

"Don't talk at me about cool, man. I been cooled down so long I don't know what hot feels like."

They went out of the cell and down a corridor. At the reception desk, two white deputies waited. Exchange papers were signed. The boy was turned over to them. One said, "Easy trip, kid?"

"Been easy my whole life."

"We're just going over to the field office."

"Can we go by way of Long Beach?"

"No."

"I sure dig those hard-assed chicks who surf out at Long Beach."

"Let's move."

"They got asses that go on forever. You ever feel ass like that? I'd sure like to walk through an acre of those asses barefoot."

"Sure."

"You know what?" the boy said, staring at one of the deputies. "White chicks got the wettest snatches in the world. White girls just drip like a faucet with a steady leak. How come is that?"

The deputy he had spoken to turned to his buddy. "You ever get the feeling you want to kick the shit out'a somebody? Like, maybe, just for the fun of it?"

The other deputy said, "Shut up, kid."

"Best head I ever got was from a chick down on Long Beach," the boy went on. "I mean, this fish really dug swinging on a joint." He stared at the first deputy. "On the beach, in daylight. Looked kind'a like you, officer. Name was Candy, only everybody called her Licorice Stick. About fifteen. You got a girlchick named Candy?"

The first deputy said to his buddy, "Let me sit in the back seat with him when we get out of here, okay?"

The other deputy said, "Quit asking for it, wise-ass. It's ten minutes over to the office. You want us to make the trip last an hour? We can do that for you."

"Me? No sir," the boy said. "I just want'a git out of here. Get socially rehabilitated, and all that."

"You going to behave?"

"Oh, surely," the boy said. "No trouble from me. Guarantee it. You got my word on that."

"That's fine," the deputy said. "Because we're going, whether you like it or not. How you go is one thing. But we are going."

"I'm easy. Don't wrong me."

"Shut your mouth then."

"I'm with you," the boy said, as they left. Each deputy had him by an arm. The prowl car was outside. As they walked out, he grinned from one deputy to the other. "You know what white girls taste like? Sweeter'n honey. Oh, my, yes. Ain't nothin' like young white gash. I could groove for hours on that scene. Got to hold 'em down with chains."

"I told you to shut up," the first deputy said. They threw him into the rear seat of the car.

"Oh, sure," the boy said. He grinned again. "You positive one of your girlchicks don't truck around Long Beach? Down by the pier? She has a resemblance, this one I'm thinking about. Licorice Stick. Takes on ten, fifteen dudes a night. I mean, like I wouldn't scam you, but she really tricks out on that kind'a train."

THE BOY WALKED into Miss Macguire's office. They knew each other. "Hey, Miz Macguire! How you makin' it?"

"Hi, Clem."

Sitting across from her was a wizened man with a cowboy hat resting on his crossed knee. He was smoking a handmade. He was old. Really old. Looked like he hadn't smiled in a hundred years. The boy gave him a casual glance. Then ignored him completely.

Jesse Slade looked up to see a tall black teen-ager, skinny in the hips, with broad, bony shoulders. The boy was still lanky, but with that frame, when he grew to size and filled out, he would be one hell of a man. He had a shiner and a bruised cheek. "Trouble," Jesse remarked, to no one in particular. "Nothing but trouble lookin' for a place to happen."

"How've you been, Clem?" Miss Macguire asked.

"Jus' fine! How *you* been?"

"Great!"

Clem grinned at her. "How's the ol' love life? Gettin' it regular?"

"Can't complain."

"Terrific!"

"How's yours?"

"At the D? Shoot! Why, they're haulin' in young chicks off Sunset for us by the busload. Regular round-the-clock orgy over at *that* place!"

"No complaints, then?"

"Me? You ever hear me complain?"

"Glad you're happy."

"Just whistlin' and snappin' the old fingers, baby," Clem said. "My, yes! Life is a feast! No use complainin'." He jerked a thumb toward Jesse. "Who he?"

"This is your grandfather."

Clem looked at the man in the chair. Then back to Miss Macguire. Rolled his eyes toward the ceiling. He had a habit, when kidding around, of imitating various dialects. Now, grinning with delight, he fell into a kind of exaggerated Alabama drawl. "Naw! You's *foolin'!* This he'ah my sho' nuff gran'pa?"

"That's right, Clem."

"You is funnin' with me! Sho' nuff?"

"Sure enough."

He stared at Jesse again. "Oh, my! Ah always *knowed* ah wuz part white. But ah never knowed ah wuz *that* white! Why, Miz Marsha, this ol' booger's *pure* white! Look like he been livin' in a flour bin."

Jesse looked up at him and said warningly, "I ain't no booger."

"Clem, cut the jive," Miss Macguire said.

"Hell, I cruise with brothers who'd turn their backs on me and never talk to me again if they found out I was related this close to white." He turned to Jesse. "So! You is my gran'pa. *Whoo-eee!* How *'bout* that!"

Jesse, looking grimmer, said to Miss Macguire, "Friendly cuss, ain't he?"

"He has some good things going for him."

"Name one."

"He's very bright."

"He don't talk like it. Don't act like it, either. You ask me, he acts like something what escaped out'a one of them freak sideshows they got at circuses."

Clem stood up straight. Looked offended and stern. Managed to get off a pretty passable mime of a bookish psychologist. "I am a culturally and ethnically deprived casualty of today's crippled social structure! It say so, right in my case record. I peeked."

"Culturally and ethnically deprived pain in the ass is more like it," Jesse said.

"Clem, cut it out," Miss Macguire said.

Clem snapped his fingers, did a small double-shuffle dance step, and slid into a Barbadian bit, with high, fluty English inflections, "Mon! Don' you know wha' de ponce is? We plays de Belefontay drums for all de ponce. All de ladies sing and play, close 'pon midnight hit de hay, lay on der backs de lib-long day, dere mon's away, but even so dey's got to play!"

"Jesus *Christ!*" Jesse said disgustedly.

"Das a sin, to be takin' de name of ou'ah Jesus-mon in vain," Clem said. "When de comin' come, bime'n by, ou'ah Jesus-mon will walk 'mongst us."

"Clem, will you quit it!" Miss Macguire said.

"Yas'm," Clem said, going back to Alabaman. "Whut's de shoot, Miz Marsha? Why fo' you got me he'ah?"

"Your grandfather wants to take you home," she said.

"Home? What you talkin' about? What home? What you mean, home?"

"He lives in New Mexico," she explained. "He wants to take you back there."

"New Mexi-*whut?* Wh'ah dat?"

"You just start headin' east," Jesse said. "Soon's you git past Arizona, you more or less got it."

"Why'd I want'a go there?" Clem said, shaking his head. "Never even heard of *that* place. Venice, Sunset, Malibu, that's where the people are. This is my town, Miz Macguire. City of the Angels. Just turn me loose. I'll make my way. I'll be good. No more trouble. No more hustling. I'll git by fine. Word of honor."

"Your word don't count for nothing with me," Jesse said.

Clem turned. "You questionin' my *wuh'd*, man?"

"Yup."

"My precious *wuh'd?*"

"My precious balls!" Jesse muttered to himself. He looked at Miss Macguire. " 'Scuse me, miss." His expression was still disgusted. "We got to sit here all day listenin' to this?"

"I hope not," Miss Macguire said. She kept her voice level. "An initial meeting like this . . . I mean, well, it's supposed to be a way for each of you to get to know the other a little."

"I already know more about him than I need," Jesse pointed out. "Fact is, I kind'a wish I knew less."

THEY KEPT AT it. A half-hour later it finally came to a head. Miss Macguire sat back and listened, with feelings of consternation, even amazement.

"What you goin' to do, *chastise* me, I don't behave? Gonna *dis*-cipline me, I don't do like you say?" Clem was demanding. "I ain't leaving L.A. What I want'a do something like that for? I ain't never been out'a this town. How you goin' to make me? Goin' to put a chain on me?"

"Nope," Jesse said.

"Well, that's just fine," Clem said. "You got some smarts, after all. I'm my own man."

"You're just a useless kid, is all I can see."

"An' you frail! That's the exact word! Just ol' . . . and *frail!*"

"And you're all mouth," Jesse said. "Just one big flappy mouth."

"You think you can push me this way and that? I can handle myself. Y'know what I do, over at the D-Home? Just to pass the time? Three hundred pushups. Two hundred situps. Just for kicks! I mean, that is my mornin' schedule! How 'bout that?"

"You ever done any real work?"

"Work? What's that?"

"Plain ol' everyday hard-assed work? Chopping firewood? Mending fence?"

Clem looked disdainful. "No. That ain't exactly in my line."

"Listen, you wanta come or not?" Jesse demanded.

"No, thanks." Clem turned to Miss Macguire. "Do I got to?"

She said, "It's your choice. But the contract reads this way, Clem: if you go, you stay with your grandfather. Split, and we have an interstate alarm out on you in half a day. You have to understand that."

"Oh, I wouldn't do nothing like that, Miz Macguire," Clem said.

"I know you wouldn't, Clem."

"Wished I did," Jesse chimed in. "Come to think about it, I wish he *would*."

Clem looked at him. "D-Home sounds good. Compared to you. Ol', frail, and foolish. Back there, I wouldn't have to listen to you. Wouldn't even have to *see* you, or look at your ol' wrinkled honkey face. You real *ugly*, you know that?"

"Make up your mind, boy."

"Don't call me boy."

"Well, goddamn it, that's all you are!" Jesse snapped. "You ever git to be a man, I might call you something else."

Clem turned back to Miss Macguire. "You mean, it's him or the Home?"

"That's about it," she said. "Clem, he'll try to take care of you. I believe that. But if you split, the contract is off. No two ways. Go with him, or take your chances on juvenile court here."

Clem stared at his grandfather. "Sometimes I wish I was daid!"

"The feeling's mutual," Jesse agreed.

"I want'a know what I'm gettin' into," Clem insisted. "I mean, if I got to call him Grandpa and all that shit, the deal's off. Just as soon take the ol' D-Home."

"Whyn't you do both of us a real favor. Don't call me nothin'," Jesse said. "Just 'cause we're related, it don't mean we got to spread the news. Bad news travels fast enough as it is."

"You got a house or an apartment?"

"House."

"You mean, you an' me got to live in it together?"

"Well, I ain't about to move out in the goddamn woodshed, y'know!"

"Cozy."

"I been cozier with scorpions I was tryin' to stomp."

"Just don't mess with me."

"Don't you mess with me," Jesse said. "I got patience. Up to a point."

"Listen to him," Clem crowed. "Ol' bag of bones. You so *feeble!* Don't worry, Frail and Feeble, I'll be gentle with you."

"Don't fret about me," Jesse said.

"Don't intend to."

"Just do as you're told. We'll git by."

"That'll be the day." Clem paused. Then he said, "Hey, ugly! You really my grandpa?"

"Jesus Christ, boy, you think I'd own up to something like that less'n I had to?"

"How 'bout that! If that don't beat all!"

"You can say that again."

"Well, I guess you're better than the D-Home," Clem said finally. "Not by much, though."

"Stay, if you want. Don't do me no favors."

"Oh, I'll go. That's for sure," Clem said. "I mean, I got to trust you, don't I? And you got to trust me, ain't that right, Miz Macguire?"

It was Jesse's turn to look scornful. "I wouldn't trust you no more'n I'd trust a back-alley Juarez Mexican tryin' to sell me a diamond stickpin."

Clem looked at Jesse and smiled, enjoying the remark. His expression was calculating, and at the same time challenging. "That's good! I'm glad we know about that. 'Cause I don't trust you either." He turned to Miss Macguire. "Say, now—just supposin'. I mean, like, for example, just supposin' I got into a mood or something, an' I came down on this ol' dude, kicked all his ribs loose, took his car maybe, an' went trashin', like goin' on the road and ballin' around, eh? How 'bout that?"

"I'd say you'd be in trouble," she said.

"You'd be in lots more'n that," Jesse said, giving the boy a dirty look. "You're big, sure. You're one part man, and ten parts talk, is all. Boy, you just remember one thing. There is one boss on this trip. You happen to be lookin' at him."

"Ain't he something!" Clem said. He shook his head again. "Oh, he is formidable!"

"I'm warning you," Jesse said. "Mebbe you're strong. But if you give me any crap, just don't turn your back on me."

"Gran'pa!'

"I mean it," Jesse said. "You give me trouble, I got a pickax handle back of my truck. It don't matter how tough you think you are. I'll fracture your skull."

Clem clapped his hands together and laughed. "Listen at that! *Whoo-eee!*"

"What d'you think, Miss Macguire?" Jesse said. "This big-talkin' loudmouth worth troublin' myself over?"

"It might or might not work." She looked down at her desk, then stroked the tip of a forefinger across her lower lip, musing. "Enormous age difference. But then . . ."

She paused. Searched mentally for an appropriate term or expression in the verbalese particular to her profession that might fit these two, the disparities in who and what they were. Searched in vain. The relationship, if any could be said to exist, seemed founded on an overt and mutual aggressiveness. She could detect nothing of symbiosis. One was young, the other elderly, yet they came on with each other like ill-tempered Alpha males. The only positive thing was that they talked. The talk was hostile. And it was not mere noise. Either of them, she sensed, had the capacity, if pushed too far, to physically strike out at the other. Yet, out of her experience, she knew that talk—any talk—was better than silence. She said finally, "Why don't we give it a try?"

"Don' worry, Miz Macguire," Clem said, still grinning. "I'll take real good care of him." He glanced at Jesse. "Say, Sprout—" this was a nickname that was to stick, "—you come on real heavy, like, I shouldn't turn my back on you, and all that. What happens if you turn your back on me?"

"And let you git your hand in my hip pocket?" Jesse replied. "Anybody that stupid would sit down in a saloon with his back to the swingin' doors. Nossir!"

Thus the contract between them was set.

THE PROCESSING OF the papers took several days. There were phone calls by Miss Macguire, who at one point explained to Jesse that the custodianship of a minor ordinarily took a great deal longer. During these days the old man and Clem did not see each other. The boy was returned to the detention home.

Along with the papers authorizing Jesse to be guardian, Miss Macguire worked a few deals with the juvenile court, the police, and the probation officer. The idea she pushed to these departments was that the boy had a chance of leaving California to take up residence in a town in New Mexico, where it was hoped that a rural and familial climate would be beneficial to his social rehabilitation. When the LAPD officer who had arrested Clem for car theft heard this, he laughed over the phone and told Miss Macguire, "Honey, you may be right, but personally, I would recommend you tell whoever is going to socially reconstruct that young hood to do it with a can of Mace and a pair of brass knucks. I'd lay odds that anything less won't make a dent on him."

The cop, though a cynic, was not exactly without objectivity. Clem had a sheet that went back to when he was eleven, and which included—besides car theft and breaking and entering—assaulting a police officer, curfew violations, chronic truancy, assault on a teacher, burglary, grand theft, drug violations (grass, speed, coke), and a rather interesting catalog of street violence and mayhem in general, which in several instances had resulted in broken bones and a certain amount of hospitalization on the part of those who had opted to challenge Clem.

Whatever, the disposition of the pending charges was finally shelved, with a stipulation from the juvenile court that periodic reports be forwarded from New Mexico, via reciprocal probation-office channels. Miss Macguire was pleased. She would at least be temporarily rid of a virtually hopeless case. And there was the vague possibility that things would work out for the best. Social workers come equipped with the self-delusion that a better world is possible: that is why so many of them end up bitter drunkards.

On the morning of the first day when all this legal and bureaucratic machinery was grinding into gear, Miss Macguire drove her car into the parking lot of the Burbank office. At the rear of the lot she spotted Jesse Slade, hunkered down beside his old truck. He was cooking breakfast over a small fire he had built out of a wood crate. Apparently, he had spent the night in his makeshift camper. For a moment she was surprised—then astonished. He had set up a camp. Right here. In a county parking lot, in the middle of Los Angeles.

She got out of her car and walked over to him and said good morning. "Mr. Slade, I don't mean to sound like I'm prying, but do you need money for a motel? We could arrange that."

"I've got money," Jesse said. He tended to his cooking arrangement, a wire folding grill that was set above the flames, and on which rested an old blue-enameled coffeepot and a frying pan with four eggs, sunnyside.

"But this lot is locked after six," she said. "How did you get back in?"

"I noticed the sign by the gate," he said. "Figured, since you told me I'd have to stick around awhile, that I might as well be comfortable. Went out and found a grocery. Got some food. Came back here a little before five. Took me a nap. There's a bunk in back. That Mojave is one hell of a tiring drive, ain't it? Reckon the attendant out front thought the truck was empty, parked for the night. Made a couple of sandwiches before it got dark. Felt like a hot meal this morning. Prices sure are sky-high out here, ain't they?"

"But it's against the law, you know," she pointed out. "This parking lot is county property."

"Shoot! Am I hurtin' anyone?" Jesse demanded. "I had a real good sleep, except my eyes burn somethin' terrible from all this smog you got. Say, how about a cup of coffee? It's about ready. I threw some eggshells in it, to calm it down. What's the schedule for today?"

"No, thank you," the social worker said. "Today I'll be working on Clem's papers."

"Always wondered what this gov'ment would do if paper'd never been invented," Jesse commented. He got out a tin plate and some bread and margarine, and began serving himself. "Supposin' we still had to use clay tablets, like them Babylonians? Mailmen'd have to be twelve feet tall and weigh five hundred pounds to lug letters like that around. Folks'd think twice about writing a thank-you note, 'cause they'd need a forklift to git it down to the mailbox. This coffee's good. What d'you say?" Without waiting for a response, he poured some in another metal cup. She accepted it. "Goddamn paperwork," he said. "Don't you ever git tired of it, girl?"

"Mr. Slade, I'm always tired of it," she said. "All of us are."

"You people ought'a ignore it, then, and just go do what needs gittin' done."

"I wish that was possible," she said, sipping the coffee.

"Well, I'd like to help you, but I can't," Jesse said. "You write up them forms, quick as you can. I'll be here, waitin' for the boy."

She thought about this, and then said, "I'll speak to the building custodian, and tell him it's all right for you to park out here."

"Thank you," he said. "You have any trouble, let me know. I can camp out on the street."

"That won't be necessary."

"Wouldn't wanta git you in hot water or anything," the old man said. "Actually, it's kind'a nice in this lot. Real quiet at night. I can't stand all that traffic noise. I already got a cat."

"A cat?"

"He moseyed by about five this morning, when I was out behind that tree tending to needs. Big red tom. I gave him the last of the baloney from supper. I stick around here a week, I'll have to take him home. Nice feller. Real polite for a cat. I named him Rojo. In Spanish that means 'red.' " He drank some of his coffee. "You live around here?"

"I have a place up near Topanga Canyon," she said.

"You married?"

"No."

"How old are you?"

She smiled. "Thirty-four."

"Maybe it's for the best, staying single," Jesse said. "Marriage don't stack up to much these days."

"Those are my feelings too."

"Actually, the only thing I got against marriage is divorce."

"Pretty chancy, a permanent relationship," she agreed.

"You're a hell of a good-lookin' girl," he said. "You got plenty of vinegar in you. Blind man could see that. Always been partial to a lively girl. The kind that can laugh and have a little fun, and look a man square in the eye. I guess you got a boyfriend?"

"I have a friend, yes."

"Is he good to you?"

"Yes. Mostly."

"Well, tell him Jesse Slade says you're okay," the old man said. "I hope he realizes that and treats you square. Most young fellers these days don't know their ass from a hole in left field. They think they got all the answers down pat. Even back in Brazos. That's my home town. They spend more time buyin' fancy clothes and lookin' at themselves in the mirror, gittin' weak in the knees with self-admiration, than they do listenin' to what a woman might have to say. Listen, I don't mind tellin' you something. I appreciate the time you took yesterday afternoon, talkin' to me and explainin' everything. Big town like this, I'm out'a my element, as they say."

"It's my job, Mr. Slade," she said.

"No, it ain't," he objected. "I mean, it's your job, but there are civilized limits to what a person has to do to pick up a paycheck. Ol' fart like me. You could'a shuffled me all over creation. But you took the time. Don't think I don't take notice of things like that. Best advice I ever got in my whole life came from women. You're a fine girl. Tell that boyfriend of yours, or whatever he is, that I said so."

"Thank you," Miss Macguire said.

"You also got about the classiest pair of legs I ever seen on a woman," Jesse went on. "You got a nice way of walking, in case no one ever told you. Don't need my eyeglasses to see that."

"I study dance," she said.

"Women ought'a take care of themselves. Most females, they hit forty, they just sit back and start spreadin' out in all directions at once. Put on weight faster'n zucchini in a wet summer. Well, I don't wanta keep you. I'll be out here when you need me. You git that boy ready. I'll do the best I can with him."

She finished the coffee and set down her cup. "Top priority, Jesse. Do you mind my calling you by your first name?"

"Hell, no."

"My name is Marsha."

"Pretty," Jesse said. "Kind'a gentle. Women's names are almost always pretty. There ain't no meanness in you, that comes clear." He peered up at her over his plate of eggs and bread. "You happy, girl? I mean, with what you're doing here in this life?"

"Yes. Mostly. It's not an easy profession," she said. "Sometimes I get to feeling shot down."

"That's usual. That's what your friend is for. Person gits low, they need to be held up sometimes. Yes, indeed. I know that feelin'."

Miss Macguire turned to go, and then paused. "You know what I think? If Clem can make it at all, he may have a chance with you, Mr. Slade."

"Told you, call me Jesse," he said, and grinned up at her, showing white false teeth. "I wouldn't want you thinkin' that because of my years I am what you call one of these senior citizens. I watch a lot of TV. I know what's what. I surely hate the way this country is forever slappin' labels on folks. Senior citizens! Juveniles! Ghetto folks! Nobody loves nobody anymore. Shit, not less'n they have a name tag on 'em, in which case the feds come in and throw a lot of weight and money in all directions, and that just makes everything worse. If there's one thing that will turn fresh milk sour, it's lettin' the gov'ment stir it. I take care of me and mine, see? I do what I think is right. If the gov'ment don't like it, it can go straight to hell as far as I'm concerned. You know what? I'm old, but I ain't about to sit on some park bench in this rotten world, leanin' my chin on a cane and bitchin' up a goddamn storm about how nobody loves me. I worked hard all my life. I git Social Security, and I take that check every month, because I paid into the damned thing for thirty-two years. But that's as far as I go. I like my independence. I don't like askin' or takin' something for nothing. Today, that is strange thinking. I live, and git by. I don't want nothin' from nobody. I like it that way. When I die, I die. I got a free plot in any national cemetery from my military service, and that is small recompense for the years I put in in the Army. I got no life insurance, because that is a way of bettin' on your own life and I am not a gamblin' person, never have been. I will go until I stop going. Anyone calls me one of these geriatrics, I'll spit right in his goddamn eye. I can work eight hours a day, and haul alfalfa wet, and chop my own firewood for the stove, and still stop off at the Emerald Bar back home and have a couple of bourbons and beers with my friends, and then go on back to the house and cook up my own dinner. I mind my own business. No one fools with me. I take care of myself. In the glove compartment of my truck I got a forty-four Colt with a six-and-three-quarter-inch barrel, and it is oiled and loaded and ready to go."

"Jesse, it's against the law here to carry a weapon concealed in a car," Miss Macguire said.

"Don't quote law at me," Jesse insisted. "At my age, I'm tired of listenin' to what the goddamn law is supposed to be about. You just go ahead and git that brown-skinned kid of mine. Hop to it, girl. My time's valuable."

ON THE FOURTH day they said goodbye to Miss Macguire. Clem in blue jeans, a knit jersey, which he figured showed off his build to advantage, and a salvaged Pan Am bag that contained underwear, socks, his toothbrush, and four copies of *Hustler* he had swiped at the D-Home.

In Miss Macguire's office the final papers were signed. Now that the time for farewells had come, there was a hint of shyness in both

the social worker and Clem. As if, behind her official propriety and
his aggravating style, they almost liked each other. Or at least understood each other. She walked out to the parking lot with Jesse and
the boy. Perhaps in her mind there was a half suspicion that Clem
might make a dash for it, once he was loose.

Right away an argument got started. Clem took a look at the 1960
Chevy pickup and snorted, "You 'spectin' me to ride in *that?*"

"What'd you want, a Rolls-Royce?" Jesse said.

"No, but I wasn't lookin' for something what just wandered away
from the city dump," Clem said. "If my 'ssociates ever saw me in
this, I'd be humiliated for life. What happened to the paint job?
Truck looks like it got skin cancer!" He walked around the vehicle,
kicking at the tires. "My, my! Ain't exactly steel-belted radials, are
they? Must be at least forty or fifty miles left in these skins." He
looked through the rolled-down windows into the cab. "Might'a
guessed. No air-conditionin'. No radio. No tape deck. No *nothin'!*
Got a steering wheel, though. That ought'a help. Springs all busted
out of the seat. What's this ol' cat doin' in here?"

Jesse said, "We're takin' him with us."

"Stray cat, stray nigger," Clem said, and laughed delightedly. He
shook his head. "Sprout, you something else! Any other redneck
tourist hits L.A., what's he lookin' for? Takes the bus tours. Hits the
movie sets. Maybe even gets to see a real TV quiz show. Eyeballs
around, trying to spot a genu-ine movie star. Ol' Sprout, he gets
back home, folks'll say, 'Hey, Sprout, how'd you dig the big town?
You see Disneyland? Marineland? You bring us back some groovy
souvenirs?' Sprout, he say, 'Souvenirs? Why, sho'! Looky here. I
found this ol' pussycat and this stray nigger, ain't they something!' "
Clem laughed again. *"Whoo-eee!"*

"Shut up and git in," Jesse said.

"You want me to sit on them busted-out springs? All the way to
New Mexico? No, thank you."

"I said git in." Jesse was looking mean, and his voice had a hard
tone to it. Despite his age, the expression and the voice carried authority. The boy sensed this. There was something of a mystery here,
because as Clem himself had pointed out, Jesse was indeed frail.
True, there was a lean wiriness to him. Probably he was tougher than
he looked. Even so, in a fair confrontation, Clem probably would
have been able to break Jesse into a neat pile of kindling.

Yet the boy did not rise to the challenge. Suddenly he got sulky, withdrawn. But it was clear that he wasn't about to try anything. In another year or two he might have told Jesse to go to hell. Or maybe he was thinking about the D-Home, and the cheerless prospect of spending the rest of the summer behind bars. Then, as quickly as it had appeared, Clem's sullen mood vanished and he was kidding around and grinning again. "Say, now, couldn't I just meet you in New Mexico?"

"No," Jesse said.

"You could buy me a bus ticket," Clem insisted. "I ain't very good company on the road. I git carsick somethin' awful."

"Bet your feet smell too."

"Cats give me an allergy," Clem said. "Cat hairs make me sneeze and break out all over in a rash."

"You'll live, I reckon," Jesse said. "We ain't got all day, damn it! Git in the truck."

And Clem did.

Jesse turned. "Well, Miss Macguire—Marsha—you take care. And thank you."

"You take care too, Jesse," she said. They shook hands.

Clem scrunched down on the seat until his knees were propped on the dash. He had the big tom on his chest and was massaging its ears. The cat didn't seem to mind. Clem mimicked the two adults. "Goo'-bye, Jesse! Goo'bye, Marsha! Y'all take care. Oh, ah sho'ly *will!* Jesse and Marsha. *Whoo-eee!* Scuba-duba-doo! Cat, you ever hear the likes of that? Sounds like they is tryin' to git it on! My very own social worker and my own flesh-and-blood grandpa. Carryin' on like they is both hot to trot. Right in front'a my eyes!"

"Shut up," his grandfather said.

"Anything you say, Sprout."

THEY GOT ON the Golden State Freeway, headed south, missed the Ventura Freeway cloverleaf, and turned into downtown Los Angeles where the freeways were stacked four high, missed another clover-leaf, and by accident got on the Santa Monica, which took them back out toward the beaches, then made another cutoff and got on the Harbor Freeway, going south again.

By now Clem was nervous. For once he was not putting on an act. Over the noise of the traffic and the pickup's horn, which Jesse was using a lot, the boy yelled, "Hey, ol' man, you trying to kill us? Where you think you going?"

"Tryin' to git on some kind'a goddamn highway headin' east, that's what I'm doin'," Jesse yelled back. "What's it look like I'm doin', admirin' the scenery?"

A raspberry-colored Porsche convertible roared past. Its driver glared and yelled something, giving Jesse the finger. Jesse said, "Flamin' asshole! Just 'cause he's got one of them fancy little roadsters, he thinks the whole world's got to make way for him."

"Man, stay on the *free*way, not the shoulder," Clem cried. By now the cat had crawled under the seat for safety. "Where in hell you takin' us? Don't you know we're drivin' south?"

"I can tell south from east, stupid. Quit yellin' at me! You're makin' me nervous."

"Guess you want'a visit all of greater L.A. before we pull out. 'Nother three, four hours and you'll have hit every freeway we got here."

"Gimme time," Jesse said.

"Where'd you learn to drive? Can't you keep this wreck in one lane? Hell! Use your rear mirror . . . don't be lookin' around like that all the time. Pay attention to what's in front of you for a change. You know something? You *scare* me, man!"

"Out where I live, there ain't this many cars."

"Probably 'cause you done run 'em all off the road," Clem said. They hit a stretch of construction where a single lane had to be formed on the left, and Jesse got onto it, knocking over a fifty-five-gallon drum and a couple of red plastic warning cones. "God almighty," Clem said. Jesse slowed the pickup to twenty and cars began stacking up behind, using their horns. He shifted down to second. Clem said, "Man, what are you *doin'?*"

"You blind or something? Road sign back there says twenty."

"You crazy?"

"Listen, I tangled with a real mean-assed cop comin' out here. Gave me a bad time. Some of these smart fuckers, they git into a uniform, right away they think they can act like Mussolini. I ain't takin' no chances."

"Out here nobody pays any mind to signs," Clem said. "Git her back up to fifty, will you?" He looked behind. "We're leading a procession. A funeral procession. Ours, probably. Hey, we git out'a this

one-lane shit, pull over and let me drive, will you? I been drivin'
since I was twelve. I know these freeways."

"I been drivin' fifty years," Jesse said.

"An' you still in one piece? My, my!"

An hour later they had finally gotten over to Riverdale, via Lake-
wood and Buena Park. The traffic had eased. "Clear sailing from
here on, Sprout," Clem said, checking the road atlas. "Get on up to
I-15 at San Berdoo. That'll take us over to Barstow. Home free, ol'
man. You sure some driver. We got anything to eat in this death
trap?" He opened the glove compartment and rummaged around
inside, found the holstered .44 Colt, and took it out. "Oh, hey now!
Lookit this, would you?"

"Put that away," Jesse said.

Clem slid the long-barreled pistol out of its holster. Hefted it.
"Oh, baby! This motherfucker ain't no Saturday-night special. This
here is what you might call a piece of genu-ine iron!"

"Goddamn it, take your finger off the trigger. It's loaded!"

Clem expertly put the hammer at half-cock and twirled the cylinder. " 'Deed she is! Lookit the size of them shells! Person could really
let some air into a dude with one of these. *Whoo-eee!*" He stuck the
pistol out the window on his side, squinting, taking aim at some
crows perched on a telephone pole. *"Pow!* Bye, bye blackbird. You
mother! You *daid! Per*-forated, through and through."

"F'Christ's sake, quit flashing that thing all over the place."

"What you doin' with a piece this big, Sprout?" Clem said. "You
got elephants out in New Mexico? Say, you know, I never been this
far out'a L.A. in my whole life. Hey, what you shoot with this thing?"

"Rabbits."

Clem had the gun back inside the cab. "Rabbits? You sure mean,
ain't you? Kinda slug this cannon tosses, wouldn't be much left of ol'
Mister Rabbit, would there? Be lucky if you could find his ears and
tail." The boy was still hefting the gun. "Hey, I got an idea. Whyn't
me an' you take this piece and knock off a gas station? Get us some
travelin' money. You want'a jump for something like that? What
say? Maybe git us a real car, while we're at it? How about a Mercedes, or a BMW? High-class wheels. You want to?"

"Put it away," Jesse muttered.

Clem looked at the old man and grinned. "I got another idea."

"You're just brimful of ideas, ain't you?"

"Supposin' I was to lay this piece on you, ol' man?" Clem said. "Like, just supposin' I was to take your wallet and this truck, and leave you an' that big lazy cat on the highway. Just take off. Have me a little fun, hey?"

"Only thing wrong with that, you'd have to shoot me," Jesse said.

"Could be, Sprout," the boy said, still grinning. "Now that you mention it, that is a distinct possibility."

"And there is only one thing wrong with that," Jesse said.

"What?"

"You ain't got the guts."

"Listen to that man! You know that, eh? I mean, you really *positive* in you' haid!"

"That's right. That is something I know."

"I sure wouldn't be takin' that kind'a chance," Clem said. "No sir! That's how people get themselves all shot fulla holes, talkin' big, and takin' on that kind'a dare. You know what they say . . . big talk's liable to lead to big trouble."

"I ain't worried," Jesse said. He stared ahead at the highway. "Talkin' don't mean that much. Man gits serious about shootin', he ain't likely to talk about it at all. He'll think on it. Then he'll just go do it. Leastways, that's been my experience."

"You ever plug a dude?" Clem said, looking over at him.

"Once. 1935."

"You kill him?"

"More or less."

"I'll be damned," Clem said wonderingly. "You spoofin' me?" For the first time he stared at Jesse with something akin to respect. "The law get on your case?"

"They judged it self-defense," Jesse said. "Now, put that thumb-buster away, will you? Let's git some miles behind us. We been drivin' for hours, and we ain't even out'a Los Angeles yet."

"*B-i-i-g* town, Sprout. It's where the action is."

"You keep your action, I'll keep mine," Jesse said. "All you been tellin' me is how tough and ornery you are. All I know is, you been in hot water since you was knee-high to a fart in a windstorm. Well, you're goin' to stay with me for a bit. Not too long. Not one minute longer'n I can help it, that is. But while you're with me, you're goin' to act halfway human. I don't want any more shit out'a you than I can tolerate. You mind your manners. We'll git along fine. Otherwise, there'll be trouble. And don't call me Sprout! Hell, I was retired when you was still shittin' yeller. You know something? You talk too goddamn much! All this jawin' away gits on my nerves. Whyn't you just shut up? Take care of that cat. Make yourself comfortable. You don't shape up, I'm liable to kick you in the ass till you bleed at the eyes. Quit complainin'. You're out'a that D-Home, ain't you? You're legal, for a change. Don't git so uppity."

Once again, there was that mercurial change of mood. Clem stared out the window with an expression that was almost glum. Jesse had said they weren't even out in the country yet. To Clem's mind they were already a thousand miles from the city. And Los Angeles was home to him. It was all he knew. He didn't feel very happy about leaving it. He said finally, "What's this little ol' town of yours like, Sprout?"

"Brazos? You pretty much got it right the first time," Jesse said. "It's little, and it's old. You could take the whole place and drop it, lock, stock, and barrel, inside one of those big shopping malls you got out here, and nobody'd even notice. 'Bout two miles off the main highway, so there ain't no tourists. Drivin' along, you sort'a have to watch out for Brazos real careful, else you're liable to find it in the past tense on the road behind you. One store, one gas station, two bars, and the post office. Most of the town is on welfare. Some ranching and lumbering. Not much else."

"What they do for fun in a place like that?"

"Oh, when the weather's pleasant, we oftentimes walk out to the main highway and watch the cars go by," Jesse said. "Winters, we git a lot of snow. Then folks mostly concentrate on doin' a little serious drinkin' and fightin'."

This information didn't make Clem any happier. He said thoughtfully, "D-Home don't sound so bad."

"Mebbe there is one thing I ought'a tell you about the town."

"What's that?"

"Population's only about a hundred and forty or so. Mostly Spanish. A few Anglos."

"How many blacks?"

"There ain't none," Jesse said.

Clem looked at him. "What?"

"You'll be the only black kid in town."

Clem stared at him unbelievingly. "'You tellin' me this, *now*? You really mean it?"

"That's right."

Clem shook his head. Attempted a blithe easiness. But it didn't come off. "I'm gittin' some funny vibes," he said finally, "and they are real heavy."

"Folks are okay there. Mostly, that is. You'll git by. Watch your step, is all."

"Oh, sure! I'll get by," Clem said somberly. "I can't wait. Get by! I'm really lookin' forward to *that*. A hundred and forty to one!" He frowned. "Hey. These people up there . . . they ever even seen a black dude?"

"Oh, sure. Lots of time. On TV."

"Oh, that's different," Clem said. "I mean, like, man, I wouldn't wanta give 'em some kinda shock or anything. *Whoo-eee!* Bye, bye, Clem. Been nice knowin' you!"

"Quit worryin'."

"Oh, *I* ain't worried. You know me! I ain't the worryin' kind. Only thing that worries me is, I hope *they* ain't worried either."

They drove along for a while in silence. Clem drummed his fingers on one knee. Jesse glanced at him and said, "It won't be all that bad. I'll be there, to vouch for you."

"What's that mean?"

"Just what I said. They don't know you. But they know me."

"Ol' Jesse Slade . . . he's so mean he's famous, eh?"

"They know me," Jesse said again.

"How long did you say I got to stay with you?"

"Till I decide otherwise."

Clem thought about what lay ahead. It was just too much. He felt deflated. Lost. What would he do in a place like that? Nothing. No hustles. No brothers. Nowheresville. Finally, casting about, he asked, a little weakly, "They got beaches or anything?"

"Nope."

"No surfing?"

"You crazy? New Mexico is a state where if somebody stops his car in the middle of the road and takes a piss, somebody else'll pull up behind him with a boat on a trailer, launch the boat in the puddle, an' go fishin'."

"Is there beaver?" Clem asked. He was still searching for a hint of something positive.

"Some. Up in the mountains. They're always damming up the cricks. More trouble than they're worth."

"Don't mean *that* kind'a beaver . . . I meant pussy beaver!"

"Yes, there is that," Jesse said. He maneuvered the truck around a long uphill curve. "I can see I'm goin' to have my hands full with you. Listen, you go messin' with girls, tryin' to see what kind'a dainties they're wearing, you better watch your step. Girls back home ain't no different than they are in Los Angeles, I reckon. They all git the itch where they can't reach to scratch. That's all they got on their minds. Only thing is, they got folks who try and keep 'em under restraint, leastways till they can git 'em married. Preserving a young female's reputation intact can be a twenty-four-hour job, Sundays and holidays included, and even then uncles and cousins got to come in and help out. Female gits antsy, she's slipperier'n axle grease. Gits all hot-eyed and in a sweat. Can't eat, can't sleep, can't do nothin' but make life a livin' hell for everyone around her. Once that happens, the only thing'll calm her down is gettin' rid of that reputation pronto, and then, of course, once that happens, nothing'll satisfy her but that she gits rid of it on a regular basis. Only thing you want'a remember is that I ain't the only one up there who carries a pistol or a rifle. Girls' families do, includin' cousins seven times removed. Hell, most of that goddamn town is interrelated anyway. Listen, I told you to put that hogleg away. Say, since you been so free and easy with my glove compartment, go back into it. I got a pint of Heaven Hill in there someplace. Also some hotdogs for the cat. See if you can coax him out from under the seat."

"Can I have a shot?" Clem said. He felt a real need for anything that might pick him up.

"You're too young."

"Well, then, can we stop for a six-pack? I get awful thirsty ridin'."

"Mebbe around sunset."

"Sprout, you ain't the easiest person in the world to get along with."

Jesse glanced at the boy. "Suffer."

BY SUNSET THEY were past Needles. Out in the desert Jesse found a place to camp, under a highway bridge, where there was a nearly dry stream bed and a thick grove of cottonwoods. Earlier, they had stopped at a 7-11 for beer and food.

Camping like that, way out in the middle of nowhere, got Clem uneasy again. The closest he had ever been to the outdoors was at beach parties, where there was stereo music, and bonfires, and drugs, and crowds of young street people partying all night. Here, they were alone. He discovered that solitude made him edgy, and started an argument with Jesse about why they hadn't stopped at one of the designated off-the-road rest areas, where everybody else in campers and trailers pulled in.

Jesse explained. "I already told you. I don't like being jammed in with a whole mess of people. Those highway camping areas are a royal pain in the ass. When I cook my dinner I want to be by myself. You ain't learned that yet. I don't want a stampeding herd of snotty-assed brats hangin' around me askin' when they can toast a goddamn marshmallow or something. I want'a be left alone. As for fancy motels, they're too expensive. All money, and nothin' to show for it. I got just about enough cash to git us back home. We do things my way."

So under the bridge by the cottonwoods Clem learned a little about putting together a one-night camp. By then he was dying of hunger. So was the cat. Actually, so was Jesse. Together, the boy and the old man gathered scraps of cottonwood. Jesse said, "This stuff doesn't burn worth a damn . . . hotter'n hell for a minute, then you got nothin' but ashes."

They unpacked water jugs and a half-gallon of milk in a waxed carton. They had a package of hamburger and a carton of eggs, the frying pan, and the coffeepot. Jesse said, "After breakfast in the mornin' you go down to that stream and clean up. We got a lot of drivin' tomorrow. I want'a git goin' early."

"What makes you think I'll be here in the mornin'?" Clem said. He was feeling sulky again.

"You will."

"You sure?"

"Pretty sure," Jesse said. "Ain't no other place to go, boy. Face up to it. You got me, or that D-Home, or, as you call it, truckin' around."

"Truckin' don't sound bad."

"That may be so. Let's have a beer while we're settin' up," Jesse said. They got the fire going, arranged the grill, washed their hands and faces in the little stream, and then opened a couple of beers. It was dusk. In the west the last glow of gold, red, and yellow. No stars showing yet through the branches of the trees, but getting darker. The cat was sitting on the hood of the truck with its tail curled around its paws. It hopped down, took a leak, and began exploring the locale. Clem and Jesse sat by the small fire, sipping beer. Clem said finally, "I feel funny out here."

"Oh?"

"I feel like I got to get away from here."

"You just stay put."

"I mean, I could just cut out," Clem said. "You'd never know. Wake up in the morning, I'd be gone. Truck, pistol, and all."

"I got the key."

"Shit! I could hotwire that ol' tin can in two seconds."

"Might be you could."

"It don't bother you?"

"No."

"Why not?"

" 'Cause you won't, that's all," Jesse said. "Right now, I'm all the family you got. Actually, I'm *all* you got. I come all this way to git you. You ain't much. I don't like you, and you don't like me. Even so, we got to git along. Say, fetch me another beer. Git one for yourself."

Clem brought the beers. Jesse molded hamburgers out of the cheap meat they had bought, and put them in the pan. It was almost dark now. He showed the boy how to toast bread over the grill. The cat smelled meat cooking, and got friendly. Jesse cracked a second six-pack, and the boy took a shot of bourbon. The smell of the cooking food got better. "You like onions?" Jesse asked. Clem shrugged, and the old man got a couple of big yellows and sliced them into the sizzling pan. He carried enough to make a meal: ketchup, green-chili relish, mayonnaise, sweet pickles, and even a package of instant potato mix, which he made into patties and then fried. He said, "Gittin' hungry?"

"I could eat."

"Nine-tenths of a meal is in the smellin'. That's what sets the juices to flowin'. Nothin' like potatoes and onions and hamburgers fryin' slow."

The stars were beginning to shine overhead now. Jesse got out the metal plates and tin cups and a couple of forks, and said, "Cat's lookin' hungry too."

It was silent and dark except for an occasional flare of head-lights as a car rushed over the bridge. Clem, sipping at his beer, said, "Don't you ever get nervous out in a place like this?"

"What for?"

"Suppose somebody was to come along and rip you off? What could you do? I mean, it's so dark."

"Miss all those lights and neon signs?"

"Hell, yes."

The hamburgers and potato patties were turning brown and crispy, and the cat was making a fool out of itself, rubbing against Clem's leg. The boy said, "Listen. This ain't goin' to work. I'm strictly a street person. I mean, like I'm tryin' to tell it to you easy. You ought'a take me back to the D-Home. I can do that scene hands down. You got no business with me."

"Quit frettin' about it."

"Well, you got to understand . . . I mean, you're right about us not diggin' each other," Clem said. He was on his fifth beer and was feeling a little more relaxed. "Like, I been listenin' to you say how you don't feel cool around me, and all that. And it's true. So, I will say the same. I'm just tellin' you how it happens to be, man. You got no business with me. I got none with you. Nothin' personal. What say we go our separate ways? Is that okay?"

"No, it ain't."

"Man, I don't *dig* hangin' out with you! Can't you get that through that bony skull of yours."

"Put up with it."

"I ain't about to," Clem said. He got indignant. "You know how I travel? First-class! This ain't that."

"You told me you never been out of L.A."

"I been to Newport Beach! You don't know what it's *like*, ol' man. You don't know my scene." He drank some of his beer, then stared glumly into the flickering campfire. "You don't know where I been. You just don't!"

"I'd as soon not hear."

Clem shook his head. "I been on the streets since I was twelve. You know what that means? No, you don't. You corny ol' asshole! You don't know nothin'. Street people, they learn how to get by. Drugs and hustlin', and a few numbers and tricks here and there, nothing big, nothing super-heavy, but, y'know, like, you get by, don't you dig that? How old was you when you got your first piece?"

"None of your business," Jesse said.

"You know how many times I've scored with chicks?" Clem said angrily. "You know how many times I hung out on Sunset, waitin' to turn a few bucks, a score, just hangin' around, y'know, movin' and groovin', waitin' to see what'll come along. Maybe some chick, maybe some ol' closet queen, gets his *en*-joys out'a dunking his head in the pisser and doin' his deep-breathin' exercises. Golden showers bring May flowers. Sprout, you know anything at *all?* Do you?"

"Don't know about any of that," Jesse said. "Supper's about ready."

"Screw supper, and screw you too."

"Suit yourself," Jesse said. "I'm eating." He put a piece of hamburger on the ground for the cat.

Clem shivered against the coolness of the night and moved closer to the campfire. "This ain't no way to live! Where we supposed to sleep?"

"Back in the camper. I take the bunk. You can have the floor."

"God almighty."

Jesse began eating. He said, "Sleep where you please. I don't care."

CLEM SETTLED FOR the camper. It had been a long day's drive, and a hot one, and this along with the beers and the supper killed any idea he had of taking off during the night. In the camper the cat curled up with him. Once he heard an owl hoot, and then the yip of a coyote, way off. The idea that there might be wild animals out there in the desert surrounding them got him nervous again, and he was wondering how they might protect themselves if something attacked them in the night, when, suddenly, he fell asleep.

When he wakened, the sun was up. He poked his head out the back of the camper, shivering in a pair of jockey shorts, his shoulders drawn up tight. Jesse was on his knees beside the fire, working on coffee and eggs. It was almost chilly. The desert air was perfectly still, and the smoke from the little fire rose straight up into a pale blue, cloudless sky. Early sunlight angled through the cottonwood grove. Clem slipped into his clothes. He felt sad and unhappy and lost. His hair was all awry. For a while he stood by the truck with a blanket wrapped around his shoulders. Then he went down to the stream and brushed his teeth. In the early light the stream was nothing, only a trickle, with a few muddy pools here and there.

Bending over, he rinsed his mouth in the alkaline water, and then jumped back, horrified. Inches from where his face had been, a dead tarantula floated, belly up. Surface bugs scooted about.

Over breakfast, Clem said, "You always travel like this?"

"Like what?"

"All this back-to-nature shit."

"Mostly. Cheaper. More fun too," Jesse said. "Hell, when I was your age, I herded sheep on Rowe Mesa. Mesas can be big, y'know. This one was sixty miles across. Ten bucks a month and keep. Good job for a kid. Out all summer. Had three dogs with me. They did the work. I just went along. That was right after World War One. Didn't even have a horse. Just a burro, for my gear. The burro and the dogs, and four hundred sheep. Once a month the boss drove up with vittles. Sack of beans, coffee, salt pork, lard. Wasn't bad. He loaned me a little .410 loaded with birdshot. Learned to shoot wild turkey. I walked that mesa from one end to the other, tending that herd. Sheep are stupid. You got to watch out for 'em. I was just a kid. Like you. Wasn't a bad life. Got tired of it. Finally quit. Went to work in a mine. We got coal mines—mostly abandoned now—out where we're goin'. Couldn't stand that. Workin' ten straight hours on your knees. Temperature up around a hundred. Nothin' but stink and yellow light underground. We'd take birds in cages down with us, to sense when the gas was dangerous. Then I went in the Army. Three years. I was in the Cavalry. That was the first time. I went back in during the Second War. After I got out, I went back to ranching. Easiest job I ever had. Ran a chuck wagon. Big ranch, millionaire-type feller owned it. He liked mountains and scenery. I had a big gray named Bill. He pulled that chuck wagon I had. I'd put up food for fifteen, twenty hands, three times a day. Had a cast-iron kettle that held fifteen gallons. Had me a bake-stove, solid steel, it would fold apart, could make me butter biscuits, cornbread, anything you wanted. Stick some more bread on that grill. You want some milk? It's warm, but it ain't sour. Kid needs milk, they say." Jesse poured some in a dish for Rojo, who came over, stared at it, and then began lapping it up.

"I just don't feel easy," Clem said finally. "Off by ourselves like this. I got to know where I'm at, is all."

"You scared out here?"

" 'Course not!" Clem said. "Only thing is, maybe I know some things you don't. Like, for example, there are some real crazies cruisin' around the highways. Man has got to watch out, see? You never know."

"No, you never do."

"Like on the beaches, y'know, people are careful how they camp out," Clem explained. "Some ol' crazy is liable to come anklin' along, and just to pass the time of night he'll kill you, pry out your teeth with a screwdriver, and bust loose your eyeballs. Wear the teeth like a necklace and the eyeballs like earrings. Sprout, you got some heavy people movin' around the country these days. They go around *lookin'* for action. You want to mess with this Boy Scout routine . . . well, I don't know."

"I'm old," Jesse said. "An old man, he sleeps real light. I tuck in with that forty-four under my pillow. Kid like you, he snores all night. Man my age, he gits his sleep in fits and snatches. Anybody fools with me is liable to git a surprise." He ate slowly, sipping at his coffee and mopping egg yolk with a piece of bread. "Listen, boy. I been thinkin'. About what we talked about last night. I reckon you're right. It's true. Actually, we don't git on. Hell, that ain't surprisin'. I'm 'most sixty years older. I'm set in my ways. I got no time left to waste on a kid like you. I don't deny it. So, if you want, we'll do this, okay? Let that niece of mine—the one over in Germany with the Air Force—take you over. She's comin' back soon. I'll write her again, and tell her to git her ass back on the double. She's used to kids. You'd be better off with her. She knows all about kids."

"How long will that take?" Clem said.

"How in hell do I know? Couple of months," Jesse replied. "You think mebbe we could stick it out for that long? I mean, just try to put up with a bad situation? Stay out'a each other's way? I don't know what else to do. How's that hit you?"

"It don't hit me at all," Clem said. "That's pie-in-the-sky talk. That's all it amounts to."

"What you want, a written guarantee?" Jesse asked. Now it was he who sounded grumpy. "Jesus, if there was ever a kid wanted to build a man a new asshole just to keep in practice, it's you."

Clem shrugged. "I got no options, do I?"

"Give that cat a piece of your breakfast. Can't you see he's makin' up to you?"

Clem did. Then he said, "You tellin' me to put up with all this?"

"Might as well try."

Clem sighed and stared off, as though the discussion was more trouble than it was worth. Ate a little off his plate, picking as though he wasn't hungry. Finally he said, "I got nothin' to lose, nothin' to gain. Either way."

After breakfast Jesse helped him wash the plates and cups in the muddy stream. "You got paper towels?" Clem asked.

"No," the old man said. "These'll dry in the sun by the time we're ready to roll. I don't believe in all that fancy paper towel and napkin stuff. Use 'em once and then throw 'em away. That's plumb extravagant, not to mention expensive."

KINGMAN, FLAGSTAFF, WHERE it rained, on to Gallup, Grants, and then into Albuquerque and up to Santa Fe for the last ninety miles north that would take them to Chama and into Brazos.

They were on the high plains by now, after nearly three days on the road, almost at eight thousand feet, past Abiqui, Canjilon, and Cebolla. The countryside was beautiful. Raw earth colors, hard ochers and dull reds and browns. Forested mountains in the distance. Clem kept repeating, "God . . . there ain't no *people* out here. I never seen anything like this in my whole life! It's like livin' on the moon! Where is everybody?"

"Oh, they're here. They just ain't easy to spot."

At the edge of the village Jesse said, "Might as well stop at the Emerald. Wet our whistle."

He pulled the truck up to a decrepit saloon with a plywood sign above its facade that read EMERALD BAR. Whatever paint that remained on the saloon's weathered front was faded to a dull brown— there was nothing green about the place at all.

Clem and Jesse rolled their windows up so that the cat would stay put. Clem said, "You trottin' me out for the local gentry?" He didn't look too pleased about going into the bar.

"Ain't showin' you off. No need to," Jesse said, getting out. "One thing you might as well learn about a town like this. Ain't no secrets in it. Everybody knows everybody else. Somebody gits an air-mail letter, folks'll wonder and talk about it for weeks. Young feller drives his girl up Brazos Canyon to drop a pebble in her well, before they git back, folks got a lottery organized like a football pool, with bets on what day the kid'll hatch. What you want to keep in mind is, whatever you do here—good or bad—people'll know. They'll judge you."

"What's that mean—judge?"

"It's a saying hereabouts. Folks judge one another. Man may be a no-good drunk, whore-hoppin' son of a bitch, but that won't slow him from judgin' his neighbor on the same grounds . . . and passin' sentence. Just keep that in mind. Judgin's a full-time hobby around here."

They went in.

The interior was dark and gloomy. People sat at the bar on stools, or at one of the half-dozen wood tables.

Someone said, "I'll be damned! Slade's back."

Someone else said, "I knew it was too good to last. Town's actually been halfway decent to live in. Hello, Jesse. Where in hell you been? Not that we care." They were talking to the old man, but everybody was staring at Clem.

"Away from this miserable hellhole, that's where," Jesse said. "Been all the way to Los Angeles."

"You went to California?"

"Sure."

"By God! Los Angeles, California!"

"People know how to live out there," Jesse remarked. "I had me a real time." He walked up to the bar. "Bitch of a drive, though. I'm knocked out. How's it goin', Woody?"

The man behind the bar was Woody Klein. He owned the Emerald. He was a big, gray-haired, sad-looking man, and his bar had the best business in town, mainly because Pacheco's Saloon down on Main Street was so broken down that not even the chairs were usable.

Lulu Uranga, the part-time waitress, came up and gave Jesse a hug. She seemed to be the only one who was really pleased to see him. Uranga was a Mexican name, not local. Lulu had town-hopped up from Juarez and El Paso years ago, whoring and waitressing, and acquiring seven kids en route, until now, at forty-eight, she was five feet tall and three feet wide, with four children still "at home" in the shack she rented on a dirt lane behind the post office. Lulu's beauty was not in her face or figure but in her feelings. She liked men. Any kind. They treated her rotten and broke her heart and sometimes even stole her welfare check, but it made no difference. She simply did not have it in her to feel bad about them. At

least not for long. Old, young, mean, gentle, they were all the same
to Lulu. In this harsh world they were a blessing.

Lulu's hair was dyed ink-black, and there was not a wrinkle in her
round face. Well, maybe a couple here and there, but they were
mostly smile wrinkles. She served drinks at the Emerald barefoot,
in an Indian squaw skirt and a white dirndl peasant blouse through
which bulged a bosom that would have made the bow of an aircraft
carrier look sick. She knew the tastes of every man who patronized
the bar. Knew how much they drank, and how much they could
hold, and how much they could pay. She knew who the deadbeats
were, and who it was safe to run a tab on. Only one man had ever
given her trouble in the Emerald, a tall lumberjack named Marty
Wilkinson, who in some long-forgotten fracas had tried to pick
Lulu up and sling her across the bar. A strict rule of Lu's was that
no one could put a hand on her until she gave the nod. No friendly
pat on the rump, no goosing, no kidding around. Lulu had dignity.
When Marty Wilkinson grabbed her in a private place she wriggled
loose and fired off a right cross that ruined eight hundred dollars'
worth of root canal work Marty had almost finished paying off. There
was a rumor that they were also lovers, but this was never discussed, at least not in front of Lulu.

After that punch, Lu commanded even more respect and dignity
in the Emerald. The patrons all liked her. With that round face and
that big, friendly grin, who could help it? And in a quiet way she
took care of the needs of a few of the lonelier men in Brazos. For
a woman who was not exactly a kid anymore she radiated more pure
sexuality than any of those Las Vegas superstars. With those ladies,
a man just knew he'd be barking his shins on a skinny tree. With
Lulu, if she said okay, a man would have a small mountain to wal-
low around on.

Also present was an enemy of Jesse's, Werner Grimmiessen,
sixty-seven, a cranky drunk. Werner had fought with General Rommel's Afrika Korps at El Alamein in '43. Werner was a neighbor, in
fact lived right alongside Jesse, and for more than twenty years
he had been trying to write the definitive memoir about the mentality
that had led Germany into the flaming chaos of World War II.
As a tank commander, he had been a national hero, and had won
an Iron Cross. His manuscript began: "Lieutenant Werner
Grimmiessen was a pure Aryan, but his hair was black as soot." For
the writing he relied heavily upon a Roget's Thesaurus and a rhym-

ing dictionary. He had rewritten the opening paragraph several thousand times over the years, and by now his hair was as white as snow. Though he had legally immigrated to America in 1954 he had done nothing to obliterate his heavy accent, which sounded like something out of an old Hollywood anti-Nazi propaganda movie.

There was also Connie—Concepción—Aragon, a lumberjack, who even sideways looked as big as a Santa Gertrudis bull. There was no cutting going on at present, so the Emerald was as good a place as any to kill time. He was sitting at a table with his buddies, Willie and Bennie Montoya, who were drinking Coors and playing pick-up-sticks with a handful of plastic wands.

Holding court at the bar, more or less coherently, were Garrison and Patsy Hurley. They came in every day to get drunk. Then they went home and got really drunk. Garrison got civil service disability due to advanced alcoholism. He had once been a mathematician at the Los Alamos Scientific Laboratory, where he had helped refine the hydrogen bomb. In his better days Garrison would commandeer hourly time with one of the big computers, until he finally designed and perfected a thermonuclear device small enough to be carried in a flight bag but big enough to blow away the lower quarter of Manhattan Island. He had finally come to his senses and abandoned his career in favor of booze, and had been fortunate enough to find Patsy at a drying-out sanitorium in Albuquerque. Both, now in their fifties, had retired to Brazos. They owned the property on the other side of Jesse's, and like Werner Grimmiessen they didn't care much for their neighbor.

Jesse walked up to the bar and said, "How about a couple of beers, Woody?"

"Is that boy with you of age?" Woody asked.

"Matter of fact, he ain't," Jesse replied. "Howsomever, the law in this state, if I remember it correct, says that a minor child can be served a drink if he's with a parent or guardian."

"So?"

"He's my grandson."

"He's what?"

"You heard me."

The other patrons exchanged looks. Jesse said, "Woody, goddamn it, do I have to stand around here all day long for a couple of cold ones?"

"This is your grandson?" Woody Klein said.

"That's right."

Connie Aragon said, "Madre de Dios!"

Woody Klein opened two Coors and placed them on the bar. "Dollar twenty, Jesse."

Jesse counted out the change. He and the boy tasted their beers. Connie Aragon said, "I never knew you had a grandkid, Jesse."

"There is lots of things you don't know, Connie," Jesse said. "Includin' how to tie your lousy shoelaces every mornin' without readin' the instruction manual. I bet you don't know that Woodrow Wilson was my uncle, on the maternal side. I bet you don't know that I'm directly hooked into the Rockefeller millions. Once or twice a year I phone 'em, collect, back East, and they mail me out a suitcase full of fifty-dollar bills. For tobacco money. Woody, don't you ever put any goddamn ice in that sonuvabitchin' cooler? Man comes in off a long haul, he don't need a beer with steam comin' out of the can."

"I just stacked those cans at noon, Jesse," Woody said. "They haven't had time to cool down yet."

"I been drinking here since you bought this place, Woody, and I have yet to see the day when your cooler ain't just been filled," Jesse said. "Only man I ever met who tries to cool eight cases of Coors with a single ice cube. How's your beer, Clem? If it's too hot, we'll just set it outside in the sun for a while to cool off."

Werner Grimmiessen came over. "Is this your son's boy?"

"That's right, Werner. And keep your hands to yourself."

"Where is your son these days?"

"Dead."

"*Ach!*" He nodded toward Clem. "So, now you have the boy?"

"You see him here, don't you?"

"He is to stay with you?"

"That's the general idea, Werner."

"Ah! Young people. We need that here," Werner said. He smiled at Clem.

Jesse stared at Grimmiessen. Then he said conversationally, "Go away, you nasty Kraut Nazi degenerate shit."

The other patrons paid no attention to this. They talked in low voices. Actually, the Emerald was a quiet place for the most part. Willie and Bennie Montoya, the two brothers with Connie Aragon, looked Clem over, as if they didn't quite know what to make of him. In a way, except for the Afro hairdo, this *mulato*, or in local talk, *este coyote negro*—black half-breed—didn't look all that much different from them. Both young men, naturally olive-complexioned, had been burned a dark brown from the summer's work up in the logging camps; in fact, their arms, with the shirtsleeves rolled, were browner than Clem's. Yet, of course, he *was* different. Lots different. Willie and Bennie exchanged glances with Connie Aragon, as if to say they had not quite figured out what to do about this, but given time, they would think of something, maybe even something unpleasant.

Garrison Hurley had a sense of decorum. His manners were always refined. Florid-faced and white-haired, he got off his stool and came over to Clem, extending a hand. "Delighted to meet you, m'boy. Welcome to Brazos. A haven for the misbegotten. Name's Hurley. Garrison Hurley. Permit me to introduce my wife, Patricia . . . Patsy. We are neighbors of your grandfather's. Not always, I fear, on the best of speaking terms. Jesse Slade is not an easy man. But, nonetheless, welcome."

"All I ever asked you and Patsy to do was quit throwing your empties over the fence into my yard," Jesse said. "Let me have another of those hot beers, Woody." He glanced at Garrison. " 'Course, it's understandable. You and Patsy got to git rid of those dead soldiers someplace. Your own yard must have two or three tons of glass layin' around by now. You ought'a hire Orly Mendocino's two-ton dump truck to tidy up."

Patsy, hanging on to Garrison's arm, smiled at Clem. "We certainly hope you like it here. It's a lovely spot. Will you be going to the high school? My! Jesse, you must be so proud. To have such a *handsome* grandson!"

"Ain't going to school," Clem said. It was the first time he had spoken.

"Oh, you must complete your education," Patsy said. "Garrison, you know, has his Ph.D. In quantum mechanics."

"Ph.D. in sousology, more'n likely," Jesse said. He told Clem, "We got a nickname for the Hurleys around here. We call 'em the Unquenchables. Werner, how's my place? You keep an eye on it, like you said you would?" This was a pact the two men had. They fought together, but if one had to go out of town, the other looked after the absentee's property.

"Couple kids were fooling around in the yard a few days ago," Werner said. "I chased them. That little Lopez kid, he was throwing rocks at the windows. I chased him too. Those kids sneaked through that hole in your fence, where I couldn't watch, and stole half my squash. You owe me two baskets of squash for that, Jesse. When are you going to pay?"

"Soon's you pay me for the four chickens your stinkin' dog chewed up when he got in the coop this spring," Jesse said.

"That's not my dog! I told you," Werner argued.

"Cochise? If he ain't yours, how come he's been livin' with you for the past six years now?" Jesse muttered under his breath, "Fuckin' dog barks with a Kraut accent!"

"Just a stray, Jesse. What am I supposed to do? I have a soft heart for animals. Can I help it?"

"Big ol' lop-eared good-for-nothin'," Jesse grumbled. "Sleeps on that moldy mattress you set up for him on your back porch. Comes over and craps in twenty different directions from one end of my front yard to the other. Won't even lift his *leg* to piss in your yard! You sure got him trained, Grimmiessen! One of these days, I'm goin' to shoot him! I'm warnin' you. By God, he's got my yard lookin' like a goddamn minefield! I'm worn out, shovelin' up after him."

"His deposits are good for the flowers."

"There's limits to having a good thing. I only got a couple of rows of geraniums, Werner, not a whole redwood forest."

Clem was beginning to get the idea that the topics of conversational interest to the street people he had hung out with back in Los Angeles were a shade different from what they were here. Yet one thing was clear to him. These were people, and people were something a hustler understood. Mountains and forests and all that outdoor jazz Jesse was into were a mystery . . . but human nature tended to be the same everywhere.

TWO

THEY HAD SEVERAL more beers at the Emerald and then left. Jesse stopped at Benavidez's Mercantile down on Main Street, where Clem was introduced to Gus Benavidez, the owner.

Gus was a large man in his fifties, with a square, expressionless face that never, or almost never, revealed what was on his mind. He did not shake hands with Clem but at Jesse's request took out the old man's credit slip so that Clem might add his own signature. This would enable the boy to charge at the store.

Like everything else in town, Gus's store looked like it was falling apart, but it was a gold mine, because the nearest other general store or grocery was eleven miles up the highway at Chama. Long ago, Gus had invented a simplistic formula for arriving at a fair price for the food and dry goods he sold. He read the Albuquerque papers, and whenever he came across an advertisement listing something he stocked on his dusty shelves he tacked thirty percent on the item. With this rudimentary form of laissez faire, most of the village was in his debt. In really bad times, Gus was known occasionally and with ostensible reluctance to accept a small parcel of land in lieu of a grocery bill that was overdue. In Gus's mind, inflation was here to stay, and real estate was the only thing that kept pace with spiraling costs. He figured only a fool would let excess money sit around in a bank where it earned minimal interest, when it might be put to better use. He had a vague idea that Brazos would, someday, experience a real estate boom. With this in mind, and by charging exorbitant interest rates on monthly credit accounts, he now owned almost one-half of the unincorporated township.

Jesse picked out a ten-pound sack of pinto beans, condensed milk, bread, margarine, some tobacco, cigarette papers, three six-packs of beer and a fifth of Heaven Hill, onions, and some hamburger from Gus's cooler that looked like it had been incubating behind glass for several weeks waiting for somebody to make up his mind to buy it.

"How much water you add?" the old man asked, as Gus weighed out a two-pound portion of the meat. Jesse looked at Clem. "Gus has the only hamburger I ever seen that you try to fry it, it ends up poached. Trim off a little of that green mold, will you, Gus? You sellin' meat or botulism?"

"It's prime ground chuck, Jesse," Gus said. He trimmed the suspect meat, then placed the butcher knife on the scale, leaned back, and peered. "Three dollars, ninety-four cents, Jesse."

"Knife included?"

Gus took the knife away. "Three sixteen. Okay?"

"Expensive, for water," Jesse said. Gus wrapped the meat and put it in with the rest of the groceries.

"That what we goin' to live on for the rest of the summer—beans and hamburger?" Clem asked at the counter.

"I like to eat simple," Jesse said. "Mebbe back there you're used to fancy stuff."

"I dig lobster," Clem said. "One time, I had *escargots*—snails. 'Nother time, I had king crab."

"What that slimy seafood garbage does to a man's liver and pancreas ain't worth describin'," Jesse said. "I wouldn't insult my system with that stuff." He added to the grocery sack two large packages of fiery red chili powder and a small bottle of tabasco sauce, the label of which carried a picture of a grinning red devil. "Chili livens up a meal," he explained. "Also, most of the time it helps disguise what you're eatin' out of Gus's store."

From there they went to the post office, which was the only new

building in town, built with federal funds, of tan stucco brick, with
a white-painted flagpole outside. The postmaster was a crippled old
man, bent over, with a locked, rheumatic spine. He had a milky
cataract in one eye and malice glaring out of the other. He wore a
pair of binoculars around his neck, and his name was Horacio
Quintana.

Horacio already had a change-of-address slip ready for Clem
when he and Jesse walked in, along with a thin stack of mail that
had accumulated for Slade.

Jesse said hello, glanced through his mail, and then looked at
the change-of-address slip. He said, "We don't need this, Horacio."

"Federal regulations say you got to send it back to the boy's
last address," Horacio explained. "Else nobody knows where to
forward his mail proper."

"He ain't got no last address."

This confused Horacio. "Everybody's got a last address," he
said.

"Well, he don't."

"It's like a precaution," Horacio went on. With the bent spine,
his chin was almost resting on the counter behind the grilled window.
As though the binoculars weighed a ton. "Mail can get lost, Jesse."

"He won't be gittin' any."

"This boy, he visits you for the summer?" Horacio said. It was
neither a statement nor really a question. It was more like an ob-
servation based on mild curiosity, a detached wish to keep the record
straight.

"Sort'a."

"Summer is already half over," Horacio pointed out. "Maybe he
stays here longer?"

"Soon's I figure that out, you'll be the first to know, Horace,"
Jesse said. He took his mail, turned, and walked out. Clem followed.

In the pickup, Jesse tossed the red cat off the dashboard, where
it had been sunning itself, and said, "Listen to me. Don't ever talk
to that man."

"I ain't much for talkin'," Clem said.

"He is full of treachery."

"He is?" Clem considered this. "Looks too ol' and beat-up to be
treacherous."

"He's an undercover agent."

"What you talkin' about?"

"You see those binoculars?"

"Sure."

"Horacio Quintana's a paid spy," Jesse said. "He is in the employment of all sorts of various gov'ment agencies besides the postal department. It's a commonly known fact here in town. Probably the FBI, the CIA, the Secret Service, and a couple of those other meddlin' outfits. That man has such gall he couldn't even hide it. Nosiest old son of a bitch in the whole state. Why, he can't figure the postage on three letters and a two-pound box of caramels without comin' up with a dozen different sets of figures, but he knows by absolute memory where any letter goes that's written in this town, and he can recite by heart the return address of every single letter that comes in. No-good spyin' bastard!" He drove off.

"How come he had that address-change card ready when we walked in?" Clem asked. "I mean, how'd he even know we were in town?"

"I told you. It's a small place," Jesse said. "Hereabouts, when you're drivin' back from someplace, first place you usually hit is the Emerald, for a beer. Then you stop at Gus's, to git groceries. Then you go to the post office, to check the mail. Probably that snoopy Horacio knew you was in town before we got to Gus's. Another hour, the whole town'll know, if it doesn't already. That's how come I wouldn't fill out that change-of-address. Jesus, all we'd have to write was the address of that D-Home and those child-welfare people. That'd sure make Horacio straighten up his rotten crippled back! He'd spread that news fast. Folks here would have enough to gabble about till next summer. Listen to me. Keep that mouth of yours shut. Ain't no one has to know our private affairs. Anybody starts cozyin' up to you real sweet and tryin' to find out what you been doin', don't tell them a goddamn thing! Whatever you do, don't tell 'em the truth. That ain't their business. Tell 'em you're a retired airplane pilot off one of them 747's. Tell 'em you're a United Nations international diplomat on vacation or something, recuperatin' from measles or leprosy. Tell 'em anything, just don't tell 'em the truth."

"Listen, is everybody in this nickels-and-dimes dump ready for the grave?" Clem demanded. "Except for a couple of dudes in that bar —and did you catch the way they was lookin' me over?—everybody I seen so far is old, drunk, or both."

"There are some young folks," Jesse said. "Not many. The smart ones leave. Can't blame 'em. No work. Only loggin' or workin' for the forest service. There was plenty of jobs six or seven years ago, when the new four-lane went in. Nothin' much now, though."

They were up by the northern outskirts of the village. The old man pulled the pickup over to the side of the dirt road. He said, "We're home."

IF ASKED, CLEM could not have described the kind of image he had built up in his mind about Jesse's house. He had seen incredible expanses of empty country on the long drive between Los Angeles and New Mexico. Maybe he had some idea of a ranch—something out of a western movie: a picturesque, rambling adobe, barns, corrals. True, in back of Jesse's place there were rolling fields, but they were knee-deep in weeds. A busted-down barbed-wire fence closed the property in, and it wouldn't have stopped a newborn calf. The whole of that end of Brazos could be described in only one way: trashy, run to seed, dirt poor.

The house itself appeared to be on its last legs. It was made of unplastered adobe—sun-dried mud mixed with straw, molded into ten-by-fourteen-inch bricks. *Vigas*—peeled, ancient spruce logs— made up the roof beams of the flat-topped structure, and their un-trimmed ends stuck right out of the mud walls. The windows were cockeyed. Most of the panes actually had glass in them, but the casements went this way and that. In back, visible from the road, was an outhouse, and to the right there was a coop with a couple of diseased-looking bantams in it. Behind it, a fair-sized wooden storage building, padlocked. A dog barked somewhere, and a couple of cats came down off the roof to say hello to whoever had come. Clem regarded this scene for a while and finally muttered, "High decor, ain't it?"

"Not bad, eh?" Jesse said.

Clem pointed toward the storage building. "What's in there?"

"Lot of old stuff of mine," Jesse said.

"Couldn't we clear it out?" Clem asked. "I could move in there. That way, we'd both have some privacy."

"We ain't changin' nothin'," Jesse said.

To the right of the fence line was another house, apparently

Werner Grimmiessen's. To the left, another property, more of a shack really, so falling apart that it made Jesse's place look elegant. This, the old man said, was the Hurley spread.

A fence made of slab sidings—scrap from the lumber mill—ran across the frontage of Jesse's property, with a little wood-slat gate that was held in place by hinges made of baling wire. The inside yard was not much different from the way the old man had described it. To get from the gate to the front door they had to plow through a minefield of dog droppings and empty whiskey bottles. Holding one of the sacks of groceries, Clem followed as Jesse broke trail. He said aloud, half to himself, "What in hell have I got myself into?"

"Kind'a cozy, ain't it?" Jesse said. He set down his sack and fumbled with a ring of keys. The front door had an old padlock-and-hasp arrangement. "I paid six hundred for this place. That was back in 'thirty. The depression was just comin' on. People laughed and swore I was robbed blind. I got forty acres on the river, and this house. Taxes run sixteen bucks a year. Took me four years to pay it off. I never complained. Man ought'a have a little place he can sit down and call his own. It ain't much."

"That's the understatement of the year," Clem observed.

"Nothin' fancy, but it'll do. Man doesn't need a whole mess of room."

"Looks like the ghetto with a view," Clem said sourly. "In Watts they pay people full-time salaries to find better-looking places than this to run bulldozers over. I mean, Sprout, back there, folks set fire to places like this just for the fun of it."

Jesse got the padlock open and unsnapped the hasp. They went in, carrying the groceries, the beer, and the whiskey. Along about then, Clem realized how low he really felt.

HE HAD NOT been feeling his usual self since they'd left Los Angeles. Was very definitely not in top form, and this awareness left him depressed and uneasy. It was like everything that could go wrong had, and it was getting steadily worse.

He felt really bad deep down inside, and didn't know what to do about it.

Felt like he'd been kicked where he didn't need it, and kissed where he didn't want it.

With that odd combination of street hustle and the sociological garbology he'd heard for years, he could have mimicked, with passable accuracy, the verbalese of the last psychologist who had interviewed him. "Man, just in case you don' happen to *know* it, you is sufferin' from what certain people might call a dislocation *syndrome!*"

He was out of his element. He thought to himself, "Clem, baby, you got yourself a real situation here! Oh, my! Yes, indeed. Fish out'a water, he got himself *good* conditions compared to this!"

It wasn't just that he was the only black in town. It wasn't just that he didn't fit in. There was nothing for him to *do* here. And it was also pretty obvious that anything he might *try* wasn't going to go down. In this crazy old town there just wasn't any way in the world he could ever make a cool move without having the whole scam go wrong. He thought, "Man, you just ain't ever goin' to hack it here! Might as well make yo' mind up about that. Yessir!"

On the loose back in Los Angeles—providing, that is, he could have sweet-talked some dumb Juvenile court judge into letting him out of the slammer—he would have been having fun. No doubt about that! There was always a lot going on in a place like the City of the Angels. In that big town, just staying alive kept a person busy. Making it took most of a man's waking hours, he had to keep his wits sharp. Yes, there was pride in the notion of just plain *making it*. Stealing and trashing. Jiving around. Dealing on the street. Back in that town, everything had a price. On the street there wasn't *nothing* that couldn't be bought. Young boys, girlchicks, guns, dope, tape decks, stereos, TV sets. Clem knew dudes who didn't deal in just any old set. You named your brand and the size screen you had a craving for, and these guys, they'd go out and come back in a couple of hours with exactly what you needed. He knew of school kids who made two, three hundred a day dealing dope. Grass, hash, acid, PCP, snort, and H, on the public school playgrounds, or in the street, they didn't care. Anything a man wanted, that's how real street people went at it. Cruising the beaches, cruising the Strip, cruising the bars, the skinflicks, the discos. Boogeying around all the livelong day, keeping on the move, never stopping longer than necessary. That was the only way to stay ahead. Nobody stood still in any one place for too long, else the Man might decide to come down on him, just to keep his hand in.

All in all, it was a fair enough life. Clem grooved on it. It was scary, and it was fun. It was rough when a person wasn't making it, but then it was cool when that person was into a good scene, like when nothing he did ever went wrong . . . when he was really "on a run." To have new threads on your back and a roll of twenties in your pocket, just trucking around and hanging in loose with friends, bragging and lying, all laid back and watching it happen, coming on big about some score you'd just made, or were about to make, or maybe might make, someday, sometime, someplace. Always thinking ahead. Never looking over your shoulder. There was nothing back there to see. Keeping on the move. Back in Los Angeles, that was how a man was judged. By what he could do and get done, whether it was money or sex or hustling. Back there, the trick was staying alive and getting your *business* taken care of, without getting busted or worked over by some strong-arm ape, or maybe just vanishing because you had done some one little thing wrong that somebody else didn't dig, to turn up, days or weeks later, in some dead-end back alley, razored, or maybe floating in belly up on the red tide. Or maybe just disappearing for good, like one minute you were right there, and the next you were blown away forever.

It was all Clem knew. For a teen-ager, he knew it well, and was getting better at it all the time. Back there, a man was careful who he messed with. And if he was worth his blood, folks were careful about messing with him. Such thinking had led Clem to become interested in the martial arts. A man might wear a blade or carry a loaded piece, but there was something very comforting in the notion that with nothing more than his bare hands and feet he could lay out heavy damage to anyone who tried to back him into a bad corner.

This philosophy had also led him to avoid the truth at all costs. In this respect he was a great deal more like Jesse than he would have cared to admit. A lie—any kind of lie—was safer. Only a fool was honest, and a really cool street person was careful who he talked to, and even more careful about what he said.

The truth was taboo. And so was trust. Clem had learned years ago to regard with suspicion anybody who seemed to like him. Especially anybody who professed an interest in doing something for him. And most especially anyone who professed an interest in doing something for him for nothing. Social workers, schoolteachers, counselors, psychiatrists, foster parents, homosexuals, white women of any age. All that shit was simple, none of it com*puted*. Nobody did you something for nothing. Not unless you did them something back. It was as simple as that.

And here. Now. What would he do in this sad, dying town, with this cranky old man? How was he even going to pass the time until that moment came when he could split? "Clem," he told himself pityingly, "you has got troubles you ain't even used yet! You think that D-Home was bad? Man, compared to this, you was livin' at the Los Angeles *Hilton* an' didn't know it!"

The inside of the house was as rundown as the exterior. Funky old sofa in the living room, with a couple of rotted-out armchairs. Television in the corner, a black-and-whiter, with half its knobs missing and a screen about as big as a postcard.

In the kitchen, a wood table, covered with peeling oilcloth—most of the design had faded or been scrubbed off, but what was left looked like yellow daisies on a field of red and blue. Four wobbly wooden chairs. Big old black-iron woodstove. Cabinets along one wall, with white-painted plywood doors that were hinged askew. The windows, fly-spotted. A vintage porcelain sink, chipped and rust-stained. Probably one of the earliest refrigerators ever invented by mankind. A sagging porch, visible through the back door, on which was stacked a couple of cords of split firewood, a second refrigerator, its door open, apparently defunct, and a collection of junk Jesse apparently treasured: a rusted hibachi, worn-out tires, pots, pans, an anvil, some aluminum sun chaises lacking most of their plastic webbing, and a four-foot-high chipped concrete birdbath statue of St. Francis, patron saint of birds. The oval birdbath, held upward and outward by the saint, in the manner of a Hindu beggar, was filled with rusted nails, spikes, bolts, and nuts that Jesse had harvested in some long-ago year. The saint's beard and most of his chin had been knocked off.

Adjoining the living room were two small bedrooms with sagging bedsteads and stacks of old hunting and fishing magazines piled on chairs. In Jesse's there were several fishing rods and, Clem noted with immediate interest, a sizable arsenal: two double-barrel shotguns and three rifles, two of them lever-actions. He thought, "Salable merchandise." Nailed to the wall over Jesse's bed, much as religious people will hang a Christ figure, was a rusted bear trap of

such immoderate proportions that it looked as though it could have
snapped the leg off a bull hippopotamus. "What you got that up there
for?" Clem asked.

Jesse took off his Stetson and placed it on one of the trap's huge
leaf springs. "Man's got'a have a place to hang his hat, don't he?"

When Clem had finished looking the place over, Jesse said,
"Where else can you git a place like this for sixteen bucks a year in
taxes? Snug, ain't it?"

"It sure is, Sprout," Clem said. "Snug ain't the word for it. Makes
a man just want to kick his shoes off and lay back and relax. Say,
how about one of those beers?"

"For a kid your age, you drink too much."

"I been drinkin' since I was twelve," Clem said.

Jesse thought about this. "Now that you mention it, so have I."

WHILE THEY WERE drinking beer, they put away the groceries. Then
they tidied up a little. Jesse opened the doors and windows to let in
fresh air. He set out dishes of food for the cats. "What are their
names?" Clem asked.

"Ain't got none," Jesse said. "I ain't much for names."

"How come Rojo's got a name?"

Jesse looked at him. "You stupid or something? What the hell
else you goin' to call a red cat?"

The two other cats weren't getting along too well with the new
tom. For a while they eyed him. He eyed them back. Eventually they
decided that teamwork was needed, and they sidled up to him. One
spat, and the other let off a swipe with a front paw. That started it.
For a while things were pretty lively in the kitchen. Then the fight
shifted to the living room. Then back to the kitchen. Jesse sat at
the table, smoking a cigarette and drinking his beer. "They're really
gittin' to know one another, ain't they," he said. "Kind of fascinatin',
the way cats go about makin' friends. It's a marvel they don't all
git killed just strikin' up an acquaintance. Give 'em time. They'll
git squared away. Cats are touchier than humans about figurin' out
how to git along together."

Finally, he opened the back door and picked up Rojo and one
other cat by the scruffs of their necks and flung them outside. The

remaining cat, a female, was up on top of the refrigerator. She went flying out too.

On the back porch, they started again. Then, suddenly, the three of them took off in different directions. Something that looked like a cross between a bear and a wolf had walked up to the open door and was poking its head into the kitchen. Clem took one look and moved away. It was a dog. A huge, mangy, malamute-shepherd mix.

Jesse said, "Howdy, Cochise." He took a sack of kibbles from one of the cupboards, poured some into a bowl, and gave it to the animal, who was sniffing Clem's legs. By then, Clem was backed against the sink. "This here is Cochise," Jesse explained. "He won't hurt you. Just looks mean. All bluff." He spoke to the dog and scratched the big head behind the ears.

"This your dog?" Clem asked.

"He's Grimmiessen's lousy mutt," Jesse said. "Comes over to visit. Full-time mooch."

Clem said, "If he's the one who's crappin' all over the place, why don't you bust him with a rock instead of feedin' him?"

"Cochise ain't so bad," Jesse said. "It's Grimmiessen I hate. I think he's one of them hidden Nazis that escaped. Looks just like the type who used to operate those concentration camps where they kept all the Jews corralled during the war."

For Jesse, all global conflicts had stopped after World War II. That had been a proper war. One worthy of patriotism. All the rest of it—Korea, Vietnam, Cambodia—were rigamaroles organized by the Democrats and Communists. Even the Chinese threat had never amounted to much, since China was, after all, way the hell around the other side of the world. But World War II, in which Jesse had served, was something real, that he could remember, where Krauts and Japs had been the enemy. His mind was still on Werner Grimmiessen. "He ain't right in the head, if you git my meaning," Jesse said.

"I'm wonderin' if anybody around here is," Clem said.

"Goddamn it, I mean he's one of them there perverts," Jesse snapped. "Oh, he's sick, clear through. You know what a pervert is, boy?"

"Oh, I've heard about 'em."

"Shoulda been run out'a town years ago," Jesse went on. "We

don't need that sort here. I mean, what's he livin' here for? There's got to be a reason! That's what makes me think he's one of them escaped sadist war criminals. Can't be anything else."

Around sunset Jesse showed Clem how to build a fire in the woodstove. Later, they cooked hamburgers and ranch-fried potatoes, and drank more beer.

Toward evening, they sat on the back porch to watch the last of the sunset. The hills and mountains to the northeast turned fiery red and gold, and the last of the light caught the steep, monolithic stone cliffs of the Brazos Box—the great Brazos Canyon.

Next door, they could hear Werner Grimmiessen, half crocked, playing some kind of German military song on an accordion. He was singing to himself. On the other side of the property, Garrison and Patsy Hurley were at times visible through their kitchen windows as they lurched around, trying to put a dinner together. They had a recording of Gregorian chants on their stereo.

Finches, wrens, doves, juncos, and jays settled down for the night in the apple trees growing behind Jesse's outhouse. Rojo, the Los Angeles cat, ambled off to case the town. He was halfway across the back field when Cochise, who was curled up on a mattress on Grimmiessen's porch, spotted him. Cochise sailed over the barbed-wire fence in a wild charge. The cat hissed, looking like it meant business. Cochise decided that caution was the better part of courage, put on the brakes, and pretended to get interested in a clump of chamiso, which he finally pissed on.

"Tired?" Jesse asked.

"Restless."

"You'll sleep."

"What do people do here at night?"

"Mostly they just go to bed."

"Oh," Clem said.

By Clem's definition, anybody who went to bed before nine o'clock was sick or maybe even mentally disturbed. Such behavior was unnatural. Yet that night he slept the sleep of the innocent. In fact, snored like whole mountainsides of timber forest being violated.

Almost a week later he snarled at his grandfather, "How come

I'm so laid back? You puttin' something in my food, Sprout? Downers?"

"You can see with your own stupid eyes I'm eatin' the exact same food," Jesse said. "What in hell are you talkin' about? You sure do complain."

"How come I got nothin' *working* for me?"

"Could be because you're breathin' actual oxygen for a change, 'stead of that poison gas they call air back in L.A.," Jesse said. They were in the kitchen, lazing around as usual, five cups of coffee, hand-rolled cigarettes, toast, eggs, salt pork, and beans for breakfast. The cats were outside. So was Cochise. He was trying to make friends with the red cat. Rojo wanted no part of it. He was sitting in St. Francis's concrete birdbath, glaring murderously at the malamute, who was acting like he wanted to get into the birdbath too but didn't know how to go about it without having his eyes clawed out.

Clem said, "How come I sleep so much? I mean, that's a waste of time. I got better things to do."

"Oh, I seen that happen before," Jesse said. "Right now, we're more'n a mile and a half above sea level. The air you're suckin' in is real clean, only there ain't much of it. Folks git kinda drunk that way. Or relaxed. That's all it is. Take it easy. Don't push at things so."

Jesse himself seemed exhausted after that long haul back and forth across the miserable Mojave. The thin, bony face was haggard, drawn. He seemed content enough to sit around and rest his bones.

Behind Clem's being laid back there was that ongoing uneasiness. In his old life, nothing went smoothly or easily. At least, not for long. Even when he was on a run, he was already worrying about the bad scenes that might be lurking around the next corner. Something bad had to happen.

Trouble was, around here nothing happened. Jesse talked a couple of times about the two of them going fishing, or hitting the high peaks to see if they could poach an out-of-season deer, but mainly they just sat around, with Clem getting more and more fidgety.

That afternoon, Jesse had a few bourbons. He seemed cranky too, and complained that his bowels were deranged from the food he had eaten during the few days he had spent in California. On a trip back from the outhouse, he stopped at the side fence to pass the time of day with Werner Grimmiessen. The chat turned into an argument, and Jesse ended up calling his neighbor an atrocity-prone, morally corrupt German son of a bitch who bred killer malamutes that might any day slash the village children to shreds. Cochise sat beside Werner, listening to this outburst, waiting for someone to toss him a Gaines doggy biscuit. Whenever his name was mentioned, Cochise laid his big ears back flat and looked sad. Cochise knew how to look sad better than any other dog in Brazos, especially when he was being cussed out. He had the saddest eyes imaginable. He also had the scurfiest coat. Up close, he looked like an old bearskin that had spent some time in a Waring blender. This could have been cured by a couple of cod-liver-oil pills and a currycombing, maybe with a garden rake, which would have taken care of some of the burs, goatsheads, prickers, cactus needles, and matted lumps of sap from the piñon trees under which Cochise loved to nap in summer, oblivious to the molasses-like goo that dripped on him.

Now, as if for the first time noting Cochise's ghastly condition, Jesse suddenly went raving off on a new tangent. "How come you don't take better care of that dog? Jesus Christ, look at the condition he's in!"

Which was another way of saying that if Jesse, who loved and fed this mutt, could not find one way to badger Werner, he would find another. Cochise-the-killer-malamute was hard to swallow. Cochise-the-canine-waif was easier. Cochise himself was walking proof. Werner said, "How many times I have to tell you, Jesse, this is not my dog!"

"I'm goin' to make a formal complaint against you with the ASPCA," Jesse said. "There's laws in this country against people like you."

"I have not done anything."

"Dog abuse! Add that to your list of crimes! One of these days, you'll git yours, Grimmiessen. Don't think you're foolin' anybody. Why, you treat that dog like an *animal!* Inhuman cruelty! You got it written all over your snively face!"

Werner got indignant. "How can you talk? Cruelty. How many times I see you kick your cats! One time I see you kick that nice old gray cat all the way from your front door to the road outside the gate. With my own eyes, *das ist bestimmt!*"

"Well, he was in my way, damn it," Jesse said. "He was deliberately provokin' me, makin' a habit of floppin' in the doorway, so's I had to step over him!"

"Ich glaub' das nicht!" Werner said.

"Listen, you! We speak American around here," Jesse warned. "You want'a talk that foreign stuff, go back where they understand it."

"Clem, please come here and help me reason with your grandfather," Werner shouted.

Clem had come out onto the kitchen porch and was leaning against a post. He waved casually to Werner. "Nothin' personal, Mr. Grimmiessen, but I don't make a habit of mixin' into other people's troubles."

The argument finally died. Not an hour later, Jesse got into it with the Hurleys, over their side of the fence line. "Goddamn profligate, mentally diseased drunken bastards, both of you! Suckin' up my hard-earned tax dollars with welfare and Social Security, like it was goin' out'a style! What in hell kind of citizens of this country d'you lyin', no-good, alcoholic, wet-brained pigs call yourselves?"

"Jesse, since when do you pay tax dollars?" Garrison said mildly. "I doubt if you've ever filed a return in your life."

"Well, I started out to, one time," Jesse said. "The intent was there."

"We're only taking aid we are legally entitled to," Garrison said.

"We can't help ourselves," Patsy pointed out, with a smile. "Jesse, you mustn't get angry at people who have problems."

"Oh, I don't blame someone for reachin' when the biscuits is passed around," Jesse said. "But that don't mean you two sots got to grab with both hands."

"I don't think you're being very fair," Patsy said, looking hurt. "As a matter of fact, I think you're being quite unkind."

Garrison put an arm around his wife's shoulder and patted her. "Now, dear. None of that. Patience and Christian forbearance. Jesse, would you care to join us in a martini?"

"Oh, that would be nice," Patsy said. She spotted Clem, who had come out on the porch again. "Clem! Yoo-hoo! Come over and join us. We're all going to have a drink."

Clem waved back. "Hi, Miz Hurley."

"Don't make a stranger out of yourself, you bad boy," Patsy said.

"Miz Hurley, I wouldn't do that for the world." Clem walked over.

"Call me Patsy."

"Sure, Patsy."

"You have lovely manners."

"Oh, where I was raised, good manners are real important," Clem said.

"Clem, git your ass back in the house," Jesse said. "We ain't havin' no drinks with nobody."

Patsy looked at Clem. "Isn't he the most dreadful old thing?"

"You ought'a try livin' with him," Clem said.

For a moment Patsy's expression was utterly, alcoholically blank. Then she put the tips of her fingers to her mouth and burst out laughing, as though this was the wildest, funniest thing she had ever heard in her life. By the time the laughter subsided there were tears in her eyes. "Oh, you dear, dear boy! How perfectly droll!"

DESPITE THE LETHARGY and a general feeling of being spaced out, Clem's mind had been working during the past week. He listened, and he watched. Additional information was provided by Jesse, who, as it turned out, loved gossiping as much, if not more, than those he condemned for the same disgusting habit. If you were out for malicious slander and purulent calumny, it paid to check with Jesse Slade. He could always find something bad to say about anybody. Clem listened and looked around him, and from this was able to begin forming certain opinions. Slowly, things were falling into place.

Patsy Hurley, for example.

A faded beauty, at fifty-three. But once—how many long years ago?—she must have been something. A truly gorgeous piece. Even now, faint signs remained. Behind the wrinkles, the complexion was clear. The blue eyes, though bleary, still betrayed an eternal girlish vivaciousness. No hint of gray in the hair. Every three weeks Patsy religiously rinsed with L'Oréal, and so maintained a pageboy of such counterfeit yellow that the whiteness of Jesse's false teeth seemed genuine in comparison. Her figure was beanpole slim, almost gaunt, really rather fetching, a lankiness that belonged to a professional mannequin who starved herself, or else a natural-born lush. And, most evident of all, was a kind of zesty, febrile femininity which communicated a message perhaps subtle, but, hell, not that subtle. She had, for example, a way of staring at Clem that reminded him of the sultry looks Werner Grimmiessen cast his way. Fat Lulu Uranga, the wetback waitress down at Woody Klein's Emerald Bar, loved men. So did Patsy, but in a somewhat more predatory manner, the way owls love mice.

Apparently, the idea, some ten years ago when they married, after falling madly for each other in that Albuquerque dry-out sanitorium, was that Garrison had contracted to take care of certain of Patsy's needs. Patsy had just been divorced from another Los Alamos physicist, so she ought to have known a little about the two-bit guarantees scientists are always making. But Garrison, even now, looked as though he could fill the bill, and back then he must have been able to come on even better.

He was a big, burly, bespectacled man, with thick, wavy hair that had turned white, but he was still virile-looking, with a wrinkled forehead, sloping brows, a long, fleshy nose, and the most sensuous mouth Patsy had ever laid eyes on. Patsy had been so entranced by all this, along with Garrison's genteel New England manners and Harvard elegance, that she stayed sober for nearly six months after they were discharged from the san. By then they had married, and she had begun to suspect two simple truths about her nifty new husband. For one, he was immensely stubborn, and for the other, this stubbornness had been channeled into an implacable determination to drink himself to death. Since their love life was pretty much a hit-or-miss affair—at his best, rested, refreshed, and stuffed to the ears with vitamin pills, Garrison was strictly a ho-hum hump—Patsy began drinking again. This at least provided them with something in common, and out of it came a sort of camaraderie. For a good part of the time they got along rather well together, perhaps better than might be expected, although on occasion Patsy cracked under the strain. Then her placid nature vanished and she would rise up, phoenix-like and aflame, in feminine indignation.

One night Clem happened to be sitting on the back porch, with Rojo curled up in his lap, when he heard loud, outraged wails coming from the Hurley residence. "Why in hell can't you ever love me up just once, like a woman needs, you phony has-been?" Their kitchen windows were open. A Liszt prelude was on the stereo.

Garrison came out the back door and pissed off the porch. He said, "My dear girl. Please."

"All talk, that's you, Garrison."

"To have what we two have . . . just contemplate that, love."

"I'm tired of contemplating it," Patsy yelled from the kitchen. "I've been contemplating it for ten years. That's all I ever think about!"

"You know you're everything to me."

She started crying. "Why aren't you ever nice to me?"

"I do my best."

"Why don't you try doing better than your best? I try to be nice to you. I really do. A fat lot of good it does me! You don't *care*."

"Can't we at least preserve the amenities?"

"Amenities aren't the only thing you've been preserving, Garrison. In alcohol."

The hostility Patsy was venting was merely a way of acknowledging a fact she had trouble accepting: in this world there are men who would rather drink than screw. At times this insight bore down mercilessly on her female psyche. That such a thing could be was enough of a mystery—what rankled was that she had had the bad luck to unite with such a man.

Garrison was sort of naturally inclined toward celibacy, as he was toward anything that interfered with his drinking. In a way, Patsy understood this, since she herself could just about match him drink for drink. But there were other urges that beset her, a slow and constant gnawing, like a worm working at the quick of a nail. Most times she put on her best face. Smiled, tittered, or pranced about nervously with a drink in her hand at the Emerald. But in her sleep she ground her teeth, and when the frustration got intolerable she turned ferocious. When Garrison, ensconced at their little kitchen table, where he spent most of his time—or at least that time when he was able to remain erect—blathered, "The world goes out not with a bang but a whimper," Patsy snapped peevishly, "You can say that again." He loved poetry and at times tried to write it, but was limited to mildly off-color limericks like, "My heart leaps up when I behold, Little Miss Pneumatic Bliss," or "Hi-diddle-diddle, it bends in the middle, the cow jumped over my moons." This disoriented eroticism was harmless enough, as Patsy knew and everyone else in the village surmised. Garrison might be a courtly intellectual with sensual features, but in terms of track record he was as horny as a mussel. You could probably have slung him into the sack with Sally Benavidez, the stunning seventeen-year-old daughter of Gus Benavidez, who owned the general store, and he would have come on all talk, wearing chamois gloves, suave, gentle, attentive, but with nothing much in the way of verifiable action. Had he ever actually been called to task for such unmanliness, Garrison, who when sober enough was an armchair Catholic, probably would have acted like a candidate to the College of Cardinals. Or else he would have fallen back on his tried-and-true fastidious New England ennui, that air of cultured disengagement which he affected until a drink was mentioned, at which point he got as frisky as a squirrel in a sack of chestnuts.

The ludicrous notion of matching Garrison against Sally Benavidez was basely cynical, and had been put forth one morning by Jesse, for whom any breakfast was not complete without a scurrilous raking-over-the-coals of anyone who came to mind. Clem, who had already met Miss Benavidez, caught the cynicism, and saw the point too. Sally was one of those devastating, caramel-skinned, flat-stomached, high-breasted, willing young handmaidens-of-destiny who crop up with unnerving and mysterious regularity every twenty years in any hick town. On the sly, she read *Playgirl, Penthouse,* and the philosophical fumblings of Erica Jong. She was much too gorgeous for Brazos, but on the other hand too dumb to leave town. She imagined she was into women's lib—or at least talked a lot about it in her sassy way—but was in essence a serenely conceited and murderously competitive young woman who spent most of her idle hours contemplating the mystique of the male penis. That was how she referred to this changeable organ, ignoring the redundancy that penises of any kind are, by and large, male. Sally was very good at making sure she was the center of attention, and would go to great lengths to ensure this. When Gus wasn't running the cash box and adding machine, Sally took over. That was when a number of people, usually young men, came in to hang out, like worshiping court attendants. Privately, Clem judged that on Sunset Strip she would have lasted maybe a week. With luck. But here in the Brazos boondocks, Sally Benavidez was queen.

It was generally acknowledged that she was just about the most beautiful creature who had ever been seen in these parts. When she walked out of the post office with the store's mail, hunched Horacio Quintana put those binoculars around his neck to far better use than the CIA and FBI could imagine. For Horacio, only Sunday was a loss. No mail then, no Sally. On that day, he went back to his regular spying.

There was a calculated sweetness about Sally, in that she knew she was lovely and saw no reason to keep the product under wraps. During the summer months she usually went around braless in a tight white polyester T-shirt, across the front of which was imprinted HANDLE WITH CARE. With the shirt, she wore navy-blue nylon jogging shorts that had patriotric white and red ribbing around the leg openings. Sally wasn't much for underwear. In the store, when she bent down over the cooler to fetch a cold one, stronger men than Willie Montoya or Connie Aragon went into cardiac arrest. Jesse might accuse her of being the Guernsey's gift to the world, but this was not true by far. Sally was lissome. She gave off an aura of hot, tense, feminine randiness.

There was also a hint of something else, dark and foul, that Clem did not discount. Again, gossip from Jesse. To the effect that when Sally emerged from her shower, all firm and tawny and tight-assed, with dewdrops twinkling in her bush, Gus was often there to hand her a towel. Gus was a widower, and as such had channeled all his energies into making money. Toward his young daughter he felt paternal love—or so he told himself. Jesse might be a cranky gossip, but in gossip lurks a grain of truth. Like having smoke without fire, but with someone to blow on the coals. The truth—and here, for once, Jesse put his finger on it—was that if there was any way in the world to do it without getting nailed, fat old Gus Benavidez would have sold his soul to get into Sally's britches. Prudishly, he might disapprove of her scanty costume, but at night he dreamed of sucking her toes. During the day, at the store, he gnawed his knuckles and was at times gruff and irritable for reasons he himself could not fathom. But of course everyone else did. In Brazos, as in other rural villages, there was a little more incest among the inhabitants than might be imagined. Clem didn't know it all yet, but he was finding out. Piece by piece. The puzzle was slowly coming together. He listened and watched. Alert. From experience, eternally suspicious. People are people, all folks hold to a path.

Another case: Werner, next door.

At times, when Jesse was not around, Clem made a point of passing the time of day with the elderly German, over the fence line. The way Clem figured it, there was no point in being antisocial. He knew that Werner liked him, and why, just as he saw that Patsy Hurley glared daggers at Grimmiessen when Clem was too attentive to him and not to her. For the present he could see no useful purpose in Werner's friendship or Patsy's jealousy, but of one thing he was sure: in this village, he was entirely alone. Not even Jesse was an ally. At least that was the way Clem saw it. If that was true, Patsy Hurley or Grimmiessen might conceivably, in some way, at some time, be useful. And so Clem made a point of giving Werner equal time.

Certainly, the tale that Grimmiessen had to tell seemed more plausible than Jesse's sinister allusions to atrocities and concentration camps. Back in those dreadful times, Werner had been a tank commander. Had had, in fact, four Tigers shot out from under him and, at the second, crucial battle of El Alamein, had led an attack point under direct radio orders from General Erwin Rommel himself, the old Desert Fox, against an approaching phalanx of British and American mediums. "That was, *natürlich*, duck soup, as you call it," Werner explained. "Back then, the Allied armor was nothing. And, of course, you know that Feldmarschall Montgomery was a paranoid-schizophrenic. Ah, those were the days! Yet . . . they won."

At this point Werner excused himself, told Clem to wait, and dashed into his house, to rummage in his collection of memorabilia, which he kept in an old green metal cashbox. He came back with an Iron Cross, ornamented with silver oak leaves, swords, and diamonds. "I have many interesting souvenirs," he said. "But you see this? It is the most important. Only a few soldiers in the entire war received such an Iron Cross. You see these swords and diamonds? You know what they signify?"

They meant that Werner had won one of the highest orders of the Iron Cross. He also produced some faded newspaper clippings that proved he was an authentic hero, with photographs showing him looking very spiffy in his Wehrmacht dress grays, crewcut and ramrod-straight of back, a lean-jawed, handsome young man smiling shyly into the camera, very different from the stiff-backed old duffer who strode down the main street of Brazos barking orders in Bavarian dialect at Cochise. Clem could not read the clippings since they were in German, and for a moment he did not link the youthful tank commander with the skinny old man babbling away on the other side of the fence . . . had difficulty in perceiving that the mere passage of years could eventually turn someone *that* young *this* old. There was one thing, however, that Clem had no trouble intuiting: Werner was telling the truth. Clem, quite simply, as a street person, could sense it.

The rest of the story was a touch vague, but Clem was able to fill in the missing pieces effectively.

There was a reason why Werner, in the early fifties, after a period of wandering about the United States, had settled in Brazos. In certain ways it reminded him of the sun-scorched coast of North Africa, where he had debarked in 1941 to participate in *Der Dritte Reich*'s noble struggle for survival. More specifically, the local youngsters reminded him of a certain sweet graciousness he had found in various brown-limbed Algerian and Moroccan lads. That slow and slumberous Moorish mentality. Such a sweet corruption of beautiful innocence, and all that was vile. That curious hint of Levantine sexuality in full-lipped young boys who were seemingly guileless but who emanated the promise of Olympian pleasures no practiced female whore ever dreamed of. *Ach Gott*, right here in Brazos! Grimmiessen had—symbolically anyway—come home.

In Chama, over at the high school, when the girls' basketball team came out to jog in baggy blue bloomers, Werner might cruise by, a classic grandfather type. But when the boys took off from the track field during the hazy autumn afternoons, in sneakers and shorts and naked from the waist up, Werner was obliged to park nearby so that he would not have to drive while in such a state of trembling intoxication.

At times a few of these boys visited him in his home. He played the accordion for them, gave them small amounts of money for tasks like yard work or waxing the kitchen floor, and acted as a surrogate father. In Brazos, this was not such a terrible thing. The Spanish townspeople were no strangers to the concept of an older man taking an interest in a youngster. The rationale was simple. If a family had eleven kids, one or two of the older boys were likely to end up in the state pen; the girls most likely would get married or go bad. So what was so wrong with one of the younger boys being sponsored by someone who might buy him a few clothes? The boys who hung out at Werner's had the permission of their parents. Over at Chama High, Werner was reputed to be the best blow job north of Albuquerque. The kids who reported this, of course, vehemently denied any first-hand knowledge. It was just a rumor they'd heard.

But it was also a rumor that had stuck around year after year, so *quién sabe*? Maybe there was some truth in it.

Grimmiessen was happy enough, and went on quietly drinking. Every few weeks he got fearfully smashed, and then, sometimes, he would dress up in his old World War II tank commander's outfit—desert tans, peaked field cap, and rubber-rimmed dust goggles. Weirdly, his dimensions had not changed at all, so that he still looked trim, tailored, and stiff-backed. He would parade around in his back yard, humming the "Horst Wessel" and kicking Cochise in the ass whenever he got a chance.

Clem's talk with Werner ended pleasantly. Werner said, "Ah, it is so good to have a young and delightful person for a neighbor again. Come visit! Please! Whenever the time permits. That I would enjoy."

"I'll do that," Clem said agreeably.

"Just as a friend. You understand?" Werner stared at him. "Nothing improper. You should understand that."

"Oh, sure."

The platonic intent seemed sincere. Next morning, however, Clem ambled out of Jesse's house in the dawn's early light and headed for the outhouse, clad only in a pair of maroon jockey shorts. That vision of Clem, all dusky brown and near naked in the mellow dawn, was something else again. From Werner's house came a faint crash and clatter, as if perhaps a chair or two had been accidentally knocked over, and an even fainter Germanic oath. Then, mere moments later, came the sound of the accordion from somewhere in the house, energetically wheezing out a romantic Sigmund Romberg operetta melody.

ONE DAY AFTER they had picked up the mail from Horacio (a flyer from *Reader's Digest* and a direct-mail offer for genuine Naugahyde seatcovers from some outfit in Iowa), Jesse and Clem stopped off at Gus's for beer. And it was then that Clem had his first gander at Sally Benavidez.

Sally was tending store. Connie Aragon, Willie Montoya, and his brother Bennie were sitting around, with a six-pack of Coors, waiting for a chance to look up Sally's crotch. Five or six young people from the high school were also there. Three of them were girls, who had figured out that the best way to hang around boys was to stick close to Sally.

Clem had his own notions of high style, and on this afternoon he was wearing one of Jesse's old Stetsons, which he figured showed off his Afro nicely, and a sheepskin vest and jeans. Below the vest was a slender waist that couldn't have gone more than twenty-eight inches at most, cinched by a leather workbelt. Clem made any kind of clothing look good, and knew it, just as Sally knew that her T-shirt and jogging shorts were not the worst ensemble she could wear.

Sally had a special weakness for tall, rangy, big-shouldered young men. She was fourteen boys away from virginity, and though she thought this was a secret, it wasn't. When she wrote in her diary, which she kept locked in the small desk in her bedroom, " 'L' came into my life last week. I lost 6½ lbs. in five days. We do what I dreamed about . . ." she might as well have published her entry on the bulletin board Horacio Quintana had hanging in the vestibule of his post office along with posters of federal criminals who were wanted by the government.

Each time Sally went up to the Brazos Box with "M" or "J" or "B," the news moved fast. At the high school, she was a legend. Most of the football team knew Sally's tastes. The star tackle, Greg Apodaca, learned that she had sharp teeth, and down by the town garbage dump at sunset one evening, amid hills of rusting tin cans, paper, and decaying matter, Orly Pacheco, a two-hundred-and-ten-pound lineman, discovered Sally's prestidigitatorial talents with a jar of vaseline. She was curious about masturbation and had a clinical interest in observing precisely how much lubricious stimulation a man could tolerate without being reduced to gibbering imbecility. Afterward, when Pacheco had become more or less coherent again, she told him, "Orly, you got one that's out'a sight, but I got to tell you, this stuff tastes like greasy soap." That night, however, in her secret diary she wrote, "I found out why O's nickname at school is 'Peanut,' but even so we did something that has never been done."

To be young and beautiful, and caught up in the age of discovery. That has to be the loveliest time, when nothing can go wrong and all the world is ready to fling itself at a girl's feet. If living was good now, how much better would it be in the future? Sally was nothing less than fiercely optimistic. Every Sunday she went to Mass, with a rebozo draped over her pretty head bent in prayer, asked the blessing, got communion via the wafer, and said to herself, "I am going to do something beautiful and different with my life!"

The trouble was, the only thing different she had seen since sixth grade was Clem, when he and Jesse came walking in.

Clem was still laid back. Sally found this interesting. The lazy, loose-hipped walk. Hands jammed into the rear pockets of the jeans. A toothpick, angled from one corner of the mouth. The antique Stetson, tilted back. Except for the vest, naked from the waist up. All of him indolent and at ease.

And while Clem might be laid back, this did not mean that he was oblivious to the flash between them. It came like a jolt. Suddenly he was alert.

So were Connie Aragon, the Montoya brothers, and the other young men. They felt as protective toward Sally, in her cute-assed shorts, as any male might feel toward a young lady who gives the promise of fun and pleasure at some future date. Around Brazos, a great deal of attention was given over to getting laid. But Sally was not just any girl—she was a mythic image. If she had been fat, dumpy, and pimpled, like Dixie Mendoza, who worked at the Dairy Queen on the highway, and who put out, when business was slow, up against the French-fry cooker in back, that would have been something else. But Sally was special. Getting it on with her had to be death and transfiguration. She knew this, and she made sure that those who courted her assumed the same.

So it got quiet in the store. The young men glanced at one another, as though tacitly acknowledging that trouble had just walked in the door. The girls with them looked on with interest. Secretly, they might hate Sally's guts, but gave credit where it was due: around *her*, something was always happening.

"Give us a case of Coors," Jesse said.

Eyeing Clem, Sally said, "Right away, Mr. Slade." It was the first time Jesse could remember her or anybody else in the village calling him mister.

She came out from behind the counter, showing off legs that were long and well developed, a dusky tan, hairless, or at least shaven closely, with firm calves and smooth thighs that rose and disappeared into the nylon shorts, the seat of which was embedded—for all apparent purposes buried until Armageddon—between her buttocks. A vision too splendorous for the eye of mere mortal man: blindness might result. Willie Montoya, who at twenty-one was not getting anywhere near as much as he bragged about, finished his beer, sighed, and stared down at the aluminum can. With forefinger and thumb, he crushed it flat. Then folded it in half, and folded it again.

Sally came back with the case of beer. She said to Clem, "You must be the new boy."

"What you mean, 'boy,' " Clem said.

Sally gave him a cool, almost disdainful look. She said archly, "Just a way of talking."

"Baby, you goin' to talk, talk right," Clem advised.

Her look got cooler. "You don't have to get bent out of shape," she said.

"Can't nothin' bend me out'a shape."

Sally had a way of taking a man's measure. Head tilted a bit to one side. Hint of a smile. The gaze direct, challenging. Weight balanced on one hip. Taking her time, she looked Clem over. When she was done, she glanced down and casually examined the fingernails of one hand. Actually, they were pretty dirty—she had spent the morning weeding the corn patch in back of her father's house. She said nothing. Held her peace for the time being. She turned to Jesse and said, "Charge the beer?"

Jesse got a half-gallon of milk, some bread, and tobacco. He signed his chit, and he and Clem left.

Willie Montoya went over to the cooler and got a fresh six-pack. He opened a can, drank, and then looked at Sally. "Listen," he said finally, "I might as well tell you something, nice and simple, so's you can understand it. There are limits. I am your cousin, so I am tellin' you. You listening to me, Sally?"

"Willie, just 'cause you're older than I am, what in hell gives you the idea that you can talk to me, or run my life, or tell me what to do?" Sally said. "You looking for trouble? Because if you are, you can just haul your big butt out'a this establishment. That'll be two fifty for the beer, please."

"Sally, what's the matter with you . . . you *stupid* or something?" Willie said angrily. He dug around in his pocket for some loose bills and change. "Get your act together, girl."

"I have got my act pulled together just great, thank you," she said. "I got it together a lot more than you do when you come out of old man Grimmiessen's place at four in the morning, so blind drunk you don't know where you are. You get off my back, you big pile of shit."

"You know something?" Willie said, frowning. "For a woman, you got a dirty mouth."

"You know something else?" she said. "For a man, you're all mouth."

"One of these days, someone's goin' to slap you flat."

"You want to try it? What day is convenient?"

"You're gettin' so that you believe all this women's-lib crap you're always braggin' on about."

"What if I am?"

"That *coyote negro* is trouble."

"You try to make any trouble for me, you better get out of this town," Sally said. She was scowling, and her lips were set in a thin line. When she got angry, she wasn't nearly as pretty. "Far as that goes, you or Connie or anybody else gets pushy around me, you'll find out what real trouble is!" She glared at them scornfully. "*Men!* I swear! To hear you, you'd think we were living back in the nineteenth century or something! Keep your noses out of my business. I mean it!"

Willie drank some of his beer, and sat down. He leaned back against the wall, frowning—really angry. "There are ways."

"Oh, shove it!"

"To think that you would look twice. At something like that."

"Actually, now that you mention it, he's kind'a cute," Sally said airily. She scratched at one hip. Her expression was contemplative. "Never saw hair like that under a Stetson."

Willie said pointedly, "Never saw hair like that on a white man, either."

"Willie, you're no one to talk," Sally said. "You got hair that makes Brillo look like silk. Also, if you don't mind my saying so, you are ugly." Neither of these statements was true. Willie's hair was as soft as hers, and he was considered one of the handsomer young men around. "Besides that, you smell funky. I bet you take a bath, you're still funky. Now, leave me be, will you?"

"I mean it. I won't put up with it," Willie insisted. His brother, Bennie, and Connie Aragon looked thoughtful. This was no small thing Willie was saying. It was a challenge—the gauntlet flung down.

Sally sensed it too. She put on an expression of girlish innocence, but at the same time she was enjoying herself immensely. "All I ever said was that he looked cute," she said. She went to the cooler and opened a Dr. Pepper. She tilted the bottle and swigged, then wiped her mouth with the back of one hand. "My goodness! To listen to some of you people talk, you'd think I'd gone and committed some kind'a *crime* or something!"

"WELL, WHAT THE hell was all that about?" Jesse said, as they drove back through town toward the house. Clem was behind the wheel.

"What was all what about?" Clem said.

"Listen, boy, I may be old, but I ain't that old!"

"What you talkin' about, Sprout?"

"I ain't blind," Jesse said sourly. "You tryin' to stir up a hornet's nest?"

"Shit, man, all I did was talk to her."

"She's goin' on eighteen. That's too old for you."

"Are you kiddin'?" Clem said. He looked amused. "Sprout, how you come on! Why, last summer I jived around with this forty-one-year-ol' chick. Leastways, she claimed she was forty-one. By my estimate, she'd clipped off a couple of years. That ol' lady, she took care of me *real* fine! Breakfast in bed, and the Grateful Dead on the stereo. Eggs Benedict! Claimed she was a retired belly dancer, only I found out she was a teacher at one of them Montessori schools. Oh, my!"

"You ain't in that degenerate Los Angeles no more!"

Clem glanced over at Jesse and laughed. "Too *old!* That is bullshit, plain an' simple. You ain't talkin' years, Sprout. That ain't what my ears are hearin'. You talkin' color, that's all. Like maybe black an' white, right?"

"You accusin' me of prejudice?"

"Why, I wouldn't do that," Clem said, grinning.

"You fuckin' well behave yourself!"

Clem got indignant. "What you think I been doin'? What in hell is there to do in a place like this? Ain't nothin' to steal. Ain't nothin' worth stealing! Can't swim. Ain't no beaches. Can't dance. Ain't no discos. No place to go. Nothin' to do. Why you comin' down on me this way? I been so straight since we got here I can't hardly stand it! I don't even recognize myself in the mirror no more! And here you are, comin' down on me. We wash the dishes, and cook the meals, and we sit around and look at that old junk TV at night."

"You bored, go out to that woodpile back of the house and start chopping. One of these days, winter'll be lookin' us straight in the eye."

"My time's too valuable."

"You go back to that D-Home, you'll find out how goddamn valuable your time is."

"Ain't goin' back there, ol' man. Take that for granted," Clem said. He shook his head. "Nossir. One way or the other, I don't see that D-Home playin' a big part in this man's future."

"Sally Benavidez is pure trash," Jesse insisted. "Everybody in this end of the county knows it."

"That little chick in the store? Don't look like trash to me."

"She's trouble on the hoof."

"Trouble like that can walk my way any time," Clem said.

"You see how those Montoya boys was lookin' at you?"

"Didn't notice," Clem said. He was still grinning.

"I guess you was too busy lookin' at her tits and ass," Jesse said.

"They do kind'a leap right out at you, don't they?"

"I wasn't payin' attention," Jesse said.

"Shoot! Come away with that talk! You said yourself you wasn't blind."

"Boy, you mess with that young tramp, you'll find yourself staring into a thirty-thirty."

Clem nodded. "She do look ripe, don't she? Yes, indeed! Prime an' *fine*."

"Pay attention, you goddamn nitwit! Every young buck that was sittin' in that store is tryin' to figure out how to be *número uno* on Sally Benavidez's list! Half the fellers in Tierra Amarilla, Chama, Canjilon, Cebolla, Lumberton, and Parkview are tryin' to figure out the same thing. Her pa is mean. I'm tellin' you. He rides herd on her with a Luger, a double-barrel shotgun, and a twenty-foot bullwhip. Even so, he can't turn his back on her for seven seconds without she's busted out'a the pen and is off somewhere, lookin' for a spoon to stir her pot of beans. She can't keep her legs crossed any more'n I can whistle through my nose. Gus knows. One of these days he'll catch someone. I feel sorry for whoever that feller is. You squirts are something, all right! Always tryin' to be *número uno*. That Sally Benavidez! Thinks she's hot shit. If she had as many *número unos* stickin' out'a her as she's had stuck in her, she'd look like a two-legged porkypine. You know what's smart, you'll keep away from her."

"Yessir."

"Goddamn it, Clem, I mean it."

"Anything you say, Sprout." He was still feeling easy. They drove up to the house. "They wouldn't lynch me, or anything, would they?"

"This ain't one of those redneck states like Alabama or Georgia," Jesse said. "You got to enroll in high school pretty soon. Don't start off with a chip on your shoulder, actin' so cocky, like you do with me all the time."

"Let's wait till next year to do that, okay?"

"You're goin' to school."

"No, I ain't."

"We'll see about that when the time comes."

"That little Benavidez chick . . . she still in school?"

"I reckon. Though why, I couldn't say, less'n she's studyin' terminal sex education," Jesse said.

"Bet she gets an 'A' for effort."

Jesse shook his head disgustedly. "You won't listen to a goddamn thing! Keepin' you on the straight and narrow is like tryin' to sweep out a house with a broom held upside down. Clem, you don't mind me, I'm gonna kick you right in the ass, y'hear? I'm your goddamn guardian, and don't you forget it. Seems like I got to keep an eye on you every second."

"You watch out for me, Sprout, and I'll look out for you, okay?" Clem said. He laughed. "We'll get by just fine." Small though this town was, there were possibilities: he was thinking of Patsy Hurley, of Werner, of Sally Benavidez.

"Trouble is, you think you're special," Jesse grumbled. "Think you can go out huntin' bear with a buggy whip. You ain't even paid your dues yet."

"What dues?"

"The dues you pay to stay alive, that's what dues," Jesse said.

"I don't owe nobody no dues. Nobody, no place, no how."

"That's what you think."

"I owe dues to myself. No one else. That is the way it goes, ol' man. You might as well understand that about me."

"We'll see."

THAT NIGHT IT RAINED. Jesse woke Clem earlier than usual. Outside, the sky was bright and clear, and the fields were cold and wet and greenly beautiful. In the scraggly apple trees, jays and starlings were already kicking up a fuss. The sun was still hidden behind the mountains to the east.

Both of them were half asleep and a little cranky. They walked around the kitchen in their underwear, moving cats out of the way with their bare feet. Cochise leaned against the door. Jesse let him inside and gave him some kibbles while Clem stoked the stove. They fed the cats and then made breakfast for themselves—beans, eggs, hamburger, toast, milk, and coffee. When they were half done, Jesse poured more coffee into their cups, and said, "What you feel like doin' today?"

"Don't know. Same thing we did yesterday, I guess," Clem said. Rojo climbed on his lap, and he stroked the cat. "What you feel like doin'?"

"I don't know," Jesse said. He rolled a smoke. "I think you need some activity."

"Boogeyin' around?"

"What's that mean? The way you talk, half the time it's a mystery."

"Boogeyin'? That means movin' around, that's all."

"I wish to hell you'd speak plain English for a change." He lit the cigarette. "A growin' kid, he's got energy to burn. I was thinking about it last night."

"Oh, you were. Matter of fact, it gets on my mind sometimes, too."

"Kid gits bored. Ain't a hundred percent your fault. Need somethin' to keep your mind occupied, is all."

"Like what?"

"I figure we might go fishin'."

"We're goin' fishin'?"

"That's right."

"Hey, man, come on!"

"You ever been fishin'?"

"What I wan'ta do something like that for?" With a look of disgust, Clem rolled his eyes ceilingward. "You're too much."

"Well, if you ain't ever tried it, how d'you know you mightn't like it?" Jesse said angrily. "How come you're always bad-mouthin' things you don't know nothin' about?"

" 'Cause there are certain things a man just knows," Clem said. "I never ate ground glass either. That don't mean I got to go out and swallow a handful just to see whether it agrees with me."

"Goddamn it, we're goin' fishin'."

"When?"

"Today, that's when."

"Sprout, do we have to?" Clem looked at him. "Hey, is that why you dragged me out'a bed this early?"

"Can't fish in bed."

"Let's wait till tomorrow, okay?"

"Boy, you don't know shit from Shinola," Jesse said. "You don't go fishin' when you feel like it. You go fishin' when you're supposed to!"

"Hell, how come we s'posed to do it today? Ain't nothin' special about today, 'cept you got a wild hair up your ass and nothin'll satisfy you but that we got to go fishin'. I'm headin' back to bed."

"No, you ain't. The reason we're goin' today is that there was a full moon last night. Trout don't like to feed on a bright night, so this mornin' they'll be hungrier than usual. Also, it rained later on. That means food has been washed into the river for 'em. It also means we can git worms real easy."

"You mean we got to shovel worms?"

"Only a fool shovels for worms. You goddamn city kids think you know it all," Jesse said, rising. "Come on, Mr. Smartass."

He took a ring of keys from a kitchen drawer. They slipped on jackets and workboots against the morning coolness and, still in their underwear, went out back to the large, decrepit storage shed. "This here's where I keep my valuables," Jesse said, unsnapping the padlock.

"I been wonderin' what you keep this locked up for," Clem said. " 'Valuables?' What you got that's so valuable, Sprout? I thought it was just a woodshed or somethin'."

Jesse swung the double doors open. Two rats and a tarantula scuttled out of sight.

The interior was crammed to the ceiling with the biggest assortment of junk Clem had ever seen. Camping and hunting equipment. Rotted canvas tarpaulins. Three old dust-covered saddles hung from nails on one wall, along with mildewed bridles, surcingles, martin-

gales, bits, spurs, and several pairs of age-stiffened leather chaps.
There were Coleman lanterns and an ornate brass Aladdin kerosene
mantel lamp with a green glass shade. Four antique rifles and a
rusted Colt single-action Frontier model pistol, in a gunbelt. Bundles
and cartons of foxed magazines, books, and newspapers. Cooking
gear, left over from the days when Jesse ran a chuck wagon: big
cast-iron kettles and a solid-copper frying pan that was two feet
across and must have weighed forty pounds. To one side stood a
Harley-Davidson '54 motorcycle, partially dismantled, with its in-
nards stacked in a couple of wood boxes. Both tires were flat. There
were axes, a ten-foot-long lumberjack's bucksaw, two peaveys and
a come-along, some logging chains, rope, a hand-operated smithy's
forge, and a string of beaver traps, as well as a pile of glazed fire-
brick, an outboard motor with no propeller, three ancient car bat-
teries, an old chain saw, a typewriter that was at least fifty years old,
two walnut-veneered Zenith table radios that looked even older, a
box of horseshoes, and all kinds of men's and women's clothing that
had gone out of style long before the Roosevelt era. Best of all, half
buried under the clutter, but clearly identifiable, was a 1934 dark
green Plymouth coupe.

Clem looked all this over and then shook his head, marveling.
"Where'd you get all this?"

"Collected it," Jesse said.

"What for?"

"Never know when you might need it."

"Sprout, you got a natural talent for surroundin' yourself with garbage," Clem said. "However, you also got some stuff in here that
looks like real antiques."

"That's why I keep the place locked up," Jesse said. He was bent
over, rummaging around in some boxes. "Where'd I put it? I just
had it out last year."

Clem looked at the Plymouth appraisingly. "You got any idea of
what this ol' heap would fetch back in Los Angeles?" he asked. "I
got a hunch it would bring real foldin' money, running or not. Lot of
this other junk is worth something, too. Guns, lamps, that ol' motorcycle. My, my! People lay out all kinds of bread for stuff like this."

Jesse was muttering to himself, "Damn it, where in hell did I put
it? Ah! I knew it was here someplace." He came up with a strange,
heavy electrical device of some kind. Wires were attached to it, and
it had a crank handle.

Clem said, "What's that supposed to be?"

"This here's a genuine magneto," Jesse said, as they went outside. The old man locked the big doors. "I stole it out of a mine one time. That must have been back in 'twenty-two or 'twenty-three. They used these to ring up the telephones that connected one level to another."

"You fixin' to catch fish with that thing?"

"No, stupid," Jesse said. "This here is our worm-getter."

Clem followed as Jesse went over to the side of the porch where he had his geranium beds. The old man took a clasp knife out of his jacket pocket and scraped the trailing ends of the wires until bright copper shone. He jabbed these into the ground, about four feet apart. Then he started cranking the magneto energetically.

"Ground's nice and wet, see?" he explained. "This magneto packs one hell of a jolt! Throws a couple of hundred volts. Shock the livin' shit out'a these worms!" Still cranking madly, he grinned at Clem, enjoying himself. "You just watch! Worms can't abide electricity! Here, slap your hand down there on the ground, where it's wet. You can feel the wallop it's puttin' out."

"No, thank you."

Jesse kept on cranking. Worms began surfacing. First one. Then a few more. Then a lot more. It was like a popcorn popper with the lid off—there were worms all over the place. Jesse said, "Look at the little bastards, just leapin' out'a the ground! Git a can, boy, to store 'em in. Move your ass!" He put down the magneto and stooped over and began collecting the worms. "One time, down in the mine, we had this big dumb Yugoslavian. He used to tamp dynamite. Every day he'd stop and piss in a puddle up by the head of the shaft, where we used to wait for the elevator. It stunk somethin' awful. Couldn't make him quit. One day, a couple of us fellers ran some wires into the puddle from the magneto that worked the telephone, and when this knothead came off shift he stopped to take his customary leak, and one of us was hid round the corner, crankin' the magneto for all it was worth. 'Course, that electricity traveled up the puddle and into the Yugoslav, and then down his body an' grounded out through his boots. He let out a screech that ruptured eardrums all over the mine, and then he bounced back about thirty feet. When he come to, we never did tell him. He had a bad temper. After that, he never pissed in the mine again, not as long as I was there anyway. He always side-stepped around any puddle. Claimed they was inhabited by devils."

Clem was using an old gallon paint can from the back porch to store the worms. He and Jesse collected thirty or forty. Jesse threw in some black dirt and a handful of wet oak leaves to keep them fresh. He said, "I happen to know a little spot on the Brazos, just below the Box. Hell to git into, even with the pickup, but we'll give it a try. Got some real lunkers in that stretch of the river."

"Say, Sprout, can I have that Plymouth?"

"Nope."

"You ain't doin' anything with it," Clem pointed out. "Maybe I could get it to run."

"I got plans for that car. Woody Klein at the Emerald has a standin' offer to buy it from me, if I ever want to sell. He collects old heaps. Rebuilds 'em."

"Well, then, can I have that busted-down motorcycle?"

"What for?"

"I don't know. Maybe I could put it back together. Harley hog like that'd be worth something."

"That was your daddy's."

"It was?" Clem looked at him. "Then it's mine by rights!"

"Who says so?"

"It's inheritance, that's what!"

"You quotin' law at me, boy?"

"Tell you what . . . you give me that ol' motorcycle, and I'll go fishin' with you today."

"I'll think about it," Jesse said. "Meanwhile, you're going fishin' whether you like it or not."

"Why's it all apart like that?"

"He was always takin' things apart," Jesse said. "That's the way he was. Always tinkerin'. Then, after he got something apart, he'd lose interest in it and forget about it, an' look around for something new to fool with." Jesse thought a moment. "Hell, I don't care. Go ahead and take it, if you want to. Mebbe it'll give you something to do. Probably half the parts is missing. I recollect that one time there was a service manual in those boxes of pieces."

In the house they dressed, and then made some sandwiches and packed a six-pack and a hip flask of bourbon into the tackle box. Jesse got out a couple of rods and spinning reels loaded with six-pound-test line.

Jesse had been right about his favorite spot not being easy to get to. The pickup made it only partway, and then they had to walk for over a mile, across boggy fields and through heavy stands of willow, to get to the river. Clem groused when he went knee-deep in a mud puddle. Towering high above them were the cliffs of the Box itself, a thousand feet of vertical granite. It was a beautiful, spooky, hidden place.

On the river, Jesse practiced with Clem until the boy got the hang of handling a spinning reel. Clem put on a big show about not being very interested in this fishing business, until he caught a small cut-throat, and then, a while later, a couple of rainbows. "Hey, man, those little fuckers go after that worm, they really smack it, don't they?"

"Oh, they can put up a bit of a fight," Jesse said.

"I mean, you can feel 'em hit, right up your arm."

"You ain't seen nothin'. These are just panfish."

"What're panfish?"

"Christ, you sure are dumb," Jesse said. He shook his head. "They're fish that're just the right size for a fry pan. What else would you call 'em panfish for?"

They moved upstream a ways. Clem said, "How come you ain't fishin'? You was the one who was all hot an' bothered about comin' up here."

"Learned a long time ago that the only way to fish with a kid is to let the kid do the fishin'," Jesse said. "Either leave the goddamn kid home and fish the way you ought'a, or take the kid along and forget your own fishin'. Kids got to be watched out for."

"Sprout, when are you goin' to wise up and quit callin' me a kid? I ain't no kid, and I don't dig bein' called one," Clem said. "Ain't nothin' here. All these big rocks. Let's go back to where we was catchin' bites."

"Don't be in such a rush," Jesse said. He pointed. "Try out there, see? Not too far. This side of that boulder."

Actually, Jesse had an idea that a big German brown might be hiding out there. Jesse had been trying to get this particular fish for two years. It didn't look as though anything worthwhile would be living in that stretch of river at all. It looked like a place where an angler maybe could dunk-fish and pick up a few small ones. But right by the boulder he had pointed out there was a deep pool in an eddy of the fast-moving current, and it was here that Jesse had hooked the German brown three times. The giant fish had taken off, breaking lines, snagging them on roots or sharp underwater rocks.

"Sprout, I'm tellin' you, there ain't nothin' here," Clem said. The fish he had caught earlier had been taken out near midstream in a running current, and on top of it he was having trouble here keeping his balance on the slippery boulders.

"Shut up and keep pokin' around." Jesse was sitting on a big granite outcropping, nipping at his bourbon. "Caught three little trout, already he's a big-mouthed expert."

Suddenly Clem said, "Shit, I think I got the line snagged." He pulled at it, then yanked.

"Jesus, take it easy, will you! That ain't no hawser."

"I'm snagged! Hell, this fishin' is too much of a hassle."

"Feel around, you fathead! That's what the fuckin' pole is for."

Clem tried this. He couldn't feel anything.

And then he did. A smooth, slow tug. "Sprout, it ain't snagged!" he yelled. "Something down there's got hold of it!"

"Take it easy."

There was another tug, still slow, but stronger. The fiberglass rod bent in a downward arc. Clem was really excited now. All tense and alert, teetering on the mossy boulder. "Hey, Sprout, I think there's something down there!"

"Play him, boy."

"What the fuck you talkin' about? Play him! He don't feel like playin'! He's just doin' whatever he wants!"

"Let the *rod* do the work. Ease up on that drag, like I showed you. Listen, will you, just for once!"

So it began. And it went on for almost an hour, with Jesse yelling orders. "Son of a bitch, will you quit operatin' that pole like it was a derrick? That's a record-size German brown you got down there. You ain't goin' to haul in something like that with just a six-pound line! Play him, you dumb shit! I know this fish! Don't push at him so! Let him do the work—wear himself out!"

"I got him!"

"You got your ass in the wind, boy."

"He's gettin' tired!"

"Shit, he ain't tired! He's foolin' you. He's just warmin' up! Playin' around. He's smart. He's been in this stream for years. He's a big, strong ol' feller. Hell, I don't know whether I'm watchin' a boy go after a fish, or a fish after a boy."

The drag-set on the spinning reel whirred as the trout made a dash for midstream. Clem yelled, *"Whoo-eee!* Lookit him go! God almighty!"

"Give him his head! Don't force him!"

"Ain't no forcin' that motherfucker, Sprout!"

"Play him, and he's yours. He'll slow down, by and by."

Time passed. The trout would make a powerful dash one way or another, and then head back to the safety of the pool beside the big boulder. Inevitably, though, he was tiring. Once Clem said, "He's easy now. Can't I just pull him in?"

"Try that just once, you'll lose him. And if you lose him, I'm goin' to kick your ass from here to Tierra Amarilla."

Clem began working him into shallower water. Finally, they were able to see the size of him. Now it was Jesse who got excited. The bourbon had loosened him up, and he was hopping up and down at the edge of the water. "Shit fire and save matches! Didn't I tell you! That ain't no little hatchery fucker. Hatchery fish always has soft flesh, scarcely worth fryin' up. This ol' boy, he's been in the river a long time! He knows what he's up to! Just take your time with him."

The trout thrashed in the shallows. Still fighting, but exhausted. Clem was exhausted too. His back and shoulders and arms ached, and he was soaked with perspiration.

Finally, very gently, he got the fish into water that was only inches deep. And, for a fact, this was a big one, heavy in the middle, almost potbellied, with a sinister prognathous jaw and killer eyes. Jesse waded into the water, crouching, slipped once and fell flat on his ass in the shallows. He got up and began stalking the fish again, like a cat after a sparrow, waiting for his moment, and then he darted quickly, grabbing it by the gills and flinging it ashore. The fish measured twenty-four inches. Jesse said, "Well, what d'you think of him?"

Clem said, "Goddamn!"

"You probably got yourself twenty-five bucks," Jesse said. "Gus runs a contest at the store for the biggest trout of the season. Personally, I'd rather keep you out'a that place, but let's enter this feller and freeze him, and then when the season's over, we'll go collect our money, and we'll git to eat the fish too. No sense lettin' twenty-five bucks go to waste. Be the first time I ever got somethin' for nothin' out'a Benavidez."

So they walked back to the pickup and drove down to the store. Clem ambled in, holding the fish by a gill. He was feeling pretty good about himself.

Sally Benavidez said, "Who caught the whale?"

"Clem did," Jesse said.

Willie Montoya and Connie Aragon were in the store too. They had been trying to talk Sally into going out on a midnight picnic with them on the Chama River, but this monster trout took precedence. Both young men turned green with envy, and what wasn't envy was all hating admiration. Connie said, "I remember that German brown that Jaime Vigil took three years ago. It was bigger, I think."

"Bullshit," Jesse said. "Besides, that was years ago. Girl, register this here fish."

"I'll have to see your license," Sally said.

"Don't talk to me about no goddamn license," Jesse said. "Just wrap this fish in plastic and mark it in the name of Clement Slade, Jr." He got out the little pocket tape measure he carried in his tackle box, tugged with all his strength at the trout's head and tail, laid it on the counter, and remeasured it. "Twenty-four and three-quarter inches."

"You ain't supposed to pull on it like that, Jesse," Willie said.

"Shut up, Montoya. I'm just compensatin' for natural dehydration. You tryin' to tell me how to measure a fish?" Jesse demanded.

Connie Aragon was at the counter, peering over Jesse's shoulder. He said, "Looked more like twenty-four and a half to me."

"We ain't goin' to quibble about a measly quarter-inch," Jesse said. "I'm nothin' if not generous."

In the freezer, where Gus kept the entries turned in by local fishermen, the other trout looked like minnows. Willie Montoya turned to Clem and said, *"Hombre,* you catch that fish all by yourself?"

Jesse said, "Sure he did! I did some advisin', naturally. First time this here boy's ever even held a rod in his hand. But I never touched the fish till he got it ashore."

"How about a Coors, on the house?" Sally said. She smiled at Clem. "How'd you learn to catch such a great big fish when you ain't even from around here?"

"Why, baby, it's all in the wrist," Clem said easily. He leaned back against the counter, hands in his pockets, and smiled down at her. "Ol' fish like that, you got to give him his room. Let him take his time. Let him make up his mind, an' make his play. Can't push at him. Fish, he don't like that." He paused, and then grinned. "All you got to do is take your time, baby. By and by, that fish sees there ain't no percentage in fightin'. Once he knows that, he's yours. Bide your time, honey, an' he'll come right to you. Once he knows who's who, all you got to do is snap your fingers an' he'll jump right into your lap."

Sally listened to this, smiling vaguely, then shivered as if chilled, although the store was warm. She got two cold beers and opened them, and handed them to Clem and Jesse.

It was the first time in thirty years that anyone had ever received a freebie at Gus's Groceries. The news went around town.

ANOTHER ARGUMENT STARTED when Jesse said it was time for Clem to register at the Chama high school. The beginning of the semester was still a long way off, but Jesse had seen an announcement on Horacio Quintana's bulletin board indicating that counselors would be interviewing new students that week.

"Sprout, I ain't cut out for school," Clem insisted.

"You're goin' anyway."

"Ol' man, I'm warnin' you, I'll split this scene first."

"You want to grow up to be a no-good, ignorant, low-down bum?" Jesse stomped around the kitchen, fuming. "Education's the whole shebang nowadays! Everybody's got to git educated, whether they want to or not. It's the goddamn law!"

"The law and yours truly ain't much for seein' eye to eye," Clem pointed out.

"Well, *you* an' *me* are goin' to see eye to eye," Jesse shouted. "Personally, I don't give a rat's ass whether you end up back in the D-Home or in some penitentiary. Wouldn't be gittin' no more than what's due you! But as long as you're my legal ward, you damn well better pay mind. And I say you go to school. Serves you right. Most places, a kid can quit school legal when he's sixteen. But you! You got nineteen thousand different kinds of criminal charges filed against you. You got probation officers and welfare workers and cops and judges and every other kind of nose-pickin' California bureaucrat bustin' their balls to make sure you act like a model citizen."

"No one has bugged us here."

"They will. Give 'em time. They know where we are. And when that time comes, you're goin' to be in school, if I have to rope you with a lariat to do it!"

Jesse got so furious that he sat right down at the kitchen table and wrote a letter to the niece in Germany:

Dear Helen:

How are you? I hope you are okay. I am writting to find out when you will be coming back to these here United States. You must be tired of being around all those Krauts by now. Things are bad here. Prices are higher than ever, with no end in sight. My health is poor and I have lots of rheumatizm. I am just about broke, and am having trouble makeing ends meet. I am writting again to find out if you can help me with my grandson, Clement Slade, Jr., since I do not have the money to raise him right, and also I am getting on in years, no spring chicken any more. How is your husband and all the kids? Please let me know about this as I have to do something pretty quick.

—Jesse R. Slade

P.S. The boy is supposed to get money from sociel security, so that will help pay for his keep.

With a glare of defiance, he showed the note to Clem. "What d'you think of *them* potatoes? There's more'n one way to skin a cat. You so goddamn miserable here, we'll just see how you like it someplace else."

"Suits me fine!"

"You ain't happy less'n you're mouthin' off all the time, like one of them uppity niggers!"

"Goddamn it, I *am* an uppity nigger," Clem said.

"First thing I intend doin' the day I git rid of you, I'm goin' to sit my ass down here in this house and relax for a solid month! Maybe two months."

"I get away from here, I'm goin' to feel so good I'm liable to dance for a whole week!"

"Meanwhile, you'll go to school."

"Don't count on it!"

The argument went nowhere. Finally Clem gave in, as much out of boredom with the old man's stubbornness as anything else. He agreed sullenly to give it a "half-assed try." "But don't 'spect too much," he added, with an ominous note. "It ain't goin' to work. I can feel it in my bones."

"Boy, just go through the motions, is all," Jesse said. "Try lookin' at it from my side of the fence. All I aim to do is keep those bureaucrats off our backs until I can git rid of you permanent."

"Sure is nice to feel wanted," Clem said glumly.

"Now, why're you talkin' that way?" Jesse said, getting angry again. "You behave like you was a bowl of strawberries an' sweet cream, when the truth is, you're as ornery as a rattlesnake with a bad wisdom tooth."

"That's a back door what swings both ways," Clem said. "You ain't no bargain yourself."

"I ain't denyin' it! Never said I was. All I'm suggestin' is that both of us act civil until things take a turn for the better, that's all."

"Well, there's one good thing about school," Clem said.

"What's that?"

"Won't have to look at your ugly ol' face all day."

Jess beamed. "Y'see! You're gittin' a better attitude about it already!"

Over at Chama High, the counselor said, "I don't know what grade he's supposed to be in, or what his level is, or what his capacities are. Why don't you write to his last school in California and have a complete transcript forwarded? We can take it from there."

Clem sprawled sulkily in a chair beside Jesse, fooling with a book of matches. The old man grew irate. "I ain't got the time to be writin' California or anyplace else! All you got to do is put him where he belongs! He's sixteen, going on seventeen. Give him tests, damn it. What the hell kind of a runaround are you tryin' to hand me? You people got tests for everything under the sun! Don't hand me this mealymouthed batshit about gittin' transcripts. *You* figure it out. Hell, don't tell me you can't test him. I seen all about it, on the TV. That's what you're bein' paid for."

As it turned out, there was a way to do this, with equivalency tests and rating scores based on NED standards.

Clem took the tests desultorily.

He turned out to have a fourteen-year-old's aptitude in English; in history and current events, he was at a twelve-year-old's level; and in simple physics and general math he scored a flat one hundred percent.

"No Slade was ever dumb when it came to figures," Jesse said.

Even so, the spread of the scores was so erratic the counselor couldn't figure out what to do. He ended by giving up and placing Clem in his general age group—third year.

Jesse was satisfied with this, even a little proud. He said, "Boy, you'll do just fine."

"That'll be the day!"

Later that week they drove down to Santa Fe to shop for some clothes for Clem. "It's cheaper down there," Jesse explained. "We ain't goin' to buy much. However, you can't start school in that vest and beat-up Stetson. You look like some kind of colored hippie. Kids can be real ballbusters that way. Judge one another on appearance. God, they're awful."

"Where'd you git the bread?" Clem asked. "How come all of a sudden you're doin' me something? You're always bitchin' about bein' broke. You got money you ain't told me about?"

"None of your business," Jesse said. "I always keep a few tens and twenties squirreled away, in case of emergencies."

In Santa Fe, they shopped at Sears Roebuck and then went over to the Montgomery Ward in DeVargas Mall and picked out a pair of lace-up logger boots, jeans, three shirts, underwear, and a sheep-skin-lined denim workjacket. When they were done, Jesse wanted a coffee at VIP's, and Clem wandered off alone to stretch his legs. They agreed to meet later at the truck.

Back in Brazos, another argument got started when they unloaded the packages in the camper. It seemed that Clem had been doing considerably more in the shopping mall than stretching his legs.

"Jesus Christ! Where'd all this come from?" Jesse demanded.

"Sprout, don't get in a sweat."

"You stole it!"

"The correct word is appropriated."

"How in hell did you *git* it?"

"That's for me to know and you to guess."

"Sonuvabitch! That mall was crawlin' from one end to the other with security guards packin' pistols."

"Strictly amateur," Clem explained modestly. "Place like that wouldn't last two days in Los Angeles. Back there, we got people who're high-class experts."

"There's enough junk back here to send you to prison for a year! We better hide it, out in the storage shed. People in this town ever saw this, they'd blab for months! Clem, you are plain dumb!"

"Just tryin' to help out, Sprout."

"Damnedest stupid thing I ever saw!"

"Sprout, stealin' ain't *that* bad."

"Oh, don't git me wrong," Jesse said. "I ain't got nothin' against stealin'. No sir. That's all capitalism is anyway, the dirty goddamn rich stealin' from the poor. I got no objection to the poor doin' a *chinga* on the rich if they git a chance. Gus Benavidez, he'd steal the pennies off a dead man's eyes. Bureaucrats and politicians are the worst thieves of all. That's a proven fact. No, boy, all I'm saying is, you took a stupid chance. Only a fool does that. With the record you got, if they'd caught you, they'd throw the goddamn key away. Now, take me. If they caught *me* heistin' a little something or other, why, I could always plead old age or senile insanity or something, and probably git off with a lecture down at the magistrate's court. But you? Clem, you hadn't ought'a taken a chance like that."

"I'm a juvenile," Clem said. "They can't do much with that."

"You're almost a man," Jesse pointed out. "That juvenile racket you been relyin' on for so long is just about behind you, in case you don't know it."

"You want we should bring all this back?"

Among the loot was a portable color television set. A new battery for the truck—the old one barely turned the engine over. An electric toaster and a tape deck. Four quarts of bourbon and a three-foot-long stick of German summer sausage bearing the imprint of Hickory Farms, as well as assorted wedges of cheeses. There were new work-gloves for Jesse and an ornate rodeo belt buckle for Clem, ammunition for the shotguns, a digital clock-radio, an electric can opener, a three-cell flashlight, and copies of *Field & Stream, Sports Afield, Playboy* and *Penthouse*. Clem said again, "I guess we could bring this stuff back, if that's what you want."

Jesse was looking at the color television admiringly. Finally, he said, "Shit, no! It ain't goin' out in the shed either! But don't do it again, y'hear?" He thought a moment. "Clem, you ain't been stealin' around here, have you?"

"Doesn't pay to liberate merchandise where you live," Clem said. "Besides, there ain't nothin' worth stealin' in this whole town."

"Nothin' out of Gus's store?"

"*Whoo-eee!* How you talk! That little Sally, in another few weeks she'll give me anything I want!"

"Her daddy catches her, he'll give you something too," Jesse said. "Your very own bullet hole, most likely."

"I'm watchin' him."

"You better watch in all directions, then. That's where real trouble comes from."

THERE WAS MORE than talk to Jesse's warnings. Behind his grumbling lay a deep uneasiness. He knew the town and the people. They took their time—often years—about letting someone new into the life of the village, such as it was. To them, Clem was a mysterious stranger, all the more so because he was as good as he boasted about being close-mouthed. Like most street people, he seemed to come on all loose and easygoing, but at the same time he never let slip a remark about what was really on his mind. Most especially he never talked about his past. For the citizens of Brazos, half the fun in having a newcomer around was guessing—often with surprising accuracy—what that person was up to, and what had brought him or her to this place. Warner Grimmiessen had not been in town a month before the word went out that he was a pansy *maricón*. The Hurleys had scarcely finished unpacking before their daily consumption was broadcast. But this new *mulato* gave them nothing, and so people like Gus Benavidez, with his expressionless eyes, looked on and waited. So did Horacio Quintana with his binoculars, and Dolores Espinoza, who was a great power in the village, and whose word—pro or con —dictated how a person ought to be treated.

What ate at Jesse was that the boy had not behaved all that badly since his arrival. True, he and Clem were constantly sniping at each other, but it could have been worse. He tried not to think about it, but at times the old man wondered when Clem would make a move. Although they knew nothing of his history, the rest of the townspeople seemed to be waiting for the same thing. The way Jesse saw it, it was inevitable. If there was truth to only a fraction of what Clem talked about in the privacy of the kitchen—his loud-mouthed bragging about his toughness and street smarts—trouble would come.

The first sign of it happened one afternoon when they stopped at Gus's. Willie Montoya happened to be there, keeping Sally company. She glanced at Clem and smiled. "Hey! I heard you're in third year. So am I."

"Where'd you hear that?" Clem said.

"Around. We'll probably have some classes together."

"Probably we will, baby."

"That'll be fun."

"Probably it will," Clem said cooly. His style with her so far was studiedly casual. As if she was not to be taken seriously. A classic putdown.

This had a certain effect on Sally that was a little like waving a red flag in front of a bull. In her scorebook, no male took her casually. She looked at him coldly. "Say, d'you have to act so snotty every time somebody tries to be friendly?"

Clem smiled at her. Then he made a show out of pretending to notice something on her forehead. Leaned across the counter a little. Wet the tip of his middle finger with his tongue. "Hey, you got a little smudge. Hold still." He cleaned the imaginary spot. "There. That's better. Say, you're a real cool chick. Anybody ever tell you that?"

At that point Willie slowly got up from where he was sitting on an upended Coca-Cola crate and said, "Keep your hands off her."

Clem turned. He was still smiling. "You talkin' to me?"

"You know something? I don't think I like you."

Clem said, "How 'bout that!"

Willie himself was over six feet, and he had an easy thirty pounds on Clem. He said, "Why don't you just get the hell out'a this town?"

There it was. Something Clem could finally understand. Trucking around with Jesse and catching trout and all that stuff might be something he wasn't into. But if somebody stood up and said straight out that they didn't dig you, well, that happened to be something he knew about.

If Willie had comprehended this, maybe he would have kept his mouth shut. Willie was not very bright. Two years earlier, at nineteen, he had finally dropped out of Chama High, still trying to absorb stuff most sixteen-year-olds had in their hip pockets. So, on top of everything else, all this scholastic garbage about Sally and Clem being third-year classmates rankled too.

Willie was tall, strong, and rugged-looking. His shoulders swelled with layers of muscle, and his stomach was flat and hard. On him a simple workshirt, skin-tight jeans, and black cycler's boots looked right. At forty, Willie would resemble a dirigible, but now this was his golden time. His dark, smooth complexion matched Clem's. His hair was two feet long, soot black, and he wore it tied in a ponytail with a piece of rawhide. He had eighteen-inch biceps and could benchpress two hundred and fifty pounds. He had thick black brows that met in a scowl, soft brown eyes fringed by long, curved lashes, and a lovely mouth that was almost feminine in the delicate curve of the upper lip. His cheeks and jaw were blue-black, no matter how closely he shaved. He had a sullen, slouching, heavy-shouldered way of moving. Looked somehow dangerous, as if possessed by that kind of smoldering temper that, once triggered, goes a long way before it cools. As a macho male, Willie ought to have been wooed by young ladies at least to a degree commensurate to the courting his cousin, Sally, got from local studs. He had a great opinion of his attractiveness as a man, but this good image was in conflict with the way life worked for him: Willie seldom scored, and when he finally did he usually loused everything up because of a tendency toward premature ejaculation. Perhaps this explained his friendship with Werner Grimmiessen. If Willie swung both ways, perhaps it was because he got some patience and understanding from Werner that he could not find elsewhere. Whatever, the narcissistic self-image he had of himself as irresistible hung on. Sally, cousin or not, ought to be his. She had to be. It was simple. Willie loved her. With those long, tanned, supple legs, the firm, nipply breasts, all of her a heavenly vision . . . how could it be otherwise?

Sally said, "Willie, you behave."

Willie glowered at Clem. "Get out'a town, while you still got two legs you can walk out on."

Clem stayed cool. "Baby, let it go."

A little nervously, at the same time enjoying the whole thing, Sally perched a thigh on the counter. "Both of you, cut it out."

Jesse said, "Clem, let's get goin'."

Willie turned to Sally. "Whyn't you just for once shut that dumb fuckin' mouth of yours?"

Clem turned to her, too. "Sugar, you take that without a fight, you'll take this without a bite."

"I hate niggers," Willie said.

Clem said, "How come is that? Mexicans is part nigger, I hear."

Willie moved forward.

Clem went into a combat stance, crouched, legs apart. "Try it," he said.

His voice was hard, his gaze steady. An implacable calm. He raised a hand toward Willie, almost gently. "No closer. That is *it!*"

Willie stared around. He was alone. No younger brother. No Connie Aragon.

He backed off. Thereby showing, perhaps for the first time in years, a sign of intelligence. But, in backing off, gave a warning. He glared stonily at Clem. "Okay. Now it starts. We'll see."

"Sho' nuff," Clem said. He relaxed.

Sally said, "What's the matter, Willie? You were talkin' just last week about slappin' me around. Where's all that macho I been hearing about?"

Willie stalked out of the store.

"He's a lot of hot air, that's all he is," Sally said. She looked at Clem. "For a second I thought you two were really going to get into it." She smiled. "Gee, that would have been something!"

Back at the house, Jesse said, "Boy, don't you know you can't bluff a dumb shit like Willie? He'll just round up his pals. Mark my words."

"Don't worry about it, Sprout."

"I ain't worried. I'm just a worn-out, tired ol' man. Any worryin' about fightin' gits done around here, that's your department, son."

WHEN JESSE WAS in a sour mood he usually ended up by going on a binge, and this was what happened the next day. He began in the morning with a few beers, and spent the following hours nipping at the bourbon Clem had stolen. When he wasn't nipping, he groused at Clem. "Christ, you must'a lived like an animal back where you come from! Can't even pick up a coffee cup after yourself. Clem, you know something? You're a full-time professional slob, that's what."

"Pot calling the kettle black," Clem said.

The cat, Rojo, was curled up by the stove. Jesse stepped on his tail, and Rojo clawed him. Jesse picked him up and he went sailing out the back door in a high, spinning arc reminiscent of a quarterback's forward pass. He landed near the outhouse, got up, and staggered off. "Fuckin' ingrates!" Jesse shouted. "That's what I'm surrounded with in my final years!" He kicked one of the kitchen chairs. "Ungrateful leeches, that's what they are! Cats and useless kids. Livin' under my roof an' moochin' off me. Eatin' me out'a house and home. Never so much as a single thank-you. Goddamn it all to hell, I've had it clear up to my eyeballs. I don't have to put up with this crap! I'm an old man! I got a right to some peace and quiet for a change, not this stinkin' hellhole I'm trapped in!"

Clem, too, was in a rotten mood. All the good things of the past week—the enormous trout, the raid at DeVargas Mall, coming down on Willie Montoya—seemed to have faded. Yesterday, on the sly, before they had left the store, he had asked Sally to go out with him. She had agreed. Yesterday, the idea seemed cool. She obviously wasn't getting it steady, and he of course had not had anything all summer. This morning, however, listening to Jesse's fuming condemnations, nothing seemed right, and Sally Benavidez, even with those nifty legs and tits, shaped up as a pain in the ass who could be trouble.

"Whyn't you clean up this crummy house for a change?" Jesse said.

"You ain't no wheelchair case," Clem replied. "Get off your lazy ass and clean it up yourself."

Around four that afternoon, Jesse was at the Emerald Bar, hoisting a few with Werner Grimmiessen, Garrison and Patsy Hurley, Connie Aragon, and a couple of other people, along with Gus Benavidez, who was having one of his periodic spells of bitter loneliness, and who was therefore driven to spend a few bucks to ease the pain. Benavidez was the most despised man in Brazos, and he knew it. Behind the counter of his store, his heavily lidded eyes were fathomless, but when it came time for a bargain to be closed or a bill paid, he was relentless and cruel, a veritable Torquemada of the account ledger. On this afternoon, he was mildly drunk. He was buying bourbon highballs for Lulu Uranga. When Gus treated anyone to a drink it meant that he was really down in the dumps.

Jesse was holding forth. "What is this goddamn country comin' to, that's what I want'a know. I remember when pinto beans was fifty cents a hundred-pound sack. You know what they cost today? I remember when cigarettes was five cents a pack, and at that you was bein' robbed. Every time the fuckin' Democrats git in, the prices shoot up all the way to the moon! How's an old man like me goin' to git by? That's all I'm askin'."

Woody Klein was behind the bar, polishing glasses with a towel. "I hear the cost of living has exactly doubled in the past eleven years."

"Tripled is more like it! Shit, you don't believe that hypocritical, two-faced, double-dealin', cotton-pickin' son of bitch they got sittin' up there in the White House, d'you? Cost of livin'! All that's just propaganda!" He tasted his drink. "I remember when beer was a nickel a glass, and a man could eat himself into the hospital at the free-lunch counters every saloon had," he said. "They had crackers and bread, an' sardines in oil, and pickled pigs' feet, an' headcheese, an' all sorts of baloney, an' everything else a man could want . . . all for a nickel beer!"

"Those days are gone forever, Jess."

"You can say that again."

Lulu stopped by Jesse. "How is Clem?"

"Don't mention that boy to me. Ain't my day gone bad enough, without you havin' to ruin it completely? That goddamn kid eats eleven times a day, just to aggravate me. I never *saw* food disappear so fast! I'm goin' to put a loggin' chain and padlock around that fridge."

"Kids got to eat," Lu said.

"Too much food is no good for a person," Jesse said. "Why, just this mornin', we finished breakfast—two eggs, beans, toast, coffee, and grape jelly—and the sonuvabitchin' dishes wasn't even cleared away before he was at the fridge. Whoever heard of makin' a sandwich with five slices of bread? It looked like some kind'a high-rise! And what he put in between those slices included everything that wasn't nailed down. Liverwurst, raw onions, mayonnaise, some real nice cheese we got down in Santa Fe that I was savin' for myself for a snack, you name it! I never saw a sandwich before that weighed three and a half pounds. It disappeared like it had been attacked by a vacuum cleaner. After that he started in on a crate of apples I been keepin' to make cider with. That kid must think I'm J. P. Morgan and Andrew Carnegie combined. Just keepin' him alive is runnin' me into the poorhouse."

"Jess, you ought to keep a ten-gallon pot of beans and salt pork going on the stove all the time," Woody said. "That's what Arlene does."

"With that tribe you got, you need a bathtub to cook beans," Jesse said.

"Beans is good for a kid," Lulu said.

"Beans often have an adverse effect on me," Patsy Hurley said.

"Don't be so polite, Patsy—we know what you mean," Jesse said. "Don't think I can't hear you over in that outhouse, mornings, thunderin' away on the ol' sousaphone. You ought'a take yourself a pair of cymbals and a harmonica out there. That way, if you ever got tuned up, it'd sound like a one-woman marchin' band in that outhouse. Every mornin', half of Brazos'd have the benefit of a free concert, and nobody'd even have to turn on their radios."

Garrison Hurley looked distressed. "Let's keep it decent, shall we?"

"Patsy brought it up, not me," Jesse observed. "The VFW ought'a hire her for their Fourth of July parade. Woody, I'll have another bourbon, if you don't mind."

"You sure you should, Jess?"

"Woody, you and me been pals for years. You ever hear me try to tell you what to do? Every year Arlene hatches another brat, and you stand in back of that bar cryin' the blues when common sense ought'a tell you that you got to draw the line somewhere! Why the hell don't you tie a knot in it? My God, you and Arlene must be out to set some kind'a endurance record. You already got most of the school system populated with Klein kids. Don't it ever git embarrassin'? Even so, you never heard a critical word from Jesse Slade. I act as godfather and offer congratulations, though what a man with a one-track mind like yours needs to be congratulated for, I couldn't say. Quit tellin' me what to do, and give me a bourbon. I know my tolerance."

Woody poured. Gus Benavidez said, "My treat, Jesse." He laid a dollar bill on the bar.

Jesse looked from him to Woody, to Werner, and then to Garrison. "Judgment Day! It's come at last. I never thought I'd live to see it. Thanks, Gus."

"My pleasure," Gus said.

"If it feels so pleasurable, how come you look like you're ready to bust out cryin'?" Jesse said.

"I got to talk to you, Jesse."

"My bill don't come due at the store until the end of the month."

"Your credit is always good with me," Gus said. "Maybe we can sit at a table alone."

"I ain't got nothin' to hide," Jesse said. "I like it up here at the bar."

"I heard what you were just saying. About how hard it is to bring up a boy right," Gus said. "Or a girl."

Jesse stared at him. "So? What's on your mind?"

"I don't want no trouble, Jesse."

"That's good. Neither do I."

"I have enough already."

"Don't we all."

"Sally tells me she has a date with your boy."

"That's news to me."

"I don't approve."

"Neither do I," Jesse said.

The Hurleys and Werner Grimmiessen exchanged glances. They looked like they didn't approve of the Clem–Sally business either, but they said nothing. Brazos was a place where a person was very careful about handing out free advice or taking sides. Partisanship of any kind was a thing to be avoided if possible. Gus Benavidez might be talking about his daughter, but it went further than that. Gus, in a way, represented a large part of the village—too many people owed him favors or money.

Jesse saw that Gus's glass was empty, and laid a dollar of his own on the bar. "Woody, git him a fresh one, will you?" Klein did, pretending not to be interested in the conversation, but not missing a word. By now everybody else was listening. It would have made no difference if the two men had gone to the farthest table. When it came to a juicy confrontation, the people who hung out at the Emerald had ears like megaphones.

With a serious look, Gus tasted his drink, then set it down and said again, "I don't want trouble."

"Won't be none," Jesse said.

"That's good. Because if there is, then I have to take care of it," Gus said. Jesse suddenly looked soberer. Gus motioned to Woody. "Give my friend here another shot."

"Thanks again, Gus," Jesse said.

"Trouble is no good."

"What kind'a trouble you talkin' about, Gus?"

Gus drank again. He had difficulty getting the words out, but he finally did. "I don't like black people."

"That's understandable, Gus," Jesse said. "Who the hell does?" He frowned, then stared at Gus. "Oh, you mean my boy."

Gus said nothing.

"He ain't such a bad kid, Benavidez."

"Sure, Jesse. I just want you should tell him to leave Sally alone."

"I already did," Jesse pointed out. "Maybe somebody ought'a tell that girl of yours the same thing."

"A boy like that, he could start some real trouble," Gus said.

"Speak plain. I want'a be sure I'm hearin' you straight."

"I got to look out for my own."

"So do I," Jesse said. He drank down his bourbon. It seemed to have the effect of sobering him up still more.

Gus thought for a while, drank again, lit a cigarette, fiddled with his lighter, then said, "*Este muchacho es un negro, qué no?* I got too many problems of my own. Life is short. Who wants trouble?"

"Who the hell does?" Jesse agreed.

"I got an arrangement, an engagement, for my girl," Gus said.

"With who? What're their names?"

That was a low blow. Everybody in the bar knew it. Woody Klein winced, shut his eyes, and turned away.

"Tell your boy to stay away," Gus said again.

"I already told him that," Jesse said again.

"Tell him harder, so that he listens," Gus said.

"I surely will, Gus."

"I mean, in this town, all of us have to live together and get along, *me parace.*"

"You want my opinion, people in this town git along like flint an' steel," Jesse said.

"No trouble, *que no?*"

"Otherwise what?" Jesse said.

Gus sipped at his drink again. Shrugged his shoulders. "What can happen, can happen."

That paid Jesse back for the cheap shot about Sally. Lulu butted in and said, "Gus Benavidez, you quit that talk! Men drink too much and then get angry an' talk that way, it's no good! You better go on home now and sleep for a while. You wake up, you feel better."

"Don't yell at me, Lulu," Gus said. "Like I said, I got to look out for my own. That's all."

Jesse sat on his bar stool, the big Stetson tilted back on his head, hunch-shouldered, over his drink, decrepit and ratty-looking, and, with his beak nose and grizzled, scrawny neck, putting one in mind of a condor. He glared down at his drink with red-rimmed eyes, in a way that could only be described as nasty. In his Sunday clothes and at his smiling best, Jesse looked like a relic from the Jurassic Era, and now he looked even meaner. Finally he turned to Gus and said, "How long we been knowin' each other, Gus?"

"Oh, thirty, thirty-five years," Gus said. "*Más o menos*. At least."

"That's right," Jesse said, finishing his drink. "You know me pretty well. Everybody knows Jesse Slade. I ain't rich, and I ain't important, and there ain't many what likes me, but when I give my word I keep it. Everybody around here knows that, right?"

"Sure, Jesse. Like I say, your credit with me is *siempre* okay," Gus said.

"Ain't talkin' about that," Jesse said. He got off the stool. Gave Gus a stony look. "Anybody lays a hand on that boy, that man answers personally to me. I mean it." He stepped closer to Benavidez. "That goes for you, or any other man in Brazos. The boy is my kin. Anything happens to him, I'll come after whoever done it."

Jesse walked out. A short time later, Gus Benavidez left too. He did not return to the store but drove down to the village garbage dump, where he could be alone. There he parked, without realizing it, near a spot frequented by his daughter, and considered the problems of life and the difficulty of raising a daughter, and how he had tried for years to do his best, and now nobody appreciated his decent qualities, and how for all his efforts there was not a single person he could call a friend. He cupped his hands to his face, leaned over the steering wheel, and wept.

THE PICNIC WAS courtesy of Gus Benavidez, only he didn't know it. Corndogs, Fritos, Cokes, bourbon, beer, hamburgers, rolls, pickled chili chips, and two sacks of Krystal Kleer ice, all filched by Sally and accounted for by her own method of bookkeeping. There was also a pack of Zig-Zag cigarette papers and a small sack of locally grown grass, which Clem, after he rolled a joint, said had as much lift as a Tetley teabag.

There was a hidden place up near a rocky crest by the great Brazos Box, with views for miles, and where no tourists ever came, at least not along the steep, rocky trail that Sally happened to know about, which led down a spruce-forested slope to a trickle of a stream. There was even a bit of a waterfall in this secret silent place. The banks of the stream were wet and mossy. It was cool and shaded. No breeze stirred among the heavy stands of timber. Together they built a fire out of aspen twigs to toast the rolls and cook the hamburgers, poured themselves bourbon-and-Cokes, smoked a couple of joints, got a little high, and fooled around.

Sally, in her irresistible shorts and T-shirt. Clem, in the old, salvaged Stetson and the sheepskin vest. She claimed a chill. Begged the vest. Now warmed by it, she openly admired what she saw of him. The slender waist and bare chest, almost hairless except for the tightly curled ringlets at the nipples. His back, as he crouched to tend the fire, showed long, smooth muscles. The shoulders bony, yet broad. The skin such a creamy brown it made her dizzy. The arms slender, yet solidly formed.

She was fascinated by his hands, and the way they moved. They were large, but unusually graceful, the fingers long and tapered, the nails clean, neatly trimmed and buffed to a sheen. The hands moved delicately, almost artfully, adjusting a twig or branch in the little fire.

They kidded around some more. His kisses were slow, exploratory—the leisureliness excited her. She laid her head against his shoulder. Her forehead was damp. Her breathing quickened, she seemed suddenly overcome by emotion. Had difficulty speaking. Her voice husky. "Promise me something."

"Sure, baby."

"Don't be mean to me."

"Now, why would I want to do a thing like that?"

"Be good to me. Be good."

"Sure."

"Oh, God. I knew it would be good. I knew it. I want everything."

She got weak. Almost went into a swoon. Felt all limp and defenseless. Dropped her head back and closed her eyes. "Hurry."

"No hurry, baby."

"Now. Please."

"Relax. That's it."

Tips of fingers pinching a nipple, then down to her bare thigh, then upward to touch crotch and stomach. The gentlest, teasing sort of caress, never ceasing, growing more insistent as the minutes slowly passed, until she cried out and flung her legs wide, lying sprawled on his lap, eyes tightly shut, teeth clenched. "God. Now. Oh, Jesus, I'm dying." Her hips arched, seeking that relentless touch, offering that slick and secret part of her. Else she would perish then and there! Her breathing quickened still more, her body felt feverish. And again and again that touch came to her, a lazy stroking, wringing from her one gasp after another until finally, almost in a dream state, frenzied and only half conscious, she tore at the belt and zipper of his jeans, tugged them down, murmuring, "Oh, my God! Oh, dear God."

Later, they smoked another joint. Clem called it popcorn. "All these seeds do is pop." They smoked still another. Got high again. Lolled around bare-assed. She kissed his fingers and toes, and said, "You are something else. You are really something else." He put her on her hands and knees, and she giggled when he spread her cheeks and examined her bottom, then gave a startled gasp as a finger deeply penetrated. "Oh, that's good," she said.

"More?"

"Yes."

"Want me to stop?"

"No. More."

Eventually he mounted her again, and they were at it when two trout fishermen—tourists—wearing chest-high waders came ambling down the path, letting off hoots of appreciation.

Toward sunset, driving back to town in the old Pontiac sedan Gus had bought for her, Sally said, "I'm crazy about you."

"Been a *fine* day," Clem said.

"I think I'm in love with you."

"Sure."

"God, you half killed me," she said. "It was wonderful."

"'Deed it was." Clem was using her orange stick to clean his fingernails. He yawned. What with Sally and the grass and the bourbon, it had been a long afternoon.

"When can we do this again?"

Clem shrugged. "Oh, sometime."

"Was it good for you?"

"Sure. Couldn't you tell?"

"Yes. But *tell* me!"

"You want another beer? There's a couple left in the cooler."

She glared at him, as though he was too stupid to understand anything.

TWO DAYS LATER Willie Montoya and Connie Aragon got into it with Clem, right out on Main Street in front of the post office. Clem was driving the pickup. Jesse sat beside him.

As Clem pulled into the post office's parking area, Willie and Connie got up from where they had been sitting on a bench and sauntered over. They looked like they'd had a few drinks. Jesse said, "Shit, I knew I shouldn't have left that forty-four home."

"Don't get in a sweat, Sprout," Clem said. "Dudes see a person's nervous, it gives 'em ideas."

"I ain't nervous. What the hell I got to be nervous about? It ain't me they're interested in. I wasn't messin' around up in the Brazos Box."

"What Brazos Box?"

"All sweetness and light, ain't you? It's all over town."

"Round here, a man has to work overtime to conduct his affairs in private, don't he?" Clem said.

"Boy, if privacy is what you hanker for, you shouldn't have picked Sally Benavidez to horse around with."

"She been talkin'?"

"Well, just the *two* of you was up there," Jesse said. "If you ain't been shootin' off your mouth, that leaves only one other person, 'cordin' to my calculations."

Clem frowned. "That's one I owe her."

Willie and Connie were by the truck now. Clem turned the ignition off, but made no move to open the door. He grinned at them and said, "How you fellers doin'?"

Jesse, however, wasted no time. He stuck his head out the window on his side, all bristling bravado, and said, "Listen, you half-baked, chicken-fuckin' black Mexican *hijos de putas cabrones,* git the fuck away from here. We ain't botherin' you, and we ain't aimin' to be bothered with!"

"*Viejo*, you talk too much," Willie said.

"I got a forty-four right here in the glove compartment talks better," Jesse said.

Either Willie or Connie, with their lumberjack muscles, could have yanked Jesse out of the truck window and flung him halfway across town, yet the old man seemed unafraid. His language said as much. In these parts, no one called a Spanish-American a black Mexican. The extra insults, about being sons of whores and chicken-fuckers, Jesse had tossed in free. So then, above and beyond whatever Sally and Clem had been up to in the Box, it looked like a real feud might be starting, between old Jesse and Willie's clan, and Connie Aragon's too.

Willie ignored Jesse's remarks, at least for the moment. He stepped up to the door on Clem's side and went to open it. From the look on his face it was more or less obvious that he intended to drag Clem out of the pickup and beat the living shit out of him, then and there, in front of the post office, right under the American flag.

The only trouble was that Clem, instead of struggling to keep the door closed, helped Willie open it. In fact, he put all his strength into ramming the door open instead of shut. The upper part of the frame caught Willie smack in the face, sending his Stetson and sunglasses flying. He went down, gagging on a couple of broken teeth. Blood spurted from a gash in the center of his forehead. Later, it was reported that sixteen stitches were needed to close the laceration.

Clem got out of the truck. Connie Aragon stepped back. His best friend was flopping around on the sidewalk, feebly groping around. No matter how Connie looked at it, the odds had been reduced to one-to-one. Connie had some second thoughts about Clem—whether or not taking him on was really so smart. Clem stepped toward Connie in a pose that reminded Connie of a picture he'd seen in a karate magazine. There was only one heartening aspect, and it was in Clem's favor. His hands were empty. That was lucky. Later, it would be judged simple self-defense.

"Ease off, fucker," Connie said. "Lemme take care of my friend."

Clem said, "You do that."

So Connie picked up Willie and helped him off. Clem and Jesse went into the post office for the mail. Horacio Quintana said, "Fighting ain't allowed around here. This is federal property. I'm reporting this to Washington."

Jesse said, "Blow it out your ass, Horacio. We got any mail?" There was none, and they left.

Driving back, the old man said, "Jesus, boy, you know you could have killed Willie that way?"

"You might have something there," Clem said.

"I never saw a human bein' move so fast in my whole life," Jesse said. "Clem where'd you ever learn to move that quick? You sure outsmarted 'em! Not that that takes much doin', considerin' Willie's brainpower."

"I couldn't just sit there, could I?" Clem said. "A person just stands around, a whole house might fall on him."

"Never saw anything like it," Jesse said. "Well, I guess I have to tell you this much . . . Willie claims he's the roughest lumberjack hereabouts. And he has proved it, more'n once. He's not so easy. That's a fact."

"Bullshit."

"You sure surprised me," Jesse said. "I mean, there it was . . . and then it *wasn't!* Goddamn!" He shook his head wonderingly. "Us Slades have always been fighters."

At this Clem smiled at him affectionately and shook his head. "You're just too much, Sprout!"

"Clem, what in God's name am I ever gonna do with you?"

"We're gettin' by, ain't we?"

"I ain't so sure of that. You'll be the death of me yet." Jesse hawked, and spat out the window. "Wished I'd never set eyes on you."

But later that day Jesse stood up for Clem.

Bill Martinez, the state cop for the district, and Milt Garcia, the local sheriff, dropped by for a talk. They were considering filing assault and battery charges against Clem, and maybe felonious assault while in possession of a deadly weapon.

Bill and Milt were cousins. Milt ran the town, and whenever there was real trouble, Bill backed him up. They sat in the kitchen and had coffee. Jesse and Clem sat on the other side of the table. Clem was quiet, outwardly docile. At the same time, he listened and watched, trying to figure out how their minds worked.

Jesse said, "I seen it with my own two eyes! They attacked us! We ought'a be filin' charges against *them*. We wasn't doin' a god-damn thing. Just gittin' our mail. There wasn't no deadly weapon at hand. Bill, what the hell are you talkin' about? How can a door on a pickup be a deadly weapon, any more'n a grand pianner or an armchair? That bastard Montoya, he started it."

"I happened to be opening the door to get out," Clem said. "The man happened to be in the way. That's all. Really, officer. His head got bumped."

Bill Martinez said, "The door just happened to fly open in a way that laid Willie's head open from eyebrows to scalp . . . is that what you're telling me?"

"I was only tryin' to get out and talk to the man," Clem said.

"Montoya's hurt pretty bad," Milt said.

"All we was doin' was goin' for the mail, like Sprout said," Clem explained. "Can't a dude get his mail around here?"

Martinez was a good state cop. His only handicap was that he had been born and raised in Brazos, and was related to practically all of the local people he had to arrest. At the age of fifty-two, his eyes were sunken and pouched with blue bags. He looked unhealthy and in pain, and he knew everyone hated him almost as much as they did Gus Benavidez. He never talked about this, but carried a stigma of treacherous betrayal because of this career he had chosen that forced him to incarcerate his own flesh and blood. Even he and Jesse Slade were related in some vague way. Somewhere, generations back, a now-dead uncle of Jesse's had married a Martinez.

Milt Garcia had a lot of relations around too. He hated having to arrest anybody because when he did, people told him he was a heartless son of a bitch, and that went down hard when the person saying it to him was liable to be a cousin or an aunt. He was a big, potbellied man in a tailored tan whipcord uniform, and perhaps secretly, like his state cop cousin sitting beside him, he wished people like Jesse did not exist. Jesse's late wife had had an aunt, also long deceased by now, who had been a half-sister of a second cousin of Milt's mother, Ermalinda Garcia, which made Jesse some kind of kin, at least by marriage, and Jesus Christ, it made this half-breed nigger *coyote* kin too! Milt sighed, as if aware for the first time that if all the intermarriages of the area could be traced, Clem Slade, Jr., might turn out to be related to three-quarters of Brazos Valley.

Bill Martinez glanced at Clem. "I got some information on you out of California, son."

"Had a few problems there," Clem said. "You run a sheet on me?"

"I didn't have to," Bill said. "Department of Probation, down in Santa Fe, wrote asking about you. Wanted to know why you hadn't been reporting in. I told them I was keeping an eye on you. That was a couple of weeks ago. They don't have a probation officer in this area. They sent up your sheet along with some other stuff that had come in from Los Angeles."

"I been clean here," Clem pointed out.

"Until today."

"Told you, that wasn't my fault."

The state trooper stared at Clem. "Don't shit me, boy."

"It's true! He didn't start it," Jesse chimed in.

"Maybe so," Bill said. "Montoya and Connie Aragon are claiming this kid jumped them. That's a lot of shit too, as far as I'm concerned. Nobody with any brains would take those two on, unless he had to." He glanced at Clem again. "The sheriff here, and me, we like a peaceful town."

"Oh, me too," Clem said.

"I got plenty to keep me busy, running drunks and tourists off the highway," Bill said. "Don't dump on me. You try that, I'll come down on you."

"Yessir."

"Around here, you behave. Okay?"

"No hassle."

"He ain't a bad kid," Jesse said.

"Tell that to Willie," Bill Martinez said.

"Fuck Willie," Jesse said. "He ain't nothin' but a big stack of horseshit tryin' to attract flies. He picked on this boy. Clem's only sixteen, and Willie's in his twenties. That ain't fair."

The two lawmen got up, placed their cups and saucers in the battered sink, and said goodbye. By now, Clem knew the one to talk to. He went up to Bill Martinez and said, "Where's it stand, man?"

Bill said, "Milt and I will talk to Montoya. His dad drove him down to the hospital in Espanola. If he doesn't press charges, we'll let it slide. If he does, you've got trouble." He put on his cap. "Even if no charges are pressed, it still stands with me, understand? I'll be watching you."

"So will I," Milt Garcia said.

"We have your sheet," Bill said. "No one else here knows much about you. Watch your step. You want to take a fall, I'll lay a real one on you that you'll never forget. Don't fuck around with me, boy. I mean it."

"Supposin' somebody tries to come down on me again? What am I supposed to do?"

"I don't know," Bill said. "Offhand, I'd say you got a problem. In this valley, Willie and Connie must have fifteen or twenty uncles and cousins. Yes, that's a problem, all right."

"Ain't no problem," Clem said somberly. "It's a major disaster, you ask me."

THREE

BUT LATER JESSE complained. "Where's it goin' to end? Now we got Bill Martinez and Fatso Garcia watchin' us like hawks! How come with you everything just goes from bad to worse?"

"Guess it would'a been easier if I'd let Montoya work me over," Clem said. "That way, there'd been no trouble. No state bull, no sheriff what looks like he just jumped out'a the Saturday mornin' cartoons. Sure, no trouble at all. Probably I'd'a been out of the hospital in five or six months at the most, right, Sprout?"

Clem angrily left the house and went off for a walk by himself, across the empty fields that stretched for miles to the east. He was irritable and depressed. When he got back, Jesse was gone. Clem made a sandwich and poured a glass of milk, and watched an afternoon soap on the new color television for a while. Then, bored, he wandered out on the back porch. The Harley-Davidson caught his eye. He had wheeled it out of the storage shed a few days earlier, and now it stood in the back yard, propped against a sagging redwood picnic table. Atop the table were the boxes of loose parts. Jesse had been right. In the bottom of one of the boxes, Clem had found a tattered maintenance manual, but so far he had not done anything with the bike except inflate the tires with a hand pump. The tires

had some tread left, and despite their age they held air, but Clem
had a feeling that the motorcycle was beyond rebuilding. He thought,
"Might'a knowed that cheap bastard wouldn't give away anything
that was worth something! Hell, if it could'a been fixed, he would've
done it years ago himself an' sold it for what he could get."

He went over to the Harley, kicked the tires a few times, and then
rummaged around idly in the boxes of parts: pistons, valve lifters,
transmission gears, a clutch in pieces, spark plugs, a disassembled
carburetor. "Ol' pile of shit," he said aloud. "Like everything else
around here."

Werner Grimmiessen was leaning on the fence separating his and
Jesse's properties.

"Hi, Werner," Clem said.

"How is your life today, my boy?"

"Lousy."

"Ah, I am sorry to hear that. I understand you have had some
difficulties today downtown."

Clem shrugged. He glanced at Werner. "What'd you hear?"

"Only that you defended yourself. That is good. Would you like
some lemonade? I made it fresh."

"No, thanks."

"A man must stand up to the world, eh?"

"If you say so."

"There are certain people who are inferior species. But, of course,
you must know that. I am proud of you, I do not mind saying. That
Willie. *Phooh!* He sticks his chest out and struts around. But
here"—Werner tapped a finger against his temple—"nothing of significance."

"Seems to me I heard you and him are real cool buddies," Clem
said.

"People gossip," Werner explained. "Yes, sometimes Willie visits.
Is there harm in that? We sit and talk. We have a little to drink. In
his mind, he is lonely. That is obvious. Everyone has loneliness. We
have conversation. That is all. I try to give him advice. He does not
listen. For Willie, life is, how do you say, simplistic. He fights. He
drinks. He looks for girls. That Sally Benavidez . . . *das Putzmädel*
. . . crazy! She is a *blitze!* You beware of that one! I have some
books I can lend you sometime, if you like to read, about her kind
of female psychodestructiveness. I tell Willie the same. But he does

not listen. He sees her. And he sees his own mind. Or what he imagines goes on in his mind." Werner paused. "Do you know, I am psychic?"

"Oh?" Clem said.

"Yes, I have psychic abilities. I know many things about people. I feel their spirits."

"I'll just bet you do, Werner."

"I know many things about you. About everyone in this terrible town."

"You do?"

"You have intelligence," Werner said. "You have sensitivity. You have the world at your feet. Some of this you do not know. Some of it you suspect. But it is not clear yet, for you. A leader! That is what you are! This interests me greatly. You are not, well, obviously, pureblooded, yet you belong to a higher order. Your genetic combination . . . ah, what can I say? Yet, the world belongs to the strong. It has always been that way. There is about you, oh, how to say, dignity. You observe the world about you. Yes, you are observant. You do not submit. That, of course, you proved today, with Willie. To be peaceful and maintain dignity, that is the mark of the supremely civilized man. You have this quality. Like me, you do not belong in Brazos. But at times, one must assume the responsibility of power. Why I am here in this place, I will never know. Sometimes I weep. An old man, waiting to die. Alone, in this *verloren gottverdammt* place!"

Clem surmised that Werner had had a few, and in this he was correct—the old German had been working on a bottle that afternoon. Werner eyed the motorcycle leaning against the redwood table, as though it had just materialized out of thin air. He said, "What have you there?"

"Old motorcycle," Clem said.

"You will fix it?"

"I'd like to."

"What is the problem?"

"I don't know where the parts go," Clem said.

"That is no problem," Werner said. He stared again at the Harley, a little vacant-eyed. "It is like a chess game. There are parts, and there are places for them to go, no?"

"Easy talk."

"If you like, I will help," Werner said.

"What the hell do you know about motorcycles, Werner?"

The old man smiled and raised a forefinger admonishingly. "I know the internal combusion engine intimately, my boy." He shook his head, as though Clem's ignorance was too much. "Both gasoline and diesel. I know transmissions. I know all about any kind of engine that drives a vehicle." He chuckled, nodding to himself. "I do not mean to boast, but all these things I know like you know the back of your hand. In *der Panzerschule,* we were taught these things. Each class had its own tank. We dismantled it, until it was in little pieces. Then we put it back together again. Believe me, that was some big job, oh boy! Do you have tools? Is there a manual?"

"Yeah, I found a manual for it."

"I have a complete set of mechanic's tools, both metric and American," Werner said. "I will have a look at it, if you like. Wheel it over, by my back porch. Your grandfather prefers that I do not come on his property. He is eccentric, but of course, I respect his rights."

So Clem moved the Harley over to Werner's side of the fence. He got the boxes of old parts and brought them over too, setting them on Werner's back porch.

Grimmiessen found a five-gallon asphalt bucket and filled it half-full with gasoline. He tossed in the loose parts. "If you must do something, do it properly," he said. "First, everything must be clean. We take *every*thing apart!"

"Werner, we don't want'a take it apart any more than it is already," Clem said.

"Down to the last nut and bolt!" Werner said. "Everything. Absolutely clean! Then we inspect. For safety, for wear, for metal fatigue!" He sounded happily enthusiastic. "Then we look in the manual. We make a list of all the parts that are missing. Many small things get lost, be sure of that. Some things will be no good. This is an old machine. All the gaskets, the oil and grease seals, these need to be replaced completely." He nodded. "With a lot of work and some luck, yes, we could have a very old motorcycle that is better than something brand-new."

"How long is this supposed to take?" Clem asked suspiciously. He had a feeling that Werner would make the job last as long as possible.

"It will take as long as is needed to make it as perfect as we know how," Werner said.

Time passed quickly as they worked. The old German got wire brushes and steel wool to scrub the parts. He went into the house and came out with a heavy metal toolbox, whose contents were immaculately clean and neatly arranged, in contrast to the kitchen drawer where Jesse kept a grab-bag assortment of rusted tools and odds and ends of junk. The afternoon sun was hot. Werner went back inside and brought out a pitcher of lemonade, a bottle of bourbon, two glasses, and a tray of cubes. They sat on the back steps and drank lemonade spiked with bourbon, and dismantled the Harley, piece by piece.

As he worked away on gas-soaked parts with a brush, Werner rambled on contentedly. "Would you like to see my photograph albums? Someday, you must make a formal visit. No, Clem, no smoking, please. With this gasoline, in two seconds we would be like toasted frankfurters, ho, ho! I have photographs from the war, and from my youth. At the University of Cologne, in 1938—ah, how long ago!—I studied to be a mechanical engineer. The army took me before I graduated. I was twenty-two. Not so much older than you. All I was interested in was mechanical science. I denied my psychic powers. Then came *der Krieg*. I was so innocent then. A simple virgin boy. I have never been brave, you know. No, I never thought of myself in that way. I could never in my entire life have done what you did today, Clem—strike another person, another human. Such a thought! Impossible. Until the war, I thought of myself as a coward. I am by nature a gentle person, you see. Yet, with the war, it turned out differently. I did what had to be done. Oh, yes, I was there. Someone had to do it. Feldmarschall Rommel would personally invite us to his command headquarters. There were over thirty of us *Panzersektionkommandanten*. Such young men we were. Like children. But we did what he asked of us. You see, Rommel was a man that other men could love. Not such a big man. Certainly not handsome. We called him *Der Alte*—the Old Man. But he was not that old, either. He died so tragically. For failing. For trying his best, and failing. He loved all of us young men like sons."

"I never knew a motorcycle had so many parts," Clem said. Even though it meant getting his hands dirty, he was growing more and more absorbed by this project.

"To think, we lost it all at El Alamein," Werner mused on. "We had better armor, better strategy. *Der Alte* was the finest armored

warfare tactician the world has ever seen. Yet we lost. Do you know
how many tanks there were, on both sides? The Allied, and ours?
Over two thousand. Can you imagine that, Clem, what a marvelous
experience it was to see so many armored vehicles maneuvering to
strike? On this great yellow-and-brown desert plain in Africa? A
vast, hot plain, surrounded by harsh mountains? A blinding sun.
Enormous clouds of brown dust kicked up by the tracks. It choked
us. Inside the tanks, the steel was too hot to touch. We drove the
tanks in shorts, or even naked, except for helmets. Tens of thousands
of young men. Foot soldiers, artillery, dive bombers. Such a
spectacle! This mass of humanity, coming together in terrible combat
on the desert plains near El Alamein, under the killing sun. And I
was there! Not in the rear. In front! I led the way. We lost, but I
led the way. They followed. Such brave young men. The best of
German manhood. They died there in the desert. So did the British,
and the Australians, and the New Zealanders, and the Americans.
High-explosive shells bursting everywhere. Clouds of black smoke
from burning and exploding tanks. The battle raged back and
forth. When it was over, we had lost. No one could understand.
Their armor was less than nothing, like a tin can you shoot with a
twenty-two. Against our mighty Tigers, their cannons were a joke—
like throwing apples at a brick wall. Yet they won. That is a
mystery. Come, let us go into the house for a cigarette, away from
this gasoline."

They carried the liquor and lemonade into the kitchen and sat at
a maple table. Like Jesse's house, Werner's home was on its last legs.
It was not the residence of anybody with money to spend. In one
corner of the kitchen, the floor sagged. There was a cast-iron woodstove for heating and cooking, similar to Jesse's. There was one
thing that was different, though. The place was neat. Despite his
complaints about Clem's sloppiness, Jesse's ideas about housekeep-
ing were rudimentary. He and the boy cleaned up more or less
when the mood took them, which wasn't often. Werner, however,
was fastidious. The panes of the windows were sparkling. There
were blue-and-white chintz curtains. The walls were clean and
painted, except for a large, unavoidable sooty halo where the stove
flue went into the wall. The floor was swept and waxed, and pictures
—mostly photographs of Werner the tank commander—hung from
the walls. In another corner there was a small, chipped mahogany

veneered writing desk. On its blotter sat a legal pad, squared neatly, and a jelly jar containing an assortment of ballpoint pens. On the floor beside the desk was an old, hair-covered blanket, and Clem suspected this was where Cochise curled up in inclement weather. As a home, the place was certainly humble enough, yet it had an austere dignity. It said that the owner strove to live in as decent a fashion as possible, regardless of his circumstances. Clem said, "Say, Werner, not that it's my business, but how do you get by?"

"My family left me a small vineyard in the Moselle area," Werner said. He pointed to a framed photograph on the wall that showed steep, terraced slopes. "That is it. That was taken in 1934. It produces an excellent wine—very light—but the annual bottling is small. I lease it to a cousin. It brings me a little, not much."

"Brings you enough so that you don't have to work. That's something."

"True. But how much does an intelligent man need? A little food, liquor, tobacco. Some clothing, a place to sleep. Once these things are taken care of, there is the brain . . . the mind. Peace of mind. That is the richest gift of all! All the money in the world cannot buy that, my boy. You will learn this as you grow older. Now you are young. A young man, he believes he must have the whole world in his hand. Otherwise, he is discontent, unhappy."

"I don't want the whole world. Want a lot more than just sittin' around this dumb town, though."

"It could be worse for you. Much worse."

"That's what Jesse's always tellin' me."

"He is right. Oh, that grandfather of yours! He is impossible to get along with. But in this case, he is right, I think."

They talked for a while longer. Werner agreed to continue helping Clem with the Harley in the coming days. "Whenever the two of us have a little spare time," the old German said. "There is no great hurry. It will be an excellent project for us. That is how men become friends. When they work together, with their hands, building, making something. You see, I would like to be your friend. That is not such a small thing, for a person to have a friend. Consider it, my boy."

"Why, sure, Werner," Clem said. "I got to admit, you weren't connin' me when you said you knew all about engines. You're something else."

BACK AT THE house, Jesse had still not returned. Clem scrubbed his hands in the kitchen sink. He got them clean enough, but could not get rid of the smell of gasoline.

Toward sunset he was caught again in another conversation, on a trip back from the outhouse, this time by Patsy Hurley. Patsy was tipsy, and for some reason she had on a blue-and-yellow flowered chiffon dress with ruffled sleeves and an enormous wide-brimmed straw hat. In her right hand, poised delicately, was a twelve-ounce glass filled with two cubes, a dash of vermouth and a lemon twist, and a lot of Tanqueray gin. This depth bomb was what Patsy called her "sundowner," and it was designed to help get her through whatever the evening ahead might hold for her and Garrison, which usually turned out to be very little. The high-quality gin was a reflection of Garrison's tastes. Though he might not fill the bill in certain ways, he believed in buying the best liquor they could afford with their disability checks. He liked to say, "Good liquor never hurt a chap's liver . . . it's that cheap stuff that will do a man in."

At the moment when Patsy called her *"Yoo-hoo!"* Garrison was passed out on the rickety bed he and Patsy shared. He believed, quite erroneously, that when he slept he could not tolerate the least light or noise—especially the noise of his own snoring—and he lay atop Patsy's handmade patchwork quilt with his entire head wrapped in a six-foot-long Harvard muffler, as if, as an alumnus of that famous old school, he felt obliged to maintain an Ivy League spirit even in sleep.

Clem ambled over to the fence line separating the Slade and Hurley properties.

"You naughty, naughty boy!" Patsy said, and shook her finger at him.

"Who, me?" Clem said. "What'd I do?"

"What were you doing in Werner's house?"

"Workin' on my motorcycle."

"In the house?"

"Went in for a break."

"You were in there almost an hour," Patsy said.

"You got a stopwatch on me or something?" Clem said. He didn't care to have anybody watching him too closely. Jesse was bad enough, but Patsy was more than he needed. He thought to himself that very possibly Werner might be spying on him and Patsy right now, from *his* kitchen window. He said, "Seems like no matter which way a cat turns, somebody in this town's got to know about it."

"I'm only trying to protect your reputation," Patsy said. "Everybody knows the sort of man Mr. Grimmiessen is."

"My reputation can take care of itself, Patsy," Clem said.

"Don't be angry with me."

"Me? Angry? How you talk. I never get mad. Man loses his cool, somebody'll dump on him for sure." He looked at the glass, and then grinned at her. "Say, could I have a little taste of that? Looks good."

"Why, of course," Patsy said. She put a forefinger to her lips and looked mischievous. "Must promise, though, not to say a word to Jesse."

"Oh, sure," Clem said. He tasted the sundowner, and then took a second drink. The gin combining with the bourbon he had had over at Werner's left a pleasant tingle in his stomach.

"We're so proud of you, Garrison and I."

"You are?"

"We heard about what happened today."

"Oh."

"I just want you to know that we're on your side," she said.

Clem had another taste. "Mellow."

"Don't you let that nasty Willie Montoya or anybody else around here try to take advantage of you," Patsy said. "The whole town will simply walk all over a person, if they think they can get away with it."

"I ain't much for lettin' people walk on me."

"Oh, bravo! Bravo! If I'd ever had a younger brother, I think I would have wanted him to be exactly like you."

Clem smiled, and leaned on a fencepost. "Well now, Patsy, that has got to be just about the nicest thing that has ever been said to me." It made no difference at all that Patsy ranked among the whitest of WASPs, and that any kind of kid brother she might have had would have been undeniably, irrefutably, as white as she was.

Patsy, overwhelmed, placed her hand on Clem's bare arm. Her girlish blue eyes were either shiny or glassy, it was hard to tell which. At any rate, her expression was intense. "You want to know a teensy secret, Clem?"

"What?"

"I think you're wonderful!"

He grinned at her again. When he smiled that way, he was exceedingly handsome. White, white teeth, and an expression that was so innocent and trusting.

The hand that had been resting on his arm moved up to stroke his cheek. "Oh, Clem," Patsy said. "Would you like to come over for a drink? It's so warm out here."

"Jesse ought'a be home pretty soon."

"We could sit in the kitchen."

"Couldn't stay long."

"Pretty please?" She pouted a little.

Clem handed her the sundowner and hopped the fence.

As they walked together toward the Hurley shack, he said, "Y'know something? You are a very classy lady."

Patsy blushed crimson and downed what was left in her glass. "I'm very glad you're here with us. You're precious."

"Nice to feel like you're wanted. Just for a change. Makes a real difference."

In the kitchen, he helped Patsy mix a drink for him and a new one for her. From the bedroom came leviathan rumblings. Clem said softly, "You sure we won't wake him up?"

She giggled. "Silly! We could set off one of those nuclear devices he used to work on—and you know what noisy things *they* are!—right under the bed, and I'd be surprised if he even twitched." Standing by the counter, they raised their glasses in a toast. Patsy said, "Would you think it . . . oh, dear, how can I put it . . . forward, if I asked you something, Clem?"

"What's on your mind?"

"Would you kiss me?" she said simply. "Just once?"

Clem thought this over. She got fidgety. Finally he said calmly, "I wouldn't mind that at all."

So they kissed, standing there in the kitchen, rather gently, almost decorously, or it would have been decorous except that Clem, in his easygoing fashion, which was made even easier by all that he'd had to drink, quite deliberately placed his free hand on her snatch. Patsy jumped as though she'd walked straight into a 7,200-volt transformer and dropped her glass. It shattered on the floor. She had been correct. The rhythmic snores from the bedroom never missed a beat.

No telling where it might have gone from there. Patsy, shaken, made the mistake of saying in a weak voice that she needed a little fresh air. They went out on the back porch, just as Jesse came out on his porch and called out to Clem, "Git your goddamn ass back in the house. What you doin' over there? We got ranch-fries to git on. The least you could do is help out once in a while, instead of bullshittin' up a storm with folks who don't need us any more'n we need them. Hell, that's why fences was invented."

Patsy said under her breath, "Oh, hell!" Then she put on a smile and called back to Jesse sweetly, "You just remember Robert Frost, Jesse. His best poem? 'Good fences make good neighbors . . .' "

"Shucks," Jesse called back. "You done recited that rotten poem at me fifty times, Patsy. All I'm askin' is that if you believe in it so much, how come you an' Garrison keep usin' the goddamn fence to toss your empties over? By God, you two should'a been in the Olympics with them discus throwers. Your pitchin' arms are so developed you'd probably fling one of them discuses clean out'a the stadium."

"I DON'T LIKE your attitude," Jesse said later, over dinner.

"How come you never let up on me?" Clem said. "How come nothin' I do is right?"

" 'Cause nothin' is, that's why."

"Old man, you got battery acid in your veins 'stead of blood," Clem said sourly. "You're one of those types who ain't content unless he's feelin' real unhappy, and the only thing that pleasures you is when you're makin' everyone around you as miserable as you are."

Jesse cut into a piece of *carne adobada*—pork in hot red chili. "I see the way you're headin'. You don't fool me none. Think the world owes you something. Think you can sweet-talk your way all around the barn. Your sort's got to have butter, while all the rest of us gits margarine. Oh, I know you smooth-talkin' types! I saw the picture the second I got home. Motorcycle's parked over in Grimmiessen's back yard, that dirty German fascist. Hang out with a dog, his fleas will rub off on you! And Patsy Hurley. Ol' Miss Goody Two-Shoes herself! What you messin' around for, over at their place? Her with her phony talk and uppity ways. Makin' out she's so goddamn high class! She don't fool no one. Makin' out she's so snooty, when half the time she's got just one thing on her mind, and the other half she's got a breath on her would paralyze a grizzly at fifty yards."

"Where were you all afternoon?" Clem said, trying to change the subject.

"Talkin' to Bill Martinez mostly," Jesse said.

"The state cop?"

"None other."

"What was you talkin' about?"

"Just makin' sure of a few things."

"Like what?"

"Like makin' sure Bill has that talk with Willie," Jesse said. "Bill Martinez happens to owe me one or two little favors. The fight wasn't a fair match."

"He already knows that. We both told him."

"Well, I told him again," Jesse said. "That's the thanks I git. Here I am, runnin' my ass off all over creation, tryin' to keep you out'a trouble, and I come home to find you rubbin' up to Grimmiessen and Patsy Hurley all at once."

"Sprout, I didn't start talkin' with them. They started it first."

"Oh, sure, and once it got started you would'a hung around till it was time to harvest the corn. You just watch your step. That's all I'm tellin' you."

"I swear, I ain't never been no place where a person gets a two-hour lecture just for openin' his mouth to say hello," Clem said.

"Listen, everybody in this town knows what Werner Grimmiessen is, and everybody knows about Patsy too. Not only that, folks are startin' to have a few ideas about *you*. I been gittin' along with the Hurleys and Werner fine for years, simply by keepin' a healthy distance from them. They ain't fit for decent folks to 'sociate with. But you won't listen! Clem, you don't watch out, you're goin' to git this whole goddamn town worked up!"

"Trouble with you is, you exaggerate everything, Sprout."

"I don't!" Jesse insisted. "Bill Martinez and Milt Garcia, they got their eye on you. So does Gus Benavidez. He knows you got that young bitch of his in a red-hot lather. I been doing business with Gus for thirty years and never had a speck of trouble with him, and now, all of a sudden, he can't look me straight in the eye, that cheatin', double-dealin' son of a bitch! You got Patsy Hurley all in a flutter, so that every time she sees you those big cow-eyes start battin' away like hummin'bird wings, an' Werner, he's ready to eat out'a your hand. You got Willie and Connie ready to slice your gizzard out, and I ain't even botherin' to take into account all their cousins and nephews and uncles. Miltie Garcia would just as soon lock you up as look at you. And you just keep on walkin' around, lookin' sweet an' innocent. You're about as innocent as a weasel in a chicken coop! Well, in case you don't know it, people in this town are takin' a real interest in you. Hell, I can't blame 'em. Ain't nothing interestin' happened around here in the last four years, since some dirty hippies got caught poachin' elk over on the Bar-O ranch, and some time before that Orly's gas station caught fire and blew up, but there hasn't been much since, until you come along, pokin' your ugly face into everybody's business. Well, I guarantee you one thing. I know these people. There ain't nothin' in the world they enjoy more than somebody in trouble. Why, it just makes their goddamn day brighter in all directions, to see a little genuine sufferin'. Hell, when someone dies, most of the town goes around grinnin' and congratulatin' one another for weeks, 'cause it didn't happen to *them,* and if there's a real tragedy, like that time when those Iowa tourists with their five kids all got killed up on the highway, why, Horacio Quintana closes down the post office and declares a legal holiday, and the VFW parades down Main Street, wavin' the flag and whackin' a bass drum!"

"I don't know what more I can do," Clem said.

"You might try not attractin' attention to yourself," Jesse said. "Person goes around attractin' attention, sooner or later it'll be the wrong kind."

"How am I goin' to do that when I'm the only black in town?"

"You do kind'a stand out, for a fact."

Later, they had coffee and watched TV. Jesse said finally, "These goddamn quiz shows git on my nerves. All they show is the natural greed an' arrogance of folks who want'a win something for nothin' and show off how smart they are. Think I'll go down to the Emerald for a drink. Want'a come along?"

"You go ahead."

"What you goin' to do?"

"Nothin'."

"I ain't goin' to make a night out of it," Jesse said. "Just feel like gittin' out for a spell. Come on along."

"You go ahead, Sprout."

"Can't sit on your ass at home all the time, y'know. School will be startin' one of these days. Then you'll be up to your ears in work. The Emerald ought'a be nice and quiet by now. What d'you say?"

"Sally may drive by."

"Oh? Her again? What's on her mind?" Jesse frowned, and drank his coffee. "As if I didn't know. That's one pot of honey you ought'a keep your finger out of, boy. Well, I guess I better hang around. Try my hand at chaperonin'." He stared at Clem. "Christ, you're stubborn!"

"We thought we might just go for a drive."

"Not less'n you take me along in the back seat."

Clem said wearily, "Sprout, cool it, will you? Just once? I'm too tired to fight with you anymore."

"Talkin' to you is like talkin' to a stone wall," Jesse said. He sighed and shook his head. "Well, don't say I didn't warn you. I reckon I know how it is. When I was your age, I used to git a lot more attention than I git now. Must be nice to have so many admirers."

"Sally's a nowhere scene, Sprout. Fun and games, that's all."

"Hope she thinks so. Hope some other folks do, too. Includin' Gus." Jesse rolled a cigarette, obviously still in a grumpy mood. "You want to use the truck?"

"She's comin' in her car."

"I don't mind walkin'."

"That's okay."

"One of these days we got to see about gittin' you a driver's license. Probably ought'a git one myself, while I'm at it."

"By and by, Sprout."

Jesse finally left, and drove the pickup down to the Emerald.

Though it was still early in the evening, Woody Klein was alone in the bar, getting ready to close up and call it a day. Lulu Uranga had gone home. The Emerald did most of its business in the afternoons and early evening, except on Friday and Saturday nights.

Everybody liked Woody because he never took sides in a dispute, and though his bar did not make much money it was a known fact that a person in a jam could usually put the bite on him for a five or a ten. When Lulu Uranga's youngest kid, Sophie, needed orthodontic braces, Woody helped. Two years ago, when Werner Grimmiessen broke out in shingles, Woody chipped in on the prescription bills. Woody liked kids and was the local scoutmaster as well as chairman of the school board, and these pursuits, plus the bar and refurbishing old cars and raising a houseful of kids, kept him more than busy. He had first seen Brazos as a young GI, thirty years ago, when his Army unit—Engineers—had been stationed in the area, doing soil-erosion work, and had fallen in love with the place, and with Arlene too, who was a Lopez girl from up the valley. After his discharge he had stayed on, forsaking his native Philadelphia and a family who to this day were mortified that their only son had not become a Talmudic scholar.

He was also Jesse Slade's friend. Or as close to being a friend as the old man could tolerate. It was a good kind of friendship in that it was seldom used. If asked, Jesse would probably have claimed that in all the world he had no friend and wanted none. Yet when Arlene developed cancer and had to have a mastectomy, it was Jesse who Woody came to, for quiet conversation. When Jesse had first received that letter from California's child welfare department, early in the summer, in which he learned that his son was dead and that his grandson was in serious trouble, he discussed the matter with Woody, who knew how to keep his mouth shut. Bill Martinez knew something about Clem, from the California dossier that had been channeled through the Santa Fe probation office. Woody Klein knew as much or more.

JESSE SAT ON one of the bar stools, tilted his Stetson back, and ordered a Coors and a single Heaven Hill. He poured the shot into a tall glass, mixed it with beer, made a cigarette, lit it, exhaled, sighed. "How you been, Woody?"

"Pretty good. Yourself, Jess?"

"So-so."

"Where's Clem?"

"Home. I felt like gittin' out for a while. Kids git on a man's nerves, don't they?"

"You can say that again." Woody got himself a Coors and pulled up a stool on his side of the bar. "You want the juke?"

"No. The quieter it is, the better it suits me. He plays that TV and radio full blast. Rock 'n' roll, quiz shows, I never heard such a racket."

They sat for a while in silence, sipping at their drinks. Then Woody said, "I heard about what happened with Willie Montoya and Connie."

"I saw it with my own eyes," Jesse said.

"Well, you know, Aragon, he's not a bad kid," Woody said. "I don't think Connie's really mean. He gets pushy, especially when he's had too many, but that's natural enough. Mostly, you can talk Connie out of it. He just wants to let off steam. But Willie, well, I don't know. He has a tricky temper. I wouldn't want to see Clem get into something he couldn't handle."

"I know," Jesse said.

"Did he really do it?"

"Do what?"

"Knock hell out of Willie, like people say, and make Connie backtrack?"

"I told you, I saw it."

"And he's only sixteen?"

"Sixteen years ten months."

Woody's brow furrowed thoughtfully as he considered this. "Think what he'll be like a couple of years from now. Well, I guess you're looking out for him as best you can."

"He's a handful."

Woody weighed his next remark carefully. "I think I'd keep an eye on Gus Benavidez while I was at it, Jesse."

"I know."

"Gus has some funny ways," Woody said. He lit a filter tip. "He's partial to that girl of his."

"Partial ain't exactly the word for it. If she was mine, I'd tie her in a gunnysack and drown her. Be doin' mankind a service."

"Did you mean it, Jess, when you told Gus to back off?" Woody asked. "I mean, I was standing right here when you told him that. Hard talk. Everybody heard."

"I meant it."

"Wouldn't want to see trouble get started," Woody said reflectively. "I've been living in this valley a long time. I've seen enough of that. Everybody has. Feud's a bad thing."

"May have started already."

"Trouble like that goes from bad to worse," Woody said. "One person, he does one thing, to get even with someone else. Then that other person does something worse. Things escalate, get out of control. Sure wouldn't want to see something like that happen."

"I know what you mean," Jesse said irritably. "But what the hell am I supposed to do?"

"Is Clem really that bad?"

"Woody, he's awful!" Jesse said. He ordered another boilermaker. While Woody was getting it, he said, "Then, on the other hand, he ain't so bad, in lots of ways. He ain't nothin' but a snot-nosed kid, but at least he's company. Actually, I've gotten kind'a used to havin' him around. Y'know what I mean?"

"Sure."

Jesse said, "Hell, I been livin' alone for so long I've plumb lost track of what it's like to live with someone else. That boy drives me just crazy. Just bugs the livin' shit out'a me, mornin', noon, and night, and then he acts like he ain't even aware of it. Yet, in some ways, he tries to do right. Only thing is, nobody ever taught him how to do anything. He doesn't mean to be bad. Leastways, I don't think he does. Not really. He just don't know any better." He rolled a fresh cigarette. "Like, you recollect the time your oldest, Ikey, got into that trouble?"

"I remember." Jesse was referring to an incident, some years back, involving Isaac, who at fourteen was caught burglarizing several of the resort lodges located along the Brazos River. It had taken a lot of backscratching on the part of Woody with Bill Martinez and Milt Garcia to get the charges killed.

Jesse said, "Ikey did a dumb thing that time. Clem's no different."

"He do something wrong?"

"Well, he didn't *mean* it to be wrong," Jesse said. He paused while he mixed his drink. "What happened was, he's been with me about a month now, right? So, durin' all this time, he's been listenin' to me talk. About how we need to git this, and how we could use that, and how money is tight. And it is, to tell the truth. So what happens is, last week we drive to Santa Fe to buy him some clothes for school, and after we're done doin' that, he moseys off all by his lonesome for a spell, over in that big DeVargas Mall they built. So, we git back home, and what do I find in the truck's camper? A brand-new color TV! I'd been complainin' about that old set, which I bought back around 1955. It's about seen its day. There was a new battery for the truck. Old battery had just about enough juice left in it to light a flashlight, and I'd made some remarks about havin' to git a new one by and by. A real electric toaster. One of them fancy clock-radios with those digit figures. More goddamn cheese and salami and German sausage and a slab of that Jewish rye bread, and crackers and that French imported mustard that makes your eyes water, than we can eat in a month of Sundays. None of that supermarket shit—

most of that cheese tastes like pink plastic—but the fancy stuff, from that Hickory Farms store they got in the mall. Y'see, I'd been bawlin' him out for hookin' snacks out of the fridge, 'cause I like snacks myself as well as the next man. I got new socks out'a that trip, and workgloves, real leather, and four boxes of twelve-gauge shells for my shotguns, only they was double-ought buck, not birdshot, which wasn't his fault, 'cause he ain't smart enough to know what size shot you need for quail and dove." Jesse puffed at his cigarette angrily. "Woody, what I suspect is that that boy was tryin' to do something nice for me."

"How could he ever get that kind of stuff out of there?" Woody said.

"He wouldn't tell. Always has to act so smart," Jesse said. "He thinks I'm old and stupid, but I ain't. You just don't walk out of a store with a color television and a truck battery that weighs forty, fifty pounds. And that German donkeydick must'a been three and a half feet long and five inches across. There was only two ways he could have done it. He got in the men's locker room and snitched a jacket and one of them lapel badges, so he looked like he worked there. Or else he stole a credit card somewhere and used it to git that stuff over the counter. And I doubt very much it was a credit card, because I heard they start checking I.D.'s pretty careful on any purchase over fifty bucks, and that color TV had a four-hundred-and-nineteen-dollar price tag on it. So now we got all this—not that it ain't useful—but if he'd been caught, that would'a been the end of him, no two ways about it."

"He must have had a pretty rough life," Woody said.

"I don't argue that," Jesse said. "Comin' out'a that kind of background, and all."

"You mean the other side of the family?"

"I mean the black side," Jesse said. "The authorities had no kind of real record, you know, on *that* side."

"Well, I guess half of him is yours."

Jesse nodded, and then said thoughtfully, "Y'know, I ain't one of these loudmouth political liberals who're always jackin' off at the jaws about how we got to lend a Christian helping hand. That's precisely the kind'a sweet cream that's just plain ol' clabber, and it's what got us involved with that do-nothin' U.N., and Korea, and Vietnam, and now, son of a bitch, if we ain't got to contend with China, which is asshole deep in slant-eyed, pigtailed Commies! All any of 'em are doin' is suckin' up to us for a handout! They all ought'a go back where they belong. Take care of your own, that's what I say. Nobody ever helped me, and I've managed to git by. But, actually, if you stop to think about it, all these poor, miserable niggers, livin' up there in them god-awful cities in ghettos . . . well, I don't know. I mean, Woody, you an' me, we know who we *are*. We know where our folks come from. Nobody clapped irons on my folks and brought 'em over here like cattle. The Slade name goes back a long way. To be honest, Slades has never been worth much of a damn. Drunks, cowpokes, homesteaders, and farmers mostly. Poor white trash, I suppose some might say. But we had a name, and it was ours. Hell, I wouldn't be a nigger if you paid me overtime."

"What're you getting at, Jess?"

"It's simple enough. We were all born free."

"Supposing you were," Woody said. "Supposing I was. What's the difference?"

"I ain't sure," Jesse said. "But there's a difference. There has to be. You know what I think? I think we did something wrong back in those days when slavery was all the thing. These coloreds today are pissed off. And I guess you can't blame 'em. Like I said, I was never much for all that lollygaggin', helping-hand shit. Most times, you hold your hand out to help a neighbor, somebody'll come along and chop it off at the wrist. The problem, though, is simple. Right is right, and wrong is wrong. That's all. And we done a wrong thing. We shouldn't have ever started messin' with those colored people." He drank some more of the boilermaker, and rolled a fresh cigarette. "It don't make any difference that *I* didn't have no part in it, nor did you, Woody, or anybody else who's alive today. The wrong was done. And that's how the fuckin' situation stands. You don't right a wrong by claimin' you had no part in it. If that wrong exists, then, by God, face up to it. Just like Grimmiessen, with his nasty Nazi ways. Like Germany today is filled to the brim with folks what claim they never had nothin' to do with Hitler and his gang of cutthroats, and extinguishin' all them Jews. Everybody's innocent, see? Howsomever, I got a strong hunch there are quite a few Jews around who don't feel the same. They don't care much for those Krauts, and they never will, not in a million years. That's because something wrong got done, and when a wrong is done there ain't no way in the world to make it right. Same with the coloreds. They had a wrong done 'em. Nobody exactly sent out any la-de-da hand-engraved RSVP invitations when they were loadin' 'em up on them ships. We rustled 'em! And now it's come back to us."

"So, what would you do about it, Jess? I mean, if you were running the show?" Woody asked.

"Ain't nothin' to be done," Jesse said. "Except to admit it. That's all, I reckon. That'd be a start. Just admit it, instead of mealy-mouthin' around."

"But, Jesse, if you don't mind my saying so, you're living with it," Woody pointed out. "This isn't some television program, where everybody has a lot of laughs, and where things work out fine at the end. You've got this overgrown kid sitting right in your lap, and you can't just turn him off, the way you do the switch on the TV."

"You sure said a mouthful," Jesse agreed. "I wish I could some-times . . . just unplug him, freeze him in dry ice, and put him in a storage locker for about twenty years. Listen, Woody, is it true? Is that boy a problem? Or is it just me? Maybe I'm too old."

"He's a hell of a problem, all right," Woody said. "All kids are. Maybe, though, he's a bigger problem than most people get stuck with."

"Ridin' herd on that boy is like tryin' to nail a lemon meringue pie to the wall with a straight pin," Jesse agreed. "He's too smart. You know, over at the high school, they tested him and found out he was real bright?"

"That can be trouble too."

"You don't have to tell me. Well, maybe that niece of mine will take him off my hands when she gits back from Europe. That might be for the best, all the way round."

"Could be. Have one on the house."

"Thanks." Jesse had a third boilermaker, and then said good-night to Woody, who was already putting out the lights at the back of the place. The old man said, "See you around. Say hello to Arlene."

"I'll do that. Take care, Jess."

Out in the street, it was dark and silent, empty save for Jesse's pickup. Clem would probably be gone by now, with Sally Benavidez. Jesse walked to the truck and stood by it for a minute, taking a piss. Back in the bar, more lights went out. Overhead, stars shone. Jesse stared up at them, and then zipped his jeans. He turned the

collar of his denim workjacket up against the night chill, took a
final drag on his cigarette, flipped it end over end into the darkness,
and got into the truck and drove home.

DESPITE THE STYLE they had evolved together—that of constant,
low-level bickering and nattering—it got so that Jesse and the boy
were thought of as a pair who hung out together. Occasionally, each
took off on his own, but more often than not if one was seen it was
likely that the other was close by. Each went to some effort to create
the impression that by some perverse fate he was forced to as-
sociate with a snarling leper, yet on many other occasions they were
spotted together engaged in activities incompatible with the behavior of born enemies—having a few beers at the Emerald, disappearing down the dirt road that led to Jesse's secret fishing holes
up in the Brazos Box, eating hamburgers out on the highway at
the Dairy Queen, where Jesse, when he was not grumbling at Clem,
would as likely be heard complaining to Dixie Mendoza, the pimply
counter girl, "Goddamn it, Dixie, don't be so tightfisted with them
greasy French fries! Give a feller his money's worth."

To Sally, Clem said, "That miserable ol' bastard is drivin' me up
the wall. Ain't no way to keep on the good side of him."

Yet each morning at breakfast the old man and the boy would
chat together while one or the other was frying the eggs and making
toast with the new appliance, listen to the early-morning news on
the radio, and drink coffee.

Sally, taking Clem's side about the old man being the devil
incarnate, said, "Well, I just don't understand why you don't tell
the old fuck to get off your back."

Clem replied, "One of these days, I'm goin' to do just that."

"That's talk."

"No, it ain't."

"Bullshit."

"What the hell you want me to do, fist him out?"

"You let him push you around."

"No one pushes me around."

"You stood up to Willie. I don't see why you take all this garbage
from a skinny old man. Besides, he doesn't like me."

Clem shrugged.

"What'd I ever do to that miserable bastard?" she demanded. "He's got no reason to hate me."

"That ol' man don't like no one, baby."

"God, I hope I never live to be that senile," Sally said.

"Ain't his fault he's so old."

"Yes, it is," she insisted. "It's horrible enough to be old and useless, but that doesn't mean he's got to hate everything the way he does. He's so old, no wonder nobody wants to be around him. He's just pissed 'cause he's so far gone and we're young. We've got the whole world ahead of us. He's got nothing but the grave staring him in the face. No wonder he's so mean! He hates me, 'cause I got you. And he doesn't have anything. I wish he'd do everybody a favor and die."

Clem stared at her and then frowned. "Shut up with that talk, woman."

Sally saw that he was angry, and eased off. Loved him up a little. She knew how to please a man. On this occasion, they were parked in her old Pontiac up by the fish hatchery. Sally was trying out some experiments she had read about in *Playgirl*. Clem's jeans were down around his ankles, and he was staring up at the ceiling light of the car, enjoying a joint Sally had brought along. Sally looked up and said, "All I'm trying to point out is that when he pushes you around it involves me too, and you sound almost pleased that he does it." Clem paid her no mind, and she took the pressurized can of whipped cream she had brought along, let off a squirt in his face, and then said, "You take me for granted."

"Not so."

"You do. Sometimes you treat me just terrible!"

"Now, baby."

"I'm a real person, you know. I'm not just a woman. I'm me. You don't seem to understand that," she said. Clem looked funny with one eye plastered with white goop, but she was not amused. She said sulkily, "I think all you goddamned men are the same. You act like you're ready to die for it, until a woman gives in. Then you couldn't care less."

Clem, who was grinning over being hit with the cream, pulled himself together. "Come on, baby. You're special. You *know* that."

"You sure don't act like I am."

He loved her up, and she licked the cream from his eye and forehead, but was still sullen. "You think a whole lot more of that old son of a bitch than you do of me!"

"How you talk!" Clem said. "You know better than that. 'Course, he is my grandpa. I mean, I guess he's about the only relation I got. So I got to put up with that, don't I?"

"I don't see why," she said moodily. "We could run off. Just the two of us together."

"Run off!"

"I been thinking about it."

"Where?"

"Los Angeles. Hollywood," she said. "You're always talking about those places."

"Why'd we want'a do that?"

"Well, we don't have anything here, do we? You wouldn't have to listen to that old man, and I wouldn't have to put up with my father's bossing me all the time. This town's a cemetery. What do you want to do, hang around here forever?"

"Ain't you got me, baby? And I got you? What's wrong with that?"

Sally gave a counterfeit yawn. "Pardon me, while I pass out with excitement."

"Why you want to go and spoil something groovy?"

"You think I'm going to sit around waiting for you until I'm too old, you better think again."

"What you mean, waitin' around? I'm right here, ain't I? Right now, this very minute?"

"Big deal! Sneaking off in my car a couple of times a week. I want our own place, with a real bed in it. This ain't my idea of a rich and varied sex life. People these days have hot saunas to do it in. They have mirrors on the ceiling. They have all sorts of nice things."

But by now her hostility had diminished a little because Clem was up to some experiments of his own. "If you really love someone, you show it by doing instead of talking," Sally said dreamily. And so Clem was. For a while, she leaned back, eyes shut.

That was how they lost those marvelous jogging shorts of hers. Eventually, they abandoned the Pontiac and made for a clump of cedar and piñon trees. Sally was dressed in a crimson halter that knotted in front, ribbed white socks, her blue Nike sneakers, and nothing else, except for an old blanket under one arm. It was sunset, and in the fading golden light she looked as good as any seventeen-year-old girl on this planet. If she was vain about her figure, or her complexion, which in that fading light seemed imbued with honey and amber, she had a right to be. She had fantastic legs and an ass that was literally divine. She walked into the woods slowly, with Clem an admiring four paces behind.

At some point while they were in the grove, Bennie Montoya, Willie's kid brother, drove past in his pickup. He pulled over and stopped to inspect the Pontiac, which he knew belonged to Sally. Saw in the front seat the famous shorts of navy-blue nylon with red and white trim at the leg openings. Without even thinking about it, Bennie, who had an even dumber sense of humor than his older brother, swiped the shorts. How Sally managed to get into her father's house without them later that evening is a mystery that has never been explained.

Next day, Bennie drove through the village of Brazos with the shorts Scotch-taped to the antenna of his CB radio, and parked in front of the grocery. There, he took them down and went in and handed them to Sally. He said nonchalantly, "Guess you must'a dropped these someplace."

Sally accepted them with serene calm. "Why, thank you, Bennie! Aren't I the most *awful* thing in the world about keeping track of things? I swear! I sometimes think I'd lose my head if it wasn't tied on to me."

Gus Benavidez was in the store too, sitting in his chair by the big potbellied stove. For a while he just sat there, picking at his cuticles. Presently, he got up and went out back, to the narrow alley behind the store, leaned his forehead against the planked side of the building, and began slowly banging his head against the weathered, unpainted wood.

DOLORES ESPINOZA WAS a tall, thin, astonishingly homely woman in her mid-fifties, with a big nose, a lantern jaw, and heavy black eyebrows that met in a dark frown, and it was inevitable that hers and Clem's paths would sooner or later cross.

She was a widow and lived with her two youngest children, now in their teens, in an old adobe behind the cemetery. There was a stern, even harsh, dignity in Dolores's expression and in the way she carried herself, erect, shoulders set square, and when she spoke to people, man or woman, she looked them right in the eye. Some claimed she was a sorceress and that she practiced witchcraft in her home, but this was not true. Dolores had graduated from high school, and if she doctored sick children on the side it was because she had studied to be a licensed practical nurse in her youth. To get by, she drew food stamps and received Social Security from the earnings of her late husband, Harvey. During the summer she worked as a cook at the Brazos Lodge, frying up trout that rich tourists had caught, and when school was in session she sometimes substituted when one of the regular teachers at the Tierra Amarilla grade school was sick. She lived with dignity. People respected her. This was as it should be. Dolores expected them to.

She and Clem and Jesse met one afternoon at the post office. Dolores was having a fight with Horacio, and it was not about mail. She never got anything anyway, except her monthly Social Security check.

"Howdy, Miz Espinoza," Jesse said. Clem noticed that he displayed something akin to respect for this old lady, who turned and looked at them briefly. Glared was more like it. "Hello," she said.

"This here is my grandson, Clement," Jesse said.

She looked Clem up and down, head tilted back a little. As if she was inspecting a bug stuck on the end of a pin. She said, "So this is the one I've been hearing about." With that, she turned back to Horacio and said, "What I want to know, is it true you reported my name to Milt Garcia?"

Horacio cringed behind the barred window and twisted his neck this way and that, as though he had on a tight collar. "I got to do my duty," he said. He looked angry and sulky.

"Up the valley those Texas summer people are using the water for their swimming pools!" Dolores said glacially. "For squash and zucchini, you got to have a *little water*. Half the people in this town use the water for their flowers. I use it for food!"

"Don't tell me about it, I know," Horacio complained. "I got Garrison Hurley for his snapdragons, and your friend Mamie Lopez with all that forsythia an' lilac. This is a democracy in this country. Everybody has to obey the same rules. No exceptions, Mrs. Espinoza. You can't have a country without rules! Even the Communists have 'em."

Jesse hissed in Clem's ear, "Didn't I *tell* you he was one of them pinkos!"

The argument was about water rights. Horacio, in addition to being postmaster, was also the *mayordomo,* or overseer, of the *acequias,* the irrigation ditches that meandered here and there through the village. When water was in surplus, like during the spring runoff, there was no problem, but during the dry times the *acequias* were empty and the town had to rely on its sixty-thousand-gallon communal water tank. It was then that the small vegetable gardens or flower plots that people grew in their back yards were likely to suffer.

That was why the postmaster wore binoculars around his scrawny neck. As *mayordomo*, bent-backed Horacio spied out malfeasance, and for this he was hated almost as much as Gus Benavidez. Some people claimed that Bill Martinez was the second most hated man in town, with Horacio ranking third, while others said it was the other way around. Whatever, all day long, when he was not busy behind the counter, Horacio glassed the village to see whom he might catch operating a garden hose. On top of the porch of his house, which was directly across the street from the post office, he had a perch with a ladder leading to it, and here he would sit in the evening hours to see what was going on, looking like a skinny, humpbacked vulture. The binoculars would slowly scan the vista that was Brazos. Searching out water thieves in the hazy violet dusk. If Horacio was a bureaucratic fascist it was only because he meant well and believed that right was right.

During the driest times, of course, nobody dared water anything. Horacio was glassing everything in sight, levying five-dollar fines, which Milt Garcia went around and collected. However, it often happened that in the evening hours, after dusk had gone, after the robins and jays had settled in and the dogs had curled up by the stoves, the garden hoses came out.

In the half dark, the flower beds and vegetable plots were watered by the men, sleeves rolled, maybe a cigarette dangling from the corner of their mouths. During these warm nights, it was a pleasure and an obligation to steal water. In the last of the twilight, the women would come out of the houses, and the kids too, to watch as pappa moved the brass nozzle of the garden hose from one patch of plants to another, slowly, leisurely. There was a certain delight in stealing this water since, after all, it was theirs to begin with. It was even a social occasion. The women would gossip over back fences, and the kids would dash around, and then everybody would sit on the steps of the back porches, with cans of beer and Dr. Pepper and Orange Fanta, and snacks of leftover frijoles, corn on the cob, and sometimes a big plastic bowl of buttered popcorn, while the man of the house moved his hose from place to place, drenching the earth in a fine, misty spray, and if they could have seen in the dark they would have discerned a solemn, dedicated expression on his face as he unhurriedly moved the hose from one plant to the next. The stars came out. Children scratched and yawned, and slapped at mosquitos. Flying beetles and big, heavy moths bounced off the lit windows. In the woods an owl did his stupid two-step call, "Hoo-hoo," and there would be a long pause, and when no other owl replied, he answered himself, "Hoo-*hoo!*" The call of the great horned. Soon he would be out and cruising the night skies with a vision incomparably superior to Horacio and his 8-power glasses. Bats came too. Black, flickering silhouettes in the last of the light, somehow alien. When the watering was done, the man of the house would turn off the hose and return to the porch and down a beer. Then he would say to the kids, "Get the hell inside and into bed, *muy pronto, ahora!*" If the kids had any sense, and they usually did, they would scoot. Now there might be a moment when the husband and wife would sit, maybe with fresh cans of cold beer. "How was your day?" "Oh, the same. How was yours?" "The same." Perhaps another cigarette. Bright spurt of flame as the match ignites. Highlighting the woman's face as she puffs. Her features already saggy. Frown wrinkles, the once girlish figure now dumpy. Already used up by life—burned out. In the dark the cigarette glows as she puffs again, and passes it to her man.

In fact, during this time of year, the water pressure in the kitchen faucets at night went down to a trickle because everybody in the village was in their back yards splashing away with garden hoses. By morning, the communal tank would be almost empty, and Horacio would be having fits. He would hobble around town nailing to telephone poles hand-lettered cardboard placards that read A WISE CITIZEN USES WATER WISELY. Everybody agreed with him that it was just awful, the way people simply ignored rules that were *good* for them, but by and large, no matter how dry it got, the flowers and vegetables of Brazos continued to be bedded in rich, moist soil.

So in a way, Dolores Espinoza had a point, and now she went on making it to Horacio. "You going to fine me five dollars, you got to fine the whole village."

"Only the ones I see," Horacio said. "That way, everything is legal."

"Horacio, you can't see the end of your nose, even with those spyglasses," Dolores said.

"I saw *you* watering!" Horacio said. "And Hurley, and that Mamie Lopez. That is pretty good seeing for a handicapped person with a cataract, if you ask me."

"Well, don't hold your breath till I pay," Dolores warned. "I'm a poor woman."

"Tell that to Sheriff Garcia when he comes around," Horacio said.

"You tell him for me, you *buitre* buzzard!" Dolores said. "I don't have any time to talk to Milt Garcia. And he knows better than to come around to my house bothering me for five dollars when I don't have it. What's he going to do, arrest me if I don't pay? That is something I would like to see him try! Those are my feelings, Horacio. You better not step on my toes." With that she turned to leave, ignoring Jesse and Clem.

Horacio yelled after her, "What sense is there in having rules, unless everybody obeys them?"

"You go to hell!" Dolores Espinoza said over her shoulder as she went out.

Later, driving back to the house, Clem said, "That ol' chick was pretty feisty, wasn't she?"

"Dolores? Oh, she's hell on wheels, all right," Jesse said. "People watch their step around her."

"Is that really why Quintana wears those dumb binoculars all the time?" Clem wanted to know. "To check on people waterin'?"

"That's one of his various spyin' activities."

"Well, he's strictly off the wall if he tries to fine that Espinoza chick," Clem said. "She looks like she wouldn't take much crap."

"She's something else, for sure," Jesse agreed. "I remember when she was young. She was one of those who left Brazos. Wanted to make something of herself. Went down to Santa Fe to work at St. Vincent's. Those people there at the hospital saw right away that Dolores had brains. She started out as a ward attendant. They put her in the school they had, to learn how to be a practical nurse, and from what I heard, she was just sailin' right through it. One day, though, she was goin' around the wards takin' people's temperatures.

Had a whole big tray of thermometers. Something happened, maybe she bumped against a bed or something, and Dolores dropped the tray. Broke every single one of them damned thermometers. The head nurse told her she'd have to dock her pay until Dolores paid for the damage—there were thirty or forty of 'em, and they cost around two bucks apiece. Dolores was makin' thirty bucks a week at the time, so it was like two, three weeks' wages. Dolores said it was an accident, but the head nurse didn't care. Said she'd have to work it off. Dolores said, 'What you're tellin' me is that I got to work for nothing, right?' 'Sort of,' this head nurse says. 'Well, the way I see it,' Dolores told her, 'the person who works for nothing is worth just that—nothing!' And she turned around and walked right out of that hospital, and never went back, and she never paid for those thermometers either. Then she got knocked up by Harvey Espinoza, and they got married. Harvey wasn't a bad feller as I recall, except that he drank. They had four kids, and then one day Harvey, he was a sort of handyman, was up on the steeple of the parish church down at Tierra Amarilla, nailin' up some new zinc siding, and he had a couple in him, and I guess he sort'a stepped back on his scaffold to admire his work, not keepin' in mind where he was, and he come down sixty feet and landed right on his head, which was downright inconsiderate of him, 'cause Dolores got stuck with the chore of raisin' those kids by herself. She seemed to think so anyway, because she never patronized that church again. Oh, she's hell on wheels, all right."

"I kind'a like her," Clem said.

Jesse stared at him. "I wouldn't like her too much if I was you."

"How come?"

"Remember how I once told you about people judging you?" Jesse said.

"Sure."

"Well, Dolores Espinoza is one of the one's who's doin' the judgin'."

SOMETHING THAT HAD been troubling Clem since his arrival was that he never had any money in his pocket, except for a few dollars that Jesse might hand over once in a while for a little gas for the pickup when Clem used it. Clem was not used to being broke. Back on the streets, a man was judged by skills that could generate real cash. It made no difference that here in Brazos he really had very little need for extra cash, living as he did with Jesse. Money counted, no matter how you looked at it.

This realization came about after one of the endless arguments they had. Jesse, as usual, had been ranting about Sally, Werner Grimmiessen, and the despicable Hurleys. "How come you can't see that such folks is out to take advantage of you?" he said.

"And how come, ol' man, you can't git it into your head that I got some smarts?" Clem countered. "You think I don't see what you see? My eyes are brown and beautiful, but they are also sharp. Twenty-twenty on a moonless night with the fog rollin' in! Don't need no eyeglasses to see what's comin' down."

"You let them use you," Jesse insisted. "And only a goddamn fool does that!"

"Maybe so . . . then again, maybe not," Clem said. "Sprout, there is one thing I know. If people wants something from you—I don't care what it is—then they are at a disadvantage. You can call the shots, that is, if you play it right. And ten times out of ten, people want something. They always do. You ever once get that straight in your mind, you can't lose. The man who understands that will end up rich an' famous!" He grinned at Jesse.

"You ain't a hundred percent right," Jesse said. "There ain't nothin' *I* want from you, boy, 'cept to put as much distance as possible twixt the two of us."

Clem stopped smiling. He finally looked at Jesse and nodded. "I know that, Sprout. You an' me, we made that clear a long time ago. About the only thing you want is never to set eyes on me again. And maybe one of these days that'll come about."

"Is that a promise?"

The conversation set Clem to thinking. If he decided to take off, he would need travel money, a stash, and this led him to consider how maybe he ought to do something about this. As the counselor over at Chama High had learned, Clem had a sharp mind. But there was an abstract complexity to his thinking too, which had its roots in what he had learned on the street. To work a scam took intelligence. But to do that same scam with finesse required something extra.

Later that morning, Jesse took off in the truck to the sawmill up in the mountains, where he had been buying loads of tailings and slash for the winter. Clem's job was to split and stack this stuff on the porch, which, to tell the truth, was a job he did not mind that much. There was a certain pleasure in using the big splitting maul out back, and the exercise was good for his physique. Of course, he complained about it and showed Jesse where calluses were developing on the palms of his hands, but even so, he enjoyed the workouts with the heavy axe.

After Jesse had left, Clem walked down to Gus's. Sally was behind the counter. She had a few customers, and when they left with their purchases, Clem had a chance to talk to her alone. They kissed a bit, and then he said, "You know, baby, I been thinkin'."

"About what?"

"About what you said."

"What was that?"

"About gettin' out'a here."

Sally looked at him suspiciously. Then she said, "You're just talking."

"No, I ain't," Clem said, with a sigh. "I don't know how much longer I can hack this scene."

"That old man at you again?"

"He's alway at me," Clem said. "I mean, that's just something I got to live with, like cancer or goin' to school. You like school?"

"I hate it."

"I'm plannin' on splittin'," Clem said.

Sally, when she was not considering the mystique of the male penis, thought a great deal about what life might be like away from Brazos. In a big city, anywhere. Where all the streets at night were brightly lit, and there was dancing, and crowds of young people, and excitement. Where maybe someone would discover her and she would become an internationally famous model, or even an actress on television, and there would be money and success, and it would never end. The farthest she had ever been was Albuquerque, on a trip taken by her eighth-grade class to the New Mexico State Fair, and all she had seen were a lot of smelly pigs and horses and cows, and tomatoes as big as cantaloupes that had been grown by hick farmers in the Four Corners area. The truth was that she was frightened by the names of places like New York City or Los Angeles. She might despise Brazos, but it was familiar, and it was also a scene where, in a very real sense, she reigned supreme. She might not do as well elsewhere. She said, "You're talking again, that's all."

"Looks like I'll split solo, then."

She gave him a hard look. "Without me?"

"I'll write you," Clem said. "That's a promise."

"Where'll you go?"

"I been thinkin' San Francisco. They say that is one swingin' town."

"When?"

"Soon's I get some bread together."

Sally's mind was working overtime. As one who knew a little about manipulation, she did not trust Clem. Also, of the pair, she figured she was the sharper, which may or may not have been a grave error on her part. What it really boiled down to was that she needed Clem. At least for the present. He knew how to get by in the city. Clem was a way out of Brazos. Perhaps the only way. She looked at him, unable to disguise the hurt in her voice. "You'd really go by yourself?"

Clem stared back at her. "You want'a come?"

"Let me think about it."

"Take your time," Clem said easily. "It'll be a while yet."

It was a relief for her to hear that there was no rush involved. She said, "Gee, for a minute you sounded like you were leaving tomorrow or something."

"Big move, you got to give it careful consideration, baby."

"And you'd take me, really? That is, if I wanted to go?"

Clem smiled and shook his head, musing. "Wouldn't we have us a time? Oh, it'd be *fine*. I'd show you off. Take you out discoing. Buy you fancy threads. We'd be on the town every night, oh, *my!* You're so beautiful. Why, I'd be fightin' dudes off right and left. You'd make all the other chicks look like real dogs. They'd hate your guts, want'a scratch out those pretty eyes, 'cause you'd be so cool and groovy."

"You'd watch out for me?" she asked suspiciously. "Really?"

Clem laughed. "Why, baby, I'd be watchin' out for you twenty-four hours a day! I'd *have* to. No need to tell Clem that!"

"Well, let me think it over."

"There's no hurry. Like I said, I got to get some bread."

"How much?"

"Much as we could hustle."

"If we go—not that I'm saying for sure, I'll have to think about it, y'know—I've got a little," Sally said.

"Probably wouldn't be enough," Clem said doubtfully.

"I've got three hundred dollars saved up," Sally said. Actually, she

had $516, and it had taken her seven years of short-changing cus-
tomers to get this much together, but she was not about to let Clem
know how much she was worth.

Clem looked thoughtful. "That'd give us a little start."

"Well, I should hope so!"

"Can you get it when you want it?"

"Yes. I don't trust banks," Sally said. "The interest is okay, but
I'd have to go all the way to the bank at Chama with my father when
he makes a deposit, and then he'd find out. This way, I lose the interest, but at least what I have is my own affair."

"You keep it handy?"

"It's in a safe place."

"I'd be nervous about keepin' that kind of money around," Clem
said. "I mean, if your ol' man ever tumbled, he might rip you off. I
wouldn't put it past him."

"He wouldn't dare," Sally said. "I'd kill him if he did."

"Well, you know what you're doin'. I'd be real careful, though,
about keepin' quiet. You sometimes got a habit of lettin' slip certain
remarks. He gets to suspectin' that you and me are splittin', he'll
begin lookin' around for money. He may not know you have it, but
if he gets a suspicion, he'll start sniffin' around. Also, I don't think
you're so smart about not puttin' that kind of money to work for
you."

"How?"

"I could invest it," Clem said.

"You mean, give it to you?"

"Not give it. I'd just be usin' it."

She stared at him. "I don't trust you."

"Baby, you leave this place with me, you're goin' to *have* to trust
me," he pointed out.

"That's all the money I have in the world," she said. "Why, you
could just take off with it, and leave me standing here. D'you think
I'm nuts?"

"Wouldn't do that," Clem said. "You know better than that."

"Well, I'll just keep it, then."

"Fine by me," Clem said. He looked thoughtful again. "Thing is,
I'd double that three hundred for you. In a couple of months. Get
you six hundred for three bills, guaranteed."

"How?"

"Six-for-fivin'," Clem explained. "Last school I went to, I had

the whole scene sewed up. Person wanted to borrow money, he came
to see Clem. Six bucks back for every fiver loaned, due on Friday.
School'll be startin' soon. If I had a little capital like that to work
with, I could double it for us, in no time. Easy. In a way, you might
even say I was just doin' my bit." He frowned. "Y'see, I'm a funny
kind'a cat. I don't like for nobody to pay my way. If we go, I'd have
to ante up my end of it. Right is right. I ain't no kept man."

They talked some more. The upshot of it was that Clem left the
store with three hundred dollars. Sally had the money hidden in a
tobacco tin that was kept on a rafter in the storeroom. She was still
suspicious, but it was also clear to her that a move had to be made,
a risk taken. Even so, she made Clem wait out in front while she was
in the storeroom. And although she was nervous and reluctant, once
she put her mind to it, she was as good or better than Clem. When
she gave him the money, she said, "We have to leave on a Thursday,
when we go."

"How come?"

"Because Friday is when he goes to the bank with the week's
receipts from the store," she explained. "I know the combination
to the safe."

"You'd hustle your own pappa?"

"What the hell has he ever done for me, that stingy bastard. No
more than that drunken Jesse has ever done for you," Sally said
coldly. "Serve both of them right."

"How much could we get?"

"Receipts usually go between eight hundred and a thousand."

"Big town, here we *come!*" Clem said. He had no objections to
doing a number on Gus Benavidez. "Why, we'd have us a real start
with that kind'a bread, baby. Shit, when we get ready to leave, we'll
do it in style!"

FROM THE STORE he went to the Hurleys'. Garrison was still upright,
since it was early in the day. In the kitchen, surrounded by dark-
green plastic bags filled with empties, Patsy served Clem milk and
cookies. Clem said, "You wouldn't happen to have a drop of vodka
I could put in my milk, would you?"

"Just a drop," Patsy cooed. She handed him a half-gallon bottle.

Clem poured a double into his glass, ate a couple of cookies, and explained his problem. "I need two hundred dollars, to fix my motor-cycle. Mr. Grimmiessen said it would cost at least that much. He says I can work it off by cleaning his house."

Patsy said, "Don't you dare!"

Garrison chuckled. "Really, my boy. You can't be that naïve."

"I'd sure like to have that cycle."

Garrison held up a forefinger and winked at Clem conspiratorially. He looked like a jovial bishop instructing an acolyte. "But at what price? You understand, I'm very fond of Werner. Intelligent old duffer. But he has his weaknesses. If you follow."

"All I'm tryin' to do is 'climatize myself to this new life," Clem explained. He drank off half his milk. "Havin' that ol' motorcycle might be fun."

"Give the lad another taste, Patricia," Garrison ordered. She did. He said, "Let us put our heads together. The real joy in any problem is finding the solution. Have you tried walking?"

"Me? Walk?" Clem said. "Not unless I absolutely have to."

"Ah, youth . . ." Garrison murmured. He placed a hand on Clem's shoulder and stared at him seriously, and for a moment Clem wondered if he was a latent. "For a boy, a motorcycle has charisma. But there is a special joy in walking. To be able to commune with nature! What do you know of the geography here? The ecology? If you like, I'll take you on walking tours. Within a few miles of here, I can show you things you could never see on a motorcycle. Walking clears the mind, tones the constitution, refreshes the soul."

"Can I come too?" Patsy asked.

Clem figured that by any given midday neither of them could have walked two hundred yards. He stuck to his point. "I got to raise some money."

Garrison smiled and nodded with tolerant amusement. "Matter of life and death, eh?" He considered this and said finally, "Well, then, if that is the case, better that we loan you a little. My dear, the bank, if you please." With that, Patsy went to the canister marked FLOUR and brought it to the table. Uncapping it, Garrison fished around inside and extracted a plastic bag containing a roll of twenties, thereby confirming to Clem a suspicion he had long had. One of them—Garrison probably—was getting an extra dole besides the disability checks, maybe out of an inheritance or something. He wished now that he had asked for four hundred.

Patsy said, "If you want to help out, come over and work for us.

I never seem to get caught up with this house. I don't know where my time goes."

"I'd be happy to do that," Clem said.

"Give the lad another drop," Garrison said.

"Thank you."

"It's uplifting to have a boy around the house," Garrison observed.

"It certainly is," Patsy agreed. She smiled at Clem. "Another cookie?"

"Vodka's fine," Clem said.

Garrison counted out ten twenties. "We live modestly," he explained, "but what we have is yours. I'd keep an eye on Werner, if I were you. I recommend, too, that this little discussion be confined to the walls of this kitchen. Do you follow? Werner need not know. Nor Jesse. As neighbors, all of us maintain a harmonious balance that is at best precarious."

"I won't tell a soul," Clem said.

"We're really poor, you know," Patsy said.

"I know what that feels like," Clem said.

An hour later Clem left their kitchen half crocked and two hundred better off than he had been when he left Gus's with Sally's three hundred, after having promised to walk the hills with Garrison and drive Patsy down to Santa Fe for a day's shopping. He went in the back door of Jesse's house and out the front, so that the Hurleys, if they were watching, would not see him.

Walked into *Hasenpfeffer mit Knödel*. Native rabbit in sour cream, and exquisite dumplings sprinkled with fresh parsley.

Werner, it seemed, in addition to being a master mechanic and a good cook, was a hunter. He proudly showed Clem the gun he used. A pistol such as Clem had never even dreamed of. An old Swiss Hammerli .22 caliber. "German marksmen used this same gun in the 1936 Olympics. I had difficulty getting it out of my homeland." Twelve-inch-long octagonal barrel, fantastically engraved in floral designs—some of the metalwork actually had inlays of real gold. A single-shot, drop-block action. Custom-carved walnut grip in polished Circassian walnut. The gun was kept in a rosewood case, lined with green velvet. Even Clem, whose knowledge of deadly weapons was mainly confined to switchblades and Saturday-night specials, could see that this item was easily worth a couple of thousand on the antiques market. He had never experienced the incredible feeling of a fine double-set hair trigger, but he understood when

Werner cocked the old target pistol and he, Clem, barely touched the second trigger, a mere contact, and there was a deadly click. "I shoot better with this old beauty than most of these peasants here can use a rifle," Werner said. "At twenty-five meters, a dime will cover ten shots from this."

"That's a terrific piece you got there," Clem said.

"I will leave her to you. In my will," Werner promised. Clem figured that the old German had made the same promise to Willie Montoya and a dozen other young men, but even so it showed that Werner's heart was in the right place.

The rabbit and dumplings were excellent. They had beer and bourbon with their meal, and later Clem and Werner got into an arm-wrestling contest.

Werner's biceps and forearms looked like the wings from a plucked chicken, and the threadbare T-shirt showed off his emaciated frame—he was, if possible, skinnier than Jesse. Clem figured a good pinch might cause a compound fracture, but he let the old man win, groaning mightily as Werner forced his arm to the tabletop. Werner exulted, "Real men, they must always compete, even in a small way. That is what builds the friendship between them. You agree?" He was out of breath from his exertions. "*Gott im Himmel!* Such strength. Incredible!"

"I am pretty strong, ain't I?"

"No, I meant me," Werner said. "At my age too!" Feeling too euphoric to contain himself, he poured a glassful of bourbon and then smacked Cochise, who was sitting beside the table, on the muzzle. "Shut up, *Scheisskopf!*" Werner commanded, though Cochise had been sitting there silently, with an attentive expression, hoping for whatever was left of the *Hasenpfeffer.* Werner regarded the dog, and then glanced at Clem. "He is a very Russian-looking dog, *nicht wahr?* With those cruel eyes and that savage expression? That, of course, is why I named him Cochise."

"But ain't that an Indian name?" Clem pointed out.

"Well? So? Why not?" Werner said, with addled mysteriousness. He smiled. "Can you give me one good reason, Clem, why such a dog should not be named with such a name?"

"Now that you mention it, Werner, it seems perfectly logical," Clem said. "It surely does."

"All Indians crossed the Aleutian land bridge, you know," Werner lectured, with sublimely drunken logic. "Show me a noble Navajo, and I guarantee you I will show you a noble Ukrainian. I know, my boy! Would you like to wrestle some more? I will teach you the Greco-Roman style. You will enjoy it."

"I'm worn out," Clem protested. He tasted his drink. "I got a problem."

"You do?"

"I thought I'd ask your advice."

"My boy, I would consider it a privilege," Werner said. He and Clem lit cigarettes. "Tell me, now, what is this great problem that is troubling you?"

"Well, in a way, it's the motorcycle," Clem explained. "And in a way, it's something else too. I been tryin' to figure out how to get the money together to buy the new parts we need." A few days earlier, he and Werner had made up a list of parts that would be needed for the Harley-Davidson. What Clem had told the Hurleys was true. Werner, using the manual, estimated that the cost would run around two hundred. Clem labored on, embarrassment in his voice, "It ain't so easy for someone my age to make a little extra money in this town."

"That is true," Werner said.

"I was thinkin' of going to Gus Benavidez and askin' him for a job, cleanin' out the store."

"*Ach so!* That Gus!" Werner laughed. "You can be sure he would pay you slave's wages, don't doubt that."

"Sally thought it might be a good idea."

"Oh, she would, that one!" Werner said. He slapped his knee with delight. "Oh, yes, *natürlich*, I just bet you she would! Women! Clem, come, come, come! You are intelligent. Can you not see what thoughts are going through that silly girl's mind?"

"I know what you mean," Clem said. "I was talking to Garrison and Patsy before. They may hire me to do chores around their place."

Werner cackled scornfully. "First Sally, then Patsy? Ho, ho! That is, how do you say, very rich! Clem, what can I tell you? You poor boy. That is like moving from the frying pan into the fire, no? I bet that Frau Hurley jumped with joy to be hiring you. Did you agree?"

"I said I'd think about it."

"You be careful!" Werner said. He leaned across the table and stared at Clem. "That is all I am telling you."

"Well, I'd like to get that motorcycle fixed."

"I know, I know," Werner said, and fell silent for a while. "Listen, it is better that I lend you the money."

"I couldn't let you do that, Werner," Clem objected. "You been too nice to me already."

"It is less than nothing," Werner said, holding up a hand. "I am a poor man, myself. But I always keep a little something put away for when it rains. I would consider it an honor. We would regard it as a loan, of course."

"I don't know when I could pay you back," Clem argued.

"A little here, a little there. Do you see me worrying? I myself sometimes have need of a little work to be done. The kitchen should be painted before winter. You could work for me, when there is time."

Their conversation ended with Clem agreeing to Werner's offer to pay for the new parts. And like the Hurleys, Werner preferred that this arrangement be kept secret. Clem said that he understood. He understood several other things too: for one, everybody in this town seemed to have money stashed away for a rainy day, and nobody wanted anybody else to know that such money existed.

At the last minute, in a fit of sentimental affection, Werner pressed a twenty-dollar bill into Clem's hand. When Clem tried to protest, Werner said, "No, no, *no!* Don't argue! I will not hear of it. A young man must have a little something to spend. Otherwise, he has no dignity. This is something I understand very well!"

Clem's day left him with a total of $520, plus Werner's promise to pay for the new Harley parts, not to mention a lot of rabbit, dumplings, beer, bourbon, and vodka. There was also the faint possibility, at some future date, of Gus's weekly receipts. That was Sally's department, but it would have to be postponed until he was ready to leave Brazos, with or without her, and more than likely it would be the latter, which did not necessarily mean that he would have to leave without Gus's money.

When Jesse found out that he had been over at the Hurleys' and Grimmiessen's again, he was furious. "Oh, it's goin' from bad to worse, day by day, as surely as the sun rises and the moon sets. Bad seed! That's what I'm stuck with in my old age."

He changed his tune, however, later that week when his old Chevy pickup blew out a head gasket with a noise that sounded like a howitzer going off. Orly Mendocino, who owned the Quick 'n' Easy gas station, shook his head. "Ain't just a head gasket, Jesse. Whole engine's all shot to hell. How many miles you figure you got on it?"

"Can't be more'n a hundred fifty thousand or so," Jesse said. "Speedometer quit workin' back around 'seventy-six, and it had about a hundred twenty then. Why, that engine's scarcely broke in."

"Broken down, not in," Orly said. "You need rings, valves, bearings, gaskets. Ain't hardly nothing left of the clutch. Brake shoes got no linings left."

"How much?"

"In the neighborhood of five hundred," Orly said.

"I ain't got that much," Jesse complained.

"Your credit's okay with me, Jesse."

"Go ahead and fix it," the old man said. He sighed. "I'll have to pay it off a few bucks at a time, though. And here I'd been savin' to git my teeth adjusted. Goddamn plates have loosened up so that I'm afraid to grin for fear they're upside down."

Later on, Clem had a little talk with Orly, and they came to an understanding. By laying a $300 advance on Mendocino, he got the price down to $400 firm. Clem also promised to do some part-time work around the station, and Orly knocked off another $50 for this. That left Jesse with a balance due of $50. Clem figured the old man could swing this. It also left Clem with $220 of his own, and if there was one thing he was sure of, it was that he would not be doing any chores for Orly, the Hurleys, Werner, or anybody else, until that sum was gone.

When Jesse heard about this, the first thing he said was, "Where'd you git so much money?"

"Don't worry about it, Sprout."

"You didn't git it honest."

"Now, how do you know that?"

" 'Cause I know *you!*"

"How you talk! You heard of anybody gettin' mugged around here?" Clem demanded. "You heard of any houses being cleaned? Any banks ripped off? Any stores stuck up? No! You ain't heard *nothin*,' ol' man, so whyn't you just shut up for once! Truck's bein' fixed. We *need* that heap to get around. What more do you want? Rest easy, Sprout."

Sally heard about it too, and she was fit to be tied. "That's my money," she said bitterly, when she got him alone. "You dirty, cheating, lying son of a bitch, you went and used my money to fix that old prick's *truck!*"

"Whyn't you just cool it, baby," Clem said easily. "I got your goddamn money right here." He took a sheaf of twenties out of his pocket and riffled them, slowly enough for her to see that no singles were spliced into the roll, but too quickly for her to count.

She was impressed. "But, honey, if it wasn't our money, where'd you get it?"

Clem smiled affectionately at her. "Now, didn't I tell you I was goin' to start investin' it?"

"How?"

He said lightly, "There's a thousand ways to make money work for you . . . and this here is one man knows 'em *all*."

She was still suspicious. "But you're supposed to be saving that money for us."

"Baby, when we leave, we're goin' to have so much that a few hundred one way or the other ain't goin' to make any difference. I wouldn't worry your head about it."

The Hurleys and Werner wanted to know about the money too. Clem told each, in turn, "I lucked into a crap game over at Chama, that's all. Not that I believe in gamblin', but I had to take the chance, and for once it paid off. But I wouldn't do it again, not ever."

To Jesse he grumbled, "I ain't ever seen a town like this before. A person tries to do someone a little favor, and right away the whole fuckin' population got to know *why*, an' *how* much, and *where* it came from. Nossir . . . no more of these favors for me! Too much explainin' involved."

"It ain't none of their business, so don't tell 'em nothin'," Jesse said.

Clem grinned. "Ain't that the truth!"

" 'Course, if you want to, you can tell me," Jesse said disinterestedly.

Clem shook his head and started laughing. "If two people knows a secret, that is one too many. *Whoo-eee!* Oh, Sprout, you are somethin' else!"

Down at the Emerald, Jesse told Woody Klein, "You got to give the devil his due. That kid is trouble on the hoof, but I do have to say that he's got a natural talent for handlin' money right. Yessir, he's a Slade, all right. Got a real head on his shoulders when it comes to horse tradin'."

Woody looked at Jesse and grinned. "Why, if I didn't know better, I'd almost think you were proud of the boy, Jess."

THE TRUCK WAS ready the following week, and that Friday there was a dance over at the VFW in Chama. Clem borrowed the pickup to take Sally. Of course they never went to the dance, because more than likely the Montoya boys and Connie Aragon and some of the other more or less violently inclined crowd they ran with would be there too, but it was an excuse to get out for the evening. Clem, who was interested in maintaining with Sally the impression he had created—that of always having money available—blew eighteen dollars on a motel outside Chama.

They returned a little before one A.M. Clem dropped her at her house, and she went inside. He drove off in a good mood. Main Street was deserted and unlit except for the truck's headlights. Just before he got to Gus's store, a car swung out of a dirt lane and began following him. For a moment, Clem merely noted its presence behind him. Then, as it speeded up and began getting closer, he grew alert. Decided that it was best to keep a little distance, and hit the gas. The car behind him speeded up too.

What developed was not really a chase—it didn't last long enough. As he went around a curve on the outskirts of the village, there was a loud noise. For a moment he thought one of the tires had blown out, but then he realized it was a shot, and with that he floorboarded the gas pedal. There was no need to. The car behind came to a halt, and as its lights receded in the rearview mirror, Clem could see it turn and head back toward town, its red rear lights growing smaller and finally vanishing. Clem kept on going.

Jesse was still up, drinking a beer and watching a late movie on TV. Clem ran in and said, "Sprout, I think someone took a shot at me." He described what had happened.

Jesse pulled on his jeans and got a flashlight, and the two of them went outside and looked the truck over. There was a neat round hole in the tailgate, and up in the front of the camper there was a heavy dent in the front panel of the truck's box. Jesse said, "Guess when school starts, I'll be drivin' you back and forth."

"No need for that."

"I'll drive you," Jesse said.

Clem was inspecting the heavy dent inside the camper. "Y'know something, Sprout? Wasn't no little twenty-two done this. It made a terrific noise when it hit."

"Huntin' rifle, most likely," Jesse said. "Or else a Magnum pistol. Folks start shootin' off guns like that, somebody could git hurt real bad."

"Killed even," Clem said soberly. He did some thinking. "Sprout, was it maybe just somebody tryin' to scare me?"

"Could be. At the same time, they didn't care one way or the other whether they scared you or hit you. No way in the world to aim that careful in a fast-movin' car. Whoever it was let off a shot, and he wasn't much worried about where it went. You were lucky it hit where it did, that's all. Let's see if we can find that slug. It ought'a be here inside the camper somewhere." They searched for almost half an hour, without luck—the slug never turned up. "I'd sure like to find it," Jesse said.

"What for?"

"See if it came from a rifle or a pistol."

"What difference does it make?"

"I'd have an idea whether it was just one person or several in that car," Jesse said. "Can't no one man drive with one hand an' aim a rifle out the window with the other. But he could do that with a pistol."

"People around here get serious, don't they?"

"They judge a person," Jesse said. "That's what I been tellin' you. Hell, there's more guns in this town than Carter's got pills."

"You got any idea who might've done it?"

"Mebbe."

"Willie Montoya?"

"Nope," Jesse said. "Willie's a bar fighter. I don't think he's got the guts to bushwhack someone. Though I know of some others. I warned you, y'know. Folks take a dislike, you got to watch 'em. Like, some years ago, we had a whole flock of hippie types come into the valley, and they organized one of them hippie camps."

"Communes?"

"That's it—communes. They were a pain in the ass, like all them hippies, but I'd have to say that they didn't particularly bother nobody, except that you had to look at 'em . . . oh, they was dirty, nasty types! One night a couple of those hippie girls got gang-raped. Miltie Garcia never could prove it on no one . . . not that he tried very hard to begin with, votes bein' as scarce to come by as they are. Then one day, this hippie boy, he was workin' around his teepee—can you imagine someone dumb enough to want'a live in one of them Injun tents?—and someone drove by and let off a thirty-thirty in his direction, just like with you tonight, and it blew off half his leg. Crippled him permanent. You got to understand these local people, boy. You got your ways. They got theirs."

"Well, who do you think done it?"

"Don't worry your mind about it," Jesse said. "Come on, let's go back in the house and have a beer."

Inside, they opened beers and sat down in the kitchen. Jesse said, "Listen, you ever shot a gun before?"

"Sure, lots of times," Clem said.

Jesse stared at him. "Goddamn it, tell me the truth. Just for once in your life."

"Well, no, I ain't," Clem admitted. "I handled plenty of 'em, though."

Jesse nodded. "Now, I want you to listen to me, and listen careful. I'm goin' to take that forty-four and git some shells for it tomorrow, and we'll go practice on tin cans, and after that I'm goin' to keep it in the glove compartment of the truck, so that if you drive anyplace you'll have it handy. You may think you're hot shit with that karate or judo business, or whatever you call it when you do those hoppin'-around exercises, gruntin' like a constipated pig. Howsomever, a gun is the only thing I know of that can stand up to another gun, and even then it's a lot smarter just to turn around and walk away. What I'm bankin' on is, if folks know you got that forty-four handy, they'll leave you alone."

"How'll they know that?"

"They'll know, all right," Jesse said. "And it'll give 'em something to think about. You don't have to act like a smartass and go flashin' it all over the place. Don't show it at all. There ain't any need to. They'll know. Like whoever shot that hippie boy and crippled him might'a thought twice if they'd knowed he could'a shot back. But he was peaceful. That whole commune crowd was, goin' around with flowers stuck in their hats and hair down to their waists, smilin' and wavin' at everybody, so stuffed full of marijuana they didn't know what month it was—some of 'em tried to plant corn right in the middle of a blizzard we had in February. Why, in warm weather

those hippie girls didn't hardly wear nothin', not even brassieres, with
their shirt fronts unbuttoned an' all, showin' off their bee stings right
and left, worse'n Sally Benavidez, no wonder the menfolks got riled,
and the womenfolk, too . . . if a female in *this* valley is really out to
be peaceful, first thing she better do is strap herself into a brassiere
like everybody else! Just 'cause someone's a hippie, it don't give 'em
the right to be different."

"There ain't no more hippies really, Sprout."

"Thank God for that," Jesse said. He frowned. "Where'd they
all go?"

"Drifted into different scenes, I guess."

"Should'a put 'em all on a boat and shipped 'em out to sea." He
finished his beer. "Well, let's git to bed."

The next morning after breakfast, he and Clem drove to Gus's.
Jesse walked into the store with the .44 stuck in his belt and bought
two boxes of 250-grain cartridges. He opened one box and, there at
the counter, depressed the pistol's catch, flipped out the cylinder,
and loaded it. Gus said, "What're you doing with the gun, Jesse?"

"Goin' to teach this boy to shoot it," Jesse said.

Gus's expression was bland, disinterested. He said nothing.

Down by the town garbage dump, Jesse let Clem use up a box
of the cartridges practicing on tin cans and rats. "Don't shoot from
the hip. Aim the goddamn thing! Hold it straight out and set that
front sight right smack in the center of the notch on the rear sight."
Clem enjoyed shooting the revolver, but he was not especially good
at it. Milt Garcia drove by to see what all the racket was about, and
Jesse said, "I'm just teachin' this boy to shoot, that's all, Miltie. Go
on about your business."

"He makes enough trouble as it is," Milt said. "He don't need any
gun. Can't you go someplace else to shoot that cannon, Jesse? Half
the town is wondering if it's the Fourth of July. You're creating a
nuisance."

"Constitution says a man's got a right to bear arms," Jesse told
him. "Git out'a here and quit botherin' us. Go find somebody to
arrest and make your day perfect."

Later, driving back to the house, Clem said, "For an ol' man, you
can be kind'a cool when you want to, Sprout."

"I don't know what you mean."

"Well, you let Gus know about this pistol. And you let Milt Garcia know too. Between the two of 'em, that means the whole valley'll know." Clem gave him a thoughtful look. "How come Gus, Sprout? You thinkin' the same thing I been?"

"What's that?"

"That he was the one. Last night?"

Jesse chuckled, but his expression was sour. "That is something I don't reckon we'll ever know. Was all the lights off when you dropped Lady Godiva off at her house last night?"

"Yeah. You want me to find out from her if Gus was home?"

"Don't you ask her a goddamn thing," Jesse said. "She wouldn't know nothin' anyway. She'd have her own room, and Gus no doubt has got his own bedroom too. Door'd be closed. She'd be tippy-toein' in, most likely, real quiet so's not to waken him and mebbe git an ass-chewin' for comin' home so late. No. She'd scoot for bed quiet as a mouse, without disturbin' him. If he was there, that is." He thought about it some more. "It don't make no difference, really. Somebody was out there last night, layin' for you. Whoever that person was, he'll hear about what we was doin' this morning. That'll caution him down a little. Let the son of a bitch do a little sweatin' of his own."

It did not quite end there, though. Two days later Clem received a letter at the post office. It was the first letter he had gotten in Brazos, and for that matter, the first letter he had ever gotten in his life. There was a single sheet inside the envelope, and on it there was a simple message printed in pencil: NO NIGGERS ALLOUD IN BRAZOS.

Clem showed it to Jesse, who got furious. "Yellow-bellied sons of bitches! They ain't got the guts to walk right up and say that face to face! They know Jesse Slade, and they know I wouldn't take it!"

"It ain't you they're talkin' about, Sprout," Clem pointed out.

"The fuck it ain't," the old man cried. "It had your name on it, but it come addressed care of me, right? Goddamn it all to hell and back, I've had about enough of this! I can't stand it when someone gits pushy with me! All that does is put a chip on my shoulder, and then I just go around lookin' for somebody to knock it off. They git me mad enough, the shit'll really hit the fan."

"What we goin' to do?"

"Defy the fuckers," Jesse said grimly. "We are goin' to go on exactly like we been." He looked at Clem. "Far as I'm concerned, boy, you got as much goddamn right to be in this town as anybody else. If they don't like it, that's too bad." He considered this for a while, and finally said bitterly, "I swear to God, sometimes I take a look at this human race an' I just want'a puke in all directions at once."

THE NEW PARTS for the motorcycle arrived from Albuquerque, where there was a Harley-Davidson distributorship. Clem and Werner got the bike reassembled in less than four days. In the process, Clem discovered something about himself: he enjoyed the work. And he was good with his hands. Dismantling the machine had been all right, but he was surprised at the satisfaction he experienced in putting it back together. Of course, he had to be shown how to do everything. But usually Werner had to show him only once—adjusting tappets, gapping plugs and points with a feeler gauge, torquing the bolts on cylinder heads.

Werner too was pleased and surprised at Clem's aptitude. By the end of the first day he said, "You have a natural understanding for mechanical things."

"I ain't plannin' on bein' no mechanic," Clem said. "I mean, this is fun, but it don't mean I'm fixin' to make a career out of nuts and bolts. Let's just get this mess of junk back together. Werner, you got to understand, these hands of mine don't like gettin' dirty."

But his disdain vanished when at last the job was done, the tank fueled, everything oiled and greased, and the body and frame wiped clean for a final time with rags. The bike, though old, did not look bad by half—a dark maroon. Most of the original chrome was pitted but still in fairly good shape. The leather seat had rotted, and Jesse donated an old sheepskin, which Werner helped fit, cut, and sew over the original leather.

Clem climbed aboard and Werner stood back, looking on proudly. He gave instructions, and Clem twisted the right handle, feeding the engine, and put the foot clutch in neutral. He kicked at the starter. Nothing happened. Kicked again, and then again. Still nothing. He kicked at it four or five more times, still with no luck. He said disgustedly, "All that work for nothin'! Somethin's wrong."

Back in Los Angeles he had sneered at the cycle gangs that cruised the city—the men dressed in funky leather outfits, with their old ladies seated behind—scorned them because he took it as a sign of weakness when people felt obliged to group or club together. The motorcycles they rode were not so bad—splendidly remodeled "hogs," with spindly little front wheels and apehanger handlebars and lots of chrome—but the people who roared around on them were creeps.

"Keep trying," Werner advised. "Don't forget, the gas must first go through the entire fuel line and carburetor, into the cylinders."

Clem hit the kick starter three or four more times, and with a cloud of blue smoke the motorcycle blasted into life. He was so astonished, he nearly fell off. He grinned at Werner and let off a *"Whoo-eee!"* Worked the gas, revving the engine, then letting it idle, then fed it again. The blue exhaust stopped as the engine warmed. It was a noisy machine. Half the baffles in the muffler were blown or rusted out.

Werner, all excited too, was hopping about Clem, waving clenched fists in the air exultantly. "You see!" he yelled. "It works! How magnificent! My boy, you have made it work!"

Jesse came out on the back porch to see what was making so much racket. Garrison and Patsy Hurley came out of their place. Jesse called to them, "I'll be damned! He's got it workin'. I never figured he'd do it. That machine has set out in the shed for over twenty years! He's something else, ain't he?"

They all had a drink on it, including Clem. The next and more formidable task was teaching him to ride the machine. Werner acted as instructor. Patsy clapped, as much as she could with a glass in one hand. Garrison beamed with pride and said to Jesse, "The Oedipal complex. That is how the child escapes and emerges fully grown!" He frowned. "No, that's wrong. To kill the father and seduce the mother."

"Lay off that filthy degenerate talk, Garrison," Jesse said. "Ain't nothin' wrong with that boy's Oedipal."

"To escape, to be off, and free! This lad of ours!"

"He's my kid, not yours," Jesse grumbled.

"Let's have a party," Patsy said.

Cochise was dancing around the motorcycle, barking up a storm. The cats, frightened by the noise and the smell of the exhaust, were on the roof of Jesse's house, looking sulky and pissed off.

After a near disaster or two and a couple of skid-outs, Clem finally got the hang of shifting the bike into first, and then into second. He was feeling very good about it all, and whirled around Werner's back yard in slow circles and figure-eights.

Werner yelled a stern warning. "The new piston rings, they are not broken in. *Dumbkopf!* With an engine there must be a marriage, a match, things must fit together, you silly boy!"

"Give it time, Clem," Garrison said.

Patsy said, "I feel like a drink."

And there was another undiscovered skill. Clem had as much of a knack for riding the bike as he had with mechanics' tools.

Jesse shouted, "You slow down! You tryin' to kill yourself?"

Clem took off out of Werner's yard onto the road, got it into third, and disappeared in a cloud of yellow dust. Could be heard returning, from some distance off. Pulled into the yard again and said, with the throttle low, "Hey, Sprout! Hop on!"

"Ain't goin' to git me on that two-wheeled death trap!" Jesse said. "Best way to git crippled I know of. Go kill yourself. I got a few good years left."

"Chickenshit!"

"Ain't."

"Are too."

"No, I ain't!"

"Yes, you is!"

This went on for a while. Finally Jesse, who had never been on a cycle and was secretly curious about it, got on. They roared off, Jesse clutching Clem around the waist with one hand and trying to hold on to his Stetson with the other. The sensation of speed was unbelievable. They roared past the post office, and Horacio Quintana scuttled out the front door, trying to focus his binoculars as they disappeared.

When they returned, Garrison got the next ride. After it was over, he got off, wheezing, "I'm too old for this."

Then Werner, clutching Clem's waist, his white hair windblown, yelling, "Motion! Movement! It is a symphony!"

Then Patsy. She was pouting and saying something about feeling left out of everything. She got the best ride of all. For once no glass in her hand. Hugging Clem, astraddle the sheepskin seat. Up on the highway, he reached sixty, which horrified her. The wind whipped at her hair and shirt, and she got into a fearful mixture of tumultuousness—frightened half to death, at the same time excited. When they returned, she got off the bike, her thighs and hips aching. Patsy had discovered something. She had orgasmed. Limping about a little dizzily, Patsy made for the Hurley household, smiling at the men around her and murmuring in a silvery voice, "Please excuse me. Got to change into something fresh."

IN THE DAYS that followed, some of Brazos' more sedate citizens began to feel that they were being terrorized by a maniac. From maintaining relatively low visibility, Clem suddenly was everywhere at once. He sped up and down the dirt lanes and alleys of the village in a cloud of dust and a spray of pebbles. People peeked out from behind parted curtains. Milt Garcia got anonymous telephone complaints, and he spoke sharply to Jesse and Clem, threatening Clem with arrest for operating a vehicle in an unsafe manner, operating an unlicensed vehicle, and operating a vehicle without even a learner's permit, let alone a regular license.

Jesse got into a fight with him. "Listen, Miltie, what in hell you bitchin' about? You quotin' state statutes at *me!* Them goddamn statutes apply to state and federal roads. You seen this boy on any regular road? I ain't."

"Why, he's driving it all over the village, you old fool," Milt argued.

"So? This here's an unincorporated township," Jesse pointed out. "Until such time as we gits incorporated, the streets of this god-forsaken hellhole ain't no different than any back country road or loggin' lane. Go read your goddamn law before you quote it! Besides which, there must be eight or ten kids in this whistle stop that got them little motorscooters an' Mopeds, or whatever they're called. They ride 'em doodley-dick wherever they please, and they ride 'em without licenses."

"Those little Tote-Goats and minibikes ain't a big, dangerous machine like that Harley," Milt said.

"Bullshit! It's got a gas propellant engine in it, just like those minibikes," Jesse said. "Technically, mechanically, and judiciously, Clem ain't breakin' the law any more'n those other kids, so long as he stays off state roads."

"Couldn't he at least put a muffler on the damned thing?" Milt said. "I get three, four calls a day. Be reasonable, Jesse. He starts that engine up, windowpanes rattle and shake from one end of town to the other."

Jesse grinned maliciously. "It's a safety device, you fathead! You just said yourself it was a big, dangerous machine. This way, every-body can hear him comin' from a good way off, and be prepared."

"People are complaining," Milt insisted.

"Ain't nothin' remarkable in that," Jesse said. "They'd complain if John the Baptist came down from heaven in a top hat and tuxedo an' sat out in front of the post office handin' around hundred-dollar bills! If the town was as silent as a tomb, they'd be complainin' that all the peace and quiet was rubbin' their rotten nerves raw. Ain't none of these bastards feel satisfied less'n they got a gutful of something to whine and gripe about. Well, let 'em! Tell 'em I said to go to hell. Tell 'em to come see me! I'll give 'em something to complain about!"

Clem continued using the bike. He and Werner worked on the engine more, tuning it and resetting tappets as the engine settled in. On Werner's advice, he ordered new tires, since the old skins were unsafe. He bought rearview mirrors, a plexiglass windshield, and black fiberglass saddlebags, delving into the money Sally had given him to invest. On warm afternoons, he rode about in jeans and boots, naked from the waist up, enjoying the feel of the wind against his body. The curtains in the windows of the houses still parted. People stared after his disappearing form and shook their heads. Party-line extensions went off like fire alarms after Clem zoomed past with Sally riding behind, arms clutching his slender waist. It was as if the two of them were simply too scandalously youthful and full of high spirits for words! Sally, in those indecent jogging shorts and tight T-shirt. Willie Montoya went pale with frustration at this outrageous spectacle. So did Connie Aragon. Gus Benavidez picked at his nails until they bled, and got in an ugly temper with customers whose bills were only a few days overdue. Horacio Quintana lurked near the window of his post office, binoculars poised. And the rest of the town looked on.

Sally, of course, relished being the center of attention—but she liked it a lot less when Clem cruised Main Street one afternoon with a tall, leggy, long-haired blonde, a Dallas girl whose family had a cabin along with other Texas summer people on a pretty stretch of the river up the valley. Sally, in fact, went through the ceiling. "Right out in public!" she screamed when she got him alone. *"Who was that bitch?"*

"Chick from up the valley, that's all," Clem said.

"You can't do this to me!"

"Didn't do nothin', baby."

"Riding around all over town! Right past the *store!*" Sally stormed. "I swear! I don't understand what goes on inside that head of yours. Why you'd let yourself be seen with a cheap bitch like that. I mean, if she was pretty, well, that would be something, but she was ugly. I saw her! Cheap and ugly!"

"Looked pretty to me."

"I'll *kill* you!"

"What you gettin' in a sweat about? Her and her people are goin' back to Texas next week."

"I bet you rode her up to the mountains."

"Just a little way," Clem said, grinning.

She looked dangerous. "Nobody treats me that way."

"Ah, come on."

"I didn't say a word when you gave everybody else a ride on that stupid motorcycle . . . that old creep Werner, and that dirty-mouthed grandfather of yours, and that ugly old Patsy Hurley. You gave them all a ride first! I didn't say a word. You think you can walk all over me. We're quits. Who was that flat-chested bitch? What's her name?"

"Susan-Jo. Calls herself Sue-Jo."

"I'll Sue-Jo her. Where'd you run into her?"

"Up by the Dairy Queen."

"Really! She was just standing around up there all by herself, I suppose. Just waiting for something to come along and happen. And that something was *you*. I bet you just snapped your fingers at her! Bet she practically threw a hip out of joint, hopping on with you."

"We were just kiddin' around and talkin'," Clem said. "Said she'd never been on a bike before."

"You son of a bitch!"

"Ain't it the truth."

"Bastard! I bet you been using my money for gas! You think I'm supposed to pay for your entertainment? You better think again!"

It took quite some time for him to mollify her. His original thought had been to irritate her to the point where she knew she could not take him for granted, but he had erred in judging the fieriness of her temper, which apparently got blistering when Sally didn't get what Sally thought she wanted. He decided that the next time he took Sue-Jo riding, they would avoid the village entirely. Sue-Jo liked it better up in the mountains anyway. For a properly brought up Texas girl, she had a certain open-mindedness, and when he finally dropped her off back at the Dairy Queen where she had left her car, she made a point of telling him that their afternoon was the best thing that had happened during her entire summer vacation, adding, "Gee, I wish my folks weren't leaving so soon." They made a date to meet again in two days.

Clem also saw that bringing a little competition into Sally's life might in a sense be constructive. Jesse himself put a finger on it, when he heard that Clem had been seen riding around town with a tall, gorgeous blonde. He told Clem, "Mebbe that'll give that highfalutin Sally something to think about! She acts like the whole world owes her a favor. One of these days she'll learn she's female. A female's got to be run with a strong hand, otherwise they git discontent and drive a man crazy. You watch out for those Texas folks, though. They don't take much stock in this desegregation business. Texans are awful notorious for bein' narrow-minded."

Clem grinned at the old man. "Sure am glad I'm livin' up here, with all you broad-minded types, Sprout."

But if the town felt negative about Clem, or the spectacle of Clem and Sally, or Clem with some other girl, it really disapproved of Clem and Lulu Uranga, Woody Klein's waitress.

In a way, Lulu was almost as much of a pariah as Clem. Like Clem—or at least until he had gotten the Harley fixed—she tried to maintain fairly low visibility, which was not easy considering the two hundred and twelve pounds she carried. Lulu technically at least was retired from whoring. In practice, she saw four or five men from time to time, including Orly Mendocino, who owned the gas station. Lu and her date would go to one of the motels on the highway outside Chama. For this she accepted small gifts, like a five-dollar bill or a sack of groceries. Such gestures helped, because it was hard for Lu to feed herself and the kids she still had at home on what she got from welfare, food stamps, and the little she earned at the Emerald Bar. Yet everyone condemned her. It made no difference that she ran a strict home and was a good mother, or that her kids did well at school—in fact, Danny, her eldest, who never came home to visit anymore, was on a straight scholarship in business administration down at UNM. The fact remained: in the minds of many, every town had its whore, and that person was Lulu. She knew Brazos, and knew enough to live quietly. At the Emerald, she was cheerful and gregarious, but away from it she minded her own business, as if she wished for nothing more than to be left alone. Even so, there were those who had it in for her. Like the time two

years ago when somebody long-distanced the welfare office down in
Espanola to complain that she was violating federal regulations by
taking welfare and working at the Emerald. The case was investigated, and Woody Klein proved Lulu innocent by opening his books
—actually, Woody paid her in cash. Woody was mad as hell about
the whole thing, and tried to find out who had ratted on Lu, but that
kind of business was hard to pinpoint. There was talk that Horacio
Quintana might have made the call, or Orly Mendocino's wife, but
then, it could have been a dozen others. Whatever, it was one more
reason why Lu had to watch her step.

Clem, with his ability to watch and listen, probably knew a little
of this, but it was not the sort of thing he would have attached importance to. What happened was that he spotted Lulu around two
o'clock one afternoon as she was walking to work, and he invited her
for a ride on the Harley. Clem liked Lu. In the Emerald, she always
had a grin for him. Would put an arm around his shoulder and tell
him how handsome he was, and ask how his life was going. To
him, she was another of life's misfits, a loser who was never going
to make it, getting by as best she could, and none too well at that.

Lulu, a little fearfully, got on the machine. Perhaps she thought
he was merely going to ride her to the Emerald. Instead, Clem took
her all over Brazos. By then Lu was letting out wild shrieks of
enjoyment and terror. The sight of them was something. The lanky,
brown-skinned troublemaker and the obese town prostitute. Both
of them howling and carrying on as if they hadn't a care in the
world. Once again, the telephones began jangling. Clem alone, on
that noisy beast of a machine, was enough to cause a stir of indignation, but Clem and Lu together, well, that was a downright insult!
By evening, the only person around who didn't feel outraged was
Sally Benavidez. She figured Lulu Uranga was no kind of competition at all.

CLEM WAS FRYING eggs in the big cast-iron skillet. He was feeling
irritable. Jesse too was in his customarily cheerful mood. He peered
over Clem's shoulder and said, "Why in flamin' hell d'you have to
cook eggs like you was usin' a weldin' torch?"

"Stove's hot."

"No one asked you to ram in thirty damned pounds of wood! Small wonder it's hot! You makin' breakfast or tryin' to smelt iron ore?"

"Kiss my ass, ol' man."

"How come the coffee ain't ready yet?" Jesse demanded. "First thing any idiot knows is to put on the pot."

"There it sits," Clem said, nodding toward the sink counter. "You don't look helpless. You want coffee, hump your lazy ass over and get it yourself for a change."

Jesse loaded the old percolator and put it on the stove. "How come you got to go struttin' around all over the goddamn place in those fancy red jockey shorts?" He snorted with disdain. "It's disgustin'! No civilized person wants to look at some freak like you, all kinky hair, prancin' around half the day with a big hard-on."

Clem glanced down and laughed. "Shoot, Sprout! You call *that* a hard?"

"Git control of yourself!"

"If you wasn't so ancient and didn't have to squat to pee, you'd know what a real hard looked like."

"All cock an' no brains! All you coloreds is the same."

Clem snapped a forefinger and thumb. "Sprout, a hard has *value*. It's better than bein' rich and famous." He grinned. "None of which *you* is, by a long shot."

"Vanity," Jesse grumbled. "That's all you got goin' for you. Figure you need a yardstick, when a magnifyin' glass would do the job nicely. All vanity. Just like the mouse climbin' up the elephant's leg with rape in mind. Git you a real woman, your ass'd be suckin' wind till next Fourth of July. Think you're something."

"I'm beautiful," Clem said, still grinning. "Don't talk at me about hards. That is something I know about. When I am genuinely in that condition, I am something else again, ol' man. Folks, they come from miles around with tape measures and Instamatics! Ol' Clem, he is a stand-up legend! In my splendor, I am splendiferous! *Every*one bows to Clem! I have beauty written all over my soul, in gilt-edge capital letters that say, 'Watch out, here he comes!' The whole world sits up and takes notice. Ladies gasp and faint dead on the spot, and I has to hand round rolls of paper towels to mop up the drool! Drag queens stand in line an' scratch each other's eyes out, waitin' for a chance to take me to Tahiti, Sain' Tropitz, anywhere! Sure wish you could get a hard, Sprout. You'd probably pass out with delight."

"In my day I had my turn."

"Back when the niggers was freed."

"Them eggs is frazzled all to hell," Jesse complained, coming over to the stove again. "I hate and despise eggs all frizzled round the edges with Irish lace. Sonuvabitch, the way you cook, they look like eyes set down in some old maid's embroidery! When are you goin' to learn to cook an egg gentle? Git that toast. Can't you see it's smokin'? That newfangled toaster ain't worth a shit. Can't you be civilized for once? That's what comes of being raised in the gutter your whole life. Hell! Might as well do it myself. Horse needs shoein', you don't hire a plumber. Git the hell out'a my way."

Clem went over and sat at the table. Then bent over on the chair, clutching his stomach.

Jesse said, "What in Christ's name's the matter with you?"

"Stomach," Clem muttered. "I got a chill." For a fact, his naked shoulders and back were goose pimpled.

"Eat some chow, you'll feel okay."

"Ain't hungry."

"Eat anyhow."

An hour later, Clem had made four trips to the outhouse and was feverish. Jesse put him to bed. Clem complained. He had never in his life been really ill. Jesse said, "You do look a touch peaky, I reckon."

"Just feel low, that's all," Clem said. He retched. Jesse got a pot, and Clem threw up into it. Mostly sour bile and slime, and a bit of the eggs and toast he'd fooled with.

"Probably appendicitis," Jesse said.

"God, I never done that before—throwin' up," Clem groaned. "Could hold my liquor, could hold my snort, could hold my motherfuckin' own." He threw up again. Sank back weakly on his pillow. Beads of perspiration on his brow. "Anyplace, anytime, Clem could hold his own. 'Cept here in Brazos. Why'd I ever come to this place?"

"Could be ulcers," Jesse said. "Might even be blood poisonin' or lockjaw."

"I'm dyin'."

"Probably it's just the summer flu," Jesse said. "Just shut up for a while." He made tea. Went down to Gus's for cans of Coca-Cola and Pepsi. "Coke's better than paregoric or any of them fancy medicines for cementin' your guts. Drink some, boy. Pretty soon, those bowels of yours'll freeze up tighter'n a bull's ass in a Montana blizzard."

When Patsy heard, she came over with a giant martini. She said, "It does wonders, Jesse, it really does." Jesse drank most of it, and let Clem have the rest. It gave him a buzz, and he felt a little better.

Garrison came in with a thick sheaf of wild parsley he had found somewhere, and said, "Stew it, Jesse, and have him drink the broth. Natural diuretic. Use it myself. Tones up the entire genito-urinary tract."

Werner came too, with a concoction of beef bouillon, rock candy, bourbon, caraway seeds, and basil strained through cheesecloth. "This helps. The formula goes back to the seventeenth century."

Sally Benavidez did not come. Instead, she went on a date all the way to a Santa Fe drive-in movie with Connie Aragon.

At his most miserable, Clem kept insisting that he wanted to die.

"Wish you would," Jesse said.

"Lot you'd care!"

"That's right."

"You don't care!"

"What you lookin' for, sympathy?"

"I feel awful."

"I've felt worse," Jesse said. "One time, in 'fifty-seven, I got pleural pneumonia and the sciatica, all at once. Came down with emphysema while I was at it. I hurt so goddamn bad I thought I was goin' to croak, and was afraid I wasn't. 'Course, I come from good stock—I'm naturally tough—elsewise, I'd've died for certain. Even so, I was so sick they put me in the hospital, and I didn't even care! Only time in my whole life I was in a hospital. Can't say I enjoyed it. Everybody in there was either dead or dyin'. That's all any of 'em thought about. You couldn't tell a joke or play checkers or do nothin' in that place, 'cause it would distract folks from doin' their dyin'. That was the year your grandma passed away. She had cancer. It was horrible."

"Can't we talk about something else?"

"I never got back my old strength after I got out'a that place," Jesse said. "The whole time I was there they wouldn't let me smoke or have a drink or do anything except lay there all day, watchin' 'em drop like flies from one end of that ward to the other. In the two weeks I was there eleven died, and at that the nurses told me it was the slow season. I wondered how much overtime the staff got when things got lively, like just before Christmas."

"God!"

"Quit whinin'. I can't abide a complainer. You don't know what sick is! Little ol' bit of summer flu is all you got. Couldn't kill you with a twelve-pound sledge and a case of dynamite. Now, you take a man my age, he's got to watch out for his health all the time. I ain't got much longer to live, but that don't mean I park my truck in front of the undertaker's any more'n I have to. I take care of myself."

"You sure do, by smokin' like a chimney and boozin' like it was goin' out of style," Clem said.

"Goddamn it, a feller my age deserves a few pleasures in life, don't he?" Jesse went out and came back with a thermometer. He shook it down, and put on his spectacles to peer at it.

Clem eyed him. "What you fixin' to do with that?"

"Well, it ain't for takin' blood pressure," Jesse said. "It's for temperature."

"Oh no you don't."

"What the hell's the matter with you?"

"You ain't stickin' that up me. Forget it!"

"Put it under your tongue, then. And don't bite down on it. They say mercury and ground glass ain't good for the system."

"Where'd you learn about temperatures?"

"Many's the time I took your daddy's," Jesse said. "When he was little he was always sick with one thing or another. Measles, whooping cough, chicken pox, hives, you name it. Every other week he'd bust out in spots. It got so when he wasn't ailin' we had to look at him three times before we could figure out who he belonged to."

Clem's temperature was 103°. When the task was finished, he asked, "Was he really as bad as you claim he was, Sprout?"

"Who?"

"My old man."

Jesse shrugged. "He was no worse than most, and mebbe a little better than some I could name. Your grandma doted on him. Yes, she did. Guess when a woman's only got one to mess with, that kid'll git the biscuits and gravy and the juicy part of the meat."

"But you never dug him?"

"Never gave it much thought," Jesse said. "First he was a baby, and then he was a little kid. I was always too busy to pay him much attention . . . ranchin', runnin' a chuck wagon. I was away from home a lot in those years. Then he got bigger. Then he went off. We never saw much of him after that. Then he died." The old man frowned. "I don't like thinkin' about things I can't do nothin' about. It ain't good to think too much. All that's in the past anyways. There ain't nothin' to be done about it. What the hell do I want to go thinkin' about stuff like that, that happened years ago? Ain't goin' to make nothin' different. I reckon you just go on with what you been doin'. Now, shut up. I got enough on my hands with you. I got to doctor you, like it or not. You just lay there in that bed and do what I tell you. I'm goin' to make you a hot mustard-plaster poultice. That'll suck the flu out of you in no time flat."

Clem didn't know what a mustard plaster was, but he found out. He bared his chest to a large square of wool that Jesse had coated with a heated mixture. At first, it felt comfortably warm. Then it got hot. Then it got flaming hot. Clem started complaining. "Ain't it been on long enough? I'm breakin' out in a sweat all over!"

"Be quiet. That's just the heat drawin' the poison out of your system."

"Take it off! It's burnin' me up!" Clem's eyes had started streaming tears. "What'd you put in this?"

"Powered mustard. Vinegar. Vicks VapoRub. Tabasco. Dash of turpentine. Pepper. If you ain't got turps, kerosene does nicely. You boil it up until it gives off a nice aroma. Then you slap it on while it's still smokin'. It's an old-time remedy. Cure anything from warts to the clap."

Clem managed to endure it for another fifteen minutes. Then he tore it off. "Look at my chest!" he yelled. "What've you done to me?" The skin was badly inflamed.

"That heat'll drizzle right down into your lungs and kill all the germs," Jesse said.

"I'm scarred! Look. I'm all burned."

"Cleans the pores, don't it?"

"You ol' son of a bitch. I'm ruined."

"You just cover up and tuck in," Jesse said. "Real soon, you'll feel lots better."

And Clem did. The chills abated. He slept awhile, then wakened and made a few more trips to the outhouse. He drank more Coca-Cola. Jesse took his temperature again. It was down to 99.8°. This time he let Clem have some bourbon with his Coke, along with four aspirin. "I got a natural talent for doctorin' a sick person, if I do say so myself," he told Clem.

"You sure do," Clem said. "By the time you get done curin' a dude, he's not only cured, he's permanently crippled for life! You ever been a doctor for real, wouldn't be none of your patients complainin' about you. They'd all be *daid,* in the cemetery."

Woody Klein brought Lulu Uranga by in his car, and she admired Clem's red-splotched chest and felt his forehead. The cats curled up on the bed, and Jesse brought the color TV in, and they all sat there for a while, drinking beer and watching an afternoon game show. Lulu gave Jesse a paper sack filled with all kinds of shrubs and weeds and foul fungoid growths, and instructed him to cook everything into a soup and feed it to Clem. "Down by Vera Cruz, where I come from, my *mamacita*, she was like a *bruja*, a *curandera*. When people were sick she would walk out in the country by herself, she knew where to look for all the plants that make powerful medicine. She was *famosa*—the famous one! People came from everywhere to buy her medicine."

"God, here we go again," Clem muttered. "I sure am glad I didn't break a leg. You people'd be flippin' coins to see who'd get to amputate!"

IN BRAZOS, AS in Tierra Amarilla, Lumberton, Chama, Cebolla, Canjilon, and other neighboring villages, all of which are poor places, outsiders are generally not welcome. Two non-residents, however, are tolerated. One is the *revisordero,* or "visitor," the welfare caseworker, who authorizes checks and food stamps. The other is Clyde Wugalter, the claims officer from Social Security. Practically everyone else is regarded with suspicion, including tourists, hippies, and other forlorn back-to-nature types, and the rich Texans, with their funny lingo and sly Houston ways, who keep summer cabins on the river. But almost two-thirds of the valley's population is dependent upon the *revisordero* and the claims officer for its food, clothing, and shelter.

This is not to say that local residents are not ready to go out and make a little money on the side. Indeed, they are eager. Brazos people are full of enterprise. But the money that changes hands is always in cash, so that no records are kept, no New Mexico gross receipts taxes paid, as in the case of Lulu Uranga, or Guadalupe Martinez, the mother of the state cop Bill Martinez, who draws Aid to the Disabled and who sells the best homemade tortillas and tamales in the county. When money isn't available, and it often isn't, the barter system is brought into play. Jesse Slade, for example, happened to own an extra forty acres near the river, and had for years leased it to Sammy Lopez, who was a second cousin of Orly Mendocino. Sammy grew pinto beans, corn, and squash on that acreage, as well as rabbits, which were housed in hutches, and through the winter Jesse could be sure that a tithe of anything produced on that land would come to him. Like others, Jesse himself traded and bartered—flour, sugar, lard, coffee, homemade wine, venison or elk, the last of which might or might not have been acquired legally.

So in a small way there was a lively commerce among the people of the valley. All this business was supposed to be a deep, dark secret that at all costs had to be kept from the "outside," because it was common knowledge that any official—state, federal, welfare, Social Security, V.A., or the IRS *bandidos*—was out to rob the poor so that the government could finance bigger atom bombs and moon rockets. Of course, this free enterprise was no secret at all—how could it be when everybody's biggest pastime was gossip? The *revisordero* and Clyde Wugalter knew all about what went on. They said nothing. There was no reason for them to. The entire area was, for a fact, in dreadful economic straits. The citizens of Brazos could have bartered and racketeered, lied and cheated, worked at odd jobs, sold firewood and illegally cut Christmas trees, poached deer and elk from now until doomsday, and still have been eligible for all the state and federal assistance that was available. It was a poverty-ridden place indeed, and if putting one over on all those sneaky bureaucrats down at the state capital and in Washington gave the people some small measure of dignity and satisfaction, well, that was all right.

While Clem was recuperating, the claims officer came to Tierra Amarilla on one of his regular visits. Wugalter used a spare office at

the courthouse—Tierra Amarilla was the county seat—and from
there conducted his business. The day before he arrived, Jesse had
a letter from him at the post office.

Horacio Quintana handed it over and said, "How come *la Seguridad Social*'s writing you at this time of month, Jesse? Ain't time
for your regular check."

"Whyn't you steam the envelope open and find out for yourself?"
Jesse said.

"I bet they goin' to launch an investigation on you," Horacio said
wickedly. "I wouldn't be at all surprised if they did that."

"Why'd they want to do that?" Jesse said, getting angry. "I ain't
done nothin'."

Horacio shrugged his bent shoulders. *"Quién sabe?* Who knows
why the government people do all these things? You know how they
are. Always ready to make trouble for a poor man."

"I know how *you* are," Jesse said. "Nosy humpback! Well, one
thing sure, I ain't done nothin' wrong."

"Maybe 'cause you got that boy in your house?" Horacio suggested.

"What's he got to do with it?" Jesse demanded.

Horacio shrugged again. "How would I know? When the government writes you a letter, it always has a reason, *qué no?"*

Jesse looked defiant, but he grew nervous. Without knowing it,
Horacio had touched a sensitive spot. Jesse didn't want anybody
meddling in his life. Especially the government. Most especially *la
Seguridad Social.* He didn't dare open the envelope in the post
office, but read it out in the truck.

Horacio had been right. The government had an interest in Clem.
The letter from Wugalter said that he wanted to interview Jesse
about benefits California Child Welfare said were due Clem. Jesse
was supposed to bring proof of his own birth, along with the papers
authorizing him to be Clem's guardian.

Jesse didn't like this at all. He stopped for a beer at the Emerald,
and had a conference with Woody about it. "Once it starts, there
ain't no end to that kind'a business. Give the gov'ment a chance, it'll
git into your private papers worse than bark borers in a spruce
viga."

Woody read the letter a second time, and argued the point. "Jess,
all it looks like to me is a routine application. Process it, would be

my advice. You'll pick up some extra money every month for the boy."

"How much?"

"I don't know. The government has to figure that out."

"I still ain't partial to it," Jesse said. "You remember the time Clyde Wugalter got Max Garcia to put in for Medicaid? Old Max hadn't ever been sick a day in his life that I know of, and not two months after he let himself git hooked into that Medicaid racket he got a coronary and dropped dead, right in his zucchini patch. Max was the picture of health, 'cept he had no teeth and was missin' an eye. They never even had time to git him down to the hospital in Espanola. So he never got a goddamn bit of use out'a the money he paid into it. He'd probably be alive today if he'd had the sense to stay away from that Medicaid. That's what comes of lettin' the gov'ment mess with your private life, and that's why this whole country is goin' straight down the drain."

"But, Jess, you get Social Security yourself," Woody pointed out.

"I got it comin', because I paid into it!" Jesse argued. "Even then, I pretty near didn't put in for it. It just gives me the cold chills to sign my name on one of them gov'ment forms. I'm always scared I've signed the wrong thing, and that I'll wake up havin' reenlisted for another three years in the Army. Besides which, Wugalter's askin' me to go to all this trouble and expense to git the boy some money, and who the hell knows how long he'll stick around? That niece over in Germany'll be comin' back one of these days. Then again, he's liable to git antsy and just take off on me any minute. He's threatened to, enough times."

"I think that's just talk," Woody said.

"No, it ain't," Jesse grumbled. "Ever since he got that motorcycle fixed, I never see him anymore. Now he's talkin' about gittin' it legally registered, with a license and all that. You know what that means! He's plannin' something, for sure. I wish to hell I'd never given him that old Harley. 'Course, it was his daddy's. I never did figure he'd git it to work. I got that traitorous Grimmiessen to thank for that!"

"I think Clem will stay," Woody decided.

"Mebbe he will, mebbe he won't," Jesse said gloomily. "Half this town must be takin' bets on whether he will or he won't. And the other half can't make up its mind whether they wish he would, or wouldn't. That damn boy is a walkin' contradiction! And, I got to admit, I feel the same about him. I can't hardly stand it when he's around the house, jabberin' away all the time and hoppin' around an' snappin' his fingers and playin' the radio and the TV both at once, like electricity was free for the takin'. And then when he goes off, it gits kind'a lonesome—I suppose if you live in a boiler factory you git used to the noise after a while—and then I git to worryin' about what mischief he's into, or tryin' to git into. I sure wish he wasn't so pesty. Why can't he live quiet and sensible, like me? But, no, he's so jumpy that bein' around him is like livin' with a houseful of grasshoppers."

Jesse was in a double bind. He needed the extra money Clem's application might bring. But once he signed his name to that paper, the government could follow him right into the grave and make his life miserable. Like most old-timers, Jesse thought a lot about death, and he liked to brag that when his time came he was assured of a decent plot in the National Cemetery, from his military service. When he was in an especially malicious mood, he liked to bug Werner Grimmiessen about this. Werner had a morbid dread of death. "That National Cemetery down in Santa Fe is so clean and neat that it'll be a pleasure to stretch out in it and turn to dust," he would tell Werner, and then add, leering, " 'stead of turnin' into something *edible,* the way you will." And it was true that in the little Brazos cemetery the latter was more likely. In addition to the cheap headstones and wood crosses, which were adorned with ornate bouquets of plastic tulips, roses, and geraniums, the cemetery had a thriving population of rats and woodchucks in underground warrens. Some of the local people claimed that the woodchucks had developed an immunity to formaldehyde and simply got drunk on it, but Garrison Hurley said this was impossible, just as he maintained that there was no way for a woodchuck to gnaw through the outer casing of one of Block's Mortuary's guaranteed ninety-nine-year bronze liners. Even so, after a heavy winter's burying, which might take off oldsters and children alike, the woodchucks that sat atop the burial mounds the following spring were fat and contented-looking. As Jesse told Werner, "They didn't git that sleek and sassy munchin' them celluloid geraniums." The old German occasionally had horrible nightmares about this, and then he would park by the cemetery fence and knock off the woodchucks one by one with the Swiss Hammerli target pistol. Once, Jesse saw a couple of twenty-pound

carcasses lying in the back of Werner's pickup, and out of the goodness of his heart offered a woodchuck-stew recipe. Werner turned
pale, and actually got shaky. "To eat something . . . that has been
eating something *else?* Jesse . . . there are limits."

THE NEXT DAY, Jesse appeared at Clyde Wugalter's desk in the
courthouse and demanded, "How much could the kid git?"

"If the application is approved, two hundred and ten a month,"
Wugalter told him, after he looked through his charts.

"Really?" Jesse was astonished. He had not thought it would
amount to so much. He himself got $230 a month. By combining
the two checks he and Clem would practically be living in the lap of
luxury. "Clyde, is that free and clear money? I got to pay taxes on
it?"

"It's free and clear."

"How come that rotten kid is worth pretty near as much as me?
He's never worked a day in his life."

Wugalter explained that the amount was computed on Clem's
father's earnings.

"How long can he git it?"

"Until he's eighteen. Or, if he stays in school, until he's twenty-
one."

Jesse did some mental figuring. That might turn out to be a tidy
sum. After thinking some more, he reluctantly produced the necessary documentation that would authorize him to receive Clem's
checks, and signed the forms. Wugalter explained that the payments
would be retroactive, back to July, when Jesse had gone to California to get the boy.

Jesse left the courthouse, and on the way into Brazos stopped at
the Emerald again. Over a beer, he told Woody the good news.
Woody listened for a while and then said, "It sounds to me like you
don't feel right about something, Jess. That extra money'll come in
handy."

"It will, at that," Jesse said.

Woody stared at him. "Seems to me you're talking like you
feel good, but you aren't acting like it."

"Reckon I'm just tryin' to git my mind clear about things," Jesse
said. Woody did not reply, and after a while Jesse went on. "The

truth is, I don't know how the kid and me would'a made it through the winter, without this new money comin' in to help. He don't know about that. He figures I always got a little something tucked away. And usually I do. But with him in the house I've about used up whatever I held on to for emergencies and such. We're pretty near flat-busted. I was figurin' on chargin' at Gus's through the winter. But with this extra money, we'll be okay, I guess."

"So, what's the problem?"

"I'm thinkin' ahead, that's all," Jesse said. "That niece in Germany may take him off my hands. Then, of course, the checks would go with him. Then again, he might take off on me. 'Course, I wouldn't be stupid enough to report that kind of thing to Clyde Wugalter, less'n he found out first . . . could be, I'd git those checks for an extra year or two before Clyde got wind of it. Wouldn't be like I was cheatin'. Why, I could even say it was a way of gittin' back some of the cash I've already laid out for the kid since he's been with me." He thought some more. "Yes, if he ran away, I'd have decent conditions for a change."

"Well, Jess, I don't have to point out to you that you've said a dozen times that you'd be better off without him," Woody said.

"Quit puttin' words in my mouth," Jesse said irritably. "Goddamn it, it ain't that simple." And then he managed to get it out. "If he stays, we'll just about git by, even with the extra check. But if he goes, I'd worry about him."

Woody stared at him and then nodded. "And miss him too, I guess."

"Mebbe." Jesse looked angrier than ever. "That surely is a puzzle, ain't it?" He stared gloomily out the open front door of the bar to the sunny street outside. "Must be gittin' soft in my old age, I reckon."

"I wouldn't go that far, Jesse," Woody said.

"I got no business lettin' a no-good kid git under my skin. I ought'a be lookin' out for Jesse Slade. Ain't no one ever done any worryin' about *him,* that's for sure!" He sipped at his beer, still gloomy. "That's what happens when a man ignores the strict rules he's laid down for himself; I hate the goddamn gov'ment, and I despise kids, and I got no tolerance for all that sentimental shit women are always blubberin' about. Christ, once a woman gits started with that weepy mush, there ain't no dryin' her up. They git geared up for a good cry, it's like havin' an artesian well on your hands. I can't stand any of that! I got no time for sentiment, and I got no time to be worryin' about someone else. Yet, here I sit! I went against my own rules. I'm in with the gov'ment, thick as thieves. Don't want no kid, yet I'm saddled with a regular nightmare. Worst of all, I fret and worry about him! He'll be the death of me yet. If that don't take all! Well, there's one thing I can tell you, Woody . . . there sure as shit ain't no justice in life!"

FOUR

TOWARD NOON OF the first day of school, Milt Garcia, the sheriff, brought Clem home with a black eye and his shirt in tatters. Jesse was mad enough about the black eye, but he went into a seething rage about the shirt, which was one of the new things he'd bought Clem on the trip to Santa Fe. He yelled, "What in hell happened?"

Clem wouldn't talk. Stood there in a slouch, glowering down at the floor.

Milt explained, "Near as I could make out, Jesse, his class was out behind the school by the track field and something got started."

"What in hell kind of goddamn school they think they're runnin' over there?" Jesse demanded. "Look at him! Lookit his clothes!"

"Now, take it easy, Jesse. Maybe you better take a look at some of the boys he mixed it up with before you start calling names," Milt pointed out. "Tony Sandoval's got a broken nose. Jerry Romero's son's missing a couple of teeth. Five or six other kids are limping pretty bad. School nurse had a busy morning. Old man Tapia, the principal, he says he wants to see you. He told me that if this is the way the school year is starting, he's going to put in for combat pay."

"How many of 'em ganged up on you, boy?" Jesse demanded. "Ain't I told you, you can't take on the whole world?"

Clem glanced up at him and sneered. "You think I'm stupid enough to go after 'em all at once? It started with one. Then it got bigger. That's all. I don't need you watchin' out for me!"

"You sure as hell need somebody," Jesse said. "Kids like that ain't about to fight fair. I'd judge they set you up. Easy pickin's. Got one to start it, then the rest piled on. Oldest dodge in the world. Only a sucker'd fall for it."

"I held up my end," Clem said. He looked almost angry enough to hit Jesse.

"Oh, sure. I can see that," the old man said dryly. "You'd held it up any better, I'd probably have you down at the hospital by now."

Later the two of them had a meeting with Emiliano Tapia, the principal, who said sternly, "If we have any more trouble with your grandson, Mr. Slade, I'll have to suspend him."

"Promises, promises," Clem said.

Tapia stared at him. "You want'a see me suspend you right now?"

"Fine by me," Clem said.

"Consider it done."

"In a horse's ass, he's suspended," Jesse broke in. His mind was filled with half-formed objections. Wugalter, the Social Security snoop, would raise hell if Clem left school. California Welfare might raise hell. Clem might even be taken back to Los Angeles. One thing was certain, nothing good would come of it. He hissed furiously at Clem, "You just sit there and keep that big, flappy mouth of yours shut, if you know what is good for you! I had about enough out'a you!" With that he turned to Tapia. "Don't bullshit me with all this talk of suspendin', Tapia. Ain't no Slade ever been suspended from school, leastways not on the very first day! I want you to find out about those boys gangin' up on him like that! And don't hand me all this horseshit about kids bein' kids! I heard that before. I know some of those boys that Miltie Garcia mentioned. Most of them are thievin', smart-assed juvenile delinquents who ought to have the shit kicked out'a them a few times. That'd straighten 'em up!"

"Running a school isn't easy," Tapia said.

"All I know is, you either run kids, or the kids run you. Looks to me like you got the latter situation here," Jesse said. "It ain't fair! This here's the only black kid you got in the whole damned herd. I heard about this school! You ain't got one teacher with guts enough to stand up to some snotnosed brat, let alone slam that kid a stiff backhand right in the mush when he's actin' out'a line. And the rotten kids *know* it! You don't run this school, Tapia. The kids do. Well, I'm tellin' you right to your face, that don't sit right with me. I ain't about to have this boy railroaded . . . *or* suspended. Not without just cause."

"Sprout, I'm glad enough to be out'a school," Clem interrupted. "Can't we leave it at that?"

"I'll *stomp* you, you don't shut up!" Jesse shouted. "And, Tapia, I'm warnin' you. I know practically all the parents of those hoodlums. If there is any more trouble, I'm goin' to speak to the fathers, and what I'll have to say won't be pleasant. While I'm at it, lemme put another tick in your ear. After I've finished raisin' sixteen different kinds of hell all over this valley, I'm goin' in front of the lousy school board. I'll write the Department of Education down in Santa Fe. I git any more horseshit, I'm goin' to make some loud noises, and it will be the kind of music no one wants to hear." Though he had never voted and was delinquent on taxes, Jesse went on undeterred. "Shit, I been payin' taxes in this county for years, and I am a registered Republican, and if those two items don't carry weight around here, I don't know what does! If this boy is in the wrong for something he done, come talk to me about it. That's fair enough. But if he's in the right, then don't push me too far. I won't have it. I can't say no more than that. Tapia, you suspend this boy, I will file a suit against you personally, as well as the rest of the entire asshole school system for contributory negligence."

"What's that?" Tapia asked worriedly.

Jesse pounded a fist on the principal's desk. "That is when you been derelict in your duty, negligent of the legal responsibilities set on you as principal, an' oblivious to thirty-five different kinds of racial prejudice you got flourishin' right under your nose, here in this school, which, in case you ain't heard about Alabama and Georgia and all those other white-trash states, happens to be against the *law,* so Congress says. I haul you into court, your ass is goin' to be on the choppin' block!"

"You can't threaten me," Tapia said.

"Ain't threatenin'. Merely declarin' my intentions."

Emiliano Tapia finally relented, to the point of agreeing to let Clem back into school on probationary status. He emphatically disclaimed the possibility of anything like racial prejudice and pointed out, "We're all proud of our high school, Mr. Slade."

"You got to be. It's the only one within fifty miles," Jesse said.

"You just have a talk with those boys, and with your teachers too, if they can be called that."

Tapia allowed as how he might do just that.

Walking back to the school parking lot, Clem got it with both barrels. "Oh, I been lookin' forward to this day," Jesse fumed. "All goddamn summer I figured that when school started I'd be rid of you, I'd have a little peace of mind, I figured I could sit myself down in the kitchen and have a cup of coffee and a smoke and watch the TV without no aggravation. I figured you'd be gittin' an educa-tion at last. Your own pa went to this school. Come pretty close to graduatin', too. I figured with you, things might be a touch easier. That just shows how foolish an old man can be. You couldn't wait a month, or even a week, to tear that school apart, not you! Oh, no! Nothing'll satisfy Clem Slade but that he surrounds himself with a major disaster on the first day! The first *mornin'!* How come trouble and calamity sticks to you like glue? I'm too old for this crap."

Clem still looked grim and sullen. "Ol' man, one of these days you'll just up and die. Then you won't have to sweat about me no more."

"I'm looking forward to it, boy."

"You an' me both."

HERMAN RODRIGUEZ, THE coach, was unhappy—in fact, miserable —and utterly confounded. He said, "Can you tell me why in God's name you won't even try out for basketball?"

"Team sports ain't in my line, that's all," Clem said. "I got better things to do than fool with that kid stuff."

Athletic competition was a big thing around the valley, mainly because Chama High ranked 135th out of the state's 137 high schools. In the course of the school year, the basketball team, the football team, the wrestling team, as well as every other kind of team Coach Rodriguez could dream up, including racquetball and soccer, neither of which he knew the first thing about teaching, participated in the regional eliminations, occasionally reaching state-wide finals that were held in Santa Fe and Albuquerque, where Chama High got its balls kicked off by Mickey Mouse teams from nowhere places like Moriarty, Wagonmound, and Truth or Conse-quences.

There were 125 boys and girls at Chama High, who were bused in from surrounding villages. In the junior class, of which Clem was a member, there were thirty-two. Athletically, the pickings were slim.

Clem might be anathema to his classmates and walking trouble to the faculty, but when Herm the Germ Rodriguez, as he was known, got a good look at him, he fell into a worshiping reverie. The way Clem looked, the way he moved, suggested one thing, and one thing only, to Rodriguez: potential star material!

Actually, Coach Rodriguez, who had been born and raised right here in the valley, wasn't the only one to stumble upon this realization. It was pointed out to him by Emiliano Tapia, who got Herman off to one side in the teacher's lounge and had a talk with him, with most of the rest of the faculty, of course, eavesdropping. What old man Tapia had to say went something like this: "You do something with that goddamn kid, Herm. He's right up your alley. I'm counting on you. Get him into athletics. Anything. I don't care. You do something with him, *muy pronto*. Some old man, claims he's the kid's grandpa—had a breath on him like a brewery—is out to make trouble. On top of it, this kid's black. Well, I guess you can see that. We ain't never had to contend with that kind of thing around here before. I ain't sure myself what to do with a black kid, without having the whole NAACP come down on us. I got more problems than I can handle as it is. Keep that kid out of my hair. You may regard that as a definite assignment."

"Yes, sir, Mr. Tapia," Herman said.

Herman loved his job. He had been coach at Chama High for eleven years, and he had tenure. He didn't want to lose his job, and he was also terrified of Emiliano Tapia. Privately, Herman figured he was the best coach in New Mexico, and he was ready to demonstrate this, if only, somehow, somewhere, he could find the right material. That was what he blamed it on: "How much can a coach do, if he doesn't have the right material?"

Herm was a tall, sturdy, dark-complexioned man in his forties, a kind of Spanish version of a Texas good ol' boy. The truth was that he really did work his ass off at being the best coach in the state, but he had no talent for the job, only perseverance. He made ten thousand dollars a year for doing nothing more than producing consistent losers. Still, he loved his work. Nobody in his entire family had ever earned nearly that much, and he had a college degree to boot, from over at Highlands, which was where, so local opinion went, a cretinous one-legged spastic could get an athletic scholarship. Herman worked hard at being coach. He read everything on the profession: knew all about triglyceride levels, oxygen content in the blood, pulmonary functions, and the advantages of a slow pulse. He knew, almost to the millimeter, the measurements of every boy on all his teams: biceps, thighs, neck, and calves. In his pep talks he did everything but get down on his knees and beg the kids to win. But they never did. When it came to losing, his teams were not merely tenacious, they were dedicated. Herman held on to his job largely because his family had a few political connections, and because no other coach in the entire country wanted it. Now, his job was imperiled because some dumb black *coyote* had cruised in from Southern California. He assured Mr. Tapia, "Don't worry. I'll shape him up in no time."

The more he thought about this task, the more enthusiastic he got. All he knew was that Clem had gotten into a terrible fight on the first day of classes, but now, as he eyed Clem in the school corridors, it became clearer and clearer: the boy *was* a natural athlete. Herm began to have visions of the fame that might come his way. The possibilities almost made him dizzy.

Which was why Clem was finally called to Herm's office. The coach was all smiles. But the enthusiasm vanished when Clem refused to cooperate and said, "Team sports ain't in my line. I got better things to do."

"But you're a natural!" Herman insisted.

" 'Course I is! Don't need you to tell me that!"

"Hasn't any other coach said the same?"

"Never hung around school long enough to listen," Clem said. "Ain't fixin' to hang in here any longer'n I have to, either."

"You could be a star player."

"Don't care about any of that."

"What do you want?"

"Bein' left alone to do my thing, mainly."

"Ain't you got pride?"

Clem stared at Herman for a long moment. Finally he said, "Sure. I got pride."

"No team spirit?"

"I am a team of one," Clem said. "That's the way it happens to be, man."

"Slade, I have to tell you, you got the wrong attitude."

"That's too bad."

"You want to be the most hated student in Chama High?" Coach Rodriguez argued.

"Figure I'm the most hated man around here already," Clem said.

"You have *star* potential."

"You talkin' to the wrong man."

"Copping out don't make you feel bad?"

"I ain't askin' anything from nobody here," Clem pointed out. "And I ain't givin' nothing, either. I'm my own man."

When Herman reported back to Emiliano Tapia, the principal shook his head. "That kid is big and strong. I'll bet he could really move on a football field."

Herman looked dejected. "I ain't had a chance to put a stopwatch on him, but I'd say you're right. He can move. He's got coordination, and power. Offhand, I'd guess we might have a teen-age combination of O. J. Simpson and Muhammad Ali on our hands." This concept was too much for him to endure. He gritted his teeth with frustration and said, "God! Right here! At Chama High! What material! A kid like that comes along maybe once every thirty, forty years! Right here! *And he won't even try!*"

Not even Sally Benavidez could sway Clem. When she heard of his refusal, she told him, "You'd look so sexy and gorgeous out there on the field in a uniform."

"I am sexy and gorgeous already," Clem pointed out. "Uniform don't mean nothin'. The body underneath is what counts. Oh, I don't mind watchin' the games on TV. They're okay to look at."

"You're just scared of getting hurt out there," Sally said.

"You know better than that," Clem said. And she did. So did all the other students. No one—not for a long time—was going to forget that fracas on the first day of school.

In a sense, though, there was no point in Clem's arguing, since P.E. was a required subject. So he finally ended up in the gymnasium every Tuesday and Thursday afternoon, working out with the barbells, to the utter disgust of Herm Rodriguez.

His attitude in class was no better. Within two weeks after school started, his pattern for the rest of the semester was set: in Spanish, algebra, science, and shop, he got straight A's. In subjects like social studies and English, he got D's and F's.

All his teachers agreed with the counselor's evaluation of Clem: he was bright, inattentive, cocky, arrogant, lazy, rebellious, profane if badgered, did not accept orders well, if at all, related poorly to his peers, and was antisocial.

This seemed to suit Clem. He stayed a loner, except, as he had promised Sally, he worked up a nice little six-for-five trade. Marijuana and pills, he stayed away from. The only apparent act of kindness to come from him was in helping Sally with her algebra homework—she had no kind of mind at all for that, and her teacher was pleased to see her assignments improve from D's to B's. Toward the rest of the student body, he affected a kind of cool disdain. This did not make him sought after, but at least there were no more fights. It wasn't that Clem was more at peace with the situation. Nobody wanted to mess with him.

ONE EVENING AFTER dinner, Clem and Jesse were drinking beer and playing checkers on the kitchen table. The cats were curled up by the stove, enjoying the heat it threw. Clem said, "Y'know, Sprout, I just ain't hackin' it here."

"Could be worse, boy," Jesse said. "You ain't doin' so bad."

"Worse like how?"

"Things can always be worse," Jesse said. "So I'm told."

"I got a cravin' to move my feet. I'm restless."

"Kids usually are."

"I mean, I'm out'a my element here. I been thinkin' of splittin' again."

"Do that, they'll fling you back in the *calabozo, pronto*," the old man warned. Clem made a double jump on the board and got his piece crowned. He usually won three games out of four. Jesse said, "Damn it, quit distractin' me with all your talk! Every time I git something lined up, first thing you do is start jabberin' and intentionally distractin' me, so's I can't concentrate. How long you been thinkin' about runnin' off?"

"Couple of weeks."

"Sweat it out, is my advice," Jesse said. "You'll be eighteen in less'n two years. Like I said, it could be worse. It ain't so bad here. We got us a house, and food and clothes on our backs. A little money comin' in regular. That's heaps more'n lots of folks have."

"High style," Clem said, shaking his head. "Besides, if I take off, they got to catch me first."

"They usually do. Sooner or later."

"I been a lot of bother to you."

"Truer words was never spoke," Jesse said. "But I guess you could'a been worse. Don't quite know how, but I guess it could'a been worse." He moved a piece. Clem jumped him again. Jesse said, "Ain't no fun playin' with you. This here is supposed to be a sportsmanlike kind'a game. I sure hate cutthroat checkers." He studied the board. He had two pieces left, against Clem's six. "You decide to take off, where you figurin' on headin'?"

"Ain't made up my mind yet," Clem said. "No place in particular. Just movin' along, y'know kind'a seein' what comes down."

"I know that feelin'."

"You ever felt like that?"

"More'n once. Mostly when I was a lot younger. Young feller likes to see different places. Do different things. Just for the hell of it. That's natural. Like you said, 'just movin' along.' " He stared at the mess he'd made of the game, trying to figure what to do next. "I hope you don't go, boy. I'd have to say that. Trouble seems to just follow you along."

"I'd be lookin' both ways, Sprout," Clem said. "I can take care of myself."

"Oh, I heard that kind'a talk before," Jesse said. "Heard plenty of it from your daddy. Used to talk that way myself." He fiddled around, drank some beer, tried to get up nerve enough to move one of his kings, then, finally, did. Clem moved a piece of his, starting to line up the final slaughter. Jesse said, "I guess I'd miss you, if you go."

"I'd stay in touch."

"That's what your daddy used to say. But he never did. He just took off, and that was the end of him. I never even knowed he was dead until I got that letter from the authorities in California. He just went off when he was seventeen. I never even learned whether he had himself a good life or a bad one. He come back here twice during all those years. Never stayed around more'n a day or two. Too nervous. To hear him tell it, he was on top of the world. A big-shot success, drivin' those semi rigs. Lots of money in his jeans, he claimed, though I never saw more than a few tens and fives. Shoot! It was like he didn't know how to come out and say he was nothin' more'n a plain ol' garden-variety truckdriver who was down on his luck most of the time. It was like he was tryin' to impress me or something. As if I cared! He got on my nerves with all that talk. Your daddy, he was one of these fellers you had to listen to real careful, to figure out what he was tryin' to tell you. All that braggin' about how things was goin' so swell for him. I knew better. His hands shook a lot. He was an awful edgy feller, couldn't sit still for two seconds. Always walkin' up and down, so moody an' restless, talkin' up a storm about himself. Last time he stopped off I could tell he wasn't takin' proper care of himself. Goin' downhill, I could see that. 'Course, I didn't talk to him about it. Wasn't none of my affair. He was losin' all his hair, and most of his teeth had been pulled. He wasn't even forty. It made me feel real bad inside to see a young feller like that just goin' all to pieces, not takin' any kind of care of himself. We all got to git old. But he was old already, and he wasn't even forty."

"That's how I remember him too," Clem said.

"When'd you see him last?"

"Must've been four, five years ago, I guess. I was in a foster home by then."

"Well, he was your daddy," Jesse said.

"That ain't enough," Clem said.

"Mebbe so."

"He never did a goddamn thing for me that I can remember."

"Could be some truth in that, boy."

"Hell, *you* done more for me than he ever did."

"He was still your daddy."

"That don't signify nothin'," Clem insisted. "It don't have any meaning at all. He never gave a shit about me. So why should I feel anything for him? All he ever looked out for was himself. I don't buy this crap about paying him respect because he was my old man, Sprout. Nossir! Don't mean nothin'. Can't trust that kind'a person. On the street, you don't trust nobody. Man on the street, he starts trustin' the wrong dudes, he is settin' himself up for a real fall. This talk about him being my ol' man, you know what that is, Sprout? It's just a hustle. All that fucker ever did to be my daddy was hustle my momma. So, when I come along, he hustled me too. He sure did. Right out'a sight. I got no respect for that, Sprout. If he was alive and sittin' right here with us, I'd tell him so. And you know what? He'd sit right here and take it. Why? Because he'd know I was speakin' true words." Clem moved another king, and Jesse saw that he'd been trapped again. The game was about over.

"I wish I could tell you that you was wrong, but it could be that you're right, boy."

"I know goddamn well I am."

"Well, I'm sorry you feel so bad about him. For a kid, you ain't really that bad. You sure keep my nerves all jangled up, but I kind'a got used to havin' you around. I still hope you change your mind . . . about leavin' an' all that."

"You goin' to tell anybody I'm thinkin' about it?"

"Ain't goin' to tell nobody nothin'," Jesse said. "You ought'a know me better'n that by now. The way I see it, if someone's made up his mind to do something, ain't nothin' in the world goin' to stop him. Clem, how can I keep you here if you don't want to stay? Chain you to the stove? Mean-assed kid like you would probably chaw through a loggin' chain with his bare teeth. No, I wouldn't tell nobody. Fuck 'em! Ain't any of their goddamn business. I hate those nosy bureaucratic bastards, one an' all! You do this, though. When you git ready to go, tell me. I got a few bucks to give you. These days a feller has to have a little cash in his pocket if he's goin' to move around. Then I want to write a letter for you. I'll make up some kind'a story to put in it, something like that I'm authorizin' you to visit a sick uncle in California, or wherever you figure on headin'. It won't be fancy, but it might help a little if you git stopped. You're goin' to need all the breaks you can git."

Clem jumped Jesse's last two pieces. The old man said, "You play checkers like a man in charge of a firin' squad . . . no mercy at all."

"Why in goddamn hell don't you learn to pay attention?" Clem said. He seemed irritated by the way the game had gone. "Before I turn my back on this town, I intend to sit you down and teach you this game *right*."

BEFORE THE END of the week Jesse got a letter from Clara Jenkins, the niece whose husband was a colonel in the Air Force in Germany.

The gist of the letter—typed on stationery with a gold-embossed letterhead that read "Colonel & Mrs. Edwin P. Jenkins, USAF"—was that she and her family (husband, three teen-age girls, the oldest of whom would enter college this year) would be returning to

Colorado Springs by winter, where the Colonel would be assigned to some kind of communications program. It also said that at the present time she felt uncertain about the idea of legally, or informally, "fitting another child into an already active and busy household."

She concluded by saying that she would take the matter up "in greater detail," with her husband. In any event, no final decision could be reached until they returned to Colorado, at which time further discussion, and perhaps a visit, could be arranged.

Jesse told Clem, "Didn't I tell you! Christian spirit comin' out'a her ears! Probably studies the Bible when she's parin' her toenails."

"When was the last time you saw this lady, Sprout?" Clem wanted to know. He was bothered by a growing suspicion.

"Clara? Oh, not since she was real little. Maybe four or five," Jesse said.

"You ain't seen her since?"

"I git Christmas and Easter cards from her, every single year," Jesse said. He went to one of the kitchen cupboards and rummaged in a shoebox full of old papers. "Here. See for yourself. This come last year."

Clem looked at the Kodacolor greeting card. Saw the Jenkins family lined up beside their Christmas three. The Colonel, in uniform, big, beefy, bespectacled. Their children, all three grinning at the camera, one of them wearing braces. And Mrs. Jenkins, in a red sweater and green slacks, hands clasped behind her back. "She's growed some, of course," Jesse said. "For a fact, looks like she needs a shoehorn to hop in the bathtub."

"She sure is white."

"Well, hell, you flamin' knothead, 'course she's white," Jesse said. "What'd you expect her to be, covered with purple and green polka dots?"

Clem was amused. He stared at Jesse. "When you first wrote her about me, you didn't, I suppose, happen to say anything about me bein' part black."

Jesse got indignant. "How in hell was I supposed to tell her about that? I didn't know about it myself until I got out there in California."

"And in that letter you wrote last month—I don't recall that you mentioned it."

"Slipped my mind."

Clem laughed delightedly. He shook his head. "And all this time, you been countin' on this fat ol' white chick to take me off your hands? She ain't laid eyes on you since she was a kid, and you think she's goin' to walk in here and fall all over herself doin' you a favor? Oh, Sprout! And you talk about *my* sweet-talkin' ways! You can sweet-talk yourself better'n anybody I ever seen! You ol' fool! You know what's goin' to happen? This chick, Clara, she's goin' to take one look at me an' disappear in a cloud of dust the like of which you never seen. Bye-bye, baby! Been nice seein' you. See you again. Sometime. Don't call me, I'll call you. Like maybe never. Oh, Sprout! You are something else again!"

"Why're you takin' that kind'a attitude?" Jesse demanded angrily. "She's a real decent lady. One time she wrote on her Christmas card how she and her husband were all involved in some kind'a CARE program with a little Vietnam girl. She sends that kid food and clothes and all kinds of things, and it ain't even hers. Never even seen the kid."

"You dummy, that's it exactly!" Clem pointed out. "That little 'Nam chick is about eight thousand miles away. Kid ain't sittin' right there in their lousy livin' room with her feet propped up on the coffee table, wigglin' her toes and munchin' popcorn and watchin' the Saturday cartoons. What's more, that 'Nam kid ain't no six-foot-four, brown-colored, flap-mouthed, spade-stud jungle bunny who's lean and mean, cool and cruel. Oh, *wow!* And this Clara's got teen-age girlchicks on top of it, lookin' like they're hot to trot! Sprout, what am I to her . . . some kind'a one-eighth nephew or something? She ain't goin' to look twice at me. You tellin' me you *serious?* Get off it!"

"Why're you gittin' all steamed up?" the old man argued furiously. "It's months yet before they git to Colorado. Don't fret so. If it doesn't work out, why, then, it doesn't. You can hang in here with me, like I been tellin' you to. If you'd ever git your ass in gear, why, I bet you could rustle one of them college scholarships or something."

"Sprout, quit connin' me. You tryin' to insult my natural intelligence?" Clem demanded. "You think I don't dig you like havin' me around so's you can collect that extra Social Security money?"

"It all gits used up on you. And more besides!"

Clem lost his temper. "You playin' both sides of the street, ol' man," he yelled. "You get my government money, and on top of it you has a servant too! Shit, you just lookin' for a *slave*. Chop the firewood! Clean out the stove! Rustle up some dinner! Wash the dishes! Sweep the floor! Sprout, who was your nigger 'fore I come along?"

"I was my own nigger," Jesse yelled back. "The wood got chopped and the stove got cleaned and the floor was swept, and damn it to hell, I lived quiet and sensible, had some peace, didn't have to listen to your bullshit. All you done since you got here is complain."

"*You's* the complainer, not me!"

"I don't complain," the old man argued. "It ain't in my nature."

"Do, too!"

"Don't, neither! God, how'd I ever git myself into this mess?"

"No one asked you to."

"That's what I git for tryin' to do right. Ain't worth the effort, for all the thanks I git."

"Don't trouble yourself no more, then," Clem said. "Pretty soon I'll be gone. For good!"

"Well, what you waitin' for, *applause?* Just go! Don't sit around forever, just talkin' about it. Go on, leave! See if *I* care."

"Well, then, I will."

"There's the door! It ain't nailed shut! Pack your gear! I don't give a good rat's ass!"

"All you complain about is how you was your own man 'fore I come along," Clem said, sneering. "Ol' man, that is a back door that swings both ways! Be good to be *my* own man again, for a change. I took care of myself for years. Long before you come stickin' your ugly ol' honky nose into my affairs!"

"Go on! End up in the penitentiary," Jesse said. "Serve you right."

"Wouldn't bother me none. I know what the slammer's like."

"I give up! I'm washin' my hands of you."

"Motherfuck this whole asshole scene! Motherfuck you too, ol' man!"

"Don't use that lowlife nigger street talk in this home!"

"Call this a home? Call this *livin'?*"

"You don't shut up, I'm goin to bend that fry pan around your skull," Jesse warned. "I will! Don't push me. I'll fetch you a clip you'll remember. You'll think you got bells and gongs and chimes goin' off inside your head for the rest of the month!"

Clem slammed out of the house. Walked around for a while in the back fields, his shirt collar turned up against the chilly September wind. Finally, he went to the outhouse and sat down to be by himself for a while. He was still an outcast. He knew this. And there was no one to be trusted. Not anywhere. He was unwanted, and unneeded. Again and again, that had been demonstrated. He'd be better off on his own. No one cared. Nothing mattered.

For the first time since he was a small boy, Clem found himself crying. The experience was so strange that he was left feeling miserable and ashamed. In the world he knew, no one wept. Women sometimes did, but not a street man. All of a sudden, he felt really low and bad and sad. Shot down. The tears kept on. He leaned his head against the wall of the outhouse and sniffled quietly to himself.

"I'M THROUGH WITH all this," Clem told himself the next morning. It was Saturday. Loafing around the house, he began to put together some plans, not speaking to Jesse any more than he had to. And for a change, the old man was relatively uncommunicative. A silent armistice of sorts.

By the time Jesse left to get the mail later that morning, Clem's thoughts went so: "It's time to go. The Harley's got a legal plate on it, and I got a license. I got almost three hundred. No sense hangin' round this place. I can make it all the way to L.A. Start out fresh. Be good to see that ol' town again. No Sally. Don't need *that,* for sure! Wouldn't mind havin' Gus's receipts, like she promised. I could strong-arm it off her and dump her on the highway. Wouldn't be no more'n she deserved. This whole town'd have a good laugh on her. But that wouldn't be smart. Use your smarts, Clem."

What was in the back of his mind was that one day—and that day might not be such a long way off—he could have a reason to return to Brazos. The old man was not going to live forever. And when he died, Clem was his only direct heir—he would get the house and the property, including that forty acres on the river. Someday that would be worth something. If he got Sally to rip off her old man, there'd be a warrant out on both of them. Or at least on him. Gus wouldn't let that pass. Sally's offer, though tempting, was a setup only a fool would go for. He thought, "Someday I will come back to this dumb town, and I'll walk right down the middle of Main Street like I own the whole show!"

It never occurred to him—at least not consciously—to think of
Jesse. Just as it did not occur to him to consider why he had wept.
There were a few other things Clem had not gotten around to
analyzing yet. But perhaps this was understandable. The summer
in Brazos had been a new and different experience. The knowledge
of life that he had been able to accumulate during his years did not
encompass much more than he had learned on the streets: hustling,
being kicked around from one foster home to another, being unwanted, and learning to survive.

With Jesse still gone, he packed his few things into the Harley's
saddlebags. No note. No farewell. Just go. He grew a little sentimental when the cats came mooching around. Cochise wandered up
to the door, looking for a snack. Clem ignored him. No farewells
for anyone. Including Sally, Werner, the Hurleys.

He shut the back door of the house, leaving it unlocked, because
no one locked anything in this crazy town, and kicked the bike's
starter. The Harley came to life. He drove out of the back yard
onto the dirt road, with money in his wallet, and a feeling of
grimness, anger, exultation, and, again, for no reason he could
discern, fierce loneliness. Farther down the road, two pickups and
an old sedan moved out, following him.

He stopped at Orly Mendocino's station, to fill the tank and
check the oil and the tires. Orly said, "How you doin', Clem?"

"Top of the world, Orly."

"When you going to start working off that little arrangement we
made when I fixed your grandpa's truck?" Orly asked. "I could
use someone an hour or so a day."

"Pretty soon, Orly." The oil checked, he kicked the motor into
life and let it idle.

The two pickups and the sedan cruised into the gas station. In
the first pickup was Willie Montoya and his brother, Bennie. In the
other was Connie Aragon. Beside him were two guys Clem had seen
around but could not identify. In the sedan were four more men.

Orly Mendocino took two dollars from Clem for the gas and said
in a low voice, "Clem, *amigo,* I think you better haul your ass out
of here, *pronto.*"

Clem was nervous. He said, "I hear you loud and clear." The
only trouble was, he was pretty well bracketed in by the people who
had come to say hello.

Orly's gas station was diagonally across the street from Gus's store. Clem happened to notice that Benavidez was standing out on the porch in front of the place, leaning against a post, arms folded, watching. Just leaning and watching. Sally nowhere around.

Willie Montoya got out of his truck and said, "Hi, man. What you up to?"

Clem said, "What's on your mind, Willie? Who let you out of your cage this early?" At the same time, he realized a mistake he'd made. The .44 was in Jesse's pickup, and the old fool was off someplace, God knows where.

"Wanted to have a talk with you," Willie said.

"How come you got company? They got to do your talkin' for you?"

"Some of the family came to visit," Willie explained. "We had us a party last night." For a fact, Willie and the others with him looked half hung over—or half drunk, it was hard to tell which.

"Should'a recognized 'em for family," Clem said. "They got a strong resemblance to you. Universally ugly."

The men in the sedan had gotten out by now. One of them said, "By God, Willie, he *is* a smartass, just like you said."

"He talks real good," Clem said to Willie. "Almost like an actual human being."

"He's my cousin, Alejandro, from over by Lumberton," Willie explained. "Alex likes to fight. Me, I don't care for trouble. But Alex, he don't mind it at all. Over there, that's Uncle Bill— Guillermo—and my nephew, little Eustacio. We call him Li'l Stuce, 'cause he's so big."

"Who're the others?"

"Friends, happened to look in for a few drinks," Willie said.

"You got that many friends? Never would'a thought it."

Willie said, "Say, we got most of two cases of beer left in the back of my truck. Whyn't you get in the car? We'll go up by the river, and all of us can have a beer."

"Too early."

"Never too early for a beer," Willie said. "Just leave your cycle here with Orly. We'll have us a time."

Clem glanced at Gus, standing on his porch across the street. He said to Willie, "Who put you up to this? Gus?"

"Now why would Gus want to do a thing like that?" Willie asked, grinning.

"Hi, Mr. Benavidez," Clem called. He waved casually to Gus. The storekeeper did not wave back, merely stood there, arms folded. "Sure is a nice day, ain't it?" Clem called. Under his breath, he added, "You fat motherfucker!" To Willie he said, "Want to try it one to one?"

"I don't like trouble," Willie said. "Cousin Alex might take you up on that, though. He likes rough-housing."

Cousin Alex, unshaven, bleary-eyed, was obviously in a sour mood. He said, "Why we talkin' like this? Let's get movin'. Get in the car, boy."

Clem had been glancing about for anything that might be used as a weapon. A tire iron. Even a broom. There was nothing. He said, "How come you waited so long, Willie? Why now?"

"Good a time as any."

"Well, you're wrong," Clem said. "Right in this saddlebag I got Jesse's forty-four. You fuck with me, there's goin' to be trouble." He made a move, unsnapped the clasp on the bag.

Willie was watching. He grinned. "You got something in there?"

"You heard me."

Willie was still grinning. He said to his brother, "You hear that, Bennie? He's got a forty-four stuck down in that bag."

Bennie, enjoying this, reached into the cab of the pickup and took out Jesse's .44. "It look anything like this?"

Clem felt deflated. He said, "How'd you heist it?"

"Leave a truck sittin' unlocked out in front of the Emerald, somebody's liable to look around inside," Willie explained. "You goin' to try bluffing someone, nigger, you ought'a make sure you got something to bluff with. Now, why don't you get in the car. We was just tryin' to be fair with you, you know. Give you a chance. You never should'a come here, never should'a stayed on. You can't say we didn't give you time enough."

"We couldn't take a raincheck?"

"Wouldn't make no difference," Willie said. "You stay on in this valley, we'd get you. Sooner or later. One way or another. Nobody wants you here. You know it. Even a nigger has brains enough for that. Come along now. Party time. Might as well come easy. Else you'll come hard."

Clem looked utterly defeated. He stood there beside the Harley, surrounded by the two pickups and the sedan, and nine men. He said, with what appeared to be a pathetic attempt at humor, "The beer cold?"

"Cold enough."

"You're callin' the shots, Willie."

"Now you're talkin' sensible."

"Lemme just wheel my machine over to the side," Clem said. He straddled the Harley, kicked back the parking stand, and began pushing the motorcycle toward the garage. The others watched.

Then he made his move. Left hand down to the gear shift. Into first. The engine still idling. Someone shouted, "Watch out! He's trying to get away."

The engine revved. Blue cloud of smoke. Foot clutch kicked in. Spray of gravel and dirt. People yelling.

Left boot on the ground. The Harley skidded in a 360-degree circle, spraying pebbles and fishtailing. Orly Mendocino dove for the doorway. Then the rear wheel caught the dirt, found traction, and with a screech of rubber the big bike shot forward.

Straight between the battered sedan and Connie Aragon's pickup. Connie and somebody else leaped out of the way. Cousin Alejandro refused to move. Or was too slow, or dumb, or hung over to think quickly. He stood to one side. Fist cocked. Ready to slug Clem out of the saddle with a single punch.

Clem connected first. A straight-armed punch as he roared past. He never even swung. Cousin Alex went down, poleaxed by a fist attached to a motorcycle.

Connecting with Alex almost tore Clem out of the saddle. The Harley went into a wild skid. But he was out in the street. He got the bike under control, and began moving out. Into second. Revving the engine into a full roar. The others behind him. Some trying to pursue on foot. Others piling into vehicles. Everybody yelling.

Clem almost didn't make it. Three hundred yards down Main Street, by the post office, he went to make the turn that would lead to the highway. Going too fast. Into another skid. This time the bike went out from under him. Stalled out. Spun around on its side. The right leg of Clem's jeans shredded. He was bleeding.

Down the street, Willie and his crowd were starting after him. Clem got up, staggering. Tugged the Harley erect. The right handlebar was bent slightly. He straddled the seat. Kicked at the starter. Nothing.

Kicked again. And again. Muttered aloud, "Werner, ol' man, don't fail me now! Come on, baby! Do your thing!"

The two trucks and the sedan were almost on him by the time

the Harley's engine coughed. Clem hit first again, and gave it the gas. The motorcycle took off. Back up Main Street toward the approaching vehicles. Clem in control of the situation now. Willie Montoya, apparently with real murder on his mind, tried to ram him. Clem took the Harley up on the wooden sidewalk. Gave Willie an exultant finger as he rode past.

Roared down the boards to the end of the street. Right past Gus Benavidez, who took off into his store at a dead run.

By then Willie had hit his brakes. His pickup did a lazy sideways skid and was plowed into by Connie, in the second pickup.

The driver of the sedan, which was moving just as fast, hit the brakes too. It skidded, barely missing the two trucks blocking the street. Hiked up on two wheels for a considerable distance. Sailed through the neat white picket fence that bordered Horacio Quintana's house, taking out most of the postmaster's patch of hollyhocks and marigolds, and finally fetching up against a corner post that held one side of the front porch. The porch collapsed onto the roof of the car. Horacio, who had come out of the post office to see what all the noise was about, screeched, "*Cabrones!* What you shits think you doin'?" He stared at his house and wailed, "*Madre de Dios!*" No one was listening. Almost sobbing, Horacio said, "Who's to pay?"

Back at the gas station, Clem sat on the bike and watched as the two pickups backed up and tried to get turned around. The sedan was completely out of action, its occupants dazedly crawling out the demolished windows.

Spread-eagled on his back near one of Orly's pumps was Cousin Alejandro.

A lot of steam was coming from Connie Aragon's truck. Radiator gone, headlights too. Willie's pickup was turned by now, and was coming slowly back toward Clem. The left front wheel wobbled eccentrically.

Clem decided it was time to leave. He took off down a side street, past Lulu Uranga's place, then turned onto another dirt lane that led behind the post office to the macadam highway into Chama.

IN CHAMA HE stopped to cool off. All kinds of emotions stormed through his mind, fear, excitement, exultation. His hands were trembling, and he felt hard and tight. He had felt like this before, back in Los Angeles. Usually after a fight, never before or during one. He thought, "You sure laid one on 'em, Clement! That was strictly a touch-and-go scene. But you came through, nigger. Yessir! Mightn't be an exaggeration to say you left in grand style. That's the way to do it, my man. Leave 'em something to remember you by."

But another part of him was in a rage. Because one other thing was true. They had, for a fact, run him out of town. Didn't make any difference that he was leaving, had already made up his mind. They'd think different, and they'd brag. That goddamn town with its miserable people. They'd finally gotten what they wanted. Willie Montoya would be a hero. Oh, would he strut and swagger! He'd let it be known far and wide that when a man was needed, it was he who had taken matters in hand. No doubt about that.

Clem told himself to ease back on this kind of thinking. "Stay cool, baby. Let 'em believe what they want. No sweat off you. You're out of it."

Something else nagged at him. But it was hidden so deep in his mind he could never have pinpointed it. The idea was too contrary, but that did not necessarily make it any the less true: he was leaving a place that had become familiar. Brazos! With its dusty dirt streets and motley assortment of crumbling shacks! Damn! In that brief summer, he had gotten used to the town. He thought, "I'm goin' to put some real distance between me and that place. Out'a sight, out'a mind!" Yet he felt nostalgia.

It still had not occurred to him—and with that crippled background he had come out of, why should it—that after Los Angeles and foster homes, and jail, and the D-Homes he'd been in, Brazos was the closest he had ever gotten to anything resembling a family life. Miserable as the place was . . . creepy old Brazos, and that cranky, bitter, complaining Jesse.

That thought was simply too far out. It had to be buried. Clem accomplished this by making plans. He thought, "Handlebar's bent, but she rides okay. Ought'a be able to make it to L.A. in two days. Look out, world!"

He had a long, shallow gash on the calf of his right leg, from the spinout. He drove to a Rexall and bought gauze, tape, and first-aid ointment. Went into the rest room at a service station and cleaned himself up. The torn jeans he had on were a mess of dried blood and caked mud. He discarded these, changed into a clean pair, put on a fresh shirt, brushed off the denim jacket, washed his face, worked on his hair. Emerged from the men's room looking fine and feeling good, except for a limp.

Rode from there to the supermarket, where he bought cheese, salami, cigarettes, and a six-pack. Had a picnic by himself in a small rest area on the north side of town, not far from the high school he had abandoned forever.

He drank four of the beers slowly, and thought. The more carefully he assessed the situation, the angrier he got. He said aloud, "You should'a *told* those freaks you was leavin'. Splittin' for good." But he knew that wouldn't have changed anything. They wouldn't have believed that he had already made up his mind to leave when they cornered him. What rankled most was that Willie and his crowd had gotten what they wanted. "They squashed you, baby. No two ways 'bout *that*." This idea gnawed at him. He could not rid himself of it.

"No one ever put you down," he told himself. "No one did a number on you, baby. Anybody tried that, they was in for trouble. Clem didn't put up with that kind'a shit! Word like that goes around, a man might as well pack up and leave town."

But that was exactly what had happened this morning. And, right now, the word would be going around.

His anger turned to Jesse. "It's his fault," he thought. "If you hadn't been busy listenin' to all his crap, you would'a handled this situation entirely in your own style, and done it right. 'Don't do this.' 'Don't do that.' 'Clem, you behave now!' Ol' peckerhead! All summer long you did what he wanted. Jumped when he snapped his fingers. Well, that was stupid. See what it got you. That's what comes of lettin' people run you to suit their own game. Hell, can't even blame that asshole Willie. You don't show people where it's at, they'll come down on you. Can't blame 'em for that. Willie, he's dumb, but he knew he had you. Right from the start. With that old man callin' the shots, he couldn't help but come out on top!"

One side of his mind kept warning him to lay back and play it cool. He wished he had a joint to mellow him out. The only thing that happened was that he got madder. "Could wrap that whole town round my little finger. Should'a done that from the very first. Listen to somebody else, you get dumped on. Every single time."

He drove the bike over to the supermarket again and got another six-pack and a pint of bourbon. Rode back and drank a little more. And got madder. His thoughts went back and forth. One side saying, "Get out." Other side saying, "Do that, you got no balls."

As simple as that. A no-win situation.

It took him a little more time to get to it. His mind was already made up, though he didn't know it. It went round and round, but always came back to the same thing. "Time has come. The mother-fuckin' time has done come at last. Oh, Clem! It ain't that you're gorgeous. You is rare!" He was working himself into a mood for warfare. But on his terms. Not theirs. "Well, now, just supposin'," he mused aloud. "Now, now, now . . . Wouldn't that be something? Just once. Do it Clem's way! Take that town." In his own fantastic style, oh, wow! That's how a man got respect. In the long run, that's what counted . . . how a dude handled himself. Screw cute-assed Sally Benavidez, Jesse, and the rest of them. He had gotten out of Brazos, but not on his own terms. They had run him out. That's what they'd be bragging about.

When the pressure was really on, a smart dude leaned with it, worked with it, used it to his own advantage. Like in karate, you used the enemy's weight and movement against him. With cops or judges or teachers or psychiatrists or foster parents, he had lied, cheated, and worked every scam he could devise, anything to fight back. You always fought. In the end, there was nothing else left to do.

"Don't wait for 'em to come to you, the way they did today," he thought. "You go to *them*. That's half the fight right there. Take 'em off guard. In daylight. Go after 'em. They wouldn't be expectin' *that,* not after the way they run you off this mornin'."

And then he said it aloud. "By God! Let 'em see, just for once, what a real low-down Los Angeles street man can do! They think they're mean? Shit, they don't know what mean *is!*"

With that, he finished the last of the beer, tossed the can into a bush, mounted the bike, and took off. Not toward Los Angeles, but back down the road to Brazos.

As BAD LUCK would have it, the first person who spotted him as he rode up Main Street was Bill Martinez, who was cruising along in the opposite direction in his prowl car. Martinez recognized Clem at a distance, and stuck his hand out the window, flagging him over. For a moment Clem thought of speeding away—Martinez could never catch him in the car—and then he said to himself, "Trouble comes in threes. First Willie. Now this fat cop. Wonder what'll be next?" He pulled the bike over to the side of the street and sat in the saddle waiting while Bill Martinez swung the prowl car around and drove back.

"Where you been, Slade?" Bill said, getting out.

"No place special."

"I been looking all over town for you."

"Well, here I am."

"Looks like you fucked up again."

Clem stared at him. "What you talkin', man?"

Bill shook his head. "Christ, you never quit, do you? What happened with you and Montoya and the others today?"

"Ask them."

"I did."

"What you askin' me for, then?"

"Thought you might have something to tell me."

"What makes you think I got something to tell *you?*"

"They said you attacked them."

"Shee-it!"

"That's what they claimed the last time," Bill agreed. "Nobody would go up against that crowd."

"You a regular Perry Mason these days, ain't you?" Clem said.

"Don't be so goddamn smart. I talked to somebody else. They said that maybe what happened might have happened a little different from Willie's version."

Clem wondered if it might be Orly Mendocino. He'd been right there at the gas station, all through it. It sure as hell couldn't have been Gus Benavidez. The idea that Orly might have stuck up for him interested Clem. He and Orly got along all right, but he couldn't see Orly sticking his neck out.

Bill said, "There was about two hundred bucks' worth of damage when that car crashed into Horacio's porch."

"You blamin' me? I wasn't drivin' that car."

"I just want satisfaction. It wasn't Horacio's fault that his house happened to be standing in the way when all of you was racing around like maniacs this morning. Willie and Connie, they agreed to come over and fix it."

"They said that?"

"After I talked to them, they did."

"You a sweet-talker, man."

"About as sweet as I'm talking to you right now," Bill said. "Those boys know me. I wish you did too. Also, I got your grandpa's pistol back."

"You frisked 'em?" Clem asked, surprised. "How'd you know it's Jesse's?"

" 'Cause I learned to shoot with that forty-four, when I was thirteen years old. Your grandpa taught me. I got some other items off them too." He stared at Clem. "No guns. I told them that, and I'm telling you the same."

"Listen, why'd you pull me over? I got things to do," Clem said.

"What's your hurry, big shot?"

"I ain't in no hurry. Got nothin' but time. If you got something on your mind, let's hear it. Otherwise, I'll just be movin' along. You want to give me that pistol, I'll see that Jesse gets it."

"It's locked in the car," Bill said. "I'll bring it by one of these days." He was still looking at Clem. "The way you took off on that cycle, I figured maybe they'd run you out of town for good."

"You hear that?"

"It was just something that occurred to me," Bill said.

"Nobody runs me out of any place. Not until I'm ready to go. I don't mind it here. Fact is, I'm gettin' to like this place. Sort'a grows on a person, don't it?"

Bill Martinez considered this. "That's the way you want it, eh?" Clem grinned at him.

"There'll be more trouble," Bill pointed out.

"Trouble for some, not for me," Clem said.

"Could be. Anyway, like I said, I talked with Willie and Connie. Besides fixing Horacio's porch, I told them something else. If they're going to mess around with you, they should do it fair, one man at a time."

"You told 'em that!"

"They agreed," Bill went on. "They know how to listen. I wish you did. I told them I didn't want to hear no more stories about how, just by accident, six or seven of them happened to run into you, and maybe, just by coincidence, a little something got started."

Clem put on an innocent face. "Why, that was real nice of you! Guess I got nothin' to worry about, then."

Bill paused, and then said, "Boy, I want you to understand something. I don't like you." Clem shrugged. "I don't like you at all. I don't want you here in this town any more than anybody else. I wish I'd never set eyes on you. I wish the fuck you had cleared out for good this morning. But here you are. That tells me you ain't smart. To me, you ain't nothing but a boil on my ass." Bill paused again. Then he said, "I just want to see things get done right, that's all. Understand? One of these days somebody in this valley is going to kick the shit out of you. I wouldn't want to hear it said that it took half a dozen guys to do it. You ain't *that* tough. I don't want no guns, and no knives. I figure there must be thirty, forty guys up and down this valley. Sooner or later, every last one of them will get a chance. That ought to keep you busy for the next four or five years at least. And one of them will take you out. That is, if you're dumb enough to hang around that long."

"You think Willie and his buddies will really go at it one to one?" Clem sneered. "You foolin' yourself, man."

"All I told them was that I wanted to see it get done right," Bill said.

"Sure am glad I got the law on my side for a change."

"Don't kid yourself. You don't break any laws here, and you don't get into trouble, I'll leave you alone, and so will Milt Garcia. But don't get the idea that we're on your side." He shook his head. "Nope. I wouldn't go around thinking that. Actually, the way I see it, there ain't nobody will stick up for you. But there ain't no sense talking to you. You'll find that out eventually. Well, you get along now, boy."

JESSE WAS NOT home. Clem put the last of his cold cuts into the fridge, fed the cats, put away the clothing he had packed in the saddlebags, and then wandered into Jesse's bedroom. On top of the bureau was a mess of junk the old man kept handy: a spare set of false teeth, a magnifying glass, loose rounds of ammunition, a couple of half-dried-out jars of "fireballs," or salmon eggs, for fishing when no worms were available, his spectacles, and a jar of quarters for the Laundromat in Chama.

Clem continued wandering around the house, practicing a few of the exercises used in the martial arts—breathing deeply, flexing various sets of muscles, stretching and straining until he could feel some of the joints in his shoulders pop. Physically, except for his injured leg, he felt all right.

From there he drove the Harley over to the Emerald Bar. No vehicles were parked out front. Still too early in the day for the regular Saturday-afternoon trade, but it was here that people came and went, to have a few drinks and pass the time. Here was as good a place as any to wait for Willie and his friends. He walked in, and Woody Klein greeted him from behind the bar. "How's it going, Clem?"

"Not so bad, Woody. You seen Jesse?"

"He hasn't been in all day."

"Anybody else?"

"Early yet."

Lulu Uranga came out of the back storeroom, lugging a case of Coors. "Hi, Clem," she called cheerfully.

"How's it goin', Lu?"

"Oh, always something, you know. Sammy, my youngest, he has the earache," Lulu said.

"Gimme a Coors, Woody."

"You ought to be with Jesse," Woody pointed out. "But okay." He got Clem a beer, and Clem laid a dollar on the bar. "Heard there was some trouble down in town this morning," Woody observed.

"Wasn't nothin'. Folks around here exaggerate."

"That's true," Woody said. "Even so, Clem, I don't know that you ought to hang around here. More'n likely, Willie and Connie will drop in. They usually do, Saturdays."

"They do, for a fact."

Woody glanced at him. "Oh." He paused. "You fixing to have it out with them?"

"That's up to them," Clem said.

"Wish you wouldn't do it here."

"Woody, look at me," Clem said. "I'm cool, ain't I? Trouble starts, it ain't goin' to be me startin' it. On the other hand, I ain't goin' to walk away neither."

"That's what I was afraid of," Woody said.

"Not no more, Woody. I am done with that."

Woody nodded. "I can see how you might feel that way. No one could exactly say you been getting a fair shake of the dice since you been here."

"I ain't even had a chance to roll 'em," Clem said. Once again, he listened with interest. Here was someone else speaking up . . . or almost speaking on his behalf. So maybe the whole village wasn't against him. Ninety percent might be, but that beat one hundred percent. Unfortunately, most of the ten percent was talk. Clem could see that much from the expression on Woody's face. Woody liked him. And Woody was Jesse's friend. But like everybody else, he hated making a choice, taking sides in something like this. It wasn't just that he was afraid of trouble starting in his bar. He simply did not want to be put in the position of coming out and saying he was for or against anyone. Clem said coolly, "Woody, don't you worry. If Willie shows up, you just stay behind that bar and tend to business."

Woody shrugged. He looked worried. "Sometimes I wonder where I ever got the idea of buying this place. I was going to open a radio and TV repair shop after I got out of the Army and Arlene and I got married. But I figured there'd be more money in a bar. And I was right, there is. More gray hair too." He paused. "You sure you wouldn't at least like to park that Harley around in back?"

"It's fine where it is, Woody."

"Like waving a flag under their noses," Woody said, shaking his head.

Clem sipped his beer and then lit a cigarette. He felt calm enough.

And, just then, the door did open. Two men came in, looked the place over, bought two beers at the bar, and then went to a far table at the rear.

One was Anglo, the other Spanish. The Anglo was a tall beanpole, with stringy blond hair that hung beneath a yellow hardhat. The headband of the hardhat was adjusted too small, so that the hat perched ludicrously atop his head. He had a snub nose, gappy teeth, a scraggly moustache that was really nothing more than a couple of droopy wisps, and practically no chin. The Spanish man was about five foot three, and a yard wide, with no fat on him. He wore a big tan Stetson, and was ugly enough to make his Anglo buddy look pretty. Both men were dressed in boots, jeans, T-shirts, and heavy leather jackets. They sat in the back at their table, in the shadows, and talked together in low voices, laughing and kidding around. Seemed real fond of each other. Heads bent close over the table, whispering, and then, the soft laughter. They glanced around at Woody, or Lu, or Clem, like maybe there was something very amusing about them. Clem was getting the idea that they were into something besides beer.

They ordered a couple of fresh ones from Lulu. While Woody was opening the cans, Clem got off his stool and casually wandered over to one of the windows. Parked beside the Harley was a beat-up Ford Econoline van, with Texas plates, wide-track tires, and an exterior that had been sprayed with Day-Glow in a sloppy attempt at van-deco. The van was parked with its rear to the bar and its front facing the highway.

Clem walked back to his stool and sat down. Woody said casually, "I don't think I've seen those fellows before."

"They ain't from around here," Clem said.

"Late in the season for tourists," Woody said.

Clem tasted his beer. "Something tells me they ain't tourists."

"Probably just passing through," Woody said.

"Could be."

"On vacation."

"Ain't on vacation. Those are city dudes."

"How can you tell?"

"I just know," Clem said. He could see that Woody wasn't feeling right about those two. He himself was uneasy. He wondered if what he'd told himself earlier might be true, about trouble coming in threes. First Willie and his crowd. Then that little talk with Bill Martinez. Now this pair.

THE SKINNY BLOND with the hardhat got up, ambled over to the juke, and fed quarters into it. Music came on. He had a taste for taco rock. He kept time with the beat, drumming his hands against his thighs and snapping his fingers. He glanced over at Clem idly and grinned. "Hey, brother, how's it going?"

"No complaints," Clem said.

The man walked over and leaned an elbow on the bar. He looked down at Clem. "Waiting for someone?"

"Could say that."

"We was just wondering," the man said. "We saw you looking out the window just now." Clem said nothing. "You get to see what you wanted?" Again Clem said nothing. "You from around here?"

"No," Clem said.

"Where you from, brother?"

"California."

"What you doing, trucking around way up here in these boonies?"

"Just lookin' the place over."

"Funny place for a black dude."

"Might say that."

"Where'd you say you was from?"

"California."

"I *know* that, brother."

"Los Angeles," Clem said reluctantly.

"What's a big-city black dude like you doing fuckin' around all by himself way up here?"

"I told you, just passin' the time."

The man nodded, still smiling. "Just having a beer and taking it easy, eh? Looking out the window, maybe to see what you can see. You maybe doing a little business around here, brother?"

"Yeah, I got something I'm waitin' on."

"We thought maybe you had a little action going for you way up here."

The man was still grinning, but everything about him was full of menace. Clem decided to be very careful with these two.

"Street dude, ain't you?"

"Yeah," Clem said.

"We clocked you for a street cat, minute we set eyes on you. You're way off the main drag up here, ain't you?"

"You fellers just passin' through?" Clem said.

"Seeing the sights," the man said. "You ask a lot of questions, don't you? Say, brother, you lonesome?"

"Not especially."

"You look lonesome. That's what we thought. What say, man, I'll jump for a round." He called to his friend. "Hey, Garza, this brother looks lonesome. Let's buy him a brew, eh?"

The dark man at the table said nothing. The man in the hardhat laid two dollars on the bar, held up three fingers to Woody, and nodded for Clem to follow.

Clem went reluctantly. He sat down at the table with them. The guy in the hardhat said, "I'm Tim. This here's Garza. Say hello to the dude, Garza." The squat Spanish man said nothing. Up close, he was the ugliest man Clem had ever seen. Tim said, "Sometimes Garza talks, other times you can't pry a word out of him. Ain't that right, Garza?" Garza grinned.

"Sounds Spanish," Clem said. "Lot of Spanish people up here, but I never heard that name."

"Tex-Mex," Tim said. "More Mex than Tex. We're Texas people. But then you probably noticed the plates on the van when you was casing the scene out front before. Down around McAllen you got Garzas crawling out'a the woodwork. I didn't catch your name."

"Clem."

"How old're you, Clem?"

"Twenty."

Tim looked at Garza and grinned. Garza grinned too, and spoke for the first time, "Fuckin' punk kid. What you doing up here, *chico?*"

"Takin' care of business."

"You dealing?" Tim asked.

"Nothin' like that," Clem said. "Town's too tight." He was beginning to feel glad that he had only five or six dollars in his billfold. The rest of the money he had left from Sally and the Hurleys he had taped to the inside of his right thigh with some of the adhesive he had bought to doctor his injured leg.

Tim grinned at Clem again. "You know what? Me'n Garza, we kind'a like you. How about that?"

"You dudes hit it off real good, don't you?" Clem said.

"We're engaged," Tim said. "You swing?"

"I'm straight," Clem said.

Garza reached into the pocket of his leather jacket and took out a plastic pharmaceutical vial. He unscrewed the lid and tapped two capsules onto the table. He said, "Be my guest."

"Beer's fine," Clem said.

Garza took one and washed it down with a drink. "You don't have to be scared. You see me take it, you know it's okay, *chico.*"

"I'll stick to beer," Clem said. He was generally leery about pills, and never popped anything unless he had a good idea of what it was he was taking and who was passing it. Even then it was scary. Pill freaks were strange types, and if they were on uppers they were considered more dangerous than junkies.

"What line of business you say you was in?" Tim asked.

"Stayin' alive."

"That's our line too!" Tim said. This, for some reason, cracked him and Garza up, and they started laughing. "Just a couple of old-timers, out to stay alive and have us a little fun."

Clem had them spotted now. Ex-cons. Maybe recently sprung. He nodded.

Tim said, "You clock us for old-timers?"

"The idea occurred to me, now that you mention it," Clem said.

Tim pushed his hardhat back on his head and looked appreciatively at Garza. "Didn't I tell you I *like* this dude?"

Garza looked at Clem with a cold stare. Clem said nothing.

"I was Canyon City," Tim said. "Garza here, he come home all the way from Rahway State. That's in New Jersey."

"You on the string?"

"Surely, surely," Tim said delightedly. "Garza sees the Man for life. Me, I only got to sweat it until two thousand thirty."

"Timmy, you talk too damn much," Garza said.

"Y'know what I'm thinking, Angie?" Tim said. "Supposing we was to cut this big groovy kid in with us. Show him how it happens."

"No way," Angie Garza said. "He ain't nothing but a punk."

"You got experience, Clem?" Tim asked.

"Some."

"This kind?" Tim asked. He nodded to Garza, who smiled at Clem and opened the front of his jacket. Inside, under the armpit, the black, checkered grips of what looked like a .45 automatic stuck out from a shoulder holster.

"Some toy," Clem said.

"That ain't no toy, brother," Tim said. "And what I got stuck in my belt ain't no toy either. We also got some very nice items locked up in the van outside. No toys, though."

Now Clem had them. He'd seen them before—or at least types like them—a few times. In the L.A. County Jail when he'd gone in the holding pen on minor raps for a couple of days, until they could get him transferred over to the juvenile section.

At the L.A.C.J. a person ran into all types—hustlers, gamblers, addicts, S-M perverts and stickup guys, strong-arm cats and flashy fast-talking pimps sweating out the bondsmen or their lawyers. But the worst were what the other inmates called the crazies, like the federal exchange habituals, who had been picked up on one count or another and were waiting to go back to Uncle Sam—some of them three- and four-time losers. Guys who had really gone off in the head. Those boys didn't care about anything—they had nothing to lose.

They almost always had that sallow, bleached, unhealthy look that Tim had, from too many years inside. Were often bird-chested, skinny-armed weasels. They were more at home on the inside than outside, and if they joked at all their humor was creepy. Those cats were really off the wall. When the U.S. marshals came in with the transfer papers, they took no crap from such types, and especially no chances. These old boys went out in stainless-steel waist chains that were linked to neck and ankle manacles, so trussed up they could hardly walk. Still laughing and joshing around with the marshals, but their eyes were always moving, casing the scene, waiting for that one little slip.

On the street, a man paid strict attention to what he was into. No other way. Otherwise, he was headed for a fall. But these old-time crazies were something else. They didn't make any sense at all . . . were completely unpredictable, and that was scary. Clem was beginning to get some very uncomfortable feelings about Tim and Angie Garza. "You was down around McAllen, you say?"

Tim shrugged. "Got fed up."

"Oh, I know that feelin'."

"Like, I was in this welding shop, and Angie here, he was on the fuckin' loading platform at UPS. We both had the same probation officer. That's how we got to know each other. Sure, we was working steady, just like regular folks."

"I dig how that shit goes down," Clem agreed.

In a way he did. On the street, he had known too many ex-cons who had clocked their time, and were now reporting to the Man weekly and working at two-bit jobs. Some of these dudes had spent most of their lives inside, and here on the outside they had to watch their step about how they behaved or who they were seen talking to. It was like a game where the P.O. or the psychiatrist or the counselor won four times out of five, because most times, sooner or later, a con would get fed up and make a move, do a little job, and that was all it took, one bad move, and somebody blew the whistle and the con got a free ride back to Soledad or wherever. And the really crazy thing was that sooner or later that con would make a move, even with the bad odds. It was a matter of going noplace if he stayed where he was . . . and boredom too, doing the old nine-to-five for a rinkydink paycheck, shit, there just wasn't any *fun* in that! There was no point in it, and no percentage, and after a while a man usually started thinking about making a move. That was the only kind of excitement some of those people understood, and in a way, it was all they really had to live for. You could give some of these guys a Cadillac and a chick and folding money, and if these items had been acquired legally, something was lacking, the fun was missing. There was nothing to brag on. Clem had personally known one ex-con who could explain it simply. "I just got fed up with all that shit, see?" he had told Clem. "So me and my pal, we do a weekend job on this nickels-and-dimes department store over at a mall in Woodland Hills. It was a piece of cake, see, no sweat, nobody gets hurt. We found out the manager's name and address, and dress up and get a tin badge, and I knock on the door of his house at five in the morning, saying I'm a detective and there's been a robbery over at the store, and we need him there, and he comes trotting right out to the car in his bathrobe, and my buddy sticks a piece into his ear and tells him to behave, which he did, and we opened the store and the safe, and came out in less'n ten minutes with fourteen grand. Shit, what a *fine* feeling that was. We lived high for six months on that, went down to Tucson and played the dog tracks, bought a Plymouth 360-Fury, and we had gash laying around all day long dropping their pants whenever we pointed a finger. Oh, it was cool!"

Maybe Tim and Angie, too. Out for fun and games.

"You dudes cruisin'?" Clem asked.

"On the road, brother."

Clem was willing to bet they had a radio in that Econoline, one with a scanner that would pick up the state police frequencies. If they were moving around, that would be one of the first things they'd put in. They'd be interested in keeping abreast of current events if they'd jumped parole, and more so if maybe they'd pulled a job someplace along the way. That might explain, too, why they were several miles off the main highway. Maybe they just wanted to stretch their legs for an hour or so. Or maybe there was a roadblock up somewhere.

One thing was sure. They wouldn't let him walk away now, not after opening up as much as they had. He wished he'd never come into the Emerald. These two had him scared. It looked to him like they were cruising around, looking for action. Like some dumb cop —maybe a creep like Bill Martinez—might flag them over for a routine check, and that big pistol of Angie's might go off right in Bill's face. Two old-timers, out on a spree. Trouble down the road. He figured this was no place for him.

Then it went from bad to worse. Garza-the-gorilla pulled out a joint and lit it, inhaled, then passed it to Tim, who took a drag and handed it to Clem, who declined.

"Better ditch that," Clem advised. "Straight place."

Garza grinned at Tim. "Didn't I tell you he was chickenshit?"

Tim took another drag, and held it. When he finally exhaled, he said, "Say, kid, is there any fun in a place like this?"

Clem grinned. "Here? You got to be kiddin'."

"The Man here?"

"Humpty-Dumpty sheriff. State cop hangs around. The sheriff is just laughs. State bull is no fall guy."

"Interesting."

By then Woody Klein had noticed the smell. He walked over to the table and said, "You trying to get my license revoked?"

"Kiss me," Garza said, staring up at him.

Woody frowned. "Whyn't you fellows move along?"

"Bring us three more beers," Tim said.

Woody nodded toward the phone on the wall behind the bar. "I'm putting in a call."

"Don't do that, Woody," Clem said.

Woody stared at Clem. He got the message. He said, "I don't want trouble in here."

"Won't be any, friend," Tim said. "You just go back behind that bar and take it easy. Tell that old cunt you got for a waitress to bring us some fresh ones. How come you don't keep your beer cold? Give her some change and tell her to play the juke. You and her can dance. We could use some entertainment. Just don't reach for the phone. That would be a mistake. And don't try reaching for anything else you might have stashed under the counter back there. Now do like you're told and get us our fuckin' beer."

Woody looked from Tim to Angie, and then to Clem. Finally, he walked back to the bar, opened three Coors, and brought them back to the table. "Dollar eighty."

"Jesus, listen to him," Tim said. "What kind of cheap joint we in? Don't you ever spring for a drink?"

Woody's face was expressionless. "Okay, this round's on the house."

"That's real friendly of you," Tim said. "Thanks. Now you get back up there and keep Two-Ton Tessie company."

Woody left. Lulu played the jukebox. Garza finished his beer and motioned for another round. That turned out to be on the house too. Lulu brought the beers to the table. She said, "Clem, I think you better get home."

"Stick around, gorgeous," Tim said to Clem. "We like your company."

Garza said something to her in Spanish. Lulu glared at him and replied back, at a machine-gun pace so fast that Clem could not catch a word. Garza spat out something else, and Lu drew back her hand, ready to take a slap at him, and Clem said desperately, "Lu, get your ass back to the bar with Woody!"

Lulu turned on him angrily. "This ain't no kind of company for you to keep." With that she turned and stomped off.

Clem was feeling more and more scared. He had been in trouble since he was eleven. But the worst offenses he had committed were small-time compared to what these two hoods were into. They were mean, and they didn't care. They might be headed toward big-time trouble, like maybe a shootout. Probably they had some kind of crazy scheme in mind, like making it to Denver or maybe Las Vegas, where there was big money, but they'd never get that far.

Clem remembered something else. Way back, on that first evening of the day when he and Jesse had left Los Angeles. Seemed like years ago. Camped out that night in the desert, in the middle of nowhere, and Clem had been nervous. His warning to Jesse. About how helpless they'd be if somebody just came along and ripped them off. Strange types cruising the highways. Old Jesse had scoffed. Was so sure he could take care of himself with that antique .44 cannon. Clem thought glumly, "Wish the ol' fucker was here right this minute! Let him see for himself I wasn't just makin' noises! Teach him a lesson for real."

Just then the Emerald's front door opened, and Clem, with his mind on Jesse, almost fainted, thinking that it was the old man who was walking in, for his Saturday-afternoon beers. Dumb as his grandfather was, that would be just like him. But it was Willie Montoya, Connie Aragon, and three of the others who had ganged up on him that morning, including Cousin Alejandro from down the valley.

Woody Klein's afternoon trade had started.

THE FIVE OF them lined up at the bar and ordered beer. Woody was so nervous by now that he spilled one of the Coors and had to replace it. Lulu had the jitters too. Connie Aragon wisecracked to her in Spanish, and instead of grinning she looked like she hadn't even heard what he said.

For a few minutes they stood there, drinking and occasionally glancing toward the rear table, where Clem and Angie and Tim were sitting. Finally, Willie and Cousin Alex strolled over. Alejandro towered over them. He didn't look good. Still hung over, and showing signs of having been in a fight—one cheek was blue and swollen. He stared down at Clem and said, "We saw your bike outside."

"How you fellers doin'?" Clem said.

"Who're your friends?" Tim said.

"How come your bike got two flat tires?" Alex said. "Looks to me like somebody let all the air out, with a knife or something."

"Ain't thinkin' about no tires right now," Clem said sourly. "Whyn't you guys take a load off your feet over at the bar?"

"That's some dirty trick, you ask me," Alex said.

"You motherfucker!" Clem said.

Tim frowned. "What's coming down?"

"Nothin'," Clem said. "We had a little discussion this mornin'. That's all."

Cousin Alex looked at Tim and then at Angie. He said to Clem, "These your friends?"

Tim smiled up at Alex. "Why don't you move your fat fuckin' ass out of here, greaser?"

"You callin' me greaser?" Alex said. "I ain't no Mexicano, for sure."

Garza looked up at Cousin Alex with a ferocious scowl. "You got something against Mexicanos, *compadre?*" he said. "I'm Mexican and I'm pure, not like you half-assed *coyotes* in this shit country."

Alejandro was a little taken aback at the insult. He said, "Ah . . . *Mexicano, sí. Como se llama?*"

"Angie," Angie said. *"Angel."* He pronounced it An-*hell.*

"Angel!" Tim laughed. "That's his goddamn name for a fact! The Angel! That's what they call him. He's some angel!"

"Soy Alejandro Montoya," Cousin Alex said.

"Fuck you, Alejandro," Angie said pleasantly.

Willie was starting to get mad. He said to Clem, "Got yourself some backup?"

"You better get back to the bar, Montoya," Clem said.

"What's with these dudes?" Tim asked again.

"Stay out of this, you want my advice," Willie said.

"You advising me?" Tim asked.

"You sidin' with this nigger?" Willie asked.

"We're just sitting here having ourselves a beer," Tim said, still in that pleasant manner. He glanced at Clem, smiling. "Hey, brother, you going to let this Mexican cocksucker call you a nigger?"

With that Willie drew back a fist. Tim reached inside his jacket and took out a big double-action Walther and pointed it in the general direction of Willie's forehead. For a clumsy-looking, gangly man, his reflexes were astonishing. Alejandro made a move. By then Angie had unlimbered the .45.

At the bar, everyone watched. No one moved. Lulu's mouth was wide open. Woody Klein said, "Oh, God!"

Willie tried a bluff. "Put that pistol away, and we'll see how good you really are."

Alejandro was standing very still. He liked fighting, but he didn't like guns, and this one that Angie had was aimed right at his stomach. The Angel looked like he didn't care much one way or another whether it went off.

Tim stood up, still smiling. He pressed the muzzle of his weapon under Willie's chin. "You talk real heavy, you know that?" he said. "You want to find out how good I am? Is that what you want?" he asked sociably. He cocked the Walther's hammer. "How would you like seeing your fuckin' brains sprayed all over this here ceiling? How'd you like to see me take the whole top of your fuckin' dumb Mexican head off?"

He pressed harder with the muzzle and then waltzed Willie backward, still easygoing and sociable, until he had him flat against the wall by the juke. By then, whatever bravado Willie had been trying to muster had fizzled out. Something told him that this tall blond *gringo* in the yellow hardhat meant business, and that the *gringo*'s Mexican sidekick was no one to screw around with either. This was odd, because in Willie's world, Spanish-speaking people always stuck together no matter what. But this *chongo*-faced Mexican was some other kind of Spanish. Willie was impressed—in fact, terrified—at how fast those pistols had appeared, almost like the way those magicians on TV could make a playing card vanish or appear, out of thin air. It happened so quickly you couldn't catch it. Whatever plans he and his friends may have had for Clem that afternoon had vanished.

Tim took the pistol away from Willie's chin and pressed it just as firmly against his stomach. Almost affectionately, he patted Willie on the right cheek a half-dozen times, only the pats were more like slaps. Willie stood still. Tim said, "That's better. Just take it easy, tough guy." Without turning his head, he called, "Angie? Everything okay?"

"No sweat," the Angel said. He raised his free hand, palm out, to Cousin Alejandro. "Move back, just a little . . . there, like that. So I can see everybody."

Tim left Willie standing against the wall and shook a forefinger at him. "You just stay there. Got that, fucker? No! Don't put your hands up. Just *stand* there. Don't move at all. That ain't smart. Angel here, he gets very quick and edgy when he's popping. You move around too much, he's liable to let one off at you, like *bang-bang-bang*. You wouldn't want that, now, would you, *amigo?* That Angel, I wouldn't fuck around with him. Why, he scares the shit out of *me* half the time, he's so quick."

Tim wandered up front, the pistol lowered, dangling loosely in his hand. "Closing time, folks. Got to drink up!" he called out. Snapped the lock on the front door, took Woody's sign that hung in the window—OPEN on one side, CLOSED on the other—flipped it to the latter, peered out the window, and laughed. "Sure seems to be a hell of a lot of vehicles out front, for a place that's closed." Called back to Clem. "Hey, brother, that fucker was right. If that's your Harley out there, it ain't going noplace, not until you get some new skins for it."

In the rear, Cousin Alex whispered desperately to Clem, "We get you new tires."

"Who asked you to say something?" the Angel said.

"I just tellin' him . . ."

Angie scowled. His expression got surly. "No one talks. You got something to say?" He swung the pistol around toward Alex. "Shut up!"

Alejandro swallowed and kept silent.

Up front, Tim was striding back and forth, grinning at everyone, clearly on an emotional high, still carrying the pistol down at his side carelessly. "Okay, folks, ante up. Wallets out, let's go," he sang out. "Get 'em on the bar." He went to the wall phone and with one jerk tore out the receiver. Went behind the bar and gave Woody a hard shove. "Get down at the far end, creep. Stay cool. Everything's okay. Right?"

Woody did as he was told. Tim checked the back of the bar for a pistol, and then stuck the Walther into the belt of his jeans, the butt sticking out in front of his stomach. Confident now that no one would make a move. Played bartender. "You guys feel like a drink? On the house. What'll you have? Come on, don't be bashful." He reached into the cooler, got out beers, and began tossing them to the men standing on the other side of the bar. They opened the cans. Connie Aragon got a faceful of foam, and tried a rueful grin. Tim set out bottles of hard liquor. "Let's have us a party, what do you say?" Leisurely, he moved down the bar, emptying the wallets that had been placed on its varnished top. The men had more money than might be expected—plenty of singles and fives, but quite a few tens and twenties. Fifty more—working bar change—came out of Woody's till. Woody had another forty-and-change in his own wallet. In the rear, the Angel frisked Willie, and got twenty-two more. Cousin Alex, who worked at the lumber mill, happily handed over most of his week's paycheck, one hundred and eighty-six dollars. Tim called, "Not bad, Angie. Must have four hundred up here."

The Angel said, "Cigarette money." He stuffed the bills he had collected into the pocket of his leather jacket, and moved up front. "What'd you expect, man?" Tim said.

Angie did not reply. He tilted a swallow of bourbon from one of the bottles Tim had set out.

"How come you're all so quiet?" Tim asked everybody. "Enjoy yourselves!"

Connie Aragon nodded toward the Angel. "He said he don't like talkin'."

Angie whirled, the pistol held out. "Who say that? Who was talkin'? Somebody's asking to get in trouble, talkin' all the time." Connie winced and shut his eyes. Angie stalked up and down before the men, scowling.

Lulu Uranga said, "You boys better go now. You had your fun. Okay?"

Angie went up to her. "You got a big mouth."

Lulu said stubbornly, "You got the money. Go now."

Angie drew back his hand for a slap, and without even thinking about it, Clem jumped up. "Lay off her."

The sudden movement was nearly his last. Tim saw it from the corner of his eye. The Walther was out, leveled before Clem even spoke. The Angel too, hearing the sound of Clem's chair scraping wood, whirled. Then, seeing who it was, relaxed, but he was coldly furious. Tim said, "Don't ever do that, punk. *Never* surprise a dude like that. I dug you for a cool guy."

"Wasn't thinkin'," Clem said.

"That's for sure," Angie said.

"It's just that a cool dude like you, why bother fistin' some ol' chick out?" Clem said. He was more scared now than he'd been before. He added nervously, "She ain't done nothin'."

"Shut up," Angie said.

Tim was thinking. He frowned and then tilted his hardhat back. Stuck the Walther into his belt. Took the can of beer that Connie Aragon was holding, drank half, and returned it to Connie. He shook his head and stared at Clem. "Man, I don't dig you."

Clem did not reply.

"I like a dude knows how to make up his mind," Tim said. "I get funny feelings around a cat who's liable to jump one way one minute and the other way the next."

"We ain't taking this punk, if that's what you got on your mind," Angie said.

"Cool it, Angel," Tim said. He smiled at Clem. "Like, I thought maybe we had a little something going with you, baby. But you can't seem to make up your mind."

"Always had that trouble," Clem said.

"Tim, you take him along, count me out, *finito!*" Angie said.

"What's the problem, kid?" Tim said. "Like, all you do is make up your mind. You dig hanging out with us, that's okay. You dig hanging out with this bunch, say so."

"I hang out solo," Clem said.

"Well, now that is okay. *That* is something I can understand," Tim said. "I'm glad to hear that. 'Cause that's important. You take a couple of people, like me and the Angel, we form a business association, well, we got to know what's coming down. So, if we start thinking about maybe cutting in a third dude, and he says he works solo, well, he is telling us something that counts a lot."

"That's how it is," Clem said.

"That's cool," Tim said. "I do think it's curious, though. I mean, what the fuck's the difference if Angie roughs up on this old cunt here? Ain't the end of the world, is it? I mean, it looks to me like we come up front for you before, right? These farmers come walking in, and it's you they got business with, not us, right? So we went up front for you. Didn't have to. Wasn't none of *our* business. Did it out of the goodness of our hearts, almost. Okay, so we got ourselves a little cigarette money while we were at it, right? Can't blame us for that, can you? I mean, it was like a *favor* we was doing for you. Seems like you don't appreciate that, though."

"I do," Clem said. "No shit."

"Don't seem that way to me. Looks to me like you're comin' up front for them. Baby, that ain't right. Makes me sad."

"Better count me out, then."

"Why, sure," Tim said. "Too bad." He shook his head sadly. "We could've had us a swell time. Break you in right." Clem knew he wasn't talking about armed robbery. He was talking sex. "Maybe we ought'a break you in right now. Out in the van. Angel, you feel like a turn?"

"I don't like standing around waiting," Angie said. He looked at Clem suspiciously. "We done our business. We better split. All you think about is balling."

"No hurry."

"We been off the highway long enough," Angie insisted.

Tim considered this. Finally, he shrugged. "Maybe you're right, Angel." He turned to Clem. "Too bad, baby. Well, you might as well join the club."

"Join how?"

Tim nodded toward the small pile of wallets on the bar. "Let's see what you got."

Clem came up to the bar and handed over his wallet. "Six crummy bucks," Tim said. "Times are hard."

Clem said nothing.

The Angel said, "Want me to shake him down?"

"No," Tim said. "Let's move." At the end of the bar where Woody Klein stood, there was an empty liquor carton. Tim began filling it with bottles, bags of cashews and peanuts, and some Mason jars containing pickles, beef jerky, and hardboiled eggs. As he worked, he talked. "Hate to leave you folks. We was getting to like it real nice here. I really dig sitting around a bar with friendly people. We'll try

and make it back through here one of these days. Send you a postcard. Angie, put this in the van."

Angie put the box under one arm and unlocked the front door,
looked out, and then left. Outside, they heard the van doors open,
and then slam. Angie came back in.

"You unlock the front door too?" Tim asked.

"It's unlocked."

Tim turned to the others. "Hate to rush off like this. We want to
thank all of you for being so decent to us." His voice was still
friendly. "Now, here's how it goes down, folks. I want you should
listen. We are going to walk out of here. I want all of you to sit here
and have another drink. Take it easy. Phone's gone. All we want is
five minutes. Is that okay with all of you? That ain't asking a lot, is
it? Don't get any ideas. We're going to sit out in front in the van for
a few minutes and let her warm up. Now, just in case there's a piece
of iron stashed away here someplace, don't get dumb. Like, I
wouldn't want to see somebody who thinks he's *brave* or something
come rushing out the front door, waving a piece around. The back
windows of that van roll down. Angel here is going to be sitting back
there. He's got himself a genuine Winchester riot gun, twelve-gauge
pump, loaded with buckshot. Anybody comes busting out of that
front door before we're good and ready to leave, the whole motherfuckin' front end of this bar is just liable to get blown away. Don't
nobody even look out the windows. Angie don't like people staring
at him. Just lay back. Hope to see you again sometime. It's been a
real pleasure."

He came out from behind the bar, and the two of them walked to
the front door and out into the sunlight.

From inside, they heard the van start, heard it revving, and then
idling. Willie Montoya said, "Wait till they drive off. Nearest phone's
down at Orly's."

"Do like they say, Willie," Clem said.

"Once they're out'a sight, we can get to the phone," Willie insisted.

"Do like they *want*, you dumb fuck," Clem said. "Guys like that're
just liable to drive off and then turn around and double back, to
make sure all the cars and trucks they counted outside are still here.
Let it go, man."

"We got to notify Bill Martinez," Willie argued. "He'll get a call
out on the radio."

"Maybe we ought'a do that," Clem said. "Knowin' that asshole, he'd jump right in his prowl car and try to capture 'em single-handed. Might even catch up with 'em. Bye-bye, Bill."

They heard the van drive off. Clem and Connie went to the window and cautiously peered out. Clem's guess had not been far off. The Day-Glow'd Econoline stopped down the road about a hundred yards away and pulled over onto the shoulder.

"They're watchin' out the back windows," Clem said.

"Shit," Connie said, "they must think we're stupid or something."

Presently, the van drove out of sight. Everybody waited. Woody served a round of free beers. Time passed. Finally Willie Montoya said, "Think it's okay to go out now?"

"I don't care," Clem said. "Sure. You make the call, if you want. Someone has to."

"You want to?" Willie asked.

"I'd be glad to," Clem said. "Only it seems I got no tires." He looked at Willie. "I don't care who did it. You owe me ninety bucks for new tires. I ain't bullshittin' you."

"Hell, ain't *none* of us got any money," Willie said.

"That's all right," Clem said, and borrowed a phrase from Gus Benavidez. "Your credit's always good with me, Montoya."

THE STICKUP AT the Emerald was the talk of Brazos. The pair got away clean. By the time the patrons got a call through to Bill Martinez, Tim and Angie were long gone. Or perhaps hidden out somewhere, on some side road or lane, munching bennies, eggs, dill pickles, and cashews, washing it all down with bourbon, and dreaming about the next big score they might make up the road somewhere. Martinez and Milt Garcia got roadblocks up by radio all the way from Abiqui to the south to Manassa, Colorado, to the north, which were the only two directions to go on Route 85, but the ex-cons never turned up, which, all things considered, may have been a lucky thing for everybody concerned.

Clem didn't come out of it too badly. For a few hours there was a rumor that he had been in with the pair, since he had sat at their table. But Martinez, when he got a sheet on them, confirmed that they had skipped parole out of Texas. So that idea was unlikely. By then, Woody Klein, who was not a brave man, had made a few remarks about Clem's standing up to them. Lulu Uranga took it from there. Her pouter-pigeon bosom swelled with pride and fierce indignation, and if she had been younger, it might have swelled with love too. She said to anyone who would listen, "That beautiful boy, he's got some *cojones*, all right, he stood up to them an' defended me. Believe me, there wasn't no one else doin' nothing! No one was even speaking a word. These *hombres* was goin' to hit me, they was bad, *rufianos bandidos*, oh, you could tell they was *muy malos!* But that Clem! *Eeee-ai!"*

Sally Benavidez said, "Oh God, they didn't get the money I let you have, did they?" Clem calmed her. She said, "I heard from the way you left after that fight at Orly's that you were gone for good, and I was sure you'd taken our money with you."

"I didn't even have it on me," Clem said. "No one but a fool carries that much in his wallet!"

Werner Grimmiessen said, "You are a hero!"

Garrison Hurley made Clem a special drink in the Waring blender, of vodka and overripe bananas, which he had bought on sale at the Chama supermarket for six cents a pound. Patsy put an arm around Clem's shoulder and kissed him wetly on the cheek. "You could have been hurt. Oh, Clem."

"Wasn't nothin'," Clem said.

"I hate violence," Patsy said. "It just gives me goose bumps from one end to the other." She gave him a hug and another kiss. Garrison was busy peeling bananas and didn't notice.

Only Jesse was discontent. In fact, he went into a rage when he got home, just before sunset. "I heard! You don't have to give me your la-de-da version! It's all over town. Associatin' with known criminals! You dumb shit! Woody Klein said they was smokin' marijuana as big as nickel panatellas, right out in public!"

"Leave me be for once!" Clem shouted. "I was just in there havin' myself a beer, and they came in. What'd you want me to do, hide in the men's room or something? How the fuck was I supposed to know they was off-the-wall crazies? Me an' Woody, we was just talkin', and they strutted in and took the joint over."

"You *sat* with 'em!" Jesse stormed. "That takes real brains. Why, I bet you felt right at home with them criminal mentalities. Woody said they was so loaded down with guns they could hardly walk. Wonder you didn't git your ass shot full of holes."

"My ass'd been shot full of holes in more ways than one, if they'd had their way," Clem said.

Jesse missed the point, and continued, "First, you and Montoya and his gang wrecked half the town this mornin', and then on top of it, you git involved up to your teeth in a stickup and armed robbery, and God knows what else. Can't you lay off for five minutes?"

"I didn't start it."

"You didn't have to," Jesse said. "Disaster sticks to you like filin's to an iron magnet. Jesus, I wish I'd never laid eyes on you!"

"I was out to fix that," Clem yelled. "I'd made up my mind to split. Ol' man, I was on my *way*."

Jesse stared at him and grew serious. "You were?"

"That's right!"

"When? Today?"

"Right on!"

"You was really goin' to leave?"

"You got it! Split, cruise, drop out, get lost."

Jesse grew thoughtful. He said finally, "So. You were really goin'?"

"You heard me."

"Just run off, on that cycle?"

"That was the idea."

The old man considered this. "Well, then, how come you didn't?"

"None of your business," Clem said. "I just changed my mind. Man's got a right to do that."

Even angry, Jesse had a shrewdness. He looked at Clem. "I'm gittin' the picture. You was afraid they'd all say they run you off. Right?"

"I got no time to worry about shit like that," Clem said.

"Goddamn it, I'm right, ain't I?"

"You never been right once in your whole life."

"You was runnin' away, only they cornered you, up by Orly's station!"

"I'm still here, ain't I?"

"You got to do it your way, every time," Jesse said. "You had any brains, you'd'a kept goin'. Truth is, they *did* run you off. Face up to it."

"Nobody runs me off," Clem insisted.

"Shoot! That ain't the way I heard it," Jesse said. "You ought'a be one of them television reporters, like ol' Cronkite on the six o'clock news . . . they tell a story to suit themselves, and actually claim the price of gasoline is goin' down and then toss in a couple of natural disasters an' earthquakes an' floods to take your mind off it, when all you got to do is look at the price on Orly's gas pump to know that they're lyin' through their teeth. From what I heard, they got you right there at the gas station. Orly saw it. So, you cold-conked Alex Montoya. That ain't nothin', boy. The last anybody saw of you, you was hightailin' it up the road to Chama doing a good eighty. And you come back! Where's the sense in that? That's all I want to know."

"Felt like stickin' around," Clem said stubbornly.

"You're just one of them deviated maso-chists, you ask me," Jesse said. "You ain't happy less'n you're miserable. If you was a canary, you wouldn't feel comfortable less'n you built your nest in a cage full of tomcats."

Clem glared at the old man. "You want me to split? Say so!"

"Hell, no! 'Course I want you to stay," Jesse said. "At the same time I don't want to have to bury you one of these days."

"I'll get by," Clem said.

"No, you won't," Jesse argued. "Listen, you think any of this makes any difference? Well, it don't. These people are as stubborn as mules. I've knowed 'em all my life. You can't trust any of 'em worth a royal shit! You got mebbe half a dozen folks here who like you, and most of them are scared to admit it straight out. The rest, they'd like you dead. They are treacherous, these Spanish. They don't want you. What they understand is Willie Montoya and his crowd, because they know him, and they know what to expect. Why, you big fool, all you're doin' is providin' entertainment! They're all sittin' back and watchin' to see what'll happen next. And whatever that is, you ain't goin' to come out on top. I can guarantee you that. Lulu and Woody are talkin' praise on you. That don't mean much. I told you when you first got here, this town will judge a person. That don't mean it's a fair judgin'. Don't git that notion, Clem. They'll be hatin' you more than ever now. And when these folks hate, they work at it overtime, weekends included. You can't win. They ain't about to let you. They'll just grudge you the more."

"I ain't leavin'," Clem said grimly.

"You really mean that?"

"You heard me."

"Don't know why you want to stay," Jesse said. "You sure ain't happy here."

"Who says so?"

"You do!"

"That's just talk."

"Well, you don't act happy."

"What you want me to do, dance all over house, snappin' my fingers?"

"Was you really fixin' to take off today?"

"I was."

"Without even sayin' goodbye?"

"I would'a written."

"And you come back?"

"Does it look like a memory sittin' here?"

"You're a mystery to me."

"No mystery. I just felt like it."

"Trouble'll keep on, boy."

"No, it won't. Listen. I been doin' it your way all summer. It got me nowhere. From here on, I'm goin' to do what I see fit. Okay? You might as well get that into your head, Sprout. I listened to you, and it got me dumped on. If you want to know the truth, I come back this afternoon huntin' for that motherfucker Montoya. I'm done takin' it from him. He don't know it, but his day has done come!"

"Boy, you really that tough?" Jesse asked. "Or are you just talkin' words at me again?"

"Talk is cheap," Clem said. "Wait and see."

"What about school?"

"I'll put up with it. For now."

"I talked to Bill Martinez this afternoon," Jesse said. "He gave me back my pistol. D'you know, these guys had swiped it out'a the truck? He said he'd stick up for you."

"Sprout, that's bullshit. Martinez hates my ass. Feeling's mutual."

Jesse thought about this. Then he said, "You really want to stay?"

Clem scowled. He did not speak.

"Not much for you here, boy," Jesse observed. He looked around the kitchen, where they were sitting. "Town ain't worth a fiddler's fart. I guess I couldn't blame you if you took off."

"You see me leavin'?"

"You do what you want," Jesse said finally. "That's all that counts, I reckon. In the end. I'm glad you're stayin'. That's all I can tell you. I don't know what goes on inside a young feller's head these days.

Mebbe the same thing that did years ago. When I was young. Only it comes out different, somehow." He paused again, and thought. Then he said, "I'd'a missed you. That's for goddamn sure."

"I guess I'd'a missed you too."

They sat there together for a while. Jesse said finally, "Hell, I'm hungry. It's almost dark. You feel like some supper?"

"How about a beer?" Clem said.

"Sure. Git the bourbon out too," Jesse said.

"Say, where the hell were you all day?"

"Doin' a little tradin'."

"You're always tradin'." He grinned at the old man. "Hell, every time I *needs* you, you're off tradin' some fool thing. You should'a seen my performance today. That was something to see, all right!"

"Didn't have to. Heard all about it."

"You'd seen me, maybe you wouldn't be worryin' so much all the time."

"Goddamn it, don't start braggin' again," Jesse said. "They say modesty's a virtue. If that's so, you ain't got a virtuous bone in your whole body. Git that beer. I'll start some ranch-fries."

Clem broke out a six-pack. He and Jesse started slicing onions and potatoes. Jesse said, "How about a nice hunk of elk steak?" Clem poured each of them a little bourbon. Jesse went on, "That's where I was today, up in the mountains, talkin' to some people I happen to know. Traded a whole haunch of elk for an ol' saddle and a couple of retread truck tires I had out in the shed. You dress out a nice cow elk, the meat is tender'n sirloin. Git one of those big cans of creamed corn, up in the cupboard. Haunch is out in the shed, curing. After a day like this, you ought'a be hungry. I ain't even seen you since this mornin', and from just what I heard around town I'm famishin'. I guess that's what they call one of them vicarious appetites. You want'a learn how to butcher an elk haunch? Still got the hide on it."

CLEM GOT A flashlight and went out with Jesse to the storage shed. He held the light while the old man sharpened a long butcher knife that had been honed to a sliver. "I like a sharp edge," Jesse said. "You ever notice how a woman ain't got the faintest notion of what a knife is? Give a woman a sharp blade, she'll dull it in two seconds and then complain at you 'cause it takes her half an hour to saw through a stick of margarine with it. See here? There's musk glands up by the hoof, and over here, under the asshole." He cut carefully with the knife. "Got to watch out for that. Git even a speck of it on the meat, it'll taste like skunk piss. Be careful about the hair on the hide. See how I do it? Just slicin' easy, there's a membrane holdin' the skin to the meat. You don't want the membrane. Nothin' worse than an elk steak that's all hair and musk and membrane. Just take it easy, like so, and everything comes away."

The haunch weighed a good seventy pounds. When Jesse was done carving, he picked up a rusty pruning saw and cut through the bones. "We'll scrub this off in the sink and throw some garlic and onions into the fry pan, put in some lard, and we got ourselves a dinner you couldn't buy in any restaurant in the world, I don't care how fancy it is."

They brought two steaks into the house—four pounds. "What's left over, we'll save for the mornin' for warmups," Jesse said. He drank off his bourbon and poured himself another. "Nothin' better than steak and eggs and hot coffee on a cold mornin'. Gittin' cool out. Winter'll be moseyin' along one of these days."

Together they cooked dinner. Good smells filled the house. Garlic, onions, the steak sizzling in hot fat on the big iron woodstove. Worcestershire, fresh green peppers, chili, and the sweet smell of caraway, which Jesse loved with his fried potatoes. He and Clem drank more beer together, and then had another bourbon. Creamed corn simmering—Jesse added a spoonful of sugar, salt, pepper, and a dash of vinegar. Clem set out plates and silverware. They put on the television to hear the local evening news and whether the hold-up guys had been caught. They had another beer.

Clem said, "Smellin' pretty good, ain't it?"

"Nine-tenths of the eatin' is in the smellin', boy."

Jesse served Clem a big plate. "That's enough for two lumberjacks and three Mexican muleskinners," he said. He got himself a plateful almost as large. "You growin' kids sure are something. Tryin' to fill you up is like tossin' food into a bottomless pit."

Clem piled in. The boards on the porch outside creaked as Cochise, smelling good things, ambled over to say hello. The gray female cat curled up in Clem's lap. Jesse said. "Whyn't you fling her ass out the door?"

"She's no bother," Clem said, cutting into his meat.

"Well, don't feed her," Jesse said. "Cats git that idea, they think they own a person."

Clem fed her a morsel. She accepted it daintily, and hopped off his lap. Rojo and the other cat were sitting on the floor by the table. Jesse said, "You can't do that, you knothead. You goin' to give to one, give to the others. That's fair. Otherwise, they'll start scrappin'." He cut off a few pieces of gristle and meat and tossed them to the cats. "That's how the floor gits all greasy. I only washed it last month."

They spent the evening quietly. Jesse, in fact, pulled back with his carping for the rest of the weekend. Which was pleasant for a change. All he said was, late the following morning, "Clem, you sure you want'a hang in here?"

"No sweat, Sprout."

Jesse stared at him over the tops of his spectacles. A Sunday-morning sports show was on the TV, but Jesse was engrossed in the *Albuquerque Journal*, reading through the classifieds. He had to use his magnifying glass to see the small print. The Sunday classifieds always fascinated him. There was nothing in them that he could ever afford —or that he really wanted—yet he spent part of every Sunday going through them from one end to the other. They were in the living room, Clem on the couch, Jesse in his falling-apart armchair. On this day he had let Cochise into the house, and was using the big malamute as a footwarmer, resting his stockinged feet on Cochise's rump. Jesse's socks were none too clean, and on the right foot two of his toes stuck through the threadbare fabric. Jesse said, "Goin' to school tomorrow?"

"Might."

"That's good. Suit yourself."

"Hang cool, Sprout."

"I am."

"Can I use the truck? Till I talk Montoya into buyin' me new skins for the Harley?"

"Just drive her careful."

"I'll do that."

Jesse seemed content with this. He went back to his classifieds. Some of the ones that interested him most he boxed in with a red ballpoint. He had never called about any of the ads, and never would, still he bracketed the ones that for one vague reason or another caught his attention. Forty rolls of tarpaper. A complete set of skiing equipment, for $175. Sky-diving lessons at the Albuquerque airport. Three hundred old copies of *National Geographic*.

Later that afternoon, they went over to the Emerald for a couple of beers. Garrison and Patsy Hurley were there, and some others. Lulu Uranga came over and kissed Clem right on the mouth in front of everybody. Werner Grimmiessen came in with four nice cottontails he had shot with the Swiss target pistol. The talk turned to Clem. Jesse said, "As kids go, he ain't a bad kid."

For a change, some of them took a position. "I'd be proud to have a son like you, Clem," Garrison said.

"So would I," Patsy said.

"Well, he sure stood up to them gangsters," Jesse agreed. "Which is more than some others can say, I reckon."

Werner said shyly, "Such magnificence!"

Clem said little. Sat and drank beer. Listened to all these old-timers gassing away. He did his thinking.

By the end of the afternoon, Jesse was drunk. He had his arm around Clem's shoulder—both out of affection and because he needed support—and was saying, "This is a good boy! He's got Slade written all over him! He's all right! Goddamn, I hate to admit it, but he's even *handsome!* He's big, he's strong, and by God, he's fearless! That's Clement Slade! People make way. Ain't that right, son?"

"We ought'a be goin' soon, Sprout," Clem said.

He finally brought Jesse home and put him to bed.

Next morning, he took the pickup. He had spent a lot of that weekend reaching his decision. Classes at the high school started at eight thirty sharp. Clem hung around town until the post office opened at nine.

When Horacio Quintana finally unlocked the front door, Clem walked in. There were no other customers.

"Mornin', Horacio," Clem said. The postmaster stared at him. "Say, you got any of them change-of-address cards around?"

"Over there," Horacio said, pointing to a table in the vestibule.

"Got a pen?"

"Not officially. People is supposed to have their own pens."

"Can I borrow yours?"

Horacio handed over a ballpoint.

Clem made out some change-of-address cards. He handed them to Horacio, who looked them over. They were addressed to various agencies in California. Los Angeles Department of Probation. Juvenile Court. Child Welfare. Department of Human Services.

Horacio's eyes glittered. "What are these places?" he said.

"I had some business with 'em."

Horacio nodded. "Well, like I told your grandpa, you got to keep everything official."

"Why sure, Horacio," Clem agreed. "I mean, I ain't expectin' anybody to be writin', but you got to keep the record straight, don't you?"

What he had printed in block letters on the cards under the blank space that read "Permanent Address" was a simple notation:

Clement Slade
Brazos, New Mexico
87511

FIVE

THE LONG WARM days passed. Autumn came to Brazos. Oak, maple, and willow turned yellow, and on the higher slopes the stands of aspen were all bright orange and gold. In the uppermost valleys rutting elk bugled challenges and pawed the turfy ground. The shores of the ponds and lakes were rimmed with frost at dawn, and the deer who came to drink had to poke through a thin crust with their hooves. In the Brazos Valley the Texas people had long since closed their summer homes and departed. The tourists too had disappeared. The afternoons were still sunny and warm, but there would be days of overcast skies, and then a cold, cutting wind blew along the main street of the village, kicking up whirlpools of dust and brown leaves, so that the place looked more forlorn and deserted than ever. The cattle and horses that had grazed all summer in the high mountain parks were rounded up and brought down to fenced pastures. The last alfalfa was cut and baled. The lumber mill laid off workers, and Gus Benavidez came down with a terrible case of hemorrhoids. When he got out of the Espanola hospital he had to sit on an air-filled rubber ring in his chair near the big potbellied iron stove, which by now was kept stoked, and everybody stopped by the store two or three times a day for a little item or two, just to hear Gus groan as he inched out of the chair to tend to customers who, all of a sudden, were coming in every five minutes.

Clem returned to school, and when he was not actually in class, operated the loan business he had started among the students. He took the school bus until new tires came in from Sears Roebuck. When they arrived, Orly Mendocino mounted them and balanced the wheels on the Harley, and Clem paid him off by helping out at the garage. He went back to using the bike to get to Chama every day. The school bus was impossible. During the brief time he had had to use it, he grumbled constantly: "Bunch of kids, always horsin' around. I'd sooner walk."

He continued to see Sally, and with her father affected an uneasy truce. Benavidez knew Clem blamed him for the entire mess that Saturday morning, or at least blamed him for being in back of it. Gus figured that there were certain subjects that were better left untouched, so that in time they might be buried and maybe even forgotten. He said little when Clem came into the store to see Sally, merely adjusted his rubber ring and put on an expression of patient resignation. For the time being, Clem let it go too.

Sally was more difficult. She had gotten suspicious, and would not abandon the notion that he had intended leaving without her. "You were fixing to run off that Saturday, weren't you?"

" 'Course not," Clem told her.

"Well, when *are* we going to get out of here?"

"One of these days."

"Just talk," she said. "You still have all that money I loaned you?"

"Got lots more'n that. Our bankroll's buildin' all the time."

"You could do better," she said sulkily. "Frankie Aguilar's selling grass all over school. He gets it from Albuquerque, and he's pulling in money hand over fist."

Clem grinned at her and shook his head. "Six-for-fiving's safe. You listen to me, and listen careful. I sold grass in L.A. And I had just two rules. I knew who I was buyin' from, and I knew who I was sellin' to. Now, without even tryin' it, I see a major problem tryin' to distribute *here*. Everybody knows everybody else, and what kind of business they happen to be in. Another problem is, nobody around here seems to know how to keep their big mouths shut. Includin' you. I'll tell you something. I already investigated the possibilities of movin' a little weed, and after thinkin' it over careful, I decided against it."

"Scared," Sally said.

"Not scared. Smart," Clem said. "Why should I set myself up? I figure everybody knows I'm loanin' money, including ol' man Tapia and Bill Martinez and Miltie Garcia. What you got to realize is, I'm special."

"And conceited too," Sally added.

"Merely statin' the facts. I'm the only black dude in this town. I'm set up. There are people who'd love to see me make a wrong move, and you know it. Now, if I start dealin' and the word gets around—and it would—well, baby, that's like I'm holdin' out both wrists to Bill Martinez and askin' for the cuffs. That's dumb."

With Willie Montoya, he came on stronger. They met one afternoon at the Dairy Queen up on the highway. Willie was alone, eating a hamburger. Clem went up to Willie's pickup and leaned an elbow on the window. "Just want you to know I personally laid out ninety-six bucks for new tires."

Willie, on this day, wanted no trouble. The hamburger he was eating suddenly seemed dry. He had trouble swallowing. He said, "I'll pay you something when I can."

"Interest rate on a hundred is twenty a week," Clem pointed out.

"You trying to hustle me, the way you do the kids over at school?" Willie demanded. "Nobody can charge interest rates like that."

"I do," Clem said.

"You ain't in California," Willie said.

"Wish I was. Meanwhile, however, that's my rate. The tariff on those bike tires now stands at a hundred twenty."

"Go fuck yourself."

"Willie, why don't you be sensible. Where I come from, if a dude don't pay his bills, well, y'know, somebody is liable to come around and talk to him. Talks real nice the first time. Second time, not so nice. Third time that man comes around, the dude usually walks away on a couple of broke ankles. And he *still* owes. Business is business. Back there, they got people who're experts at talkin' to a person. Here, I take care of my own business. Like, I could haul you out'a this pickup right here, and we could talk. Personally, I'd rather not." Clem's expression got serious. "Just get the money. I'm a man of my word, and a man has got to stand back of that, else people don't take him serious. What you got in your wallet, man?"

Willie had sixty dollars. Clem took it all. "Tariff's down. I'll be around to see you."

Later that day Willie had a beer with Connie Aragon at the Emerald. Connie had to pay, which he didn't mind doing because he was one of those who had been kept on the payroll at the lumber mill. He could see that his friend was in a low mood, and he bought several more rounds. Willie said sadly, "Winter's coming."

"Seems to do that just about every year," Woody Klein remarked.

"Connie, you got twenty I can borrow?" Willie said. Connie handed it over. Willie said, "Shit, this town is dead enough in summer. Winters it's even deader."

"Maybe we ought to cut out," Connie said.

Willie's expression brightened. "Yeah. We could go down to Albuquerque or Santa Fe. Get a job."

"We could get us an apartment," Connie said.

"Really live it up."

"By God, let's do it," Connie said. Willie nodded, and drank some of his beer.

This was something the two young men talked about every fall. Leaving Brazos. They had talked this way for years. Sometimes the destination was Albuquerque, sometimes Phoenix, or even California. Wherever it was, the life was always conceived of as incomparably better. A newer car to drive. Plenty of bars to hang out in. In their imaginations, an endless stream of gorgeous young girls who were always lonesome, sexually frustrated, and dying to make the acquaintance of a couple of virile young studs.

Every fall at about this time young fellows like Willie and Connie talked and dreamed of leaving Brazos forever. Complex plans were made, deadlines set, schedules laid out. But then the autumn deer and elk hunts would arrive, and of course no one could leave then. After that, it was one thing or another. A father or uncle would get sick or hurt, so that an extra man was needed to bring down firewood or go after some cows that had broken loose. There might be a wedding. Someone might die. Perhaps a successful liaison might start with a local girl. Always one thing or another. Usually by the time all these things had been taken care of, the first November snows had fallen, blocking the high passes, and Bill Martinez would be out on Route 85 half the time, closing it to traffic until the plows opened a lane. By then in was easier to stick to the family hearth, where there was company and three meals a day and a place to sleep at night. But in their sleep the young men of the village

dreamed: "Next year, for sure, I'll go." And next year it was the
same. The truth was that, like Sally Benavidez, they were more than
a little afraid of the outside world. The few who did escape—to
college, or a job down at the state capital—seldom returned. The
ones who stayed on would stay forever, as if in their minds they had
already accepted and set aside, in a manner of speaking, a small
space in the little cemetery at the south end of the village where the
fat woodchucks sunned themselves atop the burial mounds.

Now, at the bar, his shoulders hunched, Willie stared at his Coors
and rolled and unrolled the cover of a matchbook. He said dis-
consolately, "Only thing that makes me want to stay is the nigger."

This was how he and a number of other people referred to Clem.
"The nigger." In Brazos, there was absolutely no chance that "the
nigger" would be confused with some other nigger. No one of course
dared use the expression in conversation with Clem. There was a
possibility that he might take it the wrong way. Of course, he had
been known to refer to himself as a nigger, but then black people
had a funny way of talking about themselves sometimes, kind of
derogatory, though not nearly as insulting as they could get when
they talked about white people.

Woody Klein said, "Willie, it's none of my business, but why don't
you let the whole business with Clem go?"

"That's right, it's none of your business, Woody," Willie said. "In
fact, now that you mention it, I'm surprised to see you taking his
side."

"I'm not taking anybody's side," Woody said. He began wiping
down the top of the bar with a towel. "But I will say that I have
personally never seen him do anything that was out of order. That's
all I'm saying."

"He don't belong here," Willie said. "Just having to look at him
makes me sick."

"Willie, I think you carry it too far," Woody said. "What's he
actually ever done to you?"

Willie thought of his sixty dollars, and looked more disconsolate
than ever. He thought of that day at the gas station, and the holdup
later. He thought of Sally Benavidez. "You don't know the half of it,
Woody."

Woody finished wiping the bar. He folded the towel neatly. "Live
and let live, that's my feeling."

"And some things go on forever. Them's my feelings," Willie

said. By which he meant, perhaps, that he as well as anybody else in
this valley knew how to bide his time.

PATSY HURLEY WAS getting ready for her annual pre-Halloween
picnic. Years ago, when they had first settled in Brazos, she and
Garrison had inaugurated this ceremony as a means, to hear Garrison tell it, of "extending the hand of Christian friendship and min-
gling with the more humble but nonetheless dignified citizens of this
community."

The only trouble was that the humbler but nonetheless dignified
citizens of Brazos were not at all interested in grasping the extended
hand of friendship, not even if free chow was involved. The Hurleys
were not only Anglo, they were alcoholic Anglos. They didn't farm,
they didn't ranch, they didn't work, they didn't do anything except
sit around, pick up their disability checks, and swill liquor. Of course,
this was exactly what plenty of other Brazos residents did, and
some who did not, dearly wished they could. Whatever, nobody
came.

Patsy would thumbtack an ornately hand-lettered announcement
card on the bulletin board of the post office. At Gus's store, she
heartily greeted all the ladies she met, reminding them of the date.
They said they would come, but never did. It was the villagers' way
of snubbing the only resident who had a doctoral in quantum mechanics, along with his skinny, crazy wife, whose blond hair was
obviously *peroxidado*.

For the first few years, when Patsy still expected a big turnout,
she made thirty pounds of potato salad. When she was sober enough
to see over the rim of her glass, Patsy was a hell of a cook. The top
of the wood-burning stove would be covered with pots of boiling
Idaho russets, and in a crate by the door would be three or four
dozen ears of sweet corn she had traded off Jesse Slade. There were
also a dozen chickens, four pounds of butter for the corn, tortillas,
chili, both *verde* and *rojo, carne adobada*, sixty or seventy tamales
wrapped in corn husks, *biscochitos, empanaditas, chicharrones* made
from pork rind, enough green salad to fill a five-gallon washtub, and
six quarts of Patsy's homemade mayonnaise. For a while, Garrison
might try to help with the preparations, discoursing on the innate
brotherhood of man as he worked, but his coordination was not the

best—he would nick his thumb on the potato peeler (which was no easy thing to do) or splash boiling water on himself—and presently he would go off for his midday nap. In Garrison's world, anything approaching solid food disturbed his gastrointestinal balance.

The piles of food would be stacked around the kitchen or on a picnic table out back, attracting flies, cats, and Cochise. Woody Klein would come by. So would Werner Grimmiessen, and Milt Garcia, who was always out looking for votes. Patsy would be disconsolate. Even Jesse, who rarely displayed compassion for the minor tragedies that befall all of us in our human condition, came over from next door, bringing a bottle and his own baleful camaraderie: "Neighbors can't be fightin' all the time, even if some ain't fit to live close to. Better luck next year, Patsy. Pass that bowl of chicken, Werner, and quit guardin' it like it was Fort Knox. Ain't no need to monopolize it. This here's a democracy we're livin' in, 'case you ain't heard."

As the years passed, Patsy learned to keep her Halloween picnic small. This year, however, one idea built upon another. It started one morning after Clem had left for school. Jesse was out on the back porch getting some wood for the stove. Patsy hailed him. He walked over to the fence, and they got started on the picnic, and whether he had some corn to trade, which he did, and whether he thought Clem would enjoy her little annual fete. "If there's food and liquor around, that boy will be satisfied, long as there's enough. You better fry up a couple of extra chickens, though. Y'know how his side of the family is partial to that dish. Besides which, his birthday is November first."

"It is?" Patsy said. "Oh, my! Oh, *my!* We could make it a double celebration. What a lovely thought!"

"I ain't much for celebratin' birthdays," Jesse said. "By now, I seen so many of my own that if one comes around I wonder how I made it that far, and then I start wonderin' if I'm goin' to make it to the next. I hate playin' odds against myself. Gits a feller so that he's walkin' around on tiptoe all the time." He thought. "However, you might have an idea, for once. We could chip in on it." He thought some more. "I ain't got much to spare, though."

"Neither have we," Patsy said.

"Considerin' your overhead, that ain't surprisin'," Jesse said. "I was just goin' to buy him a new pair of blue jeans. Waste of good money. He can't keep a pair longer'n two months. Either his feet an' ankles grows out of 'em or the knees git busted. Congress ought'a pass a law to let kids like that run naked till they git their full growth."

It was at this point that Patsy had an inspiration that was on a level with some of Garrison's finest insights when he had been in nuclear weaponry at Los Alamos. "Why don't we have a garage sale?" she asked. She thought this over, and then the full impact hit her. "Yes, why don't we have a *garage* sale!"

"Patsy, we ain't got garages," Jesse pointed out.

"Pooh! That's just the term they use."

"Besides, I don't think we got anything people'd go out'a their way to buy," Jesse insisted. "I don't know what you got in that storage shed of yours, but the equipment an' stuff I got in mine is valuable mostly to me."

Patsy's eyes glittered. "Jesse, people will buy anything."

"I ain't sure of that."

"Werner could participate," Patsy mused, getting more carried away by the notion. "Why, we could have a three-family garage sale!"

"He ain't got nothin' except Cochise. Who'd buy him?"

"Jesse, you don't understand. People love garage sales."

"Sure. 'Cause it gives 'em a chance to go snoopin' and pokin' around in other folks' personal possessions, so's they can see how poor the other half lives," Jesse said.

"Nobody can resist a sale," Patsy insisted.

And this was true, even in Brazos. From time to time, people held garage sales. There was always a turnout crowd. In such a small town, people knew, or had a pretty good idea, down to the last rusty baking tin, of what their neighbors possessed. Still whenever there was a garage sale, people came, often to paw through the same junk that had been put up for sale the year before and that nobody had bought. Patsy had a hunch that a three-family sale—especially since the three families involved had never held one—would bring folks in droves.

She had a talk with Werner, who agreed. "I don't have much, but why not? A little extra money never hurt anyone. For the picnic, I will donate rabbit. Cottontails, not those jacks who are made out of shoe leather. And for Clem, I will bake a little birthday something."

"I'll bake the cake," Patsy said emphatically.

"Patricia, you are a wonderful cook, but when it comes to pastry, the Germans and Austrians cannot be surpassed," Werner said.

"That's what you think," Patsy said. They finally settled the argument by agreeing that each would bake something.

Garrison too was for the sale, with a proviso. "If we supply the food, and perhaps soft drinks for the children, that will, I think, suffice. I believe in being generous, but when it comes to liquor the adults of this village resemble walking sponges. You might indicate that it is a bring-your-own affair."

"Oh, it will be simply grand," Patsy said.

Word got out even before Patsy posted her announcement. Jesse made eight hundred dollars on the old Plymouth coupe from Woody Klein, who had coveted it for years. Woody already had a '30 Cadillac, a '39 Buick convertible, and a '26 Ford pickup. When the deal was consummated in the Emerald, over a beer, Jesse, astonished by such a sum of money, actually grinned—not his usual sour grimace, but a real smile. "Why, hellfire, we can live real decent this winter with a roll like that tucked away. Might even git my plates repaired. I go to bite a piece of elk, they have a mind of their own. I might as well be livin' with a pair of castanets in my mouth. Hell, I might even buy the kid some of those musical cassette things for his tape deck he got in Santa Fe that time, and a pair of earplugs for me. He turns that gadget on, along with the radio and TV, I got to go sit in the outhouse to have a conversation with myself, and even then I got to do it at the top of my lungs."

Patsy got out her old set of Speedball lettering pens that she had used when calligraphy was a hobby of hers, and a bottle of India ink, and produced a card, which was posted on Horacio's bulletin board:

NEIGHBORHOOD

PICNIC & GARAGE SALE!

YOUR HOSTS:
THE G. HURLEYS, THE J. SLADES,
& W. GRIMMIESSEN

VARIOUS & SUNDRY ITEMS—ALL PRICE RANGES!
ANTIQUES, JUNQUE & COLLECTIBLES!
SATURDAY OCT. 27—NOON TO 5 P.M.
FREE FOOD, REFRESHMENTS & FUN!
B.Y.O.B.

When Bill Martinez saw the announcement, he telephoned Sheriff Milt Garcia. "You going?" Bill wanted to know.

"Sure. I always go to Patsy's picnics," Milt told him. "There's plenty of food and sometimes if you can wrestle the bottle away from Garrison, there's booze too."

"Make sure you don't miss this one. I want you there all afternoon," Bill said.

"That's what I was planning on doing," Milt replied. "You going?"

"I wouldn't miss it for the world," Bill Martinez said. "I have a hunch there'll be a crowd, and around this town if three people get together, two will team up and start a fight with the third. I intend to make sure it stays peaceable."

By noon that Saturday Patsy was a nervous wreck, and everybody else was exhausted. The yards of all three residences had been cleaned and raked, and innumerable trips had been made to the garbage dump.

Werner Grimmiessen had spent the preceding days running around out in the hills like a wild man, skittering through the reeds and willows by streams with the dead-shot Hammerli, knocking off rabbits right and left. He never missed with that elderly example of Swiss gunsmithing, and carried a flour sack tied to his skinny waist to hold the day's catch, with Cochise loping along beside him, the two of them a geriatric-boy-and-his-dog.

Woody Klein brought by six long banquet tables he had borrowed from the VFW hall, and two dozen metal folding chairs. Some of the tables would be used to lay out the garage-sale merchandise, and the rest were for people to sit at.

Jesse got out his old fifteen-gallon kettle, left over from his chuckwagon days, and cooked up an elk stew with enough beans and onions and celery and bay leaves and fiery red chili in it to make a person's eyes water.

Clem helped, splitting firewood for the stoves, peeling vegetables, and hauling stuff out of the sheds. He didn't know about the birthday business, and said, "I think you're all out of your gourds, carryin' on like this."

"Lots of people have garage sales," Patsy said, winking at him conspiratorially. "But this is the first time *we*'ve had one. You just wait and see."

On Saturday morning, Werner baked an enormous tray of apple strudel with white icing that spelled out Clem's name, drinking watered-down bourbon in his kitchen and occasionally giving Cochise a kiss on a bur-ridden ear, singing *"Du, du, du bist mein Scheisskopf . . ."*

Garrison, while Clem was helping him carry out a gold-brocaded Queen Anne love seat from the Hurley storage shed, only one corner of which had been eaten by rats, paused to rest a moment, set down his end, stood erect, hit the door lintel, and knocked himself flat. Patsy ran out with a wet towel, and when he was on his feet again he said groggily, "A well-ordered existence. That's all I've ever asked for in this life."

Shortly before noon, people began arriving. In old sedans, pickups, and flatbed trucks. Orly Mendocino and his wife showed up in his dump truck. In the vehicles parked around the area were cases of beer and gallon bottles of wine, along with vodka and bourbon.

The kids went at the food, and the women gravitated like vultures toward the merchandise that had been laid out. The men, as is the custom among the Spanish, grouped by themselves, sitting or standing on the back porches, in jeans and high-heeled cowboy boots and Stetsons, wearing Levi jackets or sleeveless goosedown hunting vests against the autumn coolness, drinking cans of beer and speaking in low voices, exchanging jokes and talking about the price of cows, and how lumbering was on the way out, and whose mare had foaled, and how hard it was to get by these days, occasionally passing a pint of bourbon from one man to the next for a nip, to be chased by a beer and a cigarette and more conversation.

And what a wealth of merchandise there was. It was astonishing how much had been gotten out of three old storage sheds.

Jesse's Plymouth of course already had a "Sold" sign on it. "You sure it's really sold, Jesse?" Orly Mendocino asked. "Jesus Christ, I had a car almost exactly like that back when I was a kid in high school. Jesus!"

"It's sold," Woody Klein assured him.

Part of Patsy's treasure trove included some nice pieces of pre–World War I golden oak furniture—a server; a bookcase with real cut-glass windows in its doors; a desk, not the rolltop kind but a secretary, with genuine bronze hinges and handles—all stuff that had been left over from her first marriage.

Werner's small shed had its own gems. Nineteenth-century hand-embroidered doilies and antimacassars, done by his grandmother; an autoharp, a kind of zither that could strike whole chords; enameled bronze candlesticks, glazed in cloisonné, from his Moroccan days; a 1935 Leica camera with a cracked lens, a watchmaker's lathe with accessories, two old German chess sets, one carved in ivory and lignum vitae; several photographs of Cochise as a pup, a basswood butter churn, the prie-dieu—a small praying pew of carved walnut with a podium for a missal—that had been used by his father; two chamois bags of marbles, a set of badly chipped, egg-shell-thin cups and saucers from Austria, and a wide assortment of books on subjects that had interested Werner at one time or another: a copy of the Canadian Armed Forces Physical Fitness program, a handbook on mycology, or mushroom hunting, a book on butter-flies, a field guide to Rocky Mountain birdlife, an 1897 edition of Gray's *Anatomy*, a copy of a how-to-make-your-own-wine book, and an unexpurgated edition of Krafft-Ebing's *Psychopathia Sexualis,* which no one could read because it was in German, although perhaps not all of the material would have been that shocking or unfamiliar.

There was also the usual conglomeration of junk: rusted pots and pans, tarnished and bent silverware, two broken TV sets, radios, a dartboard with no darts, a menorah with three of its seven candle-holders missing, Jesse's old saddles and leather tack, most of which was beyond redemption; Garrison's cashmere college overcoat, sadly motheaten; five Mexican spurs, none of which matched; various elk and deer antlers that could be sawn into buttons or knife handles; tools, clothing of various kinds, wagon wheels, a piece of redwood all the way from Oregon, two Paisley shawls, four tires turned in-side out with the upper edges scalloped into a sawtooth pattern, which was a popular device hereabouts for geranium planters; an artificial left leg which Jesse had bought off a drunk Navajo for five dollars once and which he had craved because it was too good a bargain to let go by, and then kept on the chance that he might have need of it someday; a set of billiard balls complete except for the 8, 12, and 14 balls; three of Werner's lesser medals including one for good conduct, earned when he was eleven, as an acolyte in the Nazi Youth Corps; some studio portraits of Patsy when she was

twenty-two, in which she looked amazingly like the movie actress
Faye Dunaway; twelve boxes of jigsaw puzzles with all the pieces
intermixed, games of parchesi, dominoes, checkers, wahoo, back-
gammon; old potholders, frayed towels, shoes and boots, none of
which matched into a pair; all the detritus that accumulates around
a house that has been lived in for years.

On the Hurleys' stereo the Red Army Chorus sang plaintive
Russian folk songs, vibrant tenors and stentorian bassos searching
for the farthermost ranges of sweet, sad laments . . . oddly, such
strange music touched a familiar, melancholy chord in the hearts of
these Spanish men and women, who, if asked, would have claimed
a pure Iberian heritage. From Clem's room, acid rock and disco
blared forth. Kids raced around the yards, playing tag and raising
hell. The women picked through the goods that were laid out. Patsy
Hurley was in charge of receipts. No set prices were marked on the
merchandise: a reasonable price was arrived at by discussion. Some
of the junk stuff went for ten and twenty cents an item, but certain
other things, like the golden-oak desk, fetched good prices, cash on
the spot. The money rolled in.

Lulu Uranga and Mamie Lopez got into a fight over who had first
rights to a large imitation-ivory slant-eyed Buddha. Mamie wanted
it because she figured it would provide the final touch to her mantel-
piece, on which stood a collection of ceramic kewpie dolls and a
lineup of oyster shells she had harvested on her honeymoon in Morro
Bay, in 1946. Lulu wanted it because she thought the smiling idol
bore a startling resemblance to the first lover she had ever had. Lulu,
though she knew her place in the village, also had a tendency to stick
up for her rights. She had both hands locked around the Buddha's
neck. Mamie clutched the knees and rear end, and both women were
getting hot under the collar. Dolores Espinoza—the one whose word,
according to Jesse, carried weight—stepped up to them, tall and
regally glacial, and told them in Spanish that their conduct lacked
dignity and grace. Actually, her language was richer than that.
When neither woman would relinquish her hold, Dolores got angry
and said, "So, why are we arguing? Let fate decide." She took out
a quarter and flipped it. Lulu picked heads and got the Buddha.

Mamie Lopez, who was Dolores's best friend, yelled, "It's not
fair."

Dolores glared at her. "Are you telling *me* I am not fair?" she
asked in Spanish. "Is that what you are saying?"

Mamie backed off, and Dolores, who had found an eight-quart pressure cooker she figured she could use, stalked up to Patsy and said, "This is a very nice affair you are having. How much for this?"

"A dollar fifty," Patsy said. "Isn't this the best garage sale ever!"

"Seventy-five cents," Dolores said. "I am a poor woman."

"A dollar fifty."

"Do I look like I'm made of money? A dollar, take it or leave it."

"I'll take it," Patsy said happily.

Willie Montoya and his whole crowd showed up—Cousin Alejandro, another cousin named Arturo, the Jimenez boys from Canjilon, Connie Aragon, the kid brother, Bennie, and a few other rowdy types. Connie bought one of Jesse's rifles, an old 38-40 Winchester lever action with an octagonal barrel, for twenty-five dollars. On the porches, where the other men were hanging around, somebody passed the hat, and Woody was sent off to the Emerald for half a dozen cases of Coors and more bourbon.

Milt Garcia and Coach Rodriguez were in the kitchen of Jesse's house, playing their guitars. Milt was in his stocking feet, with his boots parked under the table. It was Bill Martinez who spied Willie and his pals, and he went over to talk to them. The first thing Willie said was, "This is a public gathering. So we heard."

"That's right, it is," Bill said.

"We also heard it's the nigger's birthday, so we came by to wish him our best."

"Connie, what the hell are you doing with that rifle?" Bill asked.

"Just bought it," Connie replied. "Ain't she a beauty? Hell, Bill, it ain't even in working order. I got to have it rebuilt."

Bill could see that they had had a few drinks, but their attitude, all things considered, was not that bad, or at least no worse than usual. "Let's have an easy afternoon, okay?"

"Exactly what we had in mind," Willie said.

"I mean it."

Willie grinned and raised both hands placatingly. "No problem."

Sally Benavidez came, and so did Gus, and Horacio Quintana, who went straight for the food. Emiliano Tapia, the principal, showed up and tried to talk to Clem about the importance athletics played in a student's life, only Clem and Sally were too busy discoing in the clear space between Jesse's outhouse and the back porch. Some other kids from the high school joined in. Sally had on a halter and the tightest pink hip-hugger jeans ever invented. Patsy

Hurley got sulky and mixed a fresh drink. Jesse, who was drinking too, said to her, "That Sally's got an ass that goes off in all directions at once, don't it?"

Patsy said primly, "Heard melodies are sweet, but those unheard are sweeter . . ."

"What's that mean?" Jesse said.

"Keats meant it to symbolize that the most beautiful thing was something that could not be heard, or grasped, or seen, or attained."

"Well, that sure don't fit Sally," Jesse said. "Whatever she's got, she makes sure it's seeable, graspable, *an'* attainable. Never seen a pair of pants like that on a woman. She bends over too far, they're liable to have to call out the National Guard."

Gus Benavidez wandered from one group to another, holding a beer in one hand and a paper plate loaded with food in the other, trying to be friendly, but no one believed it. Werner Grimmiessen played the accordion, dressed in his Panzerkorps desert tans. Cochise was sprawled in Jesse's geraniums, chewing up an entire roast rabbit he had swiped off one of the serving tables.

By three in the afternoon the Hurley and Slade houses and back yards were still filled with people. Many had settled in to do some serious drinking. Several more guitars had appeared, and Clem had spread out a blanket on the floor of the now empty storage shed and was operating a crap game for some of the kids from the school. Willie Montoya and Connie Aragon were feeding Sally beer and bourbon and trying to talk her into sneaking over to Werner's house for some fun.

Sally said, "With all these people around?"

Connie said, "Have another beer."

On Jesse's back porch, Milt Garcia was showing some of the other men the fast-draw technique he had learned at the law-enforcement officers' training program he had taken down at the State Police Academy. He let off two fast shots from the hip at a beer can he had placed on a tree stump. The first hit a branch in an elm tree thirty feet from the can, and the second drilled through the corrugated tin roof of Jesse's outhouse, which made Gus Benavidez, who had been sitting inside, leave in a hurry with his pants at half-mast.

That started a turkey shoot, using empty cans for turkeys. Horacio Quintana held the pot in his Stetson, a handful of dollar bills. Milt Garcia couldn't hit anything. Bill Martinez tried with his .357

Magnum, and did well. A surprising number of sidearms appeared, despite the fact that Martinez still had not returned some of the hardware he had collected on the day of the great gas-station fight. Jesse got out his .44 and sprained his thumb badly from the recoil of the first shot. Willie Montoya's cousin Arturo made a lot of noise with a .45 automatic he had swiped while in the Marine Corps, and Willie himself didn't do much better with the .25 Beretta he had. Then Werner unlimbered the old Hammerli, and though he was so drunk he could hardly hold the pistol at arm's length, or so it seemed, he won the match hands down with ten beer-can hits out of ten tries, at forty yards.

Garrison Hurley was trying to organize a garden club among the ladies. Clem and Sally were using Werner's bedroom. Patsy Hurley wandered from person to person with a giant martini, telling everybody what a wonderful day it had turned out to be, and in the next breath confessing what she imagined was her darkest secret, which was that she was not a natural blonde. From time to time she asked, of no one in particular, "Has anyone seen Clement? Where's Clement?" Somebody fell on the stereo. In Jesse's kitchen there was a strong smell of burning varnish and wood from Milt Garcia's guitar, which someone had inadvertently leaned against the wood-stove; one by one, the gut strings melted and twanged. A fight got started out back. Bill Martinez broke it up. Gus Benavidez was going around telling everyone, "The life of a small businessman is no bed of roses these days, let me assure you." Sally and Clem reappeared, and Coach Rodriguez got into a free-style wrestling match with Clem, who put up with it until he got bored, and then flipped Herm ass over teakettle into the bed of geraniums occupied by Cochise, who let out a yelp and took off. Woody Klein confessed that this was probably the finest place on the face of the earth in which to live, and Arlene, his wife, who was worried about being pregnant again, looked at him dubiously. Jesse, with his big Stetson tilted back on his head and the .44 stuck into his belt, said with some pride that he was undoubtedly the crankiest old fart in Brazos, and probably the whole county of Rio Arriba, and everybody agreed. The thumb of his right hand was wrapped in a dish towel into which ice cubes had been folded, but even so the crippled hand was able to hold on to a fifth of Heaven Hill, which Jesse leisurely sipped at as he lectured the men on the porch about the virtues of nastiness. He had his left arm around Clem's shoulder. Clem, who had had a lot of beer and a goodly sampling of Patsy Hurley's Tanqueray martinis, didn't seem to mind. "Lookin' at the situation from an overall point of view," the old man said cheerfully, "folks despise me, an' I despise 'em right back. Which is exactly as it should be. I am beholden to no one."

"How'd you get to be so mean, Jesse?" Coach Rodriguez asked.

"Patience and study."

"I guess it runs in the family."

"You mean Clem here? Shit, he ain't mean. Not really. Not *bad* mean, like some I could name. This boy thinks he's mean, and he acts mean, and he looks mean, but I seen worse. And comin' from me that's a compliment, 'cause, as you all know, next to despisin' people I despise kids most."

"Sprout, whyn't you ease off workin' at that bottle?" Clem said.

"Shut up," Jesse told him. "Don't tell me what to do. I'm cele-bratin' your birthday, is all."

"That's still six days off."

"What's wrong with startin' early?"

"I don't dig birthdays."

"Them's my exact feelin's. Every time one comes around it just means that death is one year closer."

"Ease off that bottle, will you, Sprout?"

"Don't tell me what to do. I ever tell you what to do?"

"No more'n forty times a day."

"You give me any sass, I'll ship your ugly ass straight back to Los Angeles," Jesse said. "C.O.D."

"You won't do that. Wouldn't have no one around here to pick on."

"Pickin' on you is like tryin' to eradicate the Rock of Gibraltar with a straight pin. Take twenty years, it might make a scratch."

"What you goin' to do for fun when I'm dead and gone, Sprout?"

"Goin' to do a goddamn fandango on your grave. That's what! I'm savin' the last dance I got in me for that."

"You do that, I'll reach right up out'a my coffin and lay a *hex* on you."

"Shoot! You big ugly Africans thinks you know it all. Hexes! Why, I know *curandera* and *bruja* ladies up in the mountains, they can put together a hex that'll snap your big balls clean up twixt your ears!"

The putdown talk went on. The old man's face was flushed, and

his eyes were bright—with malice or affection, there was no way
of knowing. Out in the back yard the shooters were trying to hit beer
cans tossed overhead, without much luck, and Patsy Hurley was
having a discussion with Sally. "You harlot, I know where you were
with Clem," Patsy was saying. "What were you doing in Werner's
house?"

"Someone was in my house?" Werner said. "Who was in my
house?"

Sally gave Patsy a poisonous look. "We were talking, that's all."

Patsy said disdainfully, "I'll just bet."

"No one is allowed in my house without asking," Werner insisted, frowning at Sally.

Garrison stepped between the two women to arbitrate. "Let's not
ruin a beautiful day, my dears," he kept saying. "It's been such a
lovely day."

"A person who enters my house must be invited first," Werner
was saying over and over. "That is merely reasonable respect."

"Oh, for God's sake, shut up," Sally told him.

Werner glared at her. He sought for the right word, but could
find nothing appropriate that would still be civilized, and finally,
standing almost at attention, croaked in doomsday tones, *"Du bist
eine* troublemaker!"

"Common is more like it," Patsy chimed in.

Willie and his friends had come over by now to hear what the
argument was about. Willie got the picture quickly enough. Clem
again. Less than two hours ago, Sally had been cockteasing him and
Connie about taking a break in Grimmiessen's house, and now all of
a sudden she had changed her mind, only it wasn't them she had
gone off with.

The rest of the people maintained a judicious distance. That is,
they were close enough not to miss a word, but far enough away not
to be immediately involved, should a real dispute begin. They
watched and listened, drinking beer and smoking cigarettes, glancing from one to another: *they* knew what was up. There was Patsy,
and Sally, and Werner, and Willie, and Gus, but in back of everything there was Clem.

Patsy said something else to Sally, who reached past Garrison's
shoulder and gave Patsy a hard shove. Patsy sat down in the bare
dirt, and Garrison grabbed Sally's wrist and said indignantly, "Why

are you hitting my wife? What do you think you are doing?"

Willie stepped forward and said, "Take your hands off her."

"Why is she hitting my wife, what kind of behavior is that?"

Willie hit him, and Garrison, who in his time had designed weaponry capable of taking out whole cities, but who, like Werner Grimmiessen, had never in his life raised a hand in anger against a person, went down for the second time that day.

All of a sudden Clem was there. He said to Willie, "What'd you do that for?" Willie swung, and Clem ducked and struck him in the stomach with a side kick, and with that a free-for-all started. Cousins Alejandro and Arturo and the Jimenez boys got Clem ringed in. Orly Mendocino jumped off the porch to reason with them, and got a bloody nose. Jesse came down off the porch and with his left hand reversed the .44 and used the butt on Alejandro's Stetson. Sally Benavidez was screaming that she had not done anything, and Patsy, sitting there in the dirt, leaned over and sank her teeth into Sally's calf. Somebody fired a shot, and it hit Cochise. The big dog let out a single, fearful howl and rolled in the dirt. Werner let out an anguished "*Liebchen!*" Lulu Uranga punched Arturo, Willie's other cousin, in the balls with deadly aim. Milt Garcia was trying to break it up, at the same time yelling for Bill Martinez, who was dozing in front of a bowling game on the color TV in Jesse's living room. Somebody hit Clem and he went down. Jesse ran toward him, then coughed and let out a terrible gasp. A terrible spasm took the old man, and his wiry body doubled in a convulsion. The .44 fell from his hand. Clem got to him. "You all right?" he asked. "Who hit you? You all right? What's the matter?"

Bill Martinez was on the scene by now, and he and Milt got things more or less calmed down. Patsy Hurley was cradling her husband's head in her lap, while he weakly insisted on the necessity of defending womanhood. Herman Rodriguez was helping Clem with Jesse. Herman knew all about the human body, and now, on his knees beside the old man, he yelled, "Get blankets. Get a car started."

Clem was on his knees too. Shaking the old man by the shoulder. "Sprout, what happened? You scammin' me? Quit your foolin'." He grabbed Jesse's left hand and arm. They were rigid. "What the fuck's wrong with him? Hey now, ol' man! *Hey* now!"

"I ain't sure, but I think he's had a stroke," Herman Rodriguez said.

JESSE WAS IN the hospital for almost three weeks.

The stroke was considered moderately severe. The left side of the old man's face was in a horrible sag, and his left arm and shoulder were drawn up, but these symptoms lessened by the end of the first week.

The worst thing Clem had to look at was the wild, insane glare in Jesse's eyes. During those weeks, the old man could not talk at all. It was as if he was conscious and functioning, aware of what was going on, but was sealed off by silence . . . the mind imprisoned in total helplessness. That was an ugly thing to have to see.

Jesse spent the first week in Espanola General, ninety miles to the south. Clem had a talk with Emiliano Tapia and arranged to drop out of school for an indefinite period. Every day he made the round trip to the hospital, either on the Harley or in the pickup. One afternoon, he spoke with a doctor who was treating Jesse. "How long will it take for him to get better?"

"It's too early to tell yet."

"Well, damn it, *is* he going to get better?"

"I couldn't even venture an opinion on that," the doctor told him. "Who's next of kin?"

"I am."

The doctor thought this over. "No adult in the family?"

"What the hell do I look like?"

"How old are you?"

"Seventeen." The birthday that Patsy had been looking forward to had passed unnoticed. Clem said, "He ain't got no one, except me. He's got some kind of niece over in Germany, but as far as I know . . . well, he just don't have no relations besides me. Everybody else is dead."

By then the EEG and X-rays had located the site of the stroke, in the upper right quadrant of the cerebrum. Jesse was moved by ambulance to Santa Fe, where the diagnostic facilities were better, and this meant another fifty miles a day added to the round trip. At St. Vincent's, in Santa Fe, they put him into Intensive Care. When Clem finally got to see him, the old man was hooked into so many instruments he looked like something out of a horror movie. Inverted bottles were connected to rubber tubes that fed him intravenously. Wires led from his wrists, arms, neck, and head to mysterious electronic gadgets, including an oscilloscope with a green screen that showed all kinds of interesting blips and peaks to indicate what was going on inside Jesse's body.

Clem had an enormous dislike of hospitals. Worse, he knew there was nothing he could do that would help. Nonetheless, he was there at visiting times, and he stayed until it was time to leave, talking to Jesse in a one-sided conversation:

"We made eleven hundred on that garage sale, countin' the Plymouth. The hospital here wanted to know how much bread we had. I didn't tell 'em nothin'.

"Bill Martinez put an assault-and-battery charge on Willie Montoya for startin' the fight. He's out on two hundred bail.

"Everybody's askin' about you. I tell 'em you're doin' fine.

"Ol' man, when you get your ass out'a here, you better get some smarts, and lay off throwin' so much of that cheap booze into yourself. I bet that's what brought all this on.

"You ain't young no more, y'know. Drinkin' and smokin' like a chimney. Shit! You think you Superman or something?"

Jesse stared at him with that wild-eyed expression. Clem said, "Yeah! I know! You look all pissed off. Well, it's your own goddamn fault! Not mine! Ain't no reason for you to be lookin' mean at *me*. *I* didn't do nothin'."

Jesse's right hand was in a cast too. The recoil from that shot from the .44 had fractured a bone in the thumb.

For no evident reason, his fever shot up to 103°. They gave him enemas, and then, because the bladder functions were erratic, the doctors ordered a catheter inserted, so there was one more tube hooked into the old man. By then he was able to make a little noise, nothing like real speech, only grunts and gurglings, but between these and the furious expression, Clem got the idea that Jesse did not like the catheter or the enemas or anything else that was going on.

By the time Clem got home at night it was dark, and he was too tired to see Sally or do anything more than feed the cats and fix a little dinner for himself. Sometimes the Hurleys or Werner would stop by with something for him to eat, and they would sit in the kitchen and have a drink or two while Clem reheated whatever it was they had brought. They would talk of the long drive, Jesse's condition, the approach of winter. One evening Garrison said, "My boy, it might be best to prepare yourself, you know."

Clem was in a bad mood. He had a lot on his mind. He said, "For what?"

"The worst."

"What you talkin', Garrison?"

"Jesse may never be the same. You understand that?"

"What you mean, the same?"

"I lost my own father to a stroke," Garrison explained. He sighed, shook his head, and poured himself a hooker in a jelly jar. "They linger on so. And they can be so helpless. It was a depressing time for me, to say the least."

"Well, it ain't exactly a goddamn picnic for me either, Garrison," Clem said irritably. "You think I enjoy bein' in this fix? Ridin' back and forth. Sittin' around that hospital. That is a bad scene, that place! Tryin' to talk to those doctors. You ever try to get one single word of straight talk out of a doctor? Hell. They sing so pretty, but you can never make out the lyrics. Then I got to talk to the old man. He never *says* anything, just rolls his eyes round in his head, like one of them imbeciles. I never asked for any of this! I got better things to do. I feel like I been set up. This is a nowhere scene. It ain't my natural shot."

Patsy smiled. "We'll look out for you, Clem. Don't worry."

"I don't *want* you lookin' out for me," Clem said angrily. "I been doin' that just fine for years. That is something I know how to do, thank you. Trouble is, that old man ain't got nobody lookin' out for *him*. I feel like splittin' this whole freakin' scene."

"You wouldn't leave, Clem," Garrison said.

"I don't know," Clem said. "I'd kind'a made up my mind I would hang in here until I was eighteen, like maybe another year. Then I'd be free and clear, and it would be strictly make-way-for-Clem. Watch out, world! But this . . ." He shook his head. "This puts the situation in an entirely different light. You got to remember, I never asked to leave California. I was doin' fine back there. I was gettin' by. He forced me to come here. He had no right to go and get sick on me like this. It ain't fair! For two cents, I'd just as soon pack up and go. Put this whole scene out'a my head."

"Would you really do that, Clem?" Garrison asked.

"I might," Clem said sullenly. "I don't know. Something pushes at me too hard, it don't go down good with me. I got just so much patience. Once it's used up, no tellin' what's liable to happen."

All his bad feelings deepened even further when, during the third week of Jesse's hospitalization, Werner came over at ten o'clock one night carrying a quart of bourbon and the large metal cashbox he used for his memorabilia. Cochise came along too. He was recovering slowly from his gunshot wound. The bullet had ripped out a fairsized piece of back muscle, and the wound was covered by a thick gauze bandage. Werner claimed the vet's bill in Espanola had cost over two hundred, not counting the penicillin and antibiotics Cochise had to take. The dog curled up under the kitchen table, and Werner sat down opposite Clem, with the bourbon and the cashbox between them. He asked after Jesse.

"They may let him come home this week, unless something else goes wrong with him," Clem said.

"He was most fortunate," Werner said. "At his age. He could have died on the way to the hospital." He considered this. "He is even luckier. He has you."

"I ain't no nursemaid, Werner," Clem said.

"Perhaps it will all work out," the old German went on. "My hope is that he will recover perfectly. I say this despite that your grandfather and I, we were not exactly friends. Have a drink, Clem." Clem poured a shot into a glass, and Werner continued. "Yes, that Jesse, there is no getting along with him. Very difficult, that man. But there is one thing he knew. A German can always be trusted. Implicitly."

"Is that a fact," Clem said.

"That is why he came to me," Werner said. He unlocked the cashbox. "Who else could he turn to? Here? In this village? The Hurleys? They mean well, but they are undependable. Like children, no?"

"What the hell you blabberin' about?"

"I have the papers."

"What papers?"

"The papers to the property. This house. The forty acres on the river," Werner said simply. He opened the box. In it were his medals, documents and deeds to his own house and the vineyard in Germany, a collection of snapshots of Tunisian and Moroccan lads, circa 1942, who would now, if they were still living, be fat and middle-aged; a lock of black hair, tied with thread, which had been snipped from Werner's head when he was three years old; an old photograph, now sadly faded, of his mother, who at thirty-five looked like a tackle for the Dallas Cowboys decked out in a Bavarian dirndl dress and peasant skirt; the treasured newspaper clippings that described Werner as the finest example of Teutonic warrior-hood, a long-defunct German passport, a handful of Mauser rifle cartridges, a rosary, the fragile husk of a scorpion that had some-how gotten into the box and had long ago starved to death, and the quitclaim deeds and survey plats to Jesse's properties.

Werner said, "Jesse wanted to be sure about this house and the river property. He told me he did not want the county to get it, for back taxes. He did not want the state to get it, or the *verdammt* Internal Revenue, and for sure he did not want that Gus to get hold of it, the way he has with so much other land. He wanted to give it to you."

"Give what to me?"

"This house. The forty acres."

"But it would have come to me anyway."

"Through the courts, my boy, through the courts," Werner said. "There would be the business of probate, the problem of inheritance taxes. So, last month, he came to me and left the papers, with a deed that sold everything to you. For one dollar and consideration."

"What the hell is 'one dollar and consideration'?"

"A local custom. People here do not like anybody, including the county clerk, to know what price their land is bought or sold for. So, often it is sold for a dollar and 'consideration.' You see? We have here the deeds. The clerk at Tierra Amarilla, she notarized them. When you sign them, everything is yours. That is as it should be. He did not want you to know. He said you might worry. He was, of course, thinking of dying. He could not have foreseen this." Werner handed Clem the papers.

Clem was suspicious. "Why'd he put all this on you? He could have come straight to me."

Werner shrugged. "Who knows? His mind worked in strange ways sometimes. He was not always a reasonable man. He had his own way of doing things."

"But you two hassled each other for years," Clem said.

Werner smiled and tasted his drink. "Who else could that poor old man turn to?" He placed a hand placatingly on Clem's arm. "As you must know, the word of a German is sacred. The German race is not easy to understand, but we have a system of honor that is beyond reproach, Clem."

ON THE MORNING Jesse was due for discharge, the doctor put it to Clem in the simplest terms possible. "He may act childlike."

"Been actin' that way his whole life," Clem said.

The doctor ignored this. "He'll probably improve with time. But the tests confirmed our suspicion that the damage was more extensive than we at first thought. Yes, quite serious."

"Changed your mind again, didn't you?"

"I'm speaking relatively," the doctor said. "Actually, a stroke of this severity could easily have been fatal."

Clem stared at him. "Is he goin' to die?"

The doctor glanced at the case record. "Your grandfather's an old man. He might keep going for years, but I wouldn't be fair if I didn't tell you that he might not last nearly that long."

"Don't kid yourself. He's a tough old buzzard."

"I know. As I said, he'll recuperate. To a degree. How much, we can't say. He might go for weeks, a year . . . he might very well have a second stroke. That would probably do it. Then again, there may just be a gradual debilitation."

"You tryin' to say his days are numbered?"

"So are everyone's, son."

"You medical dudes sure got a cheerful way of lookin' at life, ain't you?" Clem said.

"I just want you to have a clear picture," the doctor said. "Many stroke victims never get out of bed again. In your grandfather's case, he's sitting up, and is more or less ambulatory. He can care for himself, in a limited fashion. With help, he can go to the bathroom. He's been feeding himself. His speech is much better, and it will probably improve. Of course, he can't be left alone. Can you handle something like that? Or would you rather put him in a nursing home?"

"A neighbor said he'd never be the same," Clem said.

"I'd agree. His attention span will be erratic. His mind will probably wander."

"I'm all the family he's got."

"I know," the doctor said. He looked at Clem. "It's your decision."

"How in hell can I decide something like *that,*" Clem demanded angrily.

"Somebody has to."

"I got trouble enough just lookin' out for myself. Besides, I'm still a minor. Legally, I can't make that kind of decision."

"There are exceptions," the doctor said. "This case is one. It would be better if you were of age. But I've seen the courts assign responsibility before, in similar situations." The doctor paused. "Do you want to take him home?"

Clem slouched down in his chair, looking sullen. Finally he said, "What other choice have I got?" He felt, somehow, that he had been taken advantage of. Or, to use an old expression of Jesse's, whipsawed.

He loathed committing himself to a categorical yes or no. Was further repelled by the notion of being responsible for anybody else.

But there was really nothing he could do.

Although Jesse could walk, they brought him out in a wheelchair, dressed in the same jeans and jacket he had worn on the day of the garage sale, his Stetson propped on his head, his false teeth buttoned into a shirt pocket. Clem and a ward aide helped him into the pickup, and then they tucked blankets around his legs. Out on the highway, driving north to Brazos, Clem said, "Just don't start complainin' and talkin' down on me, okay?"

Jesse did not reply. He stared out the window on his side peacefully, taking in the familiar landscape. He seemed smaller somehow, shrunken. Maybe it was because he did not have his teeth in. Only the eyes, sunk in their sockets, glittered.

PATSY HURLEY'S WELCOME was sentimental and effusive. "We've missed you!" she kept exclaiming.

She really had a kind and gentle side to her nature. Straight off, without thinking, she did precisely the wrong thing—went up to Jesse there in the kitchen of the house and put her arms around him and gave him a hug.

Werner Grimmiessen, who with Cochise and Garrison and Patsy made up the welcome-home party, winced and shut his eyes in consternation. Turned away, waiting for the old man's blast. In former days, that kind of gesture would have elicited a profane tirade from Jesse. He might even have taken a swing at Patsy. He had always acted as though anything overtly affectionate—anything close to demonstrative love—was at best slightly obscene and at the worst grossly decadent.

Jesse just grinned, showing his gums. Seemed more than a little pleased. He spoke with difficulty. "Hello."

She stared at him. "Jesse, it's *Patsy.*"

"Nice knowin' you."

Patsy turned to Garrison with a look of anguish. Her mouth formed lip-reader's syllables: he . . . doesn't . . . *know* . . . me. Aloud she said, "Oh, dear."

Garrison went up and shook Jesse's left hand. "Glad you're back with us in the land of the living. We've missed you."

"I like it here," Jesse said slowly, looking around. He smiled again. "It's nice. That dog sure is pretty." Cochise wagged his tail.

They all sat down at the kitchen table and had a drink. Clem got out bourbon and beer, and trays of ice from the fridge. Werner had brought a huge bowl of buttered popcorn. He said sentimentally, "In times of difficulties, this is what neighbors are for, *nicht wahr?*"

"I want a drink," Jesse said.

"Well, that's one thing you ain't forgot," Clem said. "No way. The doctors told me you ain't allowed to have anything stronger than milk. That's what got you in this goddamn fix in the first place."

"Want a drink," Jesse said.

"No."

"Little one?"

Clem looked at Garrison, who shrugged and said, "Why not?"

Jesse got a cold Coors and a cigarette. Smiling again, he turned to Patsy. "You got pretty hair. I always liked blondes. Blondes have more fun. You ever hear that?" His words were hard to make out, but understandable.

Patsy blushed, and was so overcome with pleasure that she downed her bourbon in a single gulp.

Jesse leaned over with difficulty and patted Cochise on the head. "Good pup."

Soon enough the guests saw the pattern. Clem was the only one Jesse really seemed to know. It was the boy he turned to again and again, for a cigarette, a drink, a question. With the others he was pleasant enough, but none of them held his attention for very long.

Eventually, they were talking almost as if he were not there at the table.

There were inconsistencies. Jesse couldn't keep anybody's name straight, and at times seemed only half aware that he was in his own home, yet, almost without looking, he was able to get up and hobble over to the stove and absentmindedly reach into the old tin box nailed to the side of a cupboard that held wooden matches. Another time he went out the back door. They watched through the windows as he limped over to an old elm fifteen feet from the porch to relieve himself. This had been a watering spot for forty years.

He moved slowly and with care. Seemed in no great hurry about anything. Seemed, generally, in a content enough mood.

While Jesse was outside pissing, Garrison said, "It may be a blessing."

"Dear, how can you say that?" Patsy said unhappily.

"I am merely being objective," Garrison said. He tasted his drink and glumly stared out the window at Jesse. "What you must understand is that he may be happier now . . . indeed, happy for perhaps the first time in his life. It's as if a great burden has been removed from his life. Or mind. He seems almost to have gone back to some other place. Perhaps, hopefully, a happier time. We can pray for that. Poor Jesse. At his best, he did not exactly have what might be called a complex personality. For him, things were right or wrong. And, for the most part, wrong. As we can attest, my dear, having been his neighbors for years. And as you can too, Werner." Garrison sighed, and tasted his drink again. "There are inestimable difficulties in living with a contiguous neighbor whose value system is based on Old Testament harshness. That poor man was not only at war with the entire world, he was at war within himself. How tragic. It could be that his ill-temper—his constant anger—was as difficult for him to live with as it was for all of us. Now, it is gone. Perhaps forever." Garrison downed what was left of his drink, burped delicately, and went back to the table to pour a freshener. He looked at Clem with doleful affection. "However, the problem is not only with Jesse. How are you holding up, my boy?"

"We'll get by," Clem said.

"It won't be easy."

"We'll help," Patsy said.

"Suppose he lasts for years?" Garrison said.

"Well, goddamn it, supposin' he *does*," Clem said.

Werner interrupted. "Garrison, this is not the time for such talk. My opinion is that Clem has enough to think about for the present."

"And the future," Garrison pointed out. He tasted his fresh drink, and then attempted a brisk cheerfulness. "Well! One must take the bad times along with the good, eh?"

Jesse came back into the kitchen. "Want another drink." Clem poured him a quarter-ounce of bourbon and watered it down. Jesse sat with them at the table, smiling. He turned to Patsy. "You're pretty."

Patsy looked radiant. Then she jumped as Jesse pinched her thigh under the table. She hid her mouth behind a hand and murmured, "Why, Jesse Slade!"

"That's right, I'm Jesse," he said, nodding. "Jesse Slade."

LATE NOVEMBER BROUGHT the first really heavy snows, and several days after Thanksgiving there was a letter from Clara Jenkins, the niece in Germany. Clem had written her while Jesse was still in the hospital, explaining the situation. "Ed's orders have been moved up," she wrote, "and it now appears that we will leave for the States around mid-December, which means that we will be in transit over the holidays, how sad! We are all grieved to hear about Uncle Jesse's misfortune. As soon as we are settled in our new quarters at Colorado Springs, I will be in touch." Clem tossed the letter into the kitchen stove and thought to himself, "No need to worry about *her*. That is one chick don't like bad news. She won't be coming around here, not for a long time!"

In the still and silent mornings the village lay half buried under snow, except where the county plows had cleared lanes through the streets, and smoke rose from the chimneys in vertical tendrils—in the early dawn, there was no breeze at all. Down on Main, a pickup or two might be seen skidding around on the frozen ice as somebody made his way to work at the sawmill or wherever, but in the houses the women would be busy, getting kids breakfast, stoking fireplaces or wood ranges, and yelling at the children to hurry or they would be late for the school bus. And presently, at around quarter to eight, the children of the village would appear, in heavy jackets, mittened, and wearing wool hats, to stand shivering as they waited for Milt Garcia, who besides being sheriff drove the bus, to appear. They

were supposed to wait in groups at designated stops, but they only
did this if they felt like throwing snowballs or horsing around—
most times they waited in front of their homes, and this was all right,
because Milt knew every kid in town and when possible he would
pick them up or drop them right at their front doors, and sometimes,
if they were not on time in the morning, he would get pissed off and
would park the bus, with all its red warning lights blinking, and
run into a house and yell, "You think I got time to wait around all
day. Come on, *ándale,* let's move it, *pronto!*" Milt picked up an
extra hundred dollars a month for driving the old yellow bus, and
the county educational system was glad to have him because the kids
loved the idea of having the town's official gunslinger chauffering
them around: when *he* was behind the wheel, there was no wrestling
or goosing or spitballs whizzing around, no way!

The snow deepened and occasionally slid in small avalanches from
the high-angled tin roofs of the adobe houses. The cats stayed in until
nature prevailed, and then went outside to ankle miserably through
the cold white stuff. Woody Klein put a sign on the door of the
Emerald saying that it would not open until four in the afternoon.
Down at the store, Gus Benavidez stocked sweaters he had bought
in Santa Fe at the K-Mart for eight dollars, which he priced at
twenty, and sold one by one. Around the big potbellied stove at the
rear of the store all the old-timers—the *viejos*—gathered for free
warmth, rolling handmades, drinking an occasional beer, spitting
into a tin bucket Gus provided.

Clem learned that the wood he had chopped during half the
summer was for a purpose, and wished he had chopped more. The
frozen billets of piñon and spruce split with scarcely more than a tap
of the big double-bitted axe. Up at the sawmill, he bought "leftings,"
or scrap tailings, of ponderosa pine and Engelmann spruce for a
buck a pickup load. Such stuff was no good in a fireplace—it spit
and popped too much—but it was perfect for the kitchen stove
because of the heat it produced.

He kept the kitchen hot. The old man liked it that way. Clem got
up in the cold, gray, gritty dawn and made the kitchen comfortable.
Jesse hung out there most of the day, watching the TV which had
been brought in from the living room, drinking coffee, and smoking
cigarettes. Clem fed the stove until the flue whooshed and turned
red at its base. The cats got close and sat with drowsy oriental eyes
and tucked-in paws until their back fur bristled with the heat, and

then they would get up and stroke their sides against Clem's legs, making pests of themselves, until he grew aggravated and fed them. Werner and Cochise came over for coffee, and the dog sprawled on his side by the stove with the cats, to doze and, from time to time, ease off a silent, stunning fart.

"We have a nice day again," Werner would say.

"Colder'n hell, if you want my opinion," Clem replied. "I sure hate cold."

"Warm in here," Jesse said.

"The changing of seasons signifies many things," Werner said.

"Signifies gettin' colder," Clem said. "Last night, on the weather report, it was sixty-five in Los Angeles. 'Fore I come here, I never even seen snow, except on the tube or in a movie."

Jesse sat there with them, dressed in faded but clean jeans and an old cotton workshirt that Patsy Hurley had ironed. He had a bathrobe but refused to wear it. He wasn't much for keeping his teeth in either. He did use his spectacles a great deal more now, to look at the pictures in the hunting magazines that lay around the house. He would sit at the table in the kitchen with his magazines, and the glasses propped on the end of his nose, with maybe a cup of coffee and a piece of buttered toast in a saucer beside him. After the cast had been removed, it had taken him quite a while to learn how to roll a cigarette again, and even now he wasn't too good at it, certainly not as good as he had been before. His fingers trembled and tobacco got spilled, but, still, he managed—rolled and licked the skinny tube, crimped the ends, put it in his mouth, and stroked it smooth with the tips of his fingers, with a trace of that old, delicate gesture.

Clem borrowed boxes of old children's books and ancient issues of *Life* and *Look* from Woody Klein, who, like everybody else, had all kinds of treasures stored away in his garage, and Jesse enjoyed these. "Anything with lots of pictures in it," Clem told Woody. "Hell, I can't even tell if he knows what he's lookin' at, let alone whether he remembers what he's seen, but he seems to dig anything with pictures."

Clem learned how simple and boring life can be. In the morning, he hopped around barefoot on the ice-cold, creaky wood floors. Stoked the stove and got dressed. Then there was breakfast, and later dishes to be washed, and another cup of coffee and a smoke. Wood to be carried in, and then it was time to start thinking about lunch, and after that there was the afternoon, with the television going and the cats to fool with, or maybe Cochise. If it was not too cold they might start up the truck and drive over to Chama to do the laundry, or they would go to Gus's on the pretext of buying one thing or another, and there was the mail to be checked, if there was any, which there usually wasn't, and then there was dinner to start and the evening news to watch, and outside the wind blew great flurries of snow around the house. Deer searching for warmer browse areas came right down to the fields and pastures. Clem bought two poached bucks from Orly Mendocino for twenty dollars apiece, and he and Werner butchered the carcasses into portions and stored the meat in the back shed, where it would stay frozen rock-hard until spring. Woody and Arlene Klein came by to visit, and so did Lulu Uranga, and even Bill Martinez looked in to see how Jesse was doing. Sally Benavidez came too, usually at night, after the old man had been put to bed, ostensibly to have Clem help with her homework, and the two of them would drink a little or smoke a joint in his bedroom and make love until it was time for her to go home.

One night Jesse walked in on them. Sally was sitting atop Clem's quilt, naked and cross-legged, all brown and gold in the soft light cast by the bedside lamp, slender-waisted, with firm breasts, and a luxuriant bush showing between her thighs. Jesse scarcely noticed her, nor was he aware of the odor of grass. He was dressed in long underwear, and had Rojo cradled in his arms. He said to Clem, "Something woke me."

"You got to pee, Sprout?"

"No. I was havin' a dream."

"What about?"

Jesse smiled and shook his head. "I can't recollect." Then he nodded. "I remember. I was dreamin' that I was lookin' for you. I got up out'a bed, and I didn't know where you were. I couldn't find you. That's what the dream was. I went over to the kitchen windows lookin' out for you, and it was dark out there, and I was cold. Then I woke up. And that's where I was, right there by those kitchen windows, lookin' out."

"Come on. I'll tuck you in."

"I kept lookin' out the kitchen windows," Jesse said again. "It's cold out there. Seems like it's been winter forever, don't it?"

"It sure does," Clem said. He slipped on his jeans and helped Jesse back to bed.

When he returned, Sally stared at him. She said, "We got no privacy."

"Sure we do," Clem said. "This is the first time he ever come in."

"It's no kind of life."

"Can't help that."

"You're like a slave to him."

"Baby, it's been one long day," Clem pointed out, getting back into bed. "You start leanin' on me, I'm just liable to kick your ass right out the door."

"They're having a disco over at the high school this Saturday," Sally said.

"I can't go."

"Oh, fuck it." Sally thought for a while, then relit the joint. "You mean to tell me you're happy with all this?"

Clem got irritated. "No, I ain't happy! This goddamn place drives me up the walls. What a town! All anybody here is interested in is someone dyin', or hearin' about which dumb high-school chick is goin' to hatch a rug-rat by spring! The other day, down at the post office, that creep Horacio said, 'I see Jesse is still alive.' And then he looked real disappointed, like maybe it had spoiled his whole day. *'Course* I don't dig it here. I don't know what else to do, though. Take care of the house, cook meals, watch out for the old man, watch TV, look out the windows."

"I'm not going to die here," Sally insisted.

"Suit yourself."

She tried another tack. "I'm saving up my money again. You ain't earning anything for us this way. When I get enough, along with what you owe me, I'm going to leave and go to Santa Fe. They've got a beautician and hairdressers' school down there. I'm going to learn how to be a unisex hair stylist. There's big money in that."

Clem laughed. "Baby, you are out'a sight! *Whoo-eee!* Beauticians' school! I heard about that scam in Santa Fe. They got a dozen more schools like it in Albuquerque, and another up at the vocational trade school in El Rito. They turn out hairdressers like a factory assembly line, and the suckers get a genuine diploma to prove they graduated. Honey, you know how many hairdressers we got here in New Mexico? We probably got more hairdressers than we got cowboys. Got beauticians comin' out'a your ass. You want to make real money, turn whore. With your looks, you'd make it hand over fist, have to buy a wheelbarrow just to lug it all down to the bank."

Sally glared at him. "You calling me a whore?"

" 'Course not! All I'm pointin' out is, most everybody has certain natural assets and talents, that's all. And if that person is going to make her way, well, she ought'a know what her assets are. That's all. That's just usin' your head." He laughed again. "Hey, how about a little head?"

"That's all you ever think about," Sally said. "Looks to me like you're just going to sit around this place forever."

"For the time being, baby. That's all."

"How long is that?"

Clem shrugged.

She said, "You could put him in a rest home, you know. Or the Veterans Hospital or something."

"I suppose I could," Clem said. "I don't know as he'd like it in any of those places, though. I heard some no-good things about places like that."

"Bullshit," Sally insisted. "He doesn't know where he even is most of the time."

"He's gotten lots better," Clem objected. "He's comfortable right here. He knows the cats, and me, and I don't have to help him in the outhouse anymore. He's talkin' lots better."

"You'd be better off rid of him," Sally insisted. "Of course, you won't listen to me." She frowned. "You could change your whole life, just like that."

"Maybe."

"No maybe about it," she said. "You've got the property. My father would buy this place. I happen to know he's interested."

"Is he? Did he maybe ask you to do a little sweet-talkin' to me, too?"

"He doesn't tell me what to do."

"He really wants to buy me out?"

Sally nodded. "He's talkin' ten thousand for the house here, and five more for the acreage on the river."

"My, my!" Clem said. "That's real money, ain't it?"

"Clem, you got two choices. That's all I can see," Sally said. "You stay here with that dying old man. Or you can flush the whole business down the drain once and for all. Start fresh. We'd have money.

We could leave, go wherever we wanted. Nobody'd tell us what to do. Free as the air. We could live."

"Sure," Clem said.

"I'd make you happy, and keep you that way, all day long," Sally said, grinning and kissing him. She threw her arms around his neck and hugged him. "I'd eat you alive and cover you all over with kisses till you couldn't stand it, and wash you in the tub, and rub you down, and buy you some good clothes to wear, you'd be so gorgeous and beautiful!"

"Lawdy *me!*" Clem said, falling into his Alabaman dialect. "Don't *talk* at me like that! Ah's liable to have a faintin' spell just *hearin'* that kind'a talk!"

"Be serious. We could do it."

" 'Deed we could, honeybaby."

"You'll sell? You want me to tell my father?"

"Tell him I'll think it over."

"What's that mean?"

"Just what I said," Clem replied, snuggling up to her. "I will certainly give it due consideration, 'cause business is business, and there ain't nothin' ever been made that didn't have a price. Now come on over here and let's see if you're just talkin' words in the air, or if you got some real credentials workin' for you."

FOR MEDICAL REASONS, the doctors at the Veterans Hospital in Albuquerque were also in favor of permanently admitting Jesse. Clem drove him down there early in December for further tests. The case had been transferred from welfare over to the V.A.

Jesse did not like the hospital and was frightened by it. He didn't like the examination either, which took most of the day, and he pleaded with Clem to stay with him as he was wheeled on a gurney from one room to another in the enormous complex. The hospital people didn't want Clem coming along, but he did anyway, soothing the old man as best he could. Jesse kept saying, "I don't like it here, Clem. When are we goin' home? Can we go home now?"

"Pretty soon, Sprout, just take it easy," Clem told him.

When the tests were finished he had a talk with the chief neurologist, who said, "Physiologically, his recovery has been surprisingly good. Speech, coordination, and motor reflexes aren't bad at all.

However, I wouldn't let that deceive you. Don't expect any further improvement. Nothing of significance, anyway. Eventually, you can expect a decline."

"How long?" Clem asked.

"No telling. But it will come," the doctor said. "Then, of course, he will have to be admitted to this or some other facility that can provide the proper care. Understand, I'm not saying that you aren't doing a fine job. But how will you hold up if, say, he becomes a total bed patient? That's an unpleasant responsibility. It might be better for both of you if the situation were resolved right now. You see, I'm trying to think of you, as well as what may be best for your grandfather."

"You'd take good care of him here?" Clem asked doubtfully.

"As good as can be provided by anyone else," the neurologist said. "This isn't a high-class nursing home, but we do our best to take proper care of our veterans. It's our job."

Clem asked to see where Jesse would stay. The doctor phoned for a male nurse, who took Clem and the old man on a tour of the wards.

Clem hated all hospitals on general principle, because they were places people went to when they were in trouble, or sick, or dying. But he had no idea it would be like this.

The thing was, they did try to do the best for the patients, that was obvious. But the entire facility was so awesomely depressing, so fearful, that Clem's spirits went down, and then further down, and then down some more. Linoleum-floored wards, the walls painted in grays and greens, plaster peeling or mottled scabrously. Sickening odors of antiseptic, urine, feces, stale food, and the inimitable, overpowering stench of rotting flesh coming from terminal cancer patients. Men of all ages—some senile—trussed in hospital beds or in wheelchairs, or hobbling on crutches, some blind or deaf, others missing one or more limbs, or with faces that were horribly scarred or even shot away by shrapnel or explosives in some long-ago, forgotten war—one man's face was completely gone, leaving the eyes, and then nothing, nothing at all, below, no face, no chin, nothing but a gaping void and a ghastly opening out of which dangled part of a tongue. Burn victims in blue cotton bathrobes with faces and limbs shriveled and scarred. Housed in this place were all the leftovers from service to one's country, the last stop on the line for patriotism: here were kept the men who had defended their government and people, and now they were serving out the last of their time, day by day, year after year, until finally, sooner or later, they earned the release of death, and so, in a manner of speaking, were freed at last.

Jesse was as frightened as Clem. Held him by the arm as they followed after the male nurse. Kept mumbling, "I don't like this place, Clem. Clem, I sure don't like this place at all."

"Hang cool, Sprout."

"You ain't goin' to leave me here, are you, Clem? I want'a go home. I don't like it here, Clem. Can we go now?"

Before the tour was completed, Clem told the nurse that he had seen enough. He said, "Hey, man, how long some of these dudes been in here?"

"Depends," the nurse told him. "Some check in and don't last long at all. Then again, we have maybe five or six old boys, they've been here since the First World War was over."

Clem thanked him for his trouble. The nurse said, "This old-timer coming in?"

"No, he ain't," Clem said.

The nurse frowned. "Oh, I must have got it wrong. I thought he was being admitted."

"Not on your motherfuckin' life."

He and Jesse left the hospital without even bothering to see the neurologist again. Out in the huge parking lot, he put Jesse into the cab of the pickup and wrapped him in blankets. Jesse said, "Where we goin'?"

"Home," Clem said.

On the highway headed north, he got angry. Carried on a one-sided conversation, half with himself, half with Jesse. "I don't know why all the bad luck in this world has to come my way! I must'a been born under a dark cloud, that's for sure. Could be off and free, my own man, 'stead of bein' trapped in that stinkin' town! Money in my jeans. Have the whole world sittin' right in the palm of my hand. 'Stead, I got to put up with *you*, ol' man. Feedin' you and shavin' your ugly whiskers. Makin' sure you eat without sloppin' everything all over yourself. Cochise has got better table manners. Well, just don't push me too far. That's all I'm tellin' you! Don't give me a lot of shit. I don't need it. I got troubles I ain't even used yet! Washin' up after you, takin' care of you night and day. I ain't no servant, you better understand that."

Jesse said, "I'm hungry."

"Here." Clem reached over to the glove compartment and pulled out two sandwiches made with baloney and cheese and the white bread the old man liked to eat when he was not wearing his dentures. "Just eat, and shut up for a change!"

WINTER SETTLED IN with a vengeance, and half the time Bill Martinez had the highway shut down. The temperature went to thirty-five below, which amazed Clem because the impressions he had had of the Southwest before coming here included images of hot, sandy deserts, cactus, and plains and mesas with Indians riding horses. At night in the fields outside the village, coyotes howled and yipped as they ranged through the deep drifts in hunting packs. Clem burned firewood as fast as he split it, and complained to Jesse, "How'd you ever get by before I come along? God almighty, I used to complain about this no-good house bein' too small for both of us. Now I wish it was half the size. There'd be that much less to heat."

They went everywhere together. At the Emerald Bar, Clem bought them beers. This, aside from Gus's store, was the only place in the village where anything resembling a social life could be found, and on late afternoons and sometimes into the early evenings he and Jesse would sit at the bar and pass the time with Woody Klein or Lulu or whoever might come in. The Hurleys and Werner Grimmiessen were there a lot too. Connie Aragon and Willie Montoya showed up with their pals, to sit at tables near the butane stove and play penny-ante poker. They left Clem alone, and he did not speak to them. The assault charges against Willie had been dismissed for lack of evidence, and he bragged about this a few times. Clem let it go, because it had been his experience that there was no justice anywhere, especially where the law was concerned. Willie still owed him money for the Harley's tires, but for the time being, he was willing to let that slide too. He had more than enough to keep him busy with Jesse, and the way it worked out was that a truce of sorts was unofficially declared, at least for the duration of the winter. When spring came, that would be another story. Clem was sure of this. One afternoon, when the only customers were he and Jesse, he told Woody, "Oh, it's quiet enough now. But nothin's changed. They still hate me. This whole goddamn town. Things have cooled off for a while, that's all, and I ain't talkin' about the weather. Give it time, and something'll start."

"Hate's a strong word," Woody said.

"Maybe so, but it fits the situation," Clem replied. "All I want is to be left alone. It don't follow from that that I'm goin' to let anybody around here step on me. Nossir. I'm hangin' in. Doesn't mean I want to. I got all kinds of other things I'd rather be doin' than messin' around here, watchin' out for this ol' fool. You know what he did this morning? Went to the outhouse in his longjohns, no coat, no hat, barefoot, through the snow. When I got him back in the house I had to sit him by the stove for an hour to get him thawed. Watchin' out for him is worse than takin' care of six kids. Other day, I caught him eatin' the goddamn cats' kibbles! Said they tasted good. Ain't that so, Sprout?" Clem glanced at Jesse sitting beside him. "You want'a grow a tail and fur, like that Rojo? Is that what you want? You better look out, ol' man. Eat those kibbles, you'll be meowin' at me." Jesse looked from Clem to Woody and grinned.

"Those doctors down in Albuquerque ever have anything final to say about him?" Woody asked.

"Shoot! Woody, don't talk at me about no doctors," Clem replied. "I wouldn't take a doctor's word if you paid me. One says one thing. Another says something different. None of it adds up." He glanced at Jesse again. "He's comin' along just fine. Ain't you, Sprout? Ol' buzzard like him, why, that stroke would'a knocked the shit out of anybody. He'll be okay. I ought'a know. I live with him seven days a week, don't I? He'll get his act together."

"You two making it okay, then?" Woody wanted to know.

"Sittin' on top of the world. Got money to last the winter, and his and my Social Security checks comin' in regular. Got food and liquor and tobacco, and a house that's pretty near warm enough to live in. I bet I chinked up six hundred cracks in those mud walls, where the wind was whistlin' through. The ol' man, he was right about one thing—when things are tight, a person don't need a whole lot to get by. Sure, offhand, I'd say we was doin' fine."

"Glad to hear that," Woody said. "There's talk going around that you're thinking of selling out."

"You don't say!" Clem grinned, and shook his head. "Wonder what these people'd do if they didn't have something to talk about? My, my! Gus been spreadin' the good word, has he? Him or Sally."

"Gus is just land crazy," Woody said. "I'm glad it's just talk—your selling."

"Well, y'know, in a way I'd like to," Clem said. He stared at Jesse again. "Only it's his place. I got the papers and all that, but it's really his. It ain't much, but he ain't got nothin' else. I guess it's a mixed-up scene, Woody. Don't think there ain't days when I'd just like to pack up and clear out. Other days, it ain't so bad."

"Why don't you just sit on it?" Woody advised.

"That's precisely my own feelin's," Clem said. "It's dumb, makin' a fast move. Stay cool and hang loose. That is one thing I learned a long time ago. You got something they want, they got to come to you. I ain't in no hurry. I'd be kind'a curious to see how much Gus might up his offer if I let a little time coast by. Fun around with him a bit, eh? Maybe even start another rumor. Like, that I'm thinkin' of selling out to somebody else. Give him something to chew on at night, when he's lyin' in the sack figurin' up his bank accounts."

"You ever play poker, Clem?" Woody asked, smiling.

" 'Deed I have!" Clem said. "Man, that is one game I have always dug, since I was a kid. It's lots better'n shootin' craps or hittin' the roulette table, 'cause all those games depend on chance or luck, and with something like poker you got people to work with. The cards that get dealt is only part of it. You got to know how to work the people who're sittin' at that table, callin' or raisin' your hand, or foldin'. The cards you're holdin' are just luck—good or bad—but the coolest part of it is workin' your people. Makin' 'em scared of what you might be holdin' when maybe it ain't nothin'. Or makin' 'em feel brave because they *think* you ain't got nothin', and there you are sittin' with three Ladies and you're lookin' all nervous and doubtful. And they're raisin' the ante, and you're stayin', lookin' more scared. And they keep on raisin'. And you keep on stayin'. And they *know* they got you by the balls, an' they're *sure* you're just bluffin' 'em. And by and by, why, that pot is *real* big, and somebody finally calls the hand, and you spread out those three pretty Ladies, oh, *my!* Then, maybe a couple of hands later, you ain't got nothin', no more'n a pair of tens for openers, and you start raisin' the ante, and they're rememberin' those three Ladies. And then it's their turn to get scared, and that is a fine feelin', to watch your people fold, one by one, on what you're holdin', which is shit." Clem chuckled, and drank his beer. "Now, you take Gus. Tell me, Woody, how would you go about workin' him?"

"Negotiate?" Woody ventured.

"Shoot! Man, that is needless work," Clem said. He slapped the top of the bar delightedly. "Hope I never have to play poker with *you*."

"What would you do?"

"Simple. You let him do it all for you. That's what workin' a mark is all about. You got to learn how to put yourself inside your mark's head and figure out what's goin' down."

"Like how?"

"You said it yourself, Woody. You ought'a pay more attention to what you're sayin'," Clem replied. "Gus is land crazy."

"Sure."

"Well, here is how I figure he'll be thinkin'. He makes this here offer. Probably Sprout's property is worth twice the figure Gus comes up with. But that ain't important right now. So, he makes an offer, and all I'm doin' is sittin' tight, hangin' loose, actin' like I don't know what is comin' down. No matter. What counts is that I don't take the deal. So ol' Gus, he's thinkin' about how to get this property. And the more he thinks on it, the more he wants it, right? It's like I got something he wants, or thinks he wants, or believes he's *got'a* have. Presently, it gets so that he's thinkin' he can't live without gettin' his hands on this piece of property! So then he ups his offer. And I'm still sittin' around with my thumb stuck up my ass, like I just can't for the life of me make up my poor, scatterbrained mind about which way to jump. And more time goes by, and by then his mind is *set*. He starts gettin' a cravin' that is all out of proportion to the deal. By then what the property is really worth ain't important no more. He's got to have it. He's goin' to *die* unless he gets it. Then maybe he hears a little talk about how somebody else is goin' to buy it. Well, that is just *too* much! By now his ass is so bugged about that property that he's convinced he has first rights to it, that he *deserves* to own it, and now some motherfucker is goin' to steal it away from him, after all the thinkin' and schemin' and worryin' and plannin' he's put into it!" Clem drank some of his beer, scratched his head, and smiled at Woody. "That is when you got him eatin' out of your hand, man. See what I mean? That's what I mean by workin' a mark. Let him do the work for you. You can't miss. That is when he'll meet your askin' price! It may be two, three times more'n what the property is worth. That don't make no difference. He'll go away thinkin' he's got himself the best bargain of his whole life, and he'll be smilin' and congratulatin' himself on how smooth an' cool an' hip he is, and how he put one over on you. That's okay! Let him believe it. What counts is that you got his bread in your wallet. He'll brag about himself, about how sharp he is, and how dumb you are. Meanwhile, you're pussyfootin' down to the bank to make a fat deposit!"

"Clem, did you ever think of making a career out of psychology?" Woody asked.

"I don't dig any of that shit, man," Clem said, still grinning. "I been around them psychologists before, when I was a kid. Woody, they don't know from nothin'! They got a lot of fancy names for things, and it's all crap. Now, if they took the effort to know about people a little, and what makes 'em the way they are, I might have some respect for them, but as it is, they're hung up on all those fancy words they use."

Woody considered this. He said finally, "But would you really sell, Clem?"

Clem frowned. "I don't know," he said. "That is a completely different scene. I just don't know. Learnin' how to work a mark ain't so hard. Learnin' how to work with your own self is lots harder. You got to watch out that your own head don't work against your best interests. Yes, indeed, that can be a serious problem, when a person is clockin' a mark and then, for no reason at all, his own self comes tippytoein' up behind him and taps him on the shoulder and gets him really fucked up."

DURING THE WEEK before Christmas, Clem's mood worsened. It always did around this time of year. For him, holidays were bad news.

When Patsy Hurley asked what plans he had for himself and Jesse, he said, "Ain't got none."

"Oh, Clem, you can't do that," Patsy said. "Christmas is special."

"Just one more day of the year as far as this man's concerned."

"No, it's *not!*" She looked at him with a distressed expression. "Aren't you at least going to put up a tree? A little one?"

"No way," Clem replied. "Sprout never went in for any of that, did he?"

"Not that we know of."

"Well, I don't see no reason to start changin' things now."

"Will you cook a turkey?"

"Got us some nice venison steaks and chili. That'll be enough."

Patsy said angrily, "How dreary."

"Don't start on me, Patsy. It just happens to be the way I am," Clem said. "I never dug holidays. Quit tryin' to change me around. I am what I am, that's all."

"How sad," she said.

"You hear me complainin'?" Clem said irritably. "It ain't so bad! The old man and me, we're doin' okay. Why, I can remember lots of times when it wasn't so good. In fact, to tell the truth, I can't remember one goddamn time when all this Christmas jazz amounted to anything. One Christmas, I was in the slammer. Couple of other Christmases, I cruised the streets. Didn't have no place to stay, no place to go, no friends, no nothin'! That suited me fine! The other Christmases I can remember, I was stuck in some foster home. Or, when I was real little, I was dumped with neighbors or my old man's friends, while he went off someplace cruisin' on his own, I guess. I know what being poor is. I don't expect nothin', and I don't give nothin'. Just don't dig it. Christmas is one day I just want to get through as easy as I can. Maybe we'll come by for a drink. I wouldn't mind that."

Patsy said nothing more.

In the village, the front doors of all the houses were hung with wreaths made of piñon, spruce boughs, and native mistletoe. There was no holly in this part of the world, so a bright-red touch was added to the wreaths with cured chilis. Men in four-wheel-drive vehicles drove up into the mountains and cut small spruces for their families and friends. The children went on their best behavior, and frozen turkeys and fat roasting hens were brought in from storage sheds to thaw. Horacio Quintana hung a sign in the window of the post office that said Christmas was an official federal holiday and that there would be no mail, which everybody knew anyway, and Woody Klein threw his annual party at the Emerald, which featured hot toddies and endless amounts of steaming *posole* and pork spareribs cooked up by Lulu Uranga, and had a sellout crowd. Sally Benavidez and Clem got into an argument, and she quit him flat and began going around with Willie Montoya. Patsy Hurley and Werner said it was the best possible thing that could have happened, and told Clem not to grieve, that there were other fish in the pond, at which point they gave each other dirty looks.

On Christmas Eve, all the children came out and wandered through the snowy streets singing carols in Spanish, and at midnight, since there was no parish church to toll its bell, Milt Garcia drove up and down Main Street with the siren on his prowl car going full blast. By then the children were asleep, or were supposed to be. Orly Mendocino pulled an annual stunt for his youngest kids, the ones who still believed. He let the fire die in the fireplace until it was a bed of gray-white ashes, else Santa could not get down into the house. Then he dunked his boots in the soft ashes and hand-walked them all over the living room and around the spangled tree, making a terrible mess of footprints to show that Santa had actually come into the house that way during the night when everyone was asleep, and had left ashy handprints, too, all over the whitewashed adobe fireplace—well, this was one Santa who wasn't especially tidy! Tessie, his wife, who was exhausted by the long day, frowned and complained about the cleaning up she'd have to do, and Orly said, "What the hell's the harm in it?" and when he was done they drank a six-pack of beer together in the kitchen, and then went to bed and fell asleep and got some rest before the living room turned into a crazy house at six the next morning.

At seven the next morning, there was more caroling, of a different sort, in the back yard of Jesse's property. Werner with his accordion, wheezing out "Silent Night." Patsy, in Garrison's oversized rubber shoepacs and a scurfy sealskin coat that dated back thirty years. Garrison, with his big red nose and the Harvard muffler wrapped round and round his head, fearfully bleary-eyed, looking convinced that this was no fit place or time of day for a civilized man to be, but nonetheless carrying the melody in a fine, resonant baritone, while Werner yodeled and Patsy's whiskeyish coloratura cracked the soprano sound barrier when they came to *"Sleep in hea—ven—ly pe—ace!"* Cochise sat in the snow and wagged his tail. In that house, he knew, were kibbles. What else could Clem do but ask them in?

Jesse in his longjohns, two pairs of socks, and an old sweater. Clem in jeans and the sleeveless sheepskin vest. They all drank bourbon and hot coffee that morning, at first to dissipate the chill, and later because it tasted good, and by ten everybody including Jesse was half crocked.

By noon they were over at the Hurleys' because Patsy finally remembered that she had to baste the turkey. And besides, that's where the presents were. Clem was at first indignant that there was something for him and Jesse. "No way! No way!" he kept insisting. "We didn't get any of you people nothin', so there ain't no way we can take anything."

"Oh, pooh!" Patsy said. Garrison was making eggnog, leaning heavily on the rum and cinnamon and leaving out most of the cream. He said, "Don't be absurd!"

"I don't dig any of that stuff," Clem said.

Werner lurched up to him and shook a finger under his nose. "You are *most* exasperating! Do you know that? Be still! I have heard enough."

Like so many other things, accepting a gift was something Clem simply did not know how to handle. He actually got upset, and then embarrassed. For a change, he could think of nothing to say, nothing flip or sassy.

Jesse got a large canister of Prince Albert, wrapped in fancy paper, and a two-pound homemade fruitcake that Patsy's sister in Philadelphia had mailed, and which the Hurleys could not use because Patsy had cavities and Garrison didn't go in for that sort of thing.

Garrison gave Clem an old copy of Thomas Merton's *The Seven Story Mountain,* while Patsy, suddenly all sentimental and bashful, looked down at the floor as he unwrapped a knitted wool scarf that she had been working on for weeks.

Werner's present was narrow and heavy. Clem unwrapped the paper and found a short sword, with a straight blade and a staghorn handle, silver-hilted. The length of the blade was ornamented with elegant engraved scrollwork and hunting scenes. It was old. Nineteenth century. Clem, who liked weapons, was much taken with it.

"This is what you call a genuine Austrian *Haufänger,"* Werner explained. "A boar-hunting sword that the old hunters carried with them in the mountains. I could not bear to let it go at the garage sale, so I hid it. It has been in my family for years." He looked at Clem and smiled. "I hope you like it."

Clem couldn't think of anything to say, and then finally, since some sort of comment seemed to be required, mumbled, "Thanks."

By the time dinner was ready later that afternoon, everybody was soused. Patsy put too much brown sugar on the sweet potatoes and they burned, and then she spilled half her drink down Jesse's neck while dancing with Clem in a boogaloo version of a French madrigal Garrison had put on the stereo. Jesse wiped the back of his neck, smiled, and sipped at his bourbon.

Werner beat Clem four times straight at wrist wrestling, and was dumbfounded at Patsy's strength when she insisted on trying it too, and nearly broke his arm. Then she wanted to take on Clem, but he said he was too tired. Garrison went out to piss off the back porch, and fell off it. Patsy fussed with a large pot of turkey gravy made with giblets, claiming that no one in New Mexico could produce a gravy equal to hers, and absentmindedly dumped half a can of curry powder into it instead of the paprika she thought she was holding, and said, "Oh, screw it, it's Christmas in India too!" Cochise got the pope's nose and stretched out on the floor to eat it. Everybody sang, and Patsy brought down the house with a song about "There was a little girl like the choo-choo that knew it could, it could, it could . . ." Clem in a moment of camaraderie slapped Garrison on the back, and Garrison fell down again. They picked him up and set him on a chair.

Werner scientifically carved the turkey—using the razor-sharp *Haufänger*—and some of Patsy's cherished Irish-lace tablecloth too. He kept asking, *"Weiss oder dunkeln, weiss oder dunkeln?"* By then, nobody cared about white or dark. Garrison sat on his chair with a drink in one hand and a turkey leg in the other, nibbling, and explained how this animal was ranked among the noblest of birds, and that dear old Ben Franklin was on the right track about wanting to have it as the national emblem instead of the bald eagle. "Observe an eagle," Garrison said. "Its countenance, you will note, is not exactly brimming over with the spirit of benevolence. I ask you, have you ever seen an affectionate eagle, one with a mild and trusting look? I daresay not! On the other hand, the turkey has a certain depth of character. That is why the Japanese call it 'the bird with a thousand faces.' "

"Oh, Garrison, blow it out your ass," Patsy said. She smiled at the others. "Isn't he a dear? The more he drinks the more he talks, and the more I drink the less I hear, that's why we get along perfectly." She reached down and tucked a cloth napkin into his open shirt collar.

Garrison smiled and chewed at the turkey leg. "Do you know that you are a very beautiful girl? Has anyone ever told you that? It's true!"

Patsy's eyes brimmed with tears. "Why, Garrison Hurley," she said, "that is the very sweetest thing that has ever been said to me."

Werner was shouting into Jesse's ear, a cupped hand to his mouth. "You are lucky to have this boy! Do you realize that? You . . . are . . . lucky . . . Jesse!" He had somehow gotten the idea that Jesse's stroke had made him hard of hearing.

Jesse smiled. "I can hear you. Don't shout."

"He's . . . a . . . good . . . boy!"

"Yes," Jesse said. "Can I have some more stuffing? It sure is good."

"He's goin' to be all right," Clem was saying over and over. "Every day he's gettin' back to his old self. I mean, you might not see it, or other people mightn't, but *I* can tell, 'cause I'm with him all the time, y'see? That's how you can tell about someone, when you're with 'em all the time, right?" The quart of bourbon they had brought from their house was almost empty. He turned to Jesse and put an arm around him. "Ain't that right? You're goin' to be jus' fine. Right?" And, to Patsy: "He's some tough ol' dude, ain't he? Couldn't kill him if you tried. Ain't that right, Sprout? You're goin' to make it. Ain't you? You ain't goin' to die. Don't you go dyin' on me. Else I'll piss on your grave. I swear on that!"

In all of Brazos on that day there was no stranger conclave. A celebration of the misbegotten and unwanted. Clem was not the only one who had felt rejected and spurned. Werner had taken his turn. So had the Hurleys, and through the years they too had experienced joyless Christmases, when the gesture is made, the small, silly tree trimmed, the laboriously fashioned homemade wreath hung on the door that is never knocked on.

On more than one Christmas old Grimmiessen had elected to remain in bed with a bottle. It was one of the few times he allowed Cochise to curl up on the quilt with him, while the old Telefunken radio in the kitchen blared out "Adeste Fidelis."

Too many times had the Hurleys planned a private, sensible day, "just something for ourselves." And had, by late afternoon, after all the rum eggnog and all the Chablis were drunk, gone to bed to weep in each other's arms, weeping for no real reason except that it was Christmas, and all each had was the other.

Christmas is a time for cheer, and it is most of all a time for children, and in these homes, including Jesse's, there had been no child, except now Clem, who could not really be called a child, and of whom maybe the best that could be said was that he was misbegotten too, but better than nothing, indeed yes, better than nothing at all, even with his foul talk and hard ways. With all his terrible faults he brought something with him, he was *there*, and in some way that was important, it counted! It was the best of all possible days, and on this night they would all sleep peacefully, even Jesse, who was already nodding over his plate. The old man had had too much to drink. It was bad for him, but it was Christmas. Clem helped Patsy put Garrison to bed and, beside the bedroom door, they kissed, but it was such a naïve and gentle bit of affection that it meant nothing, and moments later Patsy was weeping on his shoulder.

Back in the kitchen, Werner stood militarily erect and proclaimed that Clem was a formally adopted nephew, and with that he put his arms around Clem's shoulders and kissed him on the mouth, and Clem, who when sober would have recoiled, acquiesced to his own emotions and felt affection and love.

"Merry Christmas, Clem," Patsy said.

"Merry Christmas."

"Merry Christmas, Clem," Werner said.

"Merry Christmas, Werner."

Patsy clasped her hands against her breast. "Oh, it's been the very best Christmas *ever!*" She began weeping again.

"*Ja. Bestimmt!*" Werner said. "*Fröhliche Weihnachten, es ist wunderbar, ich habe noch Freuden im diesem Welt!*"

Clem got Jesse back to the house and put him to bed. Drunkenly solicitous. "You okay, ol' man? You got to go?"

"I'm fine," Jesse said.

"You warm enough?"

"Feel good."

"Listen, you get up in the middle of the night, wake me," Clem said. "You hear me? Don't you go wanderin' around."

Jesse nodded. In a moment, he was asleep.

In the kitchen, Clem fixed a nightcap for himself, though he didn't need it. Coming back from the fridge he stepped on Rojo's tail, and the red cat squealed. "Sorry about that," Clem said. "Don't get in the way, nobody'll step on you. That's the name of the game, cat."

He went outside to piss. Against the same elm Jesse used. Too far to the outhouse.

The night was black. No moon, no stars. A solid overcast.

Low clouds scudding by overhead.

And, a rare thing: fog. A slow-moving layer of thick mist drifting down across the outer fields. Shrouding the houses in pearly gray. The yellow illumination from the kitchen windows of the three houses caught the fog, shining in the mist like angled lighthouse beacons. Clem leaned against the elm and rubbed his cheek against the hard, frozen bark. Then embraced it, locking the fingers of one hand around the wrist of the other, and squeezed with all his strength.

Sat down in the deep snow. Legs apart, elbows on knees. Felt intimations of mortality. Knew that Jesse and Patsy and Garrison and Werner, and everybody else, including himself, would one day be buried in the cold ground. They would all die. In the darkness, he stared down at snow he could not see, and shivered as a chill struck through his jacket.

Shook his head back and forth sadly. Half mournfully, half angrily.

Muttered a soliloquy of his own. "No-good sonuvabitch! Miserable, chickenshit bastard! Goddamn you! You better *not* die!"

Shook his head again. "Better not! No motherfuckin' way. That's for sure."

For a while, he let the tears come hard. Finally, he got up and went into the house, wiping his nose and eyes with the back of his hand. Said one more time, "Motherfucker! Don't you die on me! Ain't got time for any of this here dyin' shit!"

SIX

IN JANUARY A break in the bad weather arrived, and so did Clara and Colonel Jenkins. They were preceded by a note that caught Clem completely off guard: ". . . we can only visit briefly, as we will be en route to Albuquerque, to see our oldest daughter, who is enrolled at UNM."

"What in hell they comin' around now for?" he said to Jesse. "Who needs 'em? We got no time for these people. They never gave us the time of day when you was sick in the hospital, and now they think they can just drop in any ol' time the mood takes 'em."

Nonetheless, he made a stab at cleaning the house. Swept the floors and washed some of the windows, and rearranged the dust that had gathered. The place had gotten messy during the winter. He did a laundry, and changed the sheets and pillowcases. "Bet she's one of them picky types who's always stickin' her nose where it don't belong," he said. "Nothin' satisfies that kind'a chick! Well, we'll just show her what a high-rent pad is."

But the house wasn't much, even cleaned up. Clem had gotten used to the place, and now he found himself looking at it as he himself had first seen it, with the eye of a stranger. The calcimined walls were grimy, and in all the rooms the air was permeated with cooking smells.

The Colonel and his wife were exactly like their Christmas-card Kodacolor, except that in the flesh they looked heavier. When Clem opened the front door to their knock, Clara Jenkins' mouth dropped open. She did a double take. So did Edwin, her husband. He was in uniform. She wore a fur coat with a hat that matched, slacks, and sensible winter boots.

"I'm Clem Slade," Clem said.

"Oh."

"You want'a come in?"

"That would be nice," Clara Jenkins said. She was still staring at him. "It was a terribly difficult drive. La Veta Pass is barely open." Parked at the side of the road was a Volkswagen Rabbit.

Clem said, "You have any trouble findin' the house?"

"We asked at the post office."

"Well, come in, if you want to," Clem said. "No sense standin' here with the door open, lettin' the house get cold."

He led the way through the living room to the kitchen. "I'll put some coffee on," he said. Jesse was sitting at the kitchen table, looking through an old comic book. Clem said, "Sprout, this here is your relation, from over in Germany."

"Uncle Jesse," Clara Jenkins said. She was still looking at Clem.

"Hello," Jesse said.

"You remember your niece?" Clem said. "They always send Christmas cards?"

"How are you?" Jesse said, smiling.

"He don't remember," Clem informed the Jenkinses.

"It's warm in here," the Colonel said.

"Lemme have your coats," Clem said. He took them, and the Colonel's cap. Mrs. Jenkins kept her fur hat on. Clem said, "Go ahead, sit down."

They did, and she lit a cigarette. "Uncle Jesse, how are you feeling?"

"Just fine," Jesse said.

"You look well."

"I do?"

There was a silence. She and her husband looked at Clem. He said irritably, "It's okay. You can go ahead and talk in front of him, if you want. He don't mind. Half the time he doesn't know what the talkin's about, the other half he ain't payin' attention."

"I didn't think the stroke was that severe, from your letter," Clara Jenkins said.

"It was bad enough."

"What do the doctors say?"

"He's comin' along okay."

"And you've been taking care of him?"

"That's right. You people like milk and sugar?"

"Please," she said, and then, after another pause: "That's most commendable."

"What is?"

"Your shouldering such a responsibility."

Clem stared at her. "Ain't no hassle." He got up and went to the cupboards and took down cups and saucers. There was another silence. He said, "How y'all dig Colorado?"

"Oh, it's lovely," Clara said. "But of course we miss our home in Wiesbaden dreadfully. We were there three years, you know." She puffed at her cigarette.

Clem said, "Is it true, you ain't seen Sprout since you was a kid?"

"Yes."

"And you still sent all them cards at Christmas and Easter?"

"It was a custom in my family," she said. "A small way of maintaining family ties. He's the only member left in the Slade branch."

"Him and me," Clem said.

There was another pause. She said finally, "Why, I suppose that's true."

"I guess you an' me, we're some kind'a cousins."

Nobody had anything to say about this. Clem went to the stove and got the coffee and poured it, and then sat down again. Clara Jenkins stubbed out her cigarette and lit another. The Colonel got out a pipe and occupied himself cleaning the bowl with a reamer and then stuffing it with tobacco. Clem said, "You two seemed kind'a surprised when I opened the door."

"We've been looking forward so to seeing you and Jesse," Clara said.

"Oh. I thought maybe it was 'cause I was black or something," Clem said.

"Of course not," Clara Jenkins said. "Although the letters never mentioned that you were . . ." She groped for the right word. "Mulatto?"

"I guess they didn't," Clem said. "That make a difference?"

"Of course not," she said.

Colonel Jenkins stared into the bowl of his pipe. "Prejudice no longer exists in the armed forces."

"I'll just bet," Clem said. He smiled at them and leaned back in his chair. " 'Course, I told the Sprout here, way before he had his stroke, that he was crazy not to tell you I wasn't white. You know what he said? 'Even a fish can stay out'a trouble, if it can just learn to keep its big mouth shut.' He was one stubborn son of a bitch. Still is. If he made up his mind black was white, there was no movin' him. Ain't that so, Sprout?"

"That's right," Jesse said.

"You ol' fool."

Jesse smiled at the three of them. There was another silence. Clara Jenkins looked uncomfortable, and the Colonel stared down at his pipe. She said, "Of course, we want to do what is right. And we shall."

"You don't have to worry about us," Clem said.

"Oh, I'm so relieved to hear that," she said.

"I told him he was full of shit with all his talk about you people adoptin' me," Clem said. "I mean, you ain't got no obligation to me."

"Not legally," the Colonel said.

"It would be immensely difficult," Clara Jenkins said.

"I dig that."

"Of course we do feel a moral responsibility," she said.

"No need to get in a sweat."

"Family *is* family," she said. "Uncle Jesse's first letter mentioned that you were from California originally."

"That's right. Los Angeles," Clem said.

"And you have no one there?"

"Nope. Sprout here come and got me."

She looked puzzled. "But how did you get by? A young boy. You must have had someone."

"Mostly I pimped and pushed dope," Clem said.

Colonel Jenkins stared at Clem, and then at his wife, with an expression of horrified astonishment. He said, "What did you say?"

Clem said, "Had four white chicks working for me. On the side, I had a little business with hot credit cards."

"Oh, dear," Clara Jenkins said.

"You were in trouble with the law?" the Colonel asked.

"First time I was busted, I was eleven," Clem said. "I got a record as long as your arm."

Clara Jenkins and her husband thought this over. They exchanged glances while Clem poured more coffee. The Colonel said finally, "Clem, is there anything we can do for you? We have to be going soon. It's at least four hours to Albuquerque."

"Well, we sure could use a little money," Clem said. "The old man's prescriptions cost something awful, even with the discount we get, 'cause he's over sixty-five."

"Why, of course," Clara Jenkins said. "Ed?"

The Colonel reached for his wallet. "How much could you use?"

"Oh, I don't know . . . I hate to ask," Clem said. "Three hundred'd help."

The Colonel winced. "I'm afraid we don't have that much cash with us."

"Check's okay," Clem said. The Colonel got out his checkbook.

"Is there anything else we can do?" Clara Jenkins said, putting out her cigarette.

"Like what?"

"Ed and I simply want to be assured in our own minds that you two are all right here."

"Me an' Sprout? I told you. We gettin' by fine."

"Clem, I want you to understand, if you ever need help . . ." She glanced at Jesse. "I mean, if the time comes when it's necessary to do something."

"Like what?"

"The V.A. Hospital. We have to face reality. Ed could be most helpful in expediting the paperwork. Isn't that right, hon?"

"Ain't goin' to expedite shit," Clem said coldly. "I seen one of them places. That ain't no place for an old man like Sprout. You put him in there, he'd die in a month. What you want'a do, kill him? He don't dig any of those places. No way. I got something to say about that."

"Not necessarily, Clem," she said.

"What the fuck you talkin'?" Clem said, getting hostile. "I'm takin' care of him, ain't I? You tryin' to pull something? You try gettin' fancy, I'm liable to do a little expeditin' of my own. He ain't goin' in no hospital."

"I wasn't trying to be intimidating," she said, alarmed. "I only meant, well . . . if he takes a sudden turn for the worse."

"Why'd he want'a do a thing like that?" Clem demanded. "He's come back a long way. The doctors, they all say he's goin' to be okay. Why, you ought'a seen him when I first brought him home. It was like takin' care of a baby. He's in great shape now, compared to what he was. Don't talk at me about no goddamn hospitals, not after all the work I already put in on him."

They left it at that. The Jenkinses departed after finishing their coffee, with assurances from Clem that he would be in touch should anything, as Clara put it, ". . . take a turn for the worse."

"Oh, I'll do that," Clem told them, out by their car.

Clara said, "I do want you to know how relieved Ed and I are to know you're handling everything here so well."

"No sweat, like I said," Clem replied. "That three hundred'd be a real help. To tell the truth, I been worried about money."

"We'll send a little something from time to time," she said.

"Appreciate it," Clem said.

As he told Jesse later that afternoon, over a couple of beers, "That's what comes of stickin' your nose where it ain't welcome, and tryin' to do good. Yessir, ol' man, that is the best way I know of to get a surprise you don't need. First they *seen* me. Then they *heard* about me! They was in such a rush to get out'a this house, they both got stuck in the front door." He laughed and shook his head. "All that talk about family, and wantin' to do the right thing. Shoot! That's where good intentions come from . . . feelin' guilty. That's why it 'most always pays to steer clear of any dude who's tryin' to do you a favor. Usually, that dude's just tryin' to make himself feel good. You may not *need* help, and you may not *want* it, but if some asshole makes up his mind he's got to do you something, he won't give you no peace of mind till he does. Who needs it? We don't! Maybe in a couple of months we'll hit 'em for another few hundred. Be doin' 'em a favor. Make 'em feel good, and at the same time they won't come around buggin' us."

"What was they talkin' about?" Jesse asked. "Tell me what they were talkin' about, Clem?"

"Wasn't nothin'," Clem said, grinning. "Don't worry your ol' head about it, you hear? We got the world by the ass. Made in the shade. In the clear, never fear. Hey, ol' man, what say I make us up a big bowl of popcorn, eh? And we'll see what's on TV."

"CLEM?" JESSE SAID one day.

"What?"

"What's dyin' like?"

"How in hell would I know?"

"Clem, am I dyin'?"

"What the fuck you talkin', ol' man?"

Jesse began weeping quietly. "I don't want'a die."

"Why you talkin' like that? You tryin' to bug me?"

"I'm scared," Jesse said. Tears began trickling down his sunken cheeks. He shook his head. "I'm scared," he said again.

"Shut the hell up!" Clem said. "I can't stand that kind'a talk."

"I want'a go home."

"You crazy ol' off-the-wall weirdo, you *are* home."

"Wanta go where it's warm," Jesse said complainingly. "I'm cold."

"You want your sweater? Is that what you're bitchin' about?"

"I'm cold all over."

"Will you get off that talk!"

"When's summer comin'? I'm so cold. I want'a feel the sun again, one more time."

"You and me both."

"I want'a go home and sit in the sun and git warm all over," Jesse said. "Where's your mother?" He meant Clem's dead grandmother. Lately he had begun confusing Clem with his father. "Where in hell is that woman? Why ain't she here? She ought'a be at home where she belongs. Off talkin' with the neighbors again. That ain't right. Whenever there's chores and cookin' she's off somewhere. Why ain't she here? Damn that woman."

"Take it easy, ol' man."

"Chuck some wood into that stove, why don't you?" Jesse said, and Clem did.

It was March. Winter had closed in on the town again. Clem had cabin fever. There was nothing to do. Depression gripped him.

That was how it started—with Jesse himself adding to the discontent. As Clem told Patsy one afternoon, "I don't like it. He's talkin' lots better, only it's like his mind is all over the place. Gives me the creeps sometimes. One minute he knows who I am, it seems, then the next he's talkin' like I'm my old man, then after a while that'll drift off too, and he don't know who in hell I am, or where he's at, or what year it is. I don't know what I'm goin' to do with him."

Patsy had worries of her own. The week before, she and Clem had taken Garrison down to Espanola and put him in the hospital with a case of the galloping DT's. Patsy wept all the way and kept asking, "What will I do? What in the world am I going to do?" while Garrison carried on about how it was raining inside the car, and that the rain was radioactive. "It's plutonium, can't you feel it? Deuteron bombardment's out of control, beta particles everywhere." At the hospital they strapped him into bed and sedated him. He was discharged in four days and came home with enough Librium to tranquilize the whole village, and orders from the doctors to take 100 milligrams of the drug daily until his system dried out completely, which, considering the punishment he had subjected it to, might take years. Now, though still weak, he was sober. Moreover, Patsy was too.

In the hospital, Garrison had been turned on by some A.A. literature, and now he had great plans for establishing a chapter in Brazos. "Like the very best concepts, it is inherently simple," he lectured his wife. "First of all, one must admit that one is an alcoholic. Well, I've always suspected that I was. Then, one must embrace God, and through prayer ask for help. Oh, this will be the best thing that has ever happened to Brazos! Have you any inkling of how much alcohol the inhabitants of this little village put into themselves?"

"They ain't got nothin' else to do, Garrison," Clem pointed out, when Garrison gave him the same lecture. "Got to pass the time some way."

"In a stupor, half alive," Garrison said scornfully. He looked at Patsy. "Don't you feel like a different person since we stopped, darling?"

Patsy, who had not had to face her husband or herself stone sober since the early days of their marriage, said skeptically, "Well, I feel *different*, if that's what you mean." Nonetheless, if only to humor him, she got out her India ink and Speedball pens and lettered a placard inviting those who were interested in forming an A.A. chapter to get in touch. She posted it on Horacio's bulletin board, where it was ignored by everyone.

Life in Brazos drifted on. Sally Benavidez ran off to Tucson with an unemployed ski instructor from Steamboat Springs, whom she had met at the Longhorn Café in Chama. Willie Montoya's pelvis was shattered in four places by an unattended forklift that somebody had left in neutral, and it was questionable whether he would ever walk again. He had picked up a part-time job at a lumber-supply house in Chama and was stacking two-by-twelves when the forklift pinned him against the wall of the lumber shed. Connie Aragon joined the Marines and left for boot camp, and Gus Benavidez made a formal offer to buy the property from Clem, upping his price to $16,000. Clem said he would think about it. Before the conversation was finished, Gus had gone to $17,500, which, he said, was tops. "It's more than I can afford, but I want to be fair. You won't get a better deal from no one else. My advice, Clem, is to take it."

At the Emerald, over afternoon beers, Clem complained to Woody Klein, "I feel strung out. Got nothin' workin' for me no more. Ain't even got the energy to hustle Gus."

"How high do you think he might go?"

"Twenty, easy. Maybe twenty-one. If he starts feelin' real pain, he could hit twenty-two, but I doubt he'd go much higher. You want another beer, Sprout?"

Jesse smiled and nodded, and Woody opened a fresh Coors. He nodded toward Jesse. "Is it getting to you, Clem?"

Clem shrugged. "It's like he's fadin' on me. Y'know?"

"That can happen, I guess."

"I don't know what more I can do," Clem said. "You see how much weight he's lost? I make him eat five, six times a day. Things he likes. That Campbell's Chicken Noodle Soup stuff. He digs that, with Saltines busted up in it, so they get soft and he can chew 'em. I got to stay right there with him and remind him to keep eatin', else he'll forget what he's sittin' at the table for. Sometimes I feed him. He only eats a little bit at a time, then he says he ain't hungry. He'll take a whole hour to eat a little cup of soup. By then it's cold. He likes his beer. I don't begrudge him that. I think he gits as much nourishment from that as anything else. The doctors said no tobacco or liquor. What the fuck else has he got? If he enjoys a cigarette and a few beers, I say let him have 'em, right, Woody?"

"If it keeps him happy, why not?"

"Happy? I don't think anything makes him happy," Clem said. "Sometimes he just sits and cries like a little kid. I can't hack that."

"Clem, he's an old man."

"I can't help that," Clem said. "So maybe, like Garrison says, he didn't have much of a life. Ain't nothin' I can do about that either. I ain't had such a hot life myself."

"But, Clem, you're young," Woody pointed out.

"Wait fifty years," Clem said glumly. He drank some of his beer. "Sometimes I wish I'd just kept on movin', that day when Montoya and his bunch boxed me in. There ain't nothin' to do here. What d'you do here, Woody? I mean, besides havin' kids."

"Run the bar. I'm rebuilding that Plymouth," Woody said.

Clem shook his head. "I look at that ol' house sometimes, and say to myself, 'What the hell you think you doin' here?' I tell you, there are times when I feel like goin' for Gus's offer. Grab the money and run. Take the ol' man and put him in that truck and off we go, someplace where it's warm. That's a lot of bread. Take the damn cats too. Just go. You ever get that feelin'?"

"Once," Woody said. "I wanted to go to Alaska, back when the government was still giving out good homestead lands."

"Why didn't you?"

"That was the year Arlene had the twins," Woody said. "Finally, I gave up on it. You're not serious, are you? About leaving?"

"What do me and the ol' man got to stay for?" Clem said. "You know what keeps goin' through my head? We get in that truck, in two days we're down in the desert, where it's warm. In three or four, we could be at a beach, dunkin' our toes in the Pacific. Orange Juliuses spiked with rum, that is some drink! Just layin' around, soakin' it all in. He's always complainin' about how he can't get warm up here. Let him get his suntan back. Beach time, *whoo-eee!* How about that, Sprout? You see all those cute bikinis, if that don't snap your ol' ass back to normal, I don't know what will, hey?"

Woody said, "You want to do that, why not just close up the house for the winter and go? I don't think you should sell."

"You take a vacation, you need money, man," Clem said. "We got about five hundred between us. How far we goin' to get on that? Hell, I've blown that much in a weekend, all on my own. You got to pay to play, man. You goin' to make a move, don't screw around. Do it in style."

"That house is your equity," Woody insisted.

"Don't know nothin' about no equity," Clem said. "Don't know how long this ol' man's goin' to last on me. It's his house, and it's his money. I'd just as soon show him a good time, for once in his life. All he's ever known is scufflin'. Let him have good conditions, just once. What the hell is wrong with that?"

"This is his home," Woody said. "It's yours too, in case you don't know it."

"Not so," Clem said, shaking his head. "He don't know this place no more. What he knows is his Hershey bars. That is something he'll still eat. Sometime, when he was a little kid, somebody must'a bought him Hershey bars. It's things like that that count with him now." He lit a cigarette, and finished his beer. "As for me, this ain't my home. Ain't got no home. Never did have one. I'm just a rollin' stone. That's my style. Screw this town. It never gave a damn for the old man. 'Course, when he was his old self he was so mean it's under-standable why people couldn't stand him. As for me, they'll be dancin' in the streets when I go. No doubt in my mind about that. You been okay to me, and so have a few others. As for the rest of 'em, I could turn my back on this place with *no* regrets!"

He would not have thought it possible, but he finally had to admit to himself that it was not easy to live in a place where everybody ignores your existence. He was still an outcast. Except for the Hur-leys and Werner and Woody and Lulu Uranga and Orly Mendocino, he might have been invisible. There was a side of him that relished attention, even if it was critical. At least last summer there had been some fun and excitement with Willie Montoya and Connie Aragon, and Sally. There had been Jesse to fight with. Patsy Hurley and Werner to kid around with, Bill Martinez and Milt Garcia and Coach Rodriguez to bug. For a fact, he had made the most of what little the town had to offer.

Now it all seemed old. What he had told Woody was true. He was a rolling stone, he had no real home, no identity. He belonged no-where. It had always been that way, from the time he'd been born, and it would go on that way, so he might as well get used to it, be-cause none of it was going to change. The closest he had come to making it was with the old man. No arguing that. He would have liked Jesse to have understood that much. Now it was too late. The old man would not have comprehended what he was trying to say. What Jesse was tuned in on these days was hot soup, and a couple of beers, and watching TV.

"They don't care anything about us," Clem told him one evening at home. Jesse had the *Muppet Show* on, and was enjoying it.

"Damn, carryin' on a conversation with you is almost as good as talkin' to yourself. Don't you ever hear anything I say?"

"I can hear you," Jesse said. "Don't yell."

"I don't know why I got to make all the decisions around this place," Clem said. "Whyn't you help me once in a while? You want us to split this scene, say so. You want to stay, speak your piece."

Jesse said nothing.

Clem had an inspiration. He took a quarter from his pocket and flipped it. "Heads we sell, and split. Tails, we hang in. What d'you say? You want to call the shot? Heads or tails?"

Jesse looked at him and smiled. "Heads," he said without hesitation, and heads it was.

Next morning Clem saw Gus and closed the deal at $21,500. Gus said, "I'll call my lawyer in Espanola. He should have the papers drawn up by the end of the week."

ONCE THE DECISION had been made, Clem felt better. In fact, felt a growing excitement. As though a burden had been lifted from him. "Could have gotten twenty-two," he told himself. "But, what the hell, we can be generous."

To Jesse he said, "I'm goin' to show you what it is like to live, ol' man! Goin' to take you where the sun never stops shinin', where people know how to treat a man right. Yessir! You know what I'm goin' to do when we get that money? When we leave, I'm goin' to fill up the whole goddamn back of the camper with Hershey bars for you! I mean it! *Whoo-eee!* We'll go down to the Hickory Farms place and pick out all that cheese and that greaseball salami you dig. Oh, I got plans! I'm goin' to get Orly to weld a motorcycle trailer to hitch onto the back of the truck, so's we can take the Harley. Ain't about to leave that! Goin' to get you some new threads, and get your plates fixed, so's you can do some chewin' instead of gummin'. We'll have us some *real* good times. If we go to L.A., I'll take you out on the Strip, won't that be something! Let you dig all those Rolls an' Mercedes and custom Bentleys, and all that flashy snatch promenadin' up and down. Pussy comin' out'a your ears, Sprout, how about that! Gash galore! Slip a finger in that, an' they climb the walls howlin' for more. Makes you young an' well-hung. Makes the juices flow an' flow. Get us some head, Fred. We'll make a pair. They never seen nothin' like *us*. And, best of all, we'll be legal. Strictly up front. Open a bank account with that money. Maybe get us one of them condominium apartments down off La Brea. Air-conditionin', built-in bar, elevator, swimming pool. Oh, my! Spring is comin'. Springtime nights in the City of the Angels, hey? How about that? In the spring the evenings in Los Angeles are balmy, balmy like the Caribbean, and the breeze comes in off the ocean, you couldn't want anything more. Get you one of them recliner armchairs for watchin' TV, and fatten you up. I got a suspicion a change of pace might do you good, ol' man. I been suspectin' that for some time now. Man needs a jolt every now and then. We'll have us a time, that's for *sure!*"

Word got around. This time it was Clem who let it be known. He made no secret of the forthcoming arrangement with Gus Benavidez. Was almost arrogant. "Goin' to shake this town's dust out'a our asses for good."

And got varying reactions.

The hardest was from Werner Grimmiessen. "Is it true?" he asked. "What is this I have heard? Is it true?"

"It's true," Clem said.

"You can't leave."

"Who the hell says I can't?"

"Clem!"

"Werner, goddamn it, it's better, all the way around."

He was astonished when the old German became outraged, then insulted. Finally Werner turned his back on him, there in the kitchen, and when Clem put an arm around his shoulder and turned him, he saw that the old man was weeping. Werner said, "You cannot go. That is not right."

"Werner, you're wrong."

Werner shook his head emphatically and would say nothing more. He stalked out of the house, shaking his head and muttering to himself, "People today . . . they are made of ice."

Patsy Hurley was no better. She got very quiet when she heard. Looked rather helpless. "Oh. Well, I'm sure you know what's best. I certainly don't."

Garrison was pontifically enthusiastic. He said, "Youth is the time for new vistas and change and adventure. How we envy you! Patricia and I are trapped here now. We shall miss you. How I hate to think how much we will miss you. Think of us sometimes. Will you promise that? Just a passing thought . . . of us, back here. You are ours, much as you belong to Jesse. I was hoping to have you address the first A.A. meeting I am planning. For a young fellow you can hold your own surprisingly well."

"We'll write postcards, every week," Clem promised.

At the post office, Horacio Quintana said, "You're leaving, I hear."

"You heard right."

"You're smart."

"I know."

"You don't know what it's like to spend your whole life here," Horacio said.

"Ain't plannin' on findin' out."

"It's hell, believe me," Horacio said. Behind the grilled window, he tapped a forefinger on the countertop. "I believe that what is right is right! You don't know. Nobody does! All I want is to get by. I got a crippled back and terrible health problems." Through the grill, he gave Clem his best carrion-bird expression. "It is not easy for a handicapped person, believe me. You know why they hate me? It is not because of watching the water, or that I try my best to do my job. I will tell you. A postmaster is a federal appointment! It is for life! That is what they begrudge me. In this entire town I have the only steady job for life. Not so bad for a handicapped person with a back that's in pain and a cataract that can't be operated on, eh?"

Then, on the same day, outside Gus's, he met Dolores Espinoza and Mamie Lopez. On this windy and frozen day, Dolores was wearing blue jeans, lace-up lumberjack boots, and a wool mackinaw, and she had her usual arrogant expression. She said, "I hear you're going away." It was as much a statement as a question.

"That's right," Clem said.

Dolores tilted her head back and stared down that big beak of a nose. She said, "You are stupid."

"Could be."

There was something about Dolores that reminded Clem of Jesse, before he had his stroke. She had the same sort of hard-nosed nastiness. And she had judged him. He put on his coolest attitude. "Don't need you doin' a number on me, Miz Espinoza."

"Land is the only thing I know of that appreciates in value," Dolores told him. "Are you crazy, to give something like that away? Is Benavidez something special, like the church maybe, that you have to give everything you have?"

"Everybody's tryin' to tell me what to do," Clem said. "I got to say, that kind'a routine don't really turn me on."

"Somebody has to tell you, *estúpido*," Dolores said.

Clem said, "Miz Espinoza, just for once why don't you get off my fuckin' back?"

Jesse was sitting in the parked truck, with the engine going and the heater on. Mamie Lopez, when she heard Clem's remark, let off a chatter of Spanish to Dolores, in which Clem heard *negrito* several times. Dolores looked hard at her friend, and Mamie shut up. Her expression was formidable. She said, "I have heard about that dirty mouth you have. Why do you have to be so *macho* all the time? Are you such a big deal? Don't use that dirty talk around me. Last year, all you did was fight and chase girls and make trouble around bars. Why can't you behave yourself?"

"Got no time for sermons, lady," Clem said. "And I ain't in the business of livin' up to your expectations either! You don't dig me. I don't dig you. Let's leave it at that."

Mamie said something else in Spanish, and Dolores turned and gave her an even sterner look. She shook her head and said in English, "No, he isn't that bad. He takes care of his own, at least. Give him credit for that." She turned back to Clem and nodded, showing him those glittering, hard eyes. "Yes. Better than some others in this town, though I hate to admit it. He takes care of his own."

Clem thought nothing much of this remark, and dismissed it.

Later that day, however, he stopped to get some gas for the truck at Orly's station. Mendocino put in three dollars' worth and said, "Say, I heard Dolores Espinoza said you take care of your own."

"So what?" Clem said.

The next day, at the post office, Horacio said, "Dolores Espinoza said you take care of your own, I hear."

Later, that same day, at the Emerald, Lulu Uranga grinned at him and said, "Dolores Espinoza, she says you take care of your own."

"Lu, what the fuck you *talkin'*?" Clem demanded. He took off Jesse's coat and hat and hung them up on some nails Woody had driven into the wall by the door.

Woody got two Coors for him and Jesse, and explained. "That means something."

"Doesn't mean anything as far as I'm concerned," Clem said.

Woody shook his head. "It means something around here."

"All I ever heard about that bitch was that she judged me," Clem said.

"So she did," Woody agreed. "And now she's changed her mind. I'd say that means something."

"Not to me," Clem said.

"Clem, you don't know these people," Lulu put in.

"Don't want to."

"These people are strange," Woody said. "They take their time about things. Something they don't understand, it gets them edgy. And I guess you certainly were something different, all right. Clem, you hit this town last summer, and like it or not, you were something different." Woody reflected on this. "I'd say that is putting it mildly."

Clem smiled. "Shook this ol' place up, eh?"

Woody nodded. "You didn't do bad." He wiped down the bar. "What Dolores Espinoza is saying now is that you finally did something people can understand."

"Like what?"

"Taking care of Jesse."

"That ain't nothin'."

"No. You're wrong. These people place a lot of value on that. 'Taking care of your own' is a big thing. Like a custom." Woody sought for the words to explain it. "Clem, it's a poor town, this place. But people take care of their own, see? Especially old people. These Spanish people may be tough as hell, but they have a lot of respect for old folks. They don't dump them in nursing homes or anything like that. I guess what they believe in is a family staying together. I don't know how else to put it. Why, take Arlene. She made it clear to me when we got engaged that I was marrying her family as well as her. At first I never took that serious, but after a while I learned. I sure did. We still have grandpa Esteban with us. He's eighty-seven. I rebuilt the little storeroom back of the garage into a bedroom when Arlene decided he was too old to be by himself. And I had to fix it the way he wanted it. Nothing fancy. Not nearly as fancy as some nursing homes, from what I hear. It's got two beds in it. And a table and some chairs. An old radio, and a galvanized tub he does his dishes in. He gets his own water in a bucket, from a tap outside. That's what he was used to, his entire life. I put in a sheepherder stove. The kids chop and fetch wood for him. He takes supper every night with all of us. Afterward, he goes out to his room. Every single night, one of the kids takes a turn staying with him out there, so that he won't be lonesome. He really likes that. Arlene, she takes his old-age check and buys him beans and tobacco and whatever other stuff he likes. You know, he's eighty percent blind. But he's pretty good at getting around by himself, in the house or in that back storeroom. He doesn't have much, but he's got family. It's like Jews can be. I never would have thought it, until I saw it myself. You know what happens? Old Esteban, he hangs around his room all day long. But every single day at three thirty he's there in the living room, waiting for the kids to get home from school. They fool around with him. I guess it's that he has someone to talk to. He doesn't speak any English. I can't make out most of what he says, but the kids under-stand him fine. You'd think with all the years I've spent in this valley, I'd have learned Spanish by now. That's what Dolores Espinoza meant. She was talking about how you've looked out for Jesse. You took care of your own. She likes you for that."

PATSY SAID, "BUT are you sure you're doing the right thing?"

"No, I ain't," Clem said. "Ain't sure of nothin'. You askin' for a guarantee? I got to do something, that's all I know."

"It *is* his home," she said.

They were sitting in the Hurley kitchen, and for several days she had been carrying on a campaign to get him to change his mind. Gus Benavidez's lawyer was out of town until next week, so the real estate deal had been postponed. Clem figured that Patsy's arguments in-volved her own best interests as well as Jesse's, but he no longer cared for the gameplaying and manipulation that had once absorbed him. Felt too weary and dispirited.

He hated admitting it, but he was feeling a sense of loss over leaving this place. Felt something akin to, if not sharper than, his own self-admonition of last summer over leaving Los Angeles: "Man, it is a dislocation *syn*-drome, that's all. It will pass."

He felt unaccountable sadness. Concealed it. Or tried to. Told Patsy in a moment of seriousness, "Well, y'know, I guess this must be about the longest I ever spent in one place, just sittin' still. Even when they had me in foster homes, when I was a kid, I never stayed more'n five or six months. I'd run off, get on the outside, or get busted, something like that. I sure was something when I was younger. Walkin' trouble. Always movin' around from one place to the next, seein' what I could see. And now I'm leavin' here too. Well, that's how it goes. Don't pay to look behind. What's up front is what counts."

"I just don't know," she said. "I'm trying to understand, but it's hard."

That night he said to Jesse, "You sure you want'a go?"

Jesse smiled and said nothing.

"Now, you listen to me, ol' man," Clem said. "You better tell me, if you ain't sure. Once we sell, that's it. Don't you come around buggin' me later on about missin' this ol' pile of shit of a town and wishin' you was back here, or something. I ain't goin' to listen to any of that."

"What time is it?" Jesse asked.

"How the hell do I know? Why you always askin' me what *time* is it? About eight, I guess. What the hell difference does it make? What good's it do you, knowin' the time?"

"I was just wonderin'," Jesse said.

Clem looked disgusted. "You got some kind'a super-important appointment you don't want to be late for or something? You drivin' me up the wall, ol' man. You something else. I'm goin' to buy you a wristwatch, with all them dials and second hands. Then you won't be buggin' me all the time. 'What *time* is it?' Shit!"

The next day at the Emerald, he said to Woody, "What's the chance of gettin' you to open this joint at noon, Friday?"

"Why would I want to do that?" Woody said.

"Well, I want'a hire the place," Clem explained. "There's something I want to do. Sort of a little party. Nothin' big. We can't afford it. I want to ask Patsy and Garrison and Werner to come. Orly too. Drinks an' eats on me and Jesse. Maybe Lu could cook up a little something good to snack on. Could you do that for me, Lu?"

"I can do that," Lulu said.

"Just the folks I mentioned," Clem said to Woody. " 'Course, you and Lu too, and Arlene, if she can come. Will you do it, Woody?"

"I'll be glad to," Woody said.

Clem left thirty dollars with Lulu for food. Woody estimated that the liquor would cost another thirty or forty more.

Clem turned to Jesse. "How's that hit you? We're goin' to have us a party."

"A birthday party?" Jesse asked. "Is it someone's birthday?"

"No, not a *birth*-day party, you idiot. I'm talkin' about a party-type party."

"That's nice," Jesse said. "Parties are fun."

When she heard about it, Patsy Hurley said she liked parties too. "Sometimes I feel like I'm living with Saint Thomas Aquinas."

Garrison was guardedly enthusiastic. "We'll come. With the categorical proviso, however, that Patsy and I stick to ginger ale. We've made such progress! It would be anathema to backslide now, wouldn't it, dear?"

Patsy looked glum and said, "Gee, honey, Rome wasn't built in a day, you know."

"We're doing superbly."

"Well, I don't feel so superb," Patsy said. "It's all well and good for you. You're a man. You're strong, and when you make up your mind you can be so dedicated. But me. One teensy-weensy little nip wouldn't hurt. Clem's get-together will be a very special occasion."

"The ideal time to put ourselves to the test," Garrison said agreeably. "Out of the crucible comes the finest steel."

But by midmorning that Friday, Patsy lapsed. Via one excuse or another, she made numerous trips over to Jesse's place for a touch of bourbon and grapefruit juice, disguising her breath from Garrison with Saltines and peanut butter. After her sixth, she declared, "All I'm saying is that I haven't had a drop in twenty-six straight days. What the hell kind of life is that, is all I want to know? Oh, Clem, if you leave, I don't know what I'll do."

"You'll get by," Clem said.

"No, I won't! I'll kill myself."

"No way."

"You've been like a staff for me to lean on."

"You're one strong chick."

"Oh, I have to be! Have you ever tried living with a saint?"

"Can't say that I have."

"It's a pain in the ass, let me tell you," Patsy said. She poured herself another bourbon and smeared a Saltine with peanut butter. "Is it my fault if I'm human? Is that a sin?" In the living room, she kissed him moistly, smelling of peanuts and Heaven Hill. Stared at him, the lizard-lids of her eyes wrinkling angrily. "Bad, bad boy! Leaving me. If you weren't so big, I swear, I believe I'd turn you over my knee and take down your pants and give you a good spanking!"

"I'll just bet you would," Clem said.

THE PARTY STARTED shortly after noon. Werner brought his accordion and Cochise, and Woody Klein took down his NO PETS
ALLOWED sign.

Like most farewell parties, it began on a lame note. The conversation was painful and crippled. It was cold in the big bar at first,
because the butane heater had not been on long enough to warm the
place. Orly Mendocino, in his quilted parka and with a dewy pearl
dripping from his nose, came in for a double bourbon and said he
would be back later in the afternoon after he had closed the station.
Garrison said, "I took the liberty of inviting Horacio Quintana to
our little fete."

"What the hell for?" Clem asked.

"He is the first member of our Brazos chapter," Garrison explained. "That poor, poor man needs comfort."

"He ain't fit for social company," Clem said.

"You're wrong!" Garrison said. "When I heard his story!" He
sipped his ginger ale. "Clement, he *came* to me! One lost soul,
searching out another."

"Y'all find your way?"

"He confessed. He drinks two six-packs a night," Garrison said.
"Buys it by the case. In Espanola, so no one here will know. Simply
fantastic! He can't weigh more than a hundred pounds. He's drunk
two six-packs a night for twenty years! Oh, Clement. A handicapped
person. He feels ostracized. Feels unloved."

"Can't imagine why," Clem said. "If I looked like him, I'd go find
a hole in the ground to crawl into."

"Anyway, I invited him to look in," Garrison went on. "With your
permission, of course."

"Oh, he'll liven things up, all right," Clem said. He got up and
fed quarters into the juke. Had a beer, and danced with Lulu, and
then Patsy. Spread along the bar were trays and bowls of hot food
that Lulu had prepared: *posole,* tortillas, roast chicken, potato salad,
coleslaw, bean dip.

No one talked much. Clem said, "Is this a party or a burial?"

Woody Klein poured himself a bourbon-and-ginger and said,
"What the hell, why not?"

By midafternoon, things livened up. Patsy got up on a table and danced to mariachi music. She kept saying, "I have better legs than Mary Tyler Moore, don't I?"

Lulu Uranga and Woody Klein danced together on the floor, a stately country-music waltz. For a fat woman, Lu was marvelously airy on her feet. Woody was rather remarkable too, leading Lu with finesse and passing her under his arm in graceful pirouettes. When they finished, Woody's face was flushed and streaming with sweat. "I got terribly high blood pressure, you know," he said sheepishly. "Waltzing used to be a specialty of mine. That's how I won Arlene. She said I was the best waltzer she'd ever seen." He brought the bottle of bourbon over to their table, poured himself another, and sat down. "I'm fifty-four years old," he said. "That's not so young anymore."

"You look young," Patsy said.

"Sometimes I feel young," Woody said. "Except when I dance too much."

"What more could you want?" Garrison asked.

"Nothing," Woody said. He smiled at them. "Nope. I'd do it the same. I got kids. I'm the only son of an only son of an only son. With Jews, that is a thing they worry about, you know? But I got ten sons out of fifteen children, and they are all alive and well. My people back in Philadelphia, they have crossed me off, but they know too that a lot of Kleins are growing up here in New Mexico. There's Orlando, and Guillermo, and Gilberto, and Stevie, and Ricky, and Pedro—little Petey—and Patricio, and Gregorio, and, of course, Ikey, that's the closest I ever got to a Jewish name. Let's see, who've I forgot?" Woody counted on his fingers. "Eddie, who we call Mundy. Yes. Arlene gave them their first names, that's her privilege. But the last name is always Klein, and they are half Jewish. Sometimes I do a little of the holidays, like Yom Kippur, but not much. We light the candles, and I try to explain to them about where they came from, and how their great-grandfather was a rabbi, originally from Odessa, and that he knew how to live his life with grace and to study and think, and at the same time he was never more than a carpenter, he worked with his hands, a scholar who was a man who knew how to put his two hands to work. He was a wise man, from what I heard. What you have to do in this life is make concessions. The kids are growing up Catholic. That's okay, I guess. They're all healthy, and they're doing good in school, so I don't have any complaints, and their name is still Klein. That's all that counts, so what's the difference?"

"There is no difference," Jesse said. He was sitting there beside Woody, working on a beer.

"That's right," Woody agreed.

"Kids are kids," Jesse said. He turned to Clem. "Ain't that right?"

"Anything you say," Clem said.

"I raised you from a baby," Jesse said. He looked at Woody's bottle of bourbon. "Could I have some of that?"

"Sprout, today you can have anything you want," Clem told him. "Just drink it slow, ol' man. Drink it slow, it'll go down smooth."

"Bit of the hair," Patsy said.

"My dear, have you any concept of how difficult everything becomes when one member of the family abstains and the other doesn't?" Garrison was complaining. "To know that one person is in one place, and the other person is . . . someplace else?"

"I want to dance," Patsy said. She turned to the others. "Who wants to dance?"

"I think we should go home," Garrison said.

"Oh, screw it," Patsy said. "Have a drink. It's early yet. Let's be crazy."

Garrison had a small vodka. An hour later he was telling everyone, "How can something that feels so good possibly be bad?"

"Do you know you're the most gorgeous man I've ever set eyes on?" Patsy said to him. "That nose, it makes you look like a Roman emperor. Patrician."

Garrison stroked his nose and said, "It runs in the family."

Werner had had one crying spell so far and was slowly building to a second. He had an arm around Clem's shoulder and was saying, "Youth is beauty. That is why I worship youth. It goes so quick, when one is old." He began playing the accordion, and on the highest notes Cochise tilted his muzzle toward the ceiling and moaned. "He is a good dog," Werner said. He snuffled a little and then glared at Clem. "He knows where his home is, and that somebody cares for him."

Dolores Espinoza and Mamie Lopez walked into the bar. Dolores all beak and beetling brows. She said, "We heard the bar was open."

"Private party," Clem said.

"This is a public house," Dolores said. "Klein, I'll have a beer, please."

"I better do it," Woody said to Clem. "She's Arlene's aunt."

"Ain't nobody around here who's not related?" Clem asked.

"Not that I know of," Woody said. "Go back far enough, Dolores may be kin to *you*."

Dolores dragged over two chairs for herself and Mamie, and without asking, sat down with them. "Why are you leaving?" she asked Clem.

"No reason to stay," he said.

"That's a stupid reason."

"I never was bright," Clem said irritably.

"You don't have to tell me that," Dolores said. "To give away something for a little bit of money. Why don't you stay?"

"I don't dig it here, that's why."

"That has nothing to do with it."

"That's what you think."

"What do you want, an invitation?" She stared at him sourly. "The town knows you are leaving. I say you should not go. Personally, I would rather die than give that Gus Benavidez such satisfaction." She leaned forward and hissed, "You are the most *estúpido cabrito* I have ever seen! If we have to have *un negro* here, well, why not you? That's progress. Times change." She tapped her knuckles against the side of her head. "Nothing here. Nothing whatsoever."

She was too stern and grim for Clem's taste. Yet there was something about her that was formidable. Unpleasant or not, he could understand why she was a power in the village. And though she might be ridden with prejudices and judgments, she had some kind of crazy notion of fairness. At least by her definition. Clem had not seen much of that in Brazos.

Orly Mendocino returned, with his wife, Tessie. He said, "It's started snowing like hell out there again. I closed the station. No business. Can I have a bourbon, Woody? Give Tess one too."

Horacio Quintana hobbled in at four. He said, "Who comes to the post office at this time of day? It's against regulations, but I closed. Mr. Hurley, you told me you had quit drinking!"

"Have a little something for your stomach," Garrison advised, and Horacio did. "Rome was not built by bread alone," Garrison told everyone.

"Doesn't anybody want to dance?" Patsy asked.

More people drifted in. Some made the excuse that they didn't know it was a private affair, but this fooled no one. Mamie Lopez's brother, Armando, actually came up to Clem and shook his hand. "Sorry you're leaving." His words weren't too clear, because Armando had a fluty lisp and a big mouthful of beans and tortillas besides.

Gus Benavidez arrived, saying, "I closed the store. Does anyone object if I sit?"

"Sit," Clem said.

"Devil miser," Dolores muttered. "He can smell a free drink from one end of this town to the other."

"Sally is in trouble in Tucson," Gus confided to Clem.

"That's her problem," Clem said.

"That man ran off and left her," Gus said. "She wants to come home. This is where she belongs."

"Gus, I always thought that too," Clem said.

"She has good qualities, that girl."

"That's puttin' it mildly," Clem said, and let it go at that.

Some of the Montoya gang sauntered in, along with Connie Aragon, who wore Marine Corps grays and a short crew cut. He was home on emergency leave from boot camp, where he was doing poorly, and had wrangled his mother into telegramming some story about a serious illness in the family to his commanding officer, so that he could have a break. He and Willie's crowd stood at the bar and paid for their own drinks, and in general laid waste to the free food. There was Cousin Alejandro, and the Garcia clan from down the valley, and a couple of the Pachecos, and even some of the Roybals, who were known to be standoffish.

By six the Emerald was filled, and it was the best day Woody Klein had had since his Christmas party. Patsy Hurley danced with Connie and said, "You look so handsome! I've never been able to resist a uniform. I have better legs than Juliet Prowse, don't I?"

She hiked up her dress to prove her point, and Garrison said, "Patricia, decorum, please."

"*Toujours gai,* folks!" Patsy sang.

While they danced, Connie told her all about how rugged it was to be a Marine. "They get you up at five in the morning and make you run ten miles before they give you any breakfast. At home all I had to do for my mom was bring in firewood. The Marines have the highest casualty rate of any armed force, you know. But they know how to take care of their own. If it's a frontal assault, where Marines are really needed, they don't think nothing of throwing in two or three battalions. So we take eighty percent casualties, but we get to where we want to go. Do you really like my uniform? I got an expert's medal on the range, only I didn't wear it home."

Patsy felt his shoulders. "You're so big!"

Connie said proudly, "You want to feel something big, feel my thighs. Like rock. I got heavy legs. That's from logging, not the Marines."

Patsy had a feel. Her smile grew distant. She said, "Oh, dear, they really are something, aren't they?"

After the dance was over, Connie talked to Clem. "I saw Willie. He said to tell you hello. He said he's really sorry you're going."

"I'll miss him," Clem said dryly.

"He said he figures he'll be up and around by spring," Connie said. "He was looking forward to having it out with you, only you won't be here."

"Wish I could oblige him."

"Nothing's changed as far as he's concerned," Connie said.

"Didn't figure it would," Clem said.

"Nothing's changed as far as me, either."

"Go find a fuckin' war to fight," Clem said. "This is a party."

More people came. Most of them were Spanish, and many Clem had never seen. Through it all, Dolores Espinoza sat at the table like a queenly despot, respected but feared. Once, when somebody stopped by the table and spoke to her in Spanish, she said, "Speak English, can't you be polite? This big shot, Slade, he thinks he knows everything, but he doesn't know Spanish."

Clem was a little drunk. He said, "Quit pickin' on me."

"Somebody has to," Dolores told him. She made a gesture to the people who had stopped to say hello. "He's part Spanish, even if he doesn't speak it. Around the eyes and the mouth, a little *pachuco,* wouldn't you say?"

"Dolores, I'm about as much Spanish as you are Eskimo," Clem said.

"Who asked you to talk?" Dolores said. "Klein, I'll have one more beer, if you don't mind. Then I must go home." She had had seven cans of Coors already. She leaned across the table and said, "Gus, you are a stingy man."

"I'm poor," Benavidez said.

"Baloney! I should be so poor. Please tell me something new, will you?"

Gus said, "I have problems."

Dolores pinched Clem on the arm. "He has problems. Who *doesn't?*" She turned back to Gus and said grimly, "What do you want? Pity?"

Jesse was drunk. Clem said, "I better get him home."

"As a child, I studied ballet, that's where the legs come from," Patsy said.

Garrison was talking to Mamie Lopez. "We launch A.A. to-morrow evening. Would you care to hear my story? It's a modular classic. Look at my wrists. I once slashed them. See, here are the scars. I did it with a razor. It didn't hurt at all."

"He was making fifty-eight thousand dollars a year when he did that," Patsy said proudly.

"Would you like to hear my story?" Garrison asked Gus Benavi-dez.

"Nobody wants to hear your story, honey," Patsy told him. "We've all got stories of our own."

Bill Martinez and Milt Garcia came in and surveyed the crowd. They came over to Clem, and Bill said, "So, it's true. You're leav-ing."

"Right on, man."

"I thought it was just a rumor."

"Nope."

"We'll miss you," Milt said sarcastically.

"Bet you will," Clem said. "What in hell all of you goin' to do when we're gone?"

"Most likely everybody'll go back to gossiping about one another, the way we did before you came," Bill said.

Werner Grimmiessen said, "I have reached a decision. Clem? You hear me?"

"Sure, Werner."

"Cochise and I will go with you and Jesse," Werner said.

"Oh no you ain't."

"You need somebody to look out for you," Werner insisted. "You look out for Jesse, but who is to look out for you? My mind is made up."

"We'll come too," Patsy said. "I love to travel."

"No way," Clem said. "One of the reasons we're goin' is to get away from all of you."

"Clem, I'm awful tired," Jesse said. "When we goin'?"

"Pretty soon, Sprout."

"It's noisy in here."

"Soon as I finish my drink."

"Is this the party you was talkin' about?"

"That's right, ol' man."

"What we havin' a party for?"

"It's a goin'-away party," Clem said.

"Who's goin' away?" Jesse said. "I don't want to go away. I like it here."

"You changin' your fool mind already? And we ain't even got on the road yet?" Clem demanded.

"Man has to have some place he can call home," Jesse said. It was the most lucid comment he'd made in months. "I ain't goin'. You better go without me."

"Ain't leavin' without you. Make up your mind about that."

Gus Benavidez said, "You're not going to change your mind? We have an agreement."

"Who's changin' his mind?"

"You can't change your mind," Gus insisted. "That is no way to do business. We have a deal."

Clem looked at him. "You tellin' me what to do?"

"We have an agreement."

Clem said, "Don't tell me what to do. If there is one thing that bugs the shit out'a me, it's that."

"You got to keep your end of the agreement, or else I sue," Gus said.

"Sue! What you talkin'? What you goin' to sue, man? You got something in writin'? You got a piece of paper to dangle? Gus, all we did was have us a little talk."

"We talked in good faith. I offered to give you five hundred in earnest money."

"What you talkin', earnest money? No money changed hands, Gus, not that I know of. You got a receipt or something, to show that money changed hands?"

"That's dishonest."

Clem smiled. "That comes natural to a man like me." Suddenly, he was feeling good. He leaned both elbows on the table. "You know what?" he said, to no one in particular. "I'm tempted to stay. Out'a pure meanness! How 'bout that!"

He stared around at all the people in the bar, and then grinned. "What would you do, now, if we changed our minds? My, *my!* That'd be something, all right. If you had me to look forward to. Trouble is my middle name. Oh, I'd hassle you good! I'd *haunt* all of you. You'd be wishin' you'd never heard of me, let alone *seein'* me every day, 'cause I am mean and *beautiful,* an' people break their legs gettin' out'a my way when I come walkin' down the street. Why, I'd plague you so bad you'd be complainin' to Martinez here about criminal harassment!"

He took a coin from his pocket and, still smiling, said to Jesse, "Let's try it one more time, what say, ol' man, eh? Just for kicks. Heads we go. Tails we stay." He flipped the coin and expertly caught it on the back of one hand. "You called the shot last time. My turn." Carefully, he lifted the cupped hand and peeked. "Motherfucker! Tails!"

"You have to show it!" Gus said.

"Looked like tails to me," Clem said. "Didn't it look like tails to you, Sprout?"

Jesse nodded. "Can we go home now?"

"You mean, you ain't going?" Milt Garcia said.

"Ol' Lady Fate spun that coin," Clem said. "Bad luck to go contrary to *her.*"

"Did you see the coin?" Gus was asking everybody. "I didn't see it."

"He called it," Milt Garcia said, and then frowned. "I think it was tails."

Word went around the bar, "They're staying!" Patsy Hurley clapped her hands and kissed Clem. She tugged at Garrison's sleeve, but he was asleep. Werner's chin trembled. Connie Aragon came over and said, "Well, what's this goddamn party for, if you never had any intention of leaving?"

"You know me by now, Connie," Clem said. "Just a-spoofin' and a-goofin' all the time. Never let my right hand know what my left is up to, that's *this* man's style! Felt like havin' a little party. That's all. No law 'gainst that, is there? Do a little funnin' with you people. Shoot! You think I'd leave this place? You off the wall, man! Why'd I want'a do a thing like that?" I got some *plans* for this town!

Baby, you ain't heard *nothin'* yet! Y'all don't behave, why, I'm liable to run for mayor or something, maybe even sheriff, just to bug ol' Garcia here. What would y'all do then? Shit, you got nigger mayors all over this country, right up to Congress. Y'all don't straighten up, I'm just liable to bring some competition into this dump!" He put on an expression of mock ferocity and pointed a finger at Connie Aragon. "Meanwhile, you tell Willie to get himself mended, 'cause the interest on what he owes me for some tires is mountin' up, and one of these days I'll be around to collect. Trouble is, I been too soft-hearted with all you people! Soft-hearted person, he gets stepped on every time. New hand is goin' to be dealt." He laughed and slapped himself on the leg. "See how you like it. Y'all think you're mean? You don't know what *pure* mean is!"

At the bar, someone said, "Jesus, they're staying. This town would have been halfway fit to live in if they'd gone."

Someone else said, "I was actually looking forward to some peace and quiet for a change."

"Some people, they just can't never understand when they ain't welcome," someone else said.

Clem looked at all of them, and shook his head. Still enjoying himself. Downed his drink and said, "Suffer!"